"I can still hea said.

Yeah, so could he. He didn't want to tell her that she would hear them for the rest of her life. But she would. So would he. And he would remember that look of terror on her face.

There wasn't really a way to comfort her right now so Drury just slipped his arm around her and hoped that helped. It seemed to do that. For a couple of long moments anyway. Until she lifted her head, and her eyes met his.

Any chance of comforting her vanished. A lot of things vanished. Like common sense, because just like that, Drury felt the old attraction.

"I don't know how to stop this," she said. Her voice was a whisper, filled with her thin breath.

She wasn't talking about the danger now.

It would have been safer if she had been.

Before he could talk himself out of it or remember this was something he shouldn't be doing, Drury lowered his head and kissed her.

" I can still hear the gunshots ", she said.

DRURY

BY
DELORES FOSSEN

First Published in Great Britain 2017
By Mills & Boon, an imprint of HarperCollins*Publishers*
1 London Bridge Street, London, SE1 9GF

© 2017 Delores Fossen

ISBN: 978-0-263-92874-7

46-0417

Our policy is to use papers that are natural, renewable and recyclable products and made from wood grown in sustainable forests. The logging and manufacturing processes conform to the legal environmental regulations of the country of origin.

Printed and bound in Spain
by CPI, Barcelona

Delores Fossen, a *USA TODAY* bestselling author, has sold over fifty novels with millions of copies of her books in print worldwide. She's received a Booksellers' Best Award and an RT Reviewers' Choice Best Book Award. She was also a finalist for a prestigious RITA® Award. You can contact the author through her website at www.deloresfossen.com.

Chapter One

Special Agent Drury Ryland pulled into his driveway, his truck headlights slashing through the curtain of rain. Rain that nearly caused him to miss the movement behind his detached garage.

Nearly.

But Drury managed to catch a glimpse of someone darting out of sight.

He groaned because it wasn't exactly the hour or the weather for a visitor. Or the place. He was home, in one of the nearly dozen houses on the sprawling Silver Creek Ranch, and all those houses were occupied by lawmen. Anyone who'd come here to break in was a couple of steps past being stupid.

Of course, it might not be a break-in.

Because Drury's arm was still throbbing from the six stitches he had just gotten, he had no trouble recalling the encounter he'd had three hours earlier. A thug had knifed him during an FBI sting operation. Drury had managed to arrest him, but the guy had sworn on his soul that he would get even with Drury. No way could the soul-swearing guy have gotten out of jail yet, but he could have sent one of his buddies to do his dirty work.

Drury brought his truck to a stop, eased his hand over his gun and tried to pick through the darkness and rain so he could get another glimpse of the guy. Nothing. But Drury knew he was there.

"I'm Agent Drury Ryland," he shouted. "Come out so I can see you."

The guy didn't. And not only didn't he come out, he fired a shot. Before Drury could even react, the bullet slammed into his windshield.

The next two shots went straight into his truck's engine. One must have hit the radiator because steam started spewing into the air.

Drury cursed. There went his way to escape. If he wanted to escape, that is. He didn't. He wanted to confront this moron and make him pay for starting a gunfight on Ryland land.

Since the sound of the shots would no doubt alert his cousins and brothers, Drury sent a quick text to one of those cousins, Sheriff Grayson Ryland, and requested backup. However, Drury was hoping he could put an end to the situation before backup even arrived.

Drury threw open his truck door, and using it for cover, he took aim at the shadowy figure that kept peering around the garage. He couldn't just start pulling the trigger, though. It had to be a clean shot because Drury didn't want it to ricochet and risk hitting a ranch hand or someone inside one of the nearby houses.

The shooter obviously didn't have that concern because he fired off another round at Drury. Big mistake. Because he had to lean out from the garage, and Drury took the shot.

And hit the guy.

Not a kill shot, though. He must have hit him in the shoulder because the gunman took off running. A few seconds later, Drury heard the sound of an engine.

No.

He didn't want this clown getting away. Drury had to find out why the heck he'd just tried to kill him.

A dark-colored SUV sped out from behind the garage. Not coming toward Drury. But rather the driver went on the other side of the house, through the yard and onto the road. Since there weren't any houses at this angle, Drury emptied the clip into the SUV.

Drury was certain he hit the guy again, but he kept going, speeding away from the house. He was about to jump in his truck and try to go in pursuit, but then Drury saw Grayson's cruiser approaching. Grayson was not only the sheriff of Silver Creek, but he lived the closest and that's why Drury had texted him.

When Grayson reached Drury, he put down the window, and Drury saw he wasn't alone. Grayson's brother Mason was with him.

"Any idea who's in that SUV?" Grayson asked.

Drury had to shake his head, but he lifted his arm to show them the fresh bandage. "Maybe a friend of the person who gave me this."

"We'll go after him," Grayson said. "Keep watch. Make sure he doesn't double back."

Since Drury's place was the first house on the road that led to the ranch, that wouldn't be hard to do.

When Grayson drove off in pursuit, Drury had a look around the grounds. He didn't see anyone else, though. And if his attacker had left any blood by the garage, the rain was washing it all away. That made it even more critical for Grayson to find him so Drury could get some answers.

He went to his back porch and cursed when he found the door unlocked. It was possible he'd just forgotten to lock it. Just as possible, though, that someone had broken in.

Especially after what'd just happened.

Drury got his gun ready and kicked open the door that led into his kitchen.

"Don't shoot," someone said.

A woman.

Because she'd whispered that order, Drury didn't immediately recognize her voice, but he certainly knew who she was when she stepped closer.

Caitlyn Denson.

The kitchen was dark, but there was enough illumination coming from the hall light that he had no trouble seeing her long brown hair and her face.

And the blood trickling down her forehead.

Drury didn't know what shocked him the most. The blood or that she was even there at all. They weren't exactly on friendly terms and hadn't been in a long time.

He had so many questions, and he wasn't sure where to start. But his lawman's instincts kicked in, and he checked her hands for weapons. Empty. And the pale yellow dress she was wearing was wet and clinging to her, so he knew she wasn't carrying concealed.

Still, he didn't lower his gun. He kept it aimed at her. And he maneuvered himself so he could watch out the large bay window in the living room while still keeping an eye on Caitlyn.

"I heard you'd built a house here on your cousins' ranch, and your name is on the mailbox. I parked behind your barn," she said, as if that explained everything.

It didn't, not by a long shot.

"Did you have anything to do with that?" Drury tipped his head to the side yard where the shots had just been fired.

Caitlyn's eyes widened for just a second, and a thin breath left her mouth. "I think he was here because he's looking for me. I swear, I didn't know he'd follow me."

Well, it was an answer all right. But it only led to more questions. "You're going to have to give me a better explanation than that. And start with how you got that cut or whatever the hell it is." He grabbed some paper towels with his left hand and gave them to her.

She nodded and pressed the towels to her head. "I didn't break in, by the way. The door was unlocked, but you should know that I would have broken in if necessary. I needed a place to hide." She staggered, caught the back of the chair.

Drury cursed and went to her, holstering his gun so he could help her get seated and have a look at the wound that was causing her to bleed all over his kitchen floor. His stomach knotted when he saw the wound close-up.

"Did someone club you on the head?" he asked.

Caitlyn nodded, lightly touched the wound and grimaced when she saw the blood on her fingertips. "I'm not certain who did it. I didn't get a look at his face. But it could have been the same man who shot at you."

And if so, the thug had come to finish what he'd started, and Drury had gotten caught in the middle. Caught only because she'd come here. But why?

"You're sure you don't know who he is?" Drury pressed.

Even though he didn't spell it out, she obviously got what he meant. Was this connected to her late husband, Grant Denson? Grant had been dead for nearly two years now, but he'd been involved in some nasty illegal stuff when he was alive that might now have come back to haunt Caitlyn.

Of course, when you sleep with snakes, you should expect to get bitten.

Was that what had happened now?

"I honestly don't know the man's name," she explained. "But I know why he's after me." Her voice broke, and a hoarse sob tore from her mouth. "God, Drury, I'm so sorry. I didn't have anywhere else to go, and I didn't think he'd come here."

All right. That got his interest. Because she had a mother-in-law, Helen, who was loaded, not just money-wise but with all sorts of resources, including but not limited to thugs who could take care of the person who'd clubbed Caitlyn on the head.

"Start from the beginning," he demanded.

Caitlyn didn't exactly jump to do that, but she did nod again and then took a couple of seconds to gather her breath. "The year before Grant was killed, we were trying to have a baby, and we went to the Conceptions Fertility Clinic in San Antonio."

Everything inside him went still. He was well aware of the clinic because of the shady things that'd happened there just a month earlier. Specifically, embryos had been stolen and implanted in surrogates so that the former clinic manager could then "sell" the babies to the biological parents.

Ransom, extortion and black-market babies all rolled into one. Nasty business.

"All the babies were recovered and given to their parents," Drury reminded her.

Caitlyn paused a heartbeat. "Not all."

"Are you saying…?" But he stopped. "What the hell are you saying?"

"Day before yesterday I got a call from a man who said a surrogate had given birth to mine and Grant's daughter and that if I wanted the child, then I'd have to pay him a million dollars. He sent me a swab with the baby's DNA, and I had it analyzed. The man was telling the truth."

DNA could be faked. So could test results.

"And?" Drury questioned. "How did you get Grant's DNA to do a comparison?"

"From a comb I found in his things that I'd boxed up."

Drury made a circling motion for her to continue.

"I arranged payment, draining nearly every penny from Grant's estate, but when I went to get the baby, she wasn't there. Instead, the man demanded even more money."

Drury groaned. "Let me guess. They told you not to go to the cops or that you'd never see her again?" He waited for her to confirm that with a nod. "That's what criminals tell marks like you. Hell, they might not even have the baby. Or there might not be a baby at all. Even if the DNA appears to prove it's your child, they could have gotten the DNA from an embryo sample stored at the clinic."

Other than a soft moan, she didn't get a chance to respond because Drury's phone rang. "It's Grayson," he said, glancing at the screen.

That got her back on her feet, and Caitlyn shook her head. "Please don't tell him I'm here. Not yet. I'm not sure who I can trust."

"Well, you can't trust me," he snapped.

But that was a lie. He was a lawman and would do whatever it took to protect her or any other bleeding woman who showed up at his house.

"Please," she repeated, sounding just as desperate as she looked.

Drury wasn't going to let that *please* or desperation sway him. He intended to tell Grayson everything because while she might not trust his cousin, Drury darn sure did.

"We found the shooter," Grayson said the moment Drury answered the call. "He'd crashed his SUV into a tree about three miles from the ranch. He's hurt but alive."

"Who is he?" Drury asked.

"No ID, and the vehicle is registered to a woman in Austin."

Maybe that meant the SUV was stolen. Of course,

Drury already knew this guy was a criminal capable of murder. "Did he happen to say why he fired shots at me or what he was doing at my place?" Drury pressed.

Caitlyn moved closer. Too close. No doubt trying to hear the conversation.

"He's not saying much of anything. He's groggy, slipping in and out of consciousness," Grayson added. "We'll get him to the hospital, but I did find something in the SUV that was, well, disturbing. Some rope, a ski mask, duct tape and rubber gloves."

No baby. Though Drury hadn't expected there would be. Caitlyn had likely been the victim of a scam, and now that they couldn't milk any more money from her, this thug had been sent to get rid of her.

"I'll head to the sheriff's office now," Drury insisted.

"You need a ride? When I drove by earlier, I saw your truck was messed up."

"Yeah. That thug shot the radiator. But I have a car in the garage. I'll also have someone with me who can shed some light on this."

Caitlyn was shaking her head before he even finished.

"Who?" Grayson asked, but he continued before Drury could respond. "Gotta go. Ambulance is here. You can tell me when you get to the office. See you in a few."

"No," Caitlyn said, still shaking her head when Drury ended the call. "You shouldn't have done that. You shouldn't have told Grayson you were bringing someone in."

And she took off. Not toward the door but rather into the living room.

"What the heck do you think you're doing?" Drury asked.

She didn't answer that. Caitlyn hurried to the side of the sofa, and she grabbed something from the floor. Even though the room was dark, Drury had no trouble seeing the bundled-up coat.

And the stun gun.

Caitlyn picked up both, and with the coat clutched to her chest, she started running, headed to the back door this time.

Drury stepped in front of her, blocking her path, but Caitlyn tried to dart around him. He didn't want her to get a chance to use that stun gun on him, so he caught onto her arm and knocked the stun gun from her hand.

"I have to go," she insisted. "It's not safe."

Maybe it wasn't, but that didn't mean Drury was just going to let her head out. He pulled her closer and had a better look at the coat.

Damn.

In the middle of that bundle, Drury saw something move.

And that something was a baby.

Chapter Two

Caitlyn hadn't expected Drury just to let her walk out of there, but she also hadn't thought this insanity would go from bad to worse.

This definitely qualified as worse.

Now that he'd seen the baby, there was no way he'd willingly let her leave.

"The baby's yours?" he snapped.

"Maybe."

She'd figured Drury wasn't going to like that answer, and he didn't. He groaned. Then cursed.

"But I believe she's mine," Caitlyn went on. "And the man said she was. I figured I could have her tested later, but for now I have to go. That man who shot at you wants to kill me and take the baby."

"Yeah. I got that. According to Grayson, he had rope, tape, a ski mask and gloves in his SUV. All the makings of a felony or two."

Oh, God. Her stomach dropped. Even though Caitlyn had known the man didn't have good intentions, it sickened her to hear it spelled out like that. It also confirmed what she'd felt in her heart.

That he had no intention of giving her the baby.

He'd had plans to kill her then and there. She doubted he had just stopped trying to do that, either.

"The man will send someone else after me," Caitlyn tried again. Tried also to move past Drury, but, like before, he stopped her.

Mercy, she had to convince him to let her go. But how? Too bad her head was throbbing and she was dizzy because it made it hard to think.

"Look, I know you don't owe me any favors," she said. "But let me leave."

An understatement about the favors.

And the sound Drury made let her know that he didn't owe her a thing. Not after she'd walked out on him four years ago. He'd been in love with her. *Then*. Definitely not now, though. There wasn't a shred of love between them at this moment.

However, Caitlyn could still feel the tug of attraction. The one she'd had for Drury the first time she'd laid eyes on him. That attraction was all one-sided now, on her part. Drury's glare proved it.

"Please just help me by letting me leave right now," she begged.

It seemed to take him a couple of seconds to get his jaw unclenched so he could speak, and he didn't look at her when he did it. He volleyed his attention between the baby and the window. Drury was no doubt looking to see if the thug had indeed sent someone else to come after her.

Good.

Because Caitlyn was looking, too.

"How'd you get the baby?" Drury asked.

She huffed. There wasn't time for all this talk, but it was obvious he wasn't going to let her leave until he had some answers. Maybe not even then. That meant she had to get away at the first chance she got.

"I took her from that man," Caitlyn said, blinking back the tears that were burning her eyes. Her voice, like the rest of her, was trembling. "I really don't know who he is, and I didn't see his face. He was wearing a ski mask."

"Keep talking," Drury insisted when she paused again.

"I was meeting him to deliver another payment, but this time I brought a stun gun with me."

Mercy. It was hard to relive this. The memories were still so fresh and raw. The fear, too.

"When I handed him the money," she went on, "I reached for the baby. He smashed me on the head with his weapon, but I was able to hit him with the stun gun. He fell to the ground. I grabbed the baby and got away."

No groan this time. Drury cursed again instead. "You could have been killed."

"I could have lost her," Caitlyn pointed out just as quickly. "Even if she's not my daughter, she belongs to someone, and I had to get her away from that monster."

Drury didn't seem swayed in the least by that. "You should have involved the cops."

"I couldn't because the man said he'd know if I brought anyone with me." In addition to the tears and trembling, Caitlyn had to fight the sudden tightness in her chest. "He said he would hurt the baby if I wasn't alone. I couldn't risk it."

She must have looked ready to fly into a million little pieces because Drury huffed. Then did something surprising. He touched her arm. It barely qualified as a pat, but she'd take it.

Too bad he didn't offer her a hug, or she would have taken that, too.

The touch didn't last long. Drury looked at her, his gaze lingering for a moment before it also slipped away.

"During any of your conversations, did this clown say if he was working for someone or how he got the baby in the first place?" Drury asked.

"No. But I'm not sure he's connected to anyone at Conceptions Clinic." She hesitated about adding the next part. Not because it wasn't true.

It was.

But it wasn't going to shorten this conversation.

"I think the man might be working for Helen Denson."

There, she'd said it aloud. Her worst fear. Or rather, one of them. She had plenty of others at the moment, but at the top of that list was that her dead husband's rich, manipulative mother could be the one who'd orchestrated this nightmare.

Caitlyn could almost see the wheels turning in Drury's head, and he was likely trying to work out why she'd just accused her former mother-in-law of such a heinous crime.

"Helen hates me," Caitlyn explained. "And she was furious when she found out Grant left his entire estate to me. I think she would do anything, including something like this, to get back the money."

Of course, that could mean the baby wasn't hers. After all, Helen could have used any baby to carry out a scheme like that.

"Why would Helen be upset about you inheriting what belonged to your husband?" he asked.

This was another long explanation, one she didn't have time or energy to give him. Caitlyn went with the short version. "Grant and I were separated when he was killed in that car accident. I was already in the process of getting a divorce."

He pulled back his shoulders just slightly. Surprised by that. Later, if there was a later, she would tell him more. For now, though, she had to remind him of the urgency of her situation.

"That man who had the baby wasn't working alone," she continued. "When I made the first payment, there were two

of them, and I'm pretty sure they had a lookout or someone nearby because one of the men had a communicator
in his ear, and he was talking to someone. I can't stay here
because they'll come back."

"Come on," Drury said. He still had a firm grip on
her arm. "We'll go to the sheriff's office and get this all
straightened out."

"They'll look for me there if they don't attack us along
the way first. The baby could be hurt. You, too." She almost added that she couldn't live with that, but it was an
old wound best left untouched.

"If you didn't want me involved, then you shouldn't
have come here," he grumbled.

"I swear I didn't know the man would follow me. I
mean, he was out from the stun gun, and he didn't have
his partner with him this time. Didn't have the communicator in his ear, either." A heavy sigh left her mouth. "I
guess he had a lookout after all."

Caitlyn figured Drury would ignore everything she'd
just told him and demand once more that she leave with
him.

But he didn't.

His gaze volleyed from her to the baby. "Whose coat
is that?" he asked.

She had to shake her head. "It was right next to the
baby on the seat of the kidnapper's SUV, and I grabbed it
to cover her from the rain."

"Put the baby on the sofa," Drury instructed, and his
tone and body language sent a chill straight through her. "It
could have a tracking device—or something worse—in it."

Sweet heaven.

Caitlyn hurried to the sofa, easing the baby onto it. The
little girl was still sleeping, thank goodness.

"I checked her after I brought her into your house," she

explained. "No cuts or bruises." It sickened her, though, to think there could have been.

Drury didn't respond. He moved in front of the newborn, eased back the sides of the coat.

The baby was wearing a pink drawstring gown with little ducks on it. There was even an elastic headband with a bow holding back her dark brown curls from her face, and she had a thin receiving blanket around her. She was clean. Her diaper appeared to have been changed recently, and since she wasn't crying, that probably meant she'd been fed. Whoever had her had at least taken care of her.

Probably so they could protect their *investment*.

Something twisted inside Caitlyn at the thought.

She almost hated to feel this kind of anger. This kind of love for that precious little girl. Because the baby might not even be hers.

Caitlyn repeated that to herself.

It didn't seem to stop the flood of feelings that poured through her, and that love could mean she would be crushed if she had to hand over the baby to someone else.

"Lift her up," Drury said, still searching every inch of the coat. "Gently."

That gave her another jolt, and she prayed there wasn't anything on or near the baby that could hurt her.

Caitlyn eased the newborn into her arms. Of course, it wasn't the first time she'd held her, but without the coat around her, she could feel just how tiny and fragile she was.

Drury went through the coat pockets, coming up empty each time, and he turned his attention to the bow on the baby's headband.

"Hell," he mumbled.

Caitlyn watched as he gently slipped off the headband, and she saw it then.

"It's a tracking device," he said. "That's how the man was able to follow you."

Caitlyn shook her head. "I should have noticed it. Drury. I'm so sorry."

"Save it." He tossed the headband onto the coffee table. "In case I missed something, don't use the blanket to wrap her." He pulled a throw off the back of the sofa and handed it to her. "Use this."

"Where are we going?" she asked, draping it over the baby.

"Away from here. And fast." He took out his phone and sent a text. Probably to Grayson. "I don't want any other hired guns coming to the ranch. Every one of my cousins has wives and kids, and they're all right here on the grounds."

That didn't help steady her heartbeat.

Drury led her to the back door, grabbing a remote control from the kitchen counter. He used it to open the detached garage, and he stepped out onto the porch to look around.

The rain was still coming down hard, but the porch was covered so the baby was staying dry. However, she was starting to squirm, maybe because Caitlyn's dress was damp and it was cool against her. She needed dry clothes. Baby supplies.

And a safe place to take her.

But where?

The sheriff's office certainly didn't seem like an ideal location since the man's partners could go looking for her there.

"Wait here in the doorway, and I'll pull the car up to the steps," Drury said. He'd already started to walk away but then stopped and turned back around to face her. "So help me, you'd better not try to run."

Since she was indeed thinking just that, Caitlyn wondered if he'd read her mind. Or maybe he could just see the desperation on her face.

Because she didn't know what else to do, Caitlyn did wait. And she prayed. She trusted Drury, but her trust wouldn't do a darn thing to protect him or the baby.

He hurried to the garage, and it took only a few seconds before she heard the engine turn on. Only a few seconds more before he pulled the car to the steps with the passenger's side facing her.

The moment Drury threw open the door and frantically motioned for her to get in, she knew something was wrong.

"Someone's coming," Drury said.

Caitlyn saw the headlights then. There was a car on the road. And it was speeding right toward them.

Chapter Three

Drury cursed himself for not getting Caitlyn away from the house any sooner. But he'd delayed because he hadn't been sure what was going on.

Still wasn't sure.

But he couldn't wait around and find out if whoever was in that car had friendly intentions. Judging from the tracking device he'd found, his guess was no. No friendly intentions here. That vehicle was likely carrying more shooters who'd come after Caitlyn and the baby. And being inside the house wouldn't necessarily help them if these morons opened fire.

Caitlyn ran down the porch steps, and Drury reached across the seat to pull her inside. The moment she was in, he gunned the engine to get them the heck out of there.

"You're not going to drive toward that car, are you?" she asked. The fear was right back in her voice. Not that it'd completely gone away, but there was a triple dose of it now.

It was raining, they didn't have a car seat and bullets might start flying at any second.

"We're not going toward the car," he assured her, and he bolted out of the side of his yard and headed not for the highway, but toward the main house.

It was a risk, but there were no completely safe options here.

Drury tossed her his phone. "Text Grayson and tell him what's going on. And climb in the back with the baby. Get all the way down on the seat and stay there."

She gave a shaky nod, and with the baby cradled in her arms, Caitlyn scrambled into the back. Drury heard her typing the text, but he kept his attention on the other car. Even though he hadn't turned on his headlights, the driver of the vehicle must have seen him because he came after them.

Hell.

He had hoped the guy would just back off when he saw where Drury was headed. No such luck.

Drury drove toward the main house, but he certainly had no intentions of stopping. There was a security gate just ahead, and like everybody else on the ranch, he had the remote to open and close it. He started pushing the remote button the moment it came into view, and the metal gates dragged open.

It seemed to take an eternity.

And that car behind him just kept getting closer and closer.

"He's got a gun," Caitlyn said, and that's when Drury realized she'd lifted her head and was looking out the back window.

"Get back down," he warned her.

Yeah, the guy had a gun all right. Drury had no trouble spotting it because the passenger lowered his window and stuck out his hand, trying to take aim.

The moment the gates were open, Drury gunned the engine and flew through them, hitting the remote to close them.

It worked.

The gates closed before the shooter could get through.

The driver hit his brakes, slamming into the gate, but the gates held.

Thank God.

Drury kept going, and he sped past the houses that dotted the ranch. He didn't dare stop because the gunman might have a long-range rifle in the car, and Drury didn't want to give the guy any reason to keep firing.

"Grayson says his brothers and the ranch hands have been alerted," Caitlyn relayed after getting a response to the text she'd sent.

Good. Though he doubted that gunman would get out of the car and go in pursuit on foot, it was better to be safe than sorry.

Especially since Drury was already sorry enough for this fiasco.

He stayed on the road that coiled around the pastures, and once he was past the exterior security lights, it was too dark for him to see. Drury had no choice but to turn on his headlights.

"Where are we going?" she asked.

Some place she wouldn't like. "The sheriff's office. And before you remind me that these goons can follow us there, they can follow us anywhere. At least if we're at the sheriff's office, the deputies and I can protect you, and it'll get these idiots away from my family.

"Don't say you're sorry," he added, his voice a little harsher than he'd intended.

Drury had caught a glimpse of her face in the mirror and could tell from the tears that she was about to apologize again. Well, it wouldn't help. Nothing would right now except getting her and that baby to safety.

His phone rang, the sound cutting through the other sounds of his heartbeat drumming in his ears and the wipers slashing at the rain.

"It's Grayson," Caitlyn said. She passed him the phone, but since Drury still had hold of his gun, he pushed the speaker button and dropped the phone on the seat next to him.

"Where are you?" Grayson asked. "And what the heck's going on?"

"I'm at the back of the ranch on one of the trails and about to come out on Miller's Hill. The car with the gunmen didn't get past the gate."

"No," Grayson agreed. "Gage had eyes on the car, and he said the driver turned around and sped off. He got the license plate numbers, but they're bogus. Gage and Dade went in pursuit."

Both men were Grayson's brothers. And his deputies.

"I'll take the back roads to get to the sheriff's office. I should be there in about twenty minutes." Drury paused. "Caitlyn Denson is with me."

Grayson paused, too, and then cursed. A rarity for him since he was the father of a five-year-old son and had cut way back on his bad language.

"Caitlyn?" Grayson repeated like the profanity he'd just used. "You're not involved with her again, are you?"

"No, not like that." And Drury couldn't say it fast enough.

"Good. Because the last time you hooked up with her…"

Grayson didn't finish that. Didn't need to finish it. Because Drury remembered it well enough without any reminders. Caitlyn had been a CPA in those days. A CPA who'd been helping Drury investigate the crime family that had employed her.

At least Drury had believed she was helping him.

However, he'd been wrong. Because Caitlyn had ended up marrying the very man whose family Drury had been investigating. But those were old memories, and he didn't have time for them now.

"So, why is Caitlyn with you?" Grayson pressed. "And are those gunmen after her?"

"They're after her." That was the easy question to answer. The first one, not so much. "There might be another baby from Conceptions Clinic."

He gave Grayson a moment for that to sink in.

"Caitlyn and Grant Denson's baby," Grayson concluded.

"Yeah. At least that's what a man told Caitlyn." Drury could still see her in the glimpses that he was making in the rearview mirror, and she was hanging on to every word. "According to her, a man demanded a ransom. She paid it, but he reneged."

Grayson mumbled some profanity. "Where's the baby now?"

"In the backseat of my car with Caitlyn. She was waiting inside my place when I got home." He figured it wouldn't take Grayson long to fill in the blanks.

And it didn't.

"Caitlyn came to you for help."

Drury settled for another *yeah* and didn't miss Grayson's disapproval about that. Well, Drury wasn't so happy about it, either.

"I don't know for sure, but the guy you caught is probably the same one who had the baby. He should have stungun marks on…" Drury looked back at her so she could provide that.

"The left side of his neck."

Grayson made what sounded to be a weary sigh. "I'll have the doc check for it. I got a name on the guy already. Ronnie Waite. He was in the system not because he had a record but because he used to be a prison guard."

Interesting. Drury would have bet his paycheck that the

guy had a record. But then maybe whoever was behind this had made sure to use someone who was clean.

"Ronnie Waite," Drury repeated to Caitlyn. He turned onto another road and glanced around to make sure they weren't being followed. "Do you know him?"

Caitlyn repeated the name, then shook her head. "Is he in charge of this or just a lackey?"

"Don't know yet," Grayson answered. "How did Ronnie or anyone connected to this contact you?"

"Only one man contacted me," Caitlyn answered, "and he always called. I used the internet to do a reverse number lookup, but it wasn't listed."

Probably because the phone had been a burner or disposable prepaid cell. No way to trace that. But if Ronnie still had the phone on him, Grayson would have it checked.

"Does Caitlyn, or the baby, need to see a doctor?" Grayson asked.

"Yes," Drury said at the same moment that she answered.

"No. I mean, I want the baby checked out, but I'm fine. And I don't want to be in the hospital while Ronnie is still there."

"Caitlyn's not fine," Drury argued. "She might have a concussion. But I agree about not going to the hospital. She shouldn't be there until we're certain Ronnie can't get near her."

"I'll have a medic come to the office then." Grayson paused. "We'll get into all of this once you're here, but I'll need you to think of anyone who could have hired this man."

"Helen," Drury and Caitlyn said in unison.

"All right. I'll get your former mother-in-law here for a chat," Grayson agreed without hesitation. "I'll also see if there's any way to connect her to Ronnie."

"There has to be a surrogate out there, too," Caitlyn added. "I'm not sure how to find her, but she might be linked somehow to Ronnie."

"I can question Ronnie about that. And check for a Jane Doe DB who might have recently given birth."

DB as in *dead body*.

Caitlyn made a slight gasping sound. Probably because she'd just realized what Grayson was saying—that the surrogate could have been murdered after she gave birth. Whoever was behind this wouldn't have wanted to keep a surrogate alive unless, of course, the surrogate was in on the plan.

"I'll have Mason call the lead investigator who handled the Conceptions Clinic case," Grayson went on, "but if Helen's the one who did this, would she have had access to the embryo? In other words, could someone at the clinic have legally given it to her?"

"No. Not legally." Caitlyn drew in a long breath. "In fact, when Helen found out that Grant and I had visited the clinic, she tried to bribe one of the nurses to get info about what we were doing. When I found out, I had our counselor put a note in my file that no information should be given to the woman."

"That doesn't mean Helen played by the rules," Drury reminded her. In fact, he'd be surprised if she had. But there was someone else in that scummy family who was also a rule breaker. "What about Grant's brother, Jeremy?"

Drury couldn't be sure, but he thought Caitlyn shuddered. "Jeremy wouldn't have done that. And yes, I'm sure. The last thing Jeremy would want is another heir to share the inheritance he'll get from his mother."

"Okay," Grayson said, "this is enough to get things started. How far out are you now?"

"About ten minutes. No one's following us, but when

we get to the sheriff's office, I want to get Caitlyn and the baby inside ASAP."

"No problem. Park right in front of the door."

Drury hit the end-call button and took another glance back at her. "I know you don't want to go to the sheriff's office, but you can trust Grayson. If there's anything to link Helen to this, he'll find it."

And so would Drury. He hadn't especially wanted to get involved with Caitlyn, but this wasn't about her. It was about that baby in her arms.

"You think I'm a fool for getting involved with Grant," she said. "But I swear, I didn't know what Grant was when I married him."

"You should have. You knew what his family was, knew that I was investigating them."

"Yes," she whispered. And she repeated it. "His family but not him." She paused. "I think Jeremy might have been the one who killed Grant."

"Killed? I thought he died in a car accident."

"He did. One that Jeremy could have arranged." Though she shook her head right after saying that. "I don't have any proof, and knowing Jeremy, there won't be proof to find. But I meant what I said about Jeremy not wanting any competition for his mother's estate."

The last time he'd tangled with the Densons, he hadn't fared so well. Drury had ended up with a black mark on his reputation for getting involved with Caitlyn, a woman who'd clearly double-crossed him and had almost certainly been sleeping with him to get info about his investigation.

Of course, that hadn't stopped Drury from trying to go after the Densons again. Until his boss had finally gotten him to back off when Helen had threatened a lawsuit for harassment. Drury hadn't wanted to hurt the Bureau for what had essentially become a personal vendetta on his part.

"I hate being drawn back into the viper pit." He hadn't intended to say that loud enough for Caitlyn to hear.

But she heard. Because she gave him another "I'm sorry."

He kept the next comment to himself. Was she sorry she'd dumped him for Grant? Or sorry that she hadn't gotten that safe fairy tale that she wanted?

Drury wanted to tell her that she couldn't create "safe." The cut on her head and baby in her arms were proof of that. Still, he couldn't fault her for trying. After all, she'd seen her own father—a Texas Ranger—gunned down right in front of her when she was only eight.

Hard to get past memories like that.

Drury took the final turn toward town, and he tried to shut out everything so he could focus on their surroundings. It was late, nearly midnight, and with the rain there wasn't anyone out and about. Still, those thugs could be waiting on a side street, watching for them.

He held his breath and didn't release it until he saw the sheriff's office. And Grayson in the doorway. The moment Drury had brought the car to a stop, Grayson hurried Caitlyn inside, and Drury followed right behind her. He got her away from the windows—fast. Even though they were bullet resistant, he didn't want to take any chances.

After everything that'd gone on, Drury hadn't expected a warm greeting from Grayson and Mason. And he didn't get one. Mason was on the phone, scowling. But then, that was something Mason did a lot.

However, Grayson was scowling, too.

At Caitlyn.

"Is there any part of your story you want to rethink?" Grayson asked her.

That put some alarm in her eyes, and Caitlyn shook her head. "No. Why?"

"Because I just got off the phone with the doctor who's patching up Ronnie Waite, and Ronnie says that's his daughter and that you kidnapped her. He's demanding a warrant for your arrest."

Chapter Four

Caitlyn felt as if someone had knocked the breath right out of her. She shook her head, tried to deny what Ronnie had claimed, but the words were trapped in her throat.

"Is it true?" Grayson snapped.

It was more of an accusation than a question, and Caitlyn was thankful it had come from Grayson and not Drury. Still, that didn't mean Drury believed she was innocent. He was staring at her, clearly waiting for her to say something.

"Everything happened just the way I told you," she insisted.

Drury just kept staring, but Grayson made a sound, one to let her know she was going to have to do a whole lot better than that if he was to believe her.

"The baby isn't his," Caitlyn tried again. "I paid him one ransom, and he demanded a second one. Since I figured he wasn't just going to hand over the baby, I hit him with a stun gun and took her from him."

"I don't suppose you recorded any of that encounter?" Grayson, again. And he used the tone of the lawman in charge. Which he was. He also made this sound, and feel, like an interrogation.

Mercy. If she couldn't convince him of her innocence, he might take the baby. He might arrest her. That couldn't happen because if she was behind bars, she wouldn't be able to protect the baby.

"He clubbed me on the head," Caitlyn added, and she looked to Drury for help. She held her breath, hoping that he would back her up, and he finally nodded.

"When I found Caitlyn in my house, she was scared. And bleeding."

Grayson lifted his shoulder, and even though he didn't say the actual words, his expression was a reminder that she'd fooled Drury before. That's the way the Rylands would see it anyway. But she hadn't fooled him so much as she'd been fooled.

By Grant.

But that was an old wound of a different kind.

"Think this through," Caitlyn continued because she clearly had some more convincing to do with Grayson. "Why would I steal a baby and run to Drury?"

Grayson stayed quiet, probably because there was no scenario he could come up with where she'd do that. Because she wouldn't.

"So, the baby is really yours?" Grayson asked.

Caitlyn hated to hesitate, but she didn't want to withhold anything. Considering her track record with the Rylands, it would be hard enough to get them to trust her if they caught her in a lie.

She looked down at the newborn. At that precious little face, and she got that same deep feeling of love that she'd gotten the first time she saw her. Of course, she'd been wrong about her feelings before, but Caitlyn didn't think that was the case right now. In fact, she would stake her life on it.

"Other than the test I had run on the DNA sample the kidnapper sent me, I don't have any proof," Caitlyn admitted, "but she looks like the pictures of me when I was a baby."

Grayson groaned, an almost identical reaction to the one Drury had had when she'd first told him.

"I can get the proof," she insisted. "I can have her DNA tested again and compared to mine and Grant's. I just need time." She stepped closer to Grayson and looked him straight in the eyes. "But I'm not going to give her to you so you can hand her over to the very man who tried to kill us."

Grayson's attention shifted to Drury then. "You believe her?"

Drury didn't answer for several long moments. "The guy shot at me when I pulled up in front of my house. If he was truly just after Caitlyn to get his child back, then why go after me like that?" He tapped his badge. "I identified myself, and he still shot at me. Plus, he had those items in his vehicle."

No head shake from Grayson this time. He nodded. Apparently, that was enough to convince him that Ronnie was lying.

"I'll post a deputy outside his hospital room and keep digging into his background to see what turns up," Grayson said. "Why don't you two wait in my office while I call the doctor and get him down here?"

Caitlyn wasn't sure she could trust the doctor. Any doctor. But her options were limited. She couldn't just go running out into the rainy night with the baby, and she didn't even have any supplies.

"Could you please have someone get the baby some formula and diapers?" she asked.

Another nod from Grayson, and he got started on that while Drury led her to Grayson's office. It wasn't the first time she'd been there. Once when she'd still been seeing Drury, he'd brought her here to meet his cousins. Of course, they had been a lot friendlier to her than they were now.

Because her legs felt ready to give way, Caitlyn sank down into one of the chairs and looked up at Drury. "Thank you."

He huffed, clearly not meant to convey "you're welcome" because he probably hated her for getting him involved in this. Maybe soon she could convince him that she truly was sorry along with making plans to put some distance between them.

But how?

She didn't even have a phone, and besides even if she had one, Caitlyn wasn't sure who to call. Maybe a bodyguard, but at this point, she didn't even know who she could trust.

Other than Drury, that is.

And that trust was on shaky ground. Yes, he would protect her because he was an FBI agent and it was his job, but she'd already put him in danger once and didn't want to risk doing that again.

"Can you help me arrange for a safe house?" she asked.

A muscle flickered in his jaw, and he pulled a chair from the corner and sat where he was facing her. "Yes, I can do that, but I want you to do something for me. Tell me everything—and I mean everything—about who could be part of this."

Caitlyn was certain she looked confused. Because she was. "You mean about the baby?"

"For starters. You didn't have anything to do with what went on at Conceptions, did you?"

That put a huge knot in her stomach. Not because it was true. It wasn't. But because he would even consider she'd do something like that.

"No. I gave up on having Grant's baby months before he died." And she made the mistake of dodging his gaze.

Drury noticed.

He put his fingers beneath her chin, lifting it and forcing eye contact. "Explain that," he insisted.

Caitlyn hadn't wanted to get into all of this now, but it could be connected. *Could.* Still, it would mean reopening old wounds that still hadn't healed. Never would. Plus, it was hard to discuss any of this when she was holding the baby. Perhaps Grant's and her baby.

"When Grant was killed, he'd been having an affair," she said.

"Is that the reason you were divorcing him?"

"Among other things." Caitlyn paused. "The only reason I'm bringing it up now is because his girlfriend, Melanie Cordova, could be responsible for at least part of this."

Of course, he looked confused, and Drury motioned for her to continue.

Caitlyn did, after she took a deep breath. "Melanie was devastated after Grant's death, and it's possible she's the one who arranged for the baby to be born. So she could have some part of Grant."

"Even if that *part* meant the baby would be yours?" he questioned. "Because as a mistress, you'd think the last thing she would want around was her lover's baby with another woman."

"I know," Caitlyn admitted. Obviously, there were holes in her theory about Melanie's possible involvement. "But maybe Melanie was so desperate to have Grant's child that she didn't care if I was the biological mother."

Judging from the way his forehead bunched up, Drury clearly wasn't on board with this. "Then why would Melanie have demanded a ransom? Why even let you know that the child existed?"

Caitlyn had to shake her head. "Unless she just wanted the money to raise the baby. Of course, that doesn't explain why that thug Ronnie had her."

"Maybe that wasn't Melanie's choice. If she hired him to extort the ransom, he could have double-crossed her and kidnapped the baby."

Mercy. Caitlyn hadn't even thought of that. Maybe this was a sick plan that had gone terribly wrong.

"How long has it been since you've seen Melanie?" Drury asked. "Is it possible she carried the baby herself, that she's the surrogate?"

It was yet something else Caitlyn hadn't considered, but she had to nod. "I haven't seen her in over a year. For a few months after Grant died, she stalked me. Followed me, kept calling, that sort of thing, but that all stopped about a year ago."

Perhaps around the time Melanie would have been arranging for the procedure to have the baby.

Caitlyn didn't have to ask how Melanie would have gotten the fertilized embryo from Conceptions. She could have bribed someone in the clinic, possibly even the former clinic manager who'd orchestrated several births just so she could extort money from the babies' biological parents. Something that Drury knew all too well.

Since two of those babies were his twin niece and nephew.

The clinic manager was dead now, killed in a gunfight with Drury's brother Holden so she couldn't give them answers, but it was possible that Melanie could.

Drury stood. "I'll make some calls and get Melanie in for questioning."

He took out his phone, but before he could do anything, Grayson stepped into the doorway. One look at his face, and Caitlyn knew something was wrong.

"Ronnie called Child Protective Services," Grayson said. "He wants the baby in their custody."

That robbed Caitlyn of her breath, and she stood, as well. She also pulled the baby even closer to her. "It's some kind of trick. Ronnie probably figures it'll be easier to snatch the baby from foster care than from me."

Grayson made a sound of agreement. "But that won't stop CPS from taking her. They're on their way here now."

Caitlyn would have bolted for the door if Drury hadn't stopped her. No. This couldn't be happening.

"If I let them take the baby, it'd be like giving her back to Ronnie," Caitlyn pleaded. "I can't do that."

She braced herself for an argument, but one didn't come.

"Ronnie tried to kill me," Drury reminded Grayson. "Anything he does is suspect, and Caitlyn is right. He or one of his thug friends would have a much easier time getting the baby from CPS. In fact, the plan could be to kidnap her as soon as she's taken from the building."

Still no argument from Grayson, but he did stay quiet a moment. Before he nodded. "I don't trust Ronnie, either. Or rather I don't trust the person he's working for." Grayson looked at Caitlyn. "That still doesn't mean I can give you a blank check on this. How much time will you need to prove she's your daughter?"

Caitlyn had to shake her head. "How much time for you to arrange another DNA test, one that would hold up against a court order?"

"Forty-eight hours, maybe even sooner, if we put a rush on it," Drury answered. "We'll need the lab you used to process Grant's DNA, though."

Yes, because she didn't want to take the time to try to find another hair sample. "I used Bio-tech in San Antonio. They'll have both Grant's and my DNA on file there."

She could see the debate Grayson was having with himself. He was a lawman. A good one, judging from everything she'd heard. And it likely didn't set well with him that this would essentially be an obstruction of justice since he was allowing Caitlyn to walk away with the baby rather than turning her over to CPS.

"All right," Grayson finally said. "Forty-eight hours. I'll get the DNA test kit. After that, go ahead and get Caitlyn and her out of here."

The relief was instant, and it left her just as breathless as the news of Ronnie calling CPS. She wasn't going to have to give up the baby. Not just yet anyway. But that didn't mean she had a safe place to take her.

"Where?" she asked Drury and hoped he had some idea.

"Don't tell me where you're going," Grayson quickly added. "I don't want to have to lie to CPS. Oh, and figure out how the baby can get a checkup from the doctor." He walked away, no doubt to get that kit.

She certainly hadn't forgotten about the checkup but didn't know how to make it happen.

"It's not a good idea to go back to my place," Caitlyn insisted before Drury could say anything. "Or yours."

"Agreed. But there's a guesthouse on the back part of the ranch. It's out of sight from the other houses, including Grayson's, and we can use it just for tonight. Since my cousins have lots of babies, it'll be easier for us to get supplies."

"It'll also make them a target if Ronnie and his goon friends attack again," she quickly pointed out.

"We can lock down the ranch, close the security gate and use some of the hands for extra protection."

Maybe, but Caitlyn still wasn't sold on the idea. *Think.* Where else could she go? And preferably some place that didn't put others in danger.

"It's just for tonight," Drury said as if he knew what

was going through her mind. "The baby will need to be fed soon, and it won't be long before CPS arrives."

True. Still, Caitlyn didn't like it one bit.

"Are you, uh, okay with this?" But she immediately waved off her question. "Of course you're not okay. First thing in the morning, I promise, I'll start looking for bodyguards."

He didn't give her his opinion on that. "I'll pull an unmarked car to the back of the building."

Drury headed out as Grayson came in with the DNA test kit. He'd obviously done this before because he did the cheek swab in just a few seconds. The baby still stirred a little and made a whimpering sound of protest, but she went right back to sleep.

"I'll have this couriered to the lab," Grayson explained as he started toward the door again. But he stopped. "If the child's not yours, I'll expect you to turn her over to CPS. Got that?"

She nodded. Caitlyn understood that's what would have to happen. Well, she understood with her head anyway. It was her heart that was giving her some trouble because Caitlyn felt as if this baby already belonged to her. It would crush her to learn differently.

Caitlyn heard the footsteps in the hall and automatically tensed, but it was just Drury. He glanced at the DNA packet.

"I'll call you as soon as we have the results," Grayson assured them.

Drury took her by the arm and led her to the back of the building and through a break room. He paused at the exit, opening the door and glancing around. He also drew his weapon before he helped her out and into the backseat of the waiting unmarked car.

Which wasn't empty.

Drury's brother Lucas was behind the wheel.

"Lucas came when he heard about the attack," Drury said.

Since Lucas was a Texas Ranger, it made sense that he would know about the attack, but it surprised her that he would involve himself in this. Like most of the Rylands, Lucas disliked her, maybe even hated her, because of the nasty breakup between Drury and her.

Lucas didn't say a word to her, though he did spare her a glance in the rearview mirror. He took off as soon as Drury had shut the door.

Drury kept his gun drawn, and he looked all around them. No doubt for any thugs who might be watching for them to leave.

Suddenly, a new wave of fear crawled through her. As bad as it'd been inside the sheriff's office, this was worse.

"Is the car bulletproof?" she asked, and she hated the tremble in her voice.

"Bullet resistant," Drury corrected.

She wasn't certain, but Caitlyn thought that meant they could still be shot. Drury was certainly aware of that possibility, too. And this had to be bringing back god-awful memories for him.

"I'm sorry," she said.

There was no way Drury could have known what the blanket apology meant. Or at least she hadn't thought he would know, but when he glanced at her, she saw it in his eyes. The memories.

Or rather the nightmare.

Of his wife. Lily. She'd been killed by a gunman's bullet in a botched store robbery, and while Caitlyn didn't know all the details, she knew Drury had still been grieving her loss when they'd met. Heck, he probably still was.

And she hadn't helped with that.

Just as Drury had started to risk his heart again, she'd stomped on it. It didn't matter that she thought she had a good reason. Several of them in fact. No. It didn't matter.

Drury's phone buzzed, and Caitlyn prayed this wasn't another round of bad news. However, that wasn't a bad news kind of look on Drury's face when he looked at the screen.

"Don't say anything," he warned her. He pressed the answer button and put the call on speaker.

It didn't take long for her to hear the caller's voice. "What the hell did you do?" the man asked.

Caitlyn immediately recognized the voice, and it only tightened the knot in her stomach. Because it was her former brother-in-law and one of her suspects.

Jeremy.

"Well?" Jeremy snapped when Drury didn't immediately answer.

"Well what?" Drury snapped right back.

"You know. You damn well know."

Drury huffed. "I'm giving you one more chance to make sense, and if you don't, I'm ending this call. Then you can bother someone else. What is it that you think I did?"

"You sent those men after me," Jeremy insisted.

Drury looked at Caitlyn, no doubt to see if she knew anything about this, but she shook her head.

"What men?" Drury questioned.

"The men who want money. A ransom, they said. They want me to pay them for Grant's kid."

It took Caitlyn a moment for that to sink in. Had the kidnappers really contacted Jeremy? If so, they'd probably done the same to his mother, too. Of course, that was assuming that Jeremy was telling the truth, but Caitlyn didn't trust him. Trusted his mother even less.

Drury cursed. "Start talking, and tell me everything," he ordered Jeremy.

"I've already told you everything. Two men showed up at my office a couple of minutes ago. Or rather the parking lot at my office. They accosted me, showed me a picture of some kid that they claimed was Grant and Caitlyn's."

"Who were the men?" Drury pressed. "And where are they now?"

"I don't know. Never saw them before in my life. But they said something about the kid being born through a surrogate and if I wanted the kid that I was to pony up a million bucks. They said I had one hour to get the cash, and they left. They drove off in a black SUV."

"I'm still trying to figure out why you think I had anything to do with this," Drury said.

Jeremy made a sound to indicate that the answer was obvious. It wasn't. "The men told me to pay the money to you."

Because Drury's arm was touching hers, she felt his muscles tense. "Me?"

But Jeremy didn't jump to verify that. Instead, he cursed. "The men are back."

Caitlyn heard some shouts, one of them belonging to Jeremy. "Stop!" he yelled.

"Get someone out to Jeremy Denson's office," Drury told his brother. "Jeremy, are you there?"

No answer.

The line was dead.

Chapter Five

Drury waited. Something he'd been doing all night.

Patience had never been his strong suit, and that was especially true now. He wanted answers. Answers that he wasn't getting. Well, he wasn't getting the right answers anyway.

He'd certainly gotten a string of wrong ones.

No news on Jeremy. Nothing else on the kidnappers, either. Ronnie was sticking to his story about Caitlyn stealing his child. And CPS was pushing Grayson to disclose the location of the baby.

Grayson was staying quiet for now on anything about the baby, though he almost certainly knew that they were at the ranch. Drury wasn't sure how long Grayson's silence would last. Especially since CPS had said they would get protection for the little girl. If they did that, Drury wasn't even sure it was a good idea for Caitlyn and him to keep her.

Unless the child turned out to be hers, that is.

If the baby was indeed her child, then there was no way Caitlyn would give her up. A match wouldn't mean the baby was safe, though. Caitlyn, either. And that left Drury with another question for which he didn't have an answer.

What then?

The logical part of him was saying he should step away

from this. That his past with Caitlyn was just that—the past. But the illogical part of him put up an argument about it. Drury figured it had plenty to do with the old attraction. The one that was still there.

He threw back the covers and got off the sofa where he'd spent the night. Not sleeping, that's for sure. The sofa was about six inches too short for his body, and the thoughts racing through his head hadn't exactly spurred a peaceful sleep. He could still hear the shots. Could still see that look of terror on Caitlyn's face.

Of course, the shooting had brought back the old memories. Of that same look of terror on Lily's face before she'd died in his arms. Memories that he pushed aside. Like the attraction for Caitlyn, he didn't want to cloud his mind with things from the past that he couldn't change.

Since he didn't hear Caitlyn stirring in the bedroom, he tried to be quiet when he went to the kitchen and made some coffee. The small counter was dotted with baby formula and other supplies. Something Lucas had managed to get for them before he'd left the guesthouse shortly after midnight. Later, Drury would need to thank him for helping. Grayson, too.

And that thanks would include them not mentioning that he shouldn't be under the same roof with Caitlyn.

Drury sipped his coffee, went through his emails on the laptop that Lucas had also provided. No updates since the last time he checked other than Grayson was going to have the deputy at the hospital talk to Ronnie again. Maybe the man would cave on his story so that there'd be no question about Caitlyn's innocence.

She already had enough strikes against her with his family of lawmen without adding that.

He heard a slight thudding sound in the bedroom, and Drury practically threw his coffee cup on the table and hurried to find out if anything had happened. Not that he had to go far. It was literally only a few steps from the kitchen. He drew his gun from his shoulder holster and threw open the door, bracing himself for the worst. But it wasn't the *worst*.

Caitlyn was standing there naked.

Almost naked anyway. She was putting on an oversize bathrobe, and he got a glimpse of her body before she managed to yank the sides together and tie the sash.

"Sorry," she whispered. Maybe an apology for the peep show. Or maybe because she'd clearly startled him. Caitlyn picked up the plastic baby bottle that she'd obviously dropped. "I'm on edge, too," she added.

No doubt, but at the moment she didn't exactly look on edge. Their gazes connected. Held. And he saw in her eyes something he didn't want to see. The old heat.

Drury looked away and reholstered his gun. Since he was already there, he also checked on the baby. There'd been no time to get a crib, so the little girl was sleeping on the center of the bed where she'd likely spent most of the night. The covers on the floor told him that Caitlyn had probably slept there.

"I was afraid of rolling onto her during the night," Caitlyn said. "She's so little." There was some fear in her voice, but he didn't think it was from the danger but rather because it was true. The baby really was tiny.

"Did she sleep okay?" he asked.

Caitlyn nodded, then shrugged. "I guess she did. I don't really know how often a baby should be waking up."

Neither did Drury, but Caitlyn had gotten up twice in the night to warm bottles. Drury had asked if he could help. Especially since Caitlyn had had to walk right past him to get to the kitchen. But she'd declined his offer.

"Please tell me you have good news. *Any* good news," Caitlyn said.

It took Drury a couple of moments to come up with something that could possibly be considered good. "Grayson is bringing in both Helen and Melanie for questioning."

Caitlyn flexed her eyebrows. "I'm betting neither was happy about that."

"They weren't. Especially Helen. Grayson said she didn't seem too concerned when he told her about the call we'd gotten from Jeremy."

"She wouldn't be. Jeremy and she haven't been on friendly terms in years. Jeremy's a hothead."

Yeah, Drury had figured that out from the brief phone call. But the "hothead" was about to be labeled a missing person if they didn't hear from him soon.

"Someone had tampered with the security cameras in the parking garage where Jeremy made that call," he explained. "There's no footage for fifteen minutes before the call or for a half hour afterward."

She stayed quiet a moment. "You think Jeremy could have really been kidnapped?"

Drury had to lift his shoulder. "You know him better than I do. Would he fake a disappearance?"

"Yes," Caitlyn said without hesitation. "If it benefited him in some way. And this possibly could if he thought he was a suspect in the attack last night." But then she shook her head. "Of course, he wouldn't have had any part in her birth." She glanced at the baby.

"Because he wouldn't want to share his inheritance." Drury remembered Caitlyn mentioning that. "But if he's worried about splitting an inheritance, wouldn't he try to smooth things over with his mom?"

"Helen can't cut him out of the estate. That's in the

terms of his late father's will. Jeremy will inherit everything unless Grant has an heir."

Drury figured the estate had to be worth millions. Still, it took a coldhearted SOB to go after a child because of money. If that's what Jeremy had done. Considering the bad blood between him and his mother, Helen might have used this as an opportunity to get rid of Jeremy, her sole surviving son.

Especially if the woman thought she had a new heir. Grant's baby.

"I was about to take a shower." Caitlyn fluttered her fingers toward the adjoining bathroom. "That's why I wasn't dressed when you came in. I was going to put her in the carrier on the bathroom floor, but could you watch her?"

Drury nodded. And hoped the baby didn't wake up. Unlike his cousins, he just wasn't comfortable holding a newborn.

"I won't be long," Caitlyn added, and she hurried into the bathroom.

He sank down on the edge of the bed and studied the little girl's face. He could see Caitlyn's mouth and chin. Or at least he thought he could. No resemblance to Grant, though, and it surprised him a little to realize that even if he had seen it, it wouldn't have made him uneasy. His beef had never been with Grant.

But rather Caitlyn leaving him to be with Grant.

Of course, it was his own stupid fault for handing Caitlyn his heart when he knew he was the wrong man for her. She'd told him right from the get-go that she couldn't get involved with a lawman. Not after her lawman father's violent death. Even after they'd started an affair, she had continued to tell Drury that it could never be more than temporary between them.

Too bad he hadn't believed her.

Caitlyn was right about not being too long. She stayed in the shower only a couple of minutes, and it took her even less than that to dress. She hurried out while combing her wet hair.

She smelled like roses.

The soap, no doubt, but it was something he wished he hadn't noticed.

"Thanks," she said.

Since it was time for him to get the heck out of the bedroom, Drury stood, but the moment he did, the baby squirmed a little and made a fussing sound. He stepped back so that Caitlyn could go to her and take her in her arms.

They made a picture together. And Drury had no trouble seeing the love for the child in Caitlyn's eyes.

"I know," Caitlyn said, following his gaze to the baby. "I shouldn't get so attached. But I've always wanted a child, so it's hard not to have deep feelings for her."

An understatement. Caitlyn had *really* wanted a child. Something she'd made clear when they were together.

Something that had driven a wedge between them, too.

Heck, it still made him take a step back now.

Too many memories. More of those old ones that he wanted to forget. But couldn't. Because he hadn't just lost his wife the day she'd been murdered. He'd lost the child that she'd been carrying.

"Will you still help me with a safe house?" she asked. "An unofficial one, of course. I don't think you want to use FBI channels."

Neither did he. "I'll help with the house." Hell, he'd ended up helping with plenty of things he didn't want to help with, but despite their past he was still a sucker for a damsel in distress, and at the moment Caitlyn was in a lot of *distress*.

She mumbled another thanks. "I was going to get started on contacting some bodyguards, and I was hoping I could use your laptop to get some phone numbers."

He nearly offered her a protection detail. But he was also toeing the line on the law. Heck, he'd probably crossed over that line, and he didn't want to bring any of his fellow agents or family into this.

"The laptop's on the table in the kitchen," he said.

She gathered the blanket around the baby and headed that direction. Drury followed, but before he even made it there, his phone buzzed, and he saw Grayson's name on the screen. He considered not putting the call on speaker, just in case this was more bad news, but he'd end up telling Caitlyn about the conversation anyway.

"You're on speaker," Drury warned Grayson right off, though he doubted that would change anything Grayson had to say.

"Good. Because Caitlyn needs to hear this. I've arranged for the doctor to examine the baby. Yeah, I know. It's a risk, but she needs to be checked out."

"I agree." A weary sigh left Caitlyn's mouth. "And it's something I should have remembered to do."

"You've had a lot on your mind lately." There was a touch of sarcasm in Grayson's tone. "I want you two to take the baby to the hospital. And don't worry, she won't be near Ronnie. The doctor will meet you in his private office to do the exam. I've arranged for Lucas and one of the deputies to escort you there."

Escort was a nice way of saying *back up* in case someone tried to gun them down again.

"Anything new from Ronnie?" Drury asked.

"Nothing. He's lawyered up and is refusing to cooperate with us. Not CPS, though. He's still pressuring them to give him the baby. Which they won't do," Grayson quickly added. "Not without DNA proof anyway, and it'll be to-morrow before we have that."

"The DNA will show that Ronnie's not the father," Cait-lyn said like gospel, and Drury hoped that was true.

He didn't exactly relish the idea of handing over a child to someone who'd shot at him. Of course, that wouldn't happen anyway unless Ronnie was cleared of all charges.

"Ronnie said he can prove the baby is his," Grayson went on. "Because he can describe the birthmark on her ankle. Does she have a birthmark?"

"She does," Caitlyn admitted. "But Ronnie could have easily seen it when he had her."

"That was my theory, too. By the way, Melanie's on her way in," Grayson added a moment later. "Drury, if you want to be here for the interview, you could have Lucas or someone else stay with Caitlyn and the baby."

It was tempting. "When will she be there?" Drury asked.

"Within the hour." He paused. "I have plenty of ques-tions for her now that I've read the police report for Grant's car accident. Melanie's purse was found in the vehicle."

Drury had read the report, too. Not recently. But shortly after Grant had died. Why? He didn't know. It was a way of picking at those old wounds, but he hadn't been able to stop himself. So, yeah, he knew about Melanie's purse.

Obviously so did Caitlyn. "Melanie claimed that Grant and she had been together that night, but when he dropped her off at her place, she forgot her purse." She frowned. "The police cleared her as a suspect, but you think Melanie could have had something to do with his death?"

"Do you?" Grayson asked right back.

She certainly didn't jump to deny it. Caitlyn took a moment and gently rocked the baby even though the little girl was no longer fussing. "Possibly. Jeremy is still my top suspect for that. If it wasn't an accident, that is. But I suppose Melanie could have been upset with Grant about something."

"You don't know?" Grayson pressed.

"No. By then Grant and I were separated. That's why I was a suspect at first, but I was cleared, too, because it was ruled an accident. Added to that, I had an alibi."

"A ruptured appendix," Drury mumbled.

Caitlyn's gaze raced to his, and she looked a little surprised that he knew that. When it came to her, Drury always seemed to know a little too much. Like that she'd nearly died herself that night and was in emergency surgery at the same time her estranged husband swerved off the road and hit a tree. Since there'd been other skid marks nearby, the cops had first thought someone had run him off the road, but the CSIs hadn't been able to prove that the marks were made the exact same time as the accident.

"I just want to know as much about Melanie as possible before I question her," Grayson went on. "Does she have any hot buttons?"

"Me," Caitlyn answered. "Until I filed for divorce, she was harassing me. She hates me. That's why I told Drury that I didn't think she had anything to do with the baby or Conceptions Clinic."

Grayson made a sound to indicate he was withholding judgment on that. "I'll let you know if I find out anything from her, and I'll have Lucas give you a call once he's on his way there. By the way, Lucas didn't tell me exactly where you were on the ranch, and I'd like to keep it that way."

So would Drury. The fewer people who knew, the better.

Drury ended the call, and since Caitlyn had said she wanted to use his laptop, he turned it in her direction. She glanced at the baby. Then at him.

"I'll get the carrier from the bedroom," she said, not giving him a chance to decline to hold the baby. Not that he would have. But Caitlyn must have realized that it wasn't something he wanted to do.

Several moments later, she came back into the kitchen, the baby already snuggled into the carrier, and she set the carrier on the table next to the laptop.

"For a bodyguard search, try starting with Sencor Agency in San Antonio," he suggested.

She muttered a thanks and got started on that just as Drury's phone buzzed again. Not Grayson this time but rather his brother Mason, who lived at the main house on the ranch.

"We have a visitor," Mason growled the moment Drury answered. "She's at the security gate pitching a fit. I didn't tell her either of you were here, but she's insisting on seeing Caitlyn."

Even though Drury didn't have the phone on speaker, either Caitlyn heard or else she noticed the alarm on Drury's face because she slowly got to her feet.

"Who is it? Melanie?" Drury asked.

"No. It's Caitlyn's mother-in-law, Helen. And along with demanding to see Caitlyn, she says she wants her grandbaby right now."

Chapter Six

Caitlyn squeezed her eyes shut a moment. This was the last thing she'd expected—for Grant's mother to show up at the Silver Creek Ranch.

"How did Helen know Caitlyn was here?" Drury asked, taking the question right out of her mouth.

Of course, Caitlyn had an even more important question. How had Helen found out about the baby?

"She said a man called her," Mason answered. "Ronnie Waite. He told her that Caitlyn would be here."

Caitlyn had to shake her head. "Why would Ronnie have done that? He's claiming the baby is his."

"Yeah, apparently your mother-in-law doesn't believe that."

"Former mother-in-law," Caitlyn automatically corrected.

Mason grumbled something that sounded like a *whatever*. "She's on hold on the house line if you want to have a little chat with her. If not, I'll have the ranch hands *escort* her off the property."

Helen wouldn't go peacefully. She didn't do much in life that qualified as peaceful. And Caitlyn didn't want the Rylands or their ranch hands to have to deal with the woman. Heck, she didn't want to deal with Helen, either, but the fastest way to get rid of her might be to take the call.

"I'll speak to her," Caitlyn volunteered.

"Not a smart idea," Drury snapped. "It'll confirm to her that you're here."

"I can tell her that I transferred the call to your location," Mason suggested. "I won't have to tell her where, exactly, that location is."

"Yes, please do that," Caitlyn said, ignoring Drury's huff. She picked up the landline phone and waited.

Despite Drury not agreeing to this, he used the laptop to tap into the ranch's security system. There were multiple screens, and he zoomed in on the one at the security gate. Helen was there all right, her phone pressed to her ear while she glared at the two armed ranch hands who were blocking her from getting past the gate.

Helen was aware of the camera because she was volleying glances between it and the ranch hands. The October wind had kicked up some and was rifling through her blond hair. Hair that was usually perfect. Ditto for her dark jacket, but she definitely looked a little disheveled this morning.

At least the baby had fallen back to sleep and Helen wouldn't be able to hear her, but just in case she woke up, Caitlyn would keep her voice soft. Also for the baby's sake, she would make this conversation short.

"Start talking," Caitlyn *greeted* Helen the moment the woman came on the line.

"No, you start talking. Tell these goons to let me onto the ranch so I can see the baby."

"We're not at the ranch," Caitlyn lied. "So, you need to leave before they arrest you. It's not very smart to go to a ranch with a family of lawmen and start making a scene."

"It's not right for you to withhold my granddaughter from me," Helen countered. "Did you think you could hide her?"

Caitlyn took a moment to consider her answer, but a moment was too long because Drury took the phone from her and put it on speaker. "What did Ronnie tell you?" he demanded.

"Special Agent Drury Ryland, I presume?" Helen spat out his name like profanity. "Ronnie said you'd be with Caitlyn, that you were helping her hide the baby."

"No, I'm helping her stay alive. Someone tried to kill the baby and her last night. What do you know about that?"

Helen gasped. Shocked, or else faking that she was. "The baby was in danger?"

"Not what you'd planned, huh?" Drury asked. "Did you tell Ronnie not to fire shots around the baby?"

Since Drury had just accused Helen of hiring a thug like Ronnie to get the baby and kill Caitlyn, it wasn't much of a surprise that her eyes narrowed to slits.

"I know what you're doing," Helen said. "You're trying to put the blame on me for this. Well, I didn't do it. Hell, I didn't even know I had a grandchild until this morning when he called me."

"And did he tell you that the child was his?" Caitlyn countered.

"He said it was possibly his. Or my granddaughter. But he said the odds are that she was Grant's daughter."

Caitlyn groaned. The man was playing both sides.

"What did he want in exchange for the information he was giving you?" Drury asked.

Helen paused. No, it was a hesitation. "He wants me to help him get out of any possible charges that might be filed against him."

"He shot at me, and I won't be giving him a get-out-of-jail-free card on that," Drury stated. "Now tell me everything you know about Ronnie and Conceptions Clinic."

Caitlyn expected the woman to launch into a verbal

tirade and blast Drury for the order. She didn't. Helen pushed her hair from her face and sighed.

"I did go to Conceptions," Helen finally admitted. "Not recently, but I went there when Grant told me that Caitlyn was having her eggs harvested. I wanted to find out more about the procedure."

Caitlyn knew Helen well enough to know that she was leaving something out of that explanation. And she thought she might know exactly what.

"You tried to bribe someone into stopping the in vitro," Caitlyn said. Yes, it was a bluff, but she knew she'd hit pay dirt when again Helen didn't jump to deny it.

Helen glanced away from the camera, but her defiance quickly returned. "I knew your marriage to Grant wouldn't last. You weren't in love with him, and he was seeing another woman. That bimbo, Melanie."

Not defiance that time but anger. Apparently, Melanie and Helen had clashed. Or maybe Helen blamed Melanie in some way for her son's death.

"No one at the clinic would listen to me," Helen went on. "And then Grant died and I forgot all about Conceptions."

"Really?" Drury challenged. "You're sure you didn't arrange to use their stored embryo so you could have a grandchild?"

"No." Helen was adamant about it, too. "I had nothing to do with that. But someone must have seen this as a way to make some money. They did with others at Conceptions."

They had, and other than his niece and nephew, there'd been another child, as well. One not connected to the Ryland family or Caitlyn.

"You paid them a ransom," Helen snapped. "Didn't you, Caitlyn?"

It was probably a guess on her part, but Caitlyn saw no

reason to deny it. "I did. And when Ronnie reneged on the deal, that's when I hit him with a stun gun and took the child." Caitlyn paused long enough to draw in a long breath. "Helen, if you hired him, tell me now because I need to know if there are others who'll try to kidnap the baby."

"I didn't hire him." No hesitation whatsoever. "But if my granddaughter is in danger, I can help."

"She doesn't need your help," Drury fired back.

Judging from the profanity that he mumbled, he hadn't intended to say that. Probably because it sounded as if he was volunteering to make sure she was safe. Caitlyn wouldn't hold him to that, though. As soon as she had a safe place to go, she and the baby would leave.

"You have no right to keep my granddaughter from me," Helen argued. She didn't wait for either of them to respond. "I know Caitlyn's always been in love with you, but you're not the baby's father. My son is."

Caitlyn tried not to react to that. Hard to do, though, when she felt as if someone had slapped her. It must have felt that way to Drury, too, because he stared at her, mumbled more of that profanity and looked away.

"You went to Conceptions to stop Caitlyn from having Grant's baby," Drury reminded Helen. "Now you want me to believe that you have a right to see a child that you never wanted to exist?"

Helen didn't fire off a quick answer that time. "My son is dead, and this baby is part of him. Part of *me*. You can't stop me from seeing her."

"I can and will if it means keeping her safe," Drury insisted.

"You can't mean that. You really want to protect Grant's child? Any child for that matter."

Caitlyn saw Drury's old wounds rise to the surface.

Helen probably knew all about Drury's past. Knew that her comment would pick at those old wounds. And Caitlyn hated the woman for it.

"I'm an FBI agent," Drury finally said. "I'll do my job, and right now my job is protecting Caitlyn and the baby. A baby whose paternity doesn't matter to me because it won't stop me from protecting her. You won't stop me, either."

Helen flinched. "What does that mean? I told you that I want this child. I wouldn't hurt her."

"Then who would?" Drury snapped. "Who would hire a man like Ronnie to kidnap her?"

"I don't know."

"Then guess!" His voice was so loud that it startled the baby.

Drury mumbled an apology, and Caitlyn gently rocked the carrier so the baby would go back to sleep.

"Jeremy," Helen said.

It didn't take Caitlyn any time at all to realize that Helen had just accused her son of some assorted felonies. Or rather she'd *guessed* he was involved.

"You have proof?" Drury asked.

"No." The woman's shoulders dropped. "I'm sure Caitlyn told you all about how much Jeremy hated Grant. I'm sure Caitlyn told you a lot of things. Pillow talk reveals lots of secrets."

Caitlyn had to bite her lip to keep from shouting out a denial that Drury and she were involved again. Besides, Helen wouldn't believe her no matter what she said, especially since Drury and she were under the same roof.

For the moment anyway.

"Why don't you tell me more about Jeremy?" Drury countered. "Is he really missing or did he fake his disappearance?"

"Who knows?" There was no concern in her expression

or her tone. She could have been discussing the weather. "I gave up trying to figure Jeremy out a long time ago."

Drury made a sound of disagreement. "And yet you just accused him of attempted murder. Are you sure you're not trying to put the blame on your son so you won't look guilty?"

Helen glanced around, and when she looked back at the camera, Caitlyn could see new resolve in the woman's eyes. "I'm done with this conversation. If you don't let me see my granddaughter, then I'll call your boss and tell him exactly what you're doing."

"Call him," Drury responded.

Obviously, that wasn't the reaction Helen expected because she shot a glare into the camera. "This isn't over," Helen said, and she stormed back to her car, slamming the door once she was inside.

"She means it." Caitlyn eased the baby carrier back onto the table. "Helen will make trouble for you."

Drury kept his attention focused on the screen where they could see Helen driving away. "She'll try."

Yes, and Helen would keep trying until she got what she wanted. But she wouldn't just want the baby if it turned out that she was her granddaughter. Helen would want the baby without Caitlyn in the picture.

Drury glanced at her and no doubt saw that she was trying to blink back tears. "Don't apologize again," he warned Caitlyn.

She did anyway, but she doubted it would be the last of the apologies that she would owe him. Caitlyn sank down in the chair next to him.

"If you're going to talk about those things Helen just said about us, don't bother," Drury added. He dismissed it with a shake of his head.

However, it dismissed nothing for Caitlyn. "I was in love with you when we were together," she said.

Drury didn't dismiss that, but he did stare at her for a long time before he looked away. "Do you really want to dig up these old bones?"

No. But she couldn't seem to stop herself. "We didn't really talk when things ended between us." In fact, Drury hadn't said a word when she'd told him she was leaving. He wasn't saying a word now, either. "I left because I couldn't be there, not after what happened."

There was no reason for her to explain that. Because Drury hadn't forgotten that he'd nearly been killed just the day before she'd ended things. Nearly killed while doing his job.

A job he would never give up.

"I saw the pictures of the attack," she went on.

Again, she didn't need to add to that because he knew which pictures she meant. Drury had been caught in the middle of a gunfight while on a task force to arrest a serial killer, and there'd been bystanders around who'd taken photos that had appeared in every news outlet in the state. On social media, too.

Everywhere she looked, she'd seen Drury on the ground after taking a bullet to the chest. Thankfully, the Kevlar had prevented him from being killed, but he'd had several cracked ribs. Along with escaping death by only a couple of seconds. The killer had taken aim at Drury again, but Drury's partner had stopped him before he could pull the trigger.

In Caitlyn's mind, however, she saw the trigger being pulled. She felt the pain of losing yet another man she loved.

Drury's gaze came back to her. "Is there a reason you're going through all of this now?"

"Yes. I just wanted you to know that it wasn't you. It was me."

For a moment Caitlyn wasn't even sure he was going to acknowledge that. But then he huffed, got to his feet and went to the window.

"We were both in a bad place at that time," he finally said.

Yes, because he was trying to get over the loss of his wife and unborn child. Heck, he was no doubt still trying to get over that. Losing them wasn't a wound that was ever going to heal.

"Does that mean you can forgive me?" she asked.

"No."

Caitlyn had steeled herself up for that answer, but it still cut to the bone. Because it was true.

But Drury waved it off, spared her a glance. "I don't want to forgive you," he amended. "It's easier to hang on to the hurt than it is the pain."

She nodded, and while it wasn't exactly a truce, it was a start. A start that she would take.

His phone buzzed again, and Caitlyn automatically checked the computer screen to make sure Helen hadn't returned. Or that kidnappers hadn't shown up to storm the ranch. But other than the ranch hands, there was no one else at the gate.

"It's Grayson," Drury relayed.

Unlike some of the other calls, he didn't put this one on speaker, and since the air was practically zinging between them, Caitlyn didn't go closer. Best not to risk being so close to him when everything felt ready to explode.

Caitlyn couldn't hear a single word of what Grayson was saying, but she had no trouble interpreting Drury's response. He cursed.

Mercy, what had gone wrong now?

"How did that happen?" Drury snapped.

Again, she couldn't hear Grayson's response. Whatever it was, though, it didn't help Drury's suddenly tight muscles. It seemed to take an eternity for him to finish the conversation and another eternity before he turned to her.

"Ronnie's gone," he said.

"He escaped?" And her mind automatically thought the worst. That he'd gotten away and was coming after the baby and her. "We should leave now."

Drury shook his head. "He didn't escape. Two men sneaked into the hospital, knocked out the deputy and took him at gunpoint. According to several eyewitnesses, Ronnie's been kidnapped."

Chapter Seven

"I don't like being here," Drury heard Caitlyn say under her breath. She probably hoped that would make the doctor speed up the exam that he was giving the baby.

Drury hoped that as well, but Dr. Michelson sure didn't move any faster. Too bad because being in the hospital was an in-your-face reminder that only a couple of hours earlier, those gunmen had stormed in.

And kidnapped Ronnie.

Well, maybe that's what had happened. But Drury wasn't about to buy it just yet. It was just as likely that Ronnie's comrade-thugs had pretended to take him by force. Or maybe the person who'd hired Ronnie had done that. Not necessarily to rescue him, though, but to silence him after he'd failed to get his hands on the baby.

"There are two deputies outside the door," Drury reminded Caitlyn.

He hadn't figured that would erase the worry on her face. It didn't. Maybe because she remembered that a deputy had been outside Ronnie's room as well, and that hadn't stopped the attack. In fact, the deputy had been hurt. Not seriously. But it could have been a whole lot worse.

"Well, she appears to be fine," the doctor finally said. "Since you don't know the exact day of her birth, I'm estimating that she's at least a week old. She's been well fed, no signs of any kind of injury or trauma."

Caitlyn released the breath that she must have been holding. Of course, Drury had expected the child to be in good health since he hadn't seen any signs to indicate otherwise.

"Can you tell if she was born with a C-section?" Drury asked. "It might make it easier for us to find the surrogate who carried her."

"It's hard to say in her case. Her head is well shaped, which could mean a C-section delivery, but the surrogate could have also had a very short labor. Therefore, the baby wouldn't have been in the birth canal that long."

This seemed like way too much personal information. And it brought back the memories.

Always the memories.

His wife, Lily, had been only three months pregnant when she died, but she'd started reading books about pregnancy and delivery even before they'd conceived. What the doctor had just told him rang some bells. But Drury pushed those bells and memories aside and forced himself to look at the situation from a lawman's point of view.

Basically, the information didn't help at all because it didn't rule out any woman who'd given birth within the past couple of weeks. Plus, Drury figured whoever was responsible for this hadn't delivered the child in a hospital. Too much of a paper trail.

Caitlyn made a sharp sound, and it not only grabbed Drury's attention. It caused him to reach for his gun. False alarm. The sound was the doctor giving the baby a blood test. The baby didn't like it much and kicked and squirmed. Drury figured it was necessary, but he had to look away. Yeah, he was plenty used to seeing blood, but it was different when it was an innocent baby.

"I'll get this to the lab," the doctor said when he finished. Caitlyn immediately got up and scooped the child into her arms.

"I thought you said nothing was wrong with her," Drury reminded him.

"This is just routine, something all newborns have done." Dr. Michelson headed for the door but then stopped. "I won't put your name on it," he said to Caitlyn. "I'll just list it as Baby Ryland. There are enough of those around here that it won't raise any suspicions."

He was right about the sheer number of Rylands, but Drury figured it still might get some attention. The wrong attention, too. That's why Drury didn't want to stick around the hospital much longer. Even though they were in the clinic section, on the other side of the building from where Ronnie had been, that didn't mean someone didn't have the place under surveillance.

"How soon can we leave?" Drury asked the doctor.

"Soon. I just need to get the paperwork for Caitlyn to sign." He headed out, shutting the door behind him.

The baby didn't fuss for long. Probably because Caitlyn was rocking her and looking down at the baby's face with an expression he knew all too well. Love. She'd gotten attached to the child, and that could turn out to be a bad thing if the DNA tests proved the baby belonged to someone else.

But who else?

There'd been no reports of missing newborns in the area, and if the child had been kidnapped from her parents, someone would have almost certainly reported it. If they were still alive, that is.

Caitlyn glanced at him. "I'm sorry about the doctor putting *Ryland* on the lab test."

They were talking about those blasted memories again.

The ones Drury didn't want to discuss with her. With anyone.

Instead he took out his phone to make a call about the safe house, but before he could do that, Caitlyn sat down beside him. "I really think you should just walk away from this," she said. "I know how hard this is for you."

Yeah, it was hard, but that pissed him off.

"Walk away? *Right*. I'm a lawman, and even if I weren't, I'm not a coward. There's someone after the baby. Someone who's free as a bird right now." He had to get his teeth unclenched before he could continue. "No, I won't walk away until I'm sure she's safe."

Drury hadn't intended to blurt all that out. Hadn't intended to make a commitment that would keep Caitlyn right by his side. And she would be. Because the baby and Caitlyn were a package deal. At least until the DNA results came back anyway and the person responsible for the danger was caught.

He looked at her and saw that she was staring at him. He also saw just how close they were to each other. Close enough for him to draw in her too-familiar scent. That scent had his number because it slid right through him. Silk and heat.

Apparently, this was his morning for doing things he hadn't planned on doing because he made the mistake of dropping his gaze to her mouth. He remembered how she tasted, knew how it felt to kiss her long and deep.

Worse, his body remembered it, too.

She took in a quick breath, and he saw the pulse flutter on her throat. There was some of that heat in her eyes. Her body seemed to be remembering, as well.

Drury suddenly wanted to kiss her. Or maybe it wasn't so sudden after all. Kissing, and other things, had a way of coming to mind whenever he saw Caitlyn.

He was so caught up in the notion of that kiss that Drury nearly jumped when the sound of his phone startled him. Great. Talk about losing focus.

Grayson's name was on the screen, and Drury pressed the answer button as fast as he could. Maybe his cousin had found something to put an end to all of this.

"Are you still at the hospital?" Grayson asked right off.

"Yeah. But we're nearly finished."

"Good. How would you feel about leaving the baby with the deputies and coming here to the sheriff's office for a short visit?"

"I wouldn't feel good about it at all," Caitlyn answered, which meant she'd heard every word.

Drury put the call on speaker anyway. "What's going on?"

"Melanie's here, and she's in a very chatty mood. Well, up to a point anyway. She's been telling us about Helen's visits to Conceptions, and she claims she knows who Helen might have hired to steal Grant and Caitlyn's embryo."

"She has a name?" Drury quickly asked.

"Says she does, but she's insisting on talking to Caitlyn face-to-face. She says she has questions for her."

Drury didn't want to speculate as to what those questions might be, but he was plenty skeptical that Melanie had any information that would help.

"This could be a ploy to get Caitlyn out into the open," Drury reminded him.

"I know. I could give you a protection detail to get here. A second detail for the baby so she can be taken back to the ranch. But I can't tie up that kind of manpower for long."

No, because that would include four deputies, and that was a third of the lawmen working there.

"You really think my seeing Melanie would help anything?" Caitlyn asked. "And what if CPS finds out I'm there?"

"I can't guarantee you that CPS won't show up, but if they do, I could stall them. As for whether or not Melanie can help, who knows? Right now, I'd like nothing more than to charge her with obstruction of justice for withholding possible evidence, but I doubt I could get the charges to stick. Melanie could just claim she doesn't have any real info and that she was bluffing so she could speak to Caitlyn."

Drury agreed, and it would also likely rile the woman to the point where she wouldn't give them any info.

"It's your decision," Drury told Caitlyn.

She glanced at the baby, then at Drury before she nodded. "Let's do it," Caitlyn said, getting to her feet.

Drury certainly didn't feel any relief over that decision. Even if Melanie did manage to give them something, it could come at a very high price.

"Go ahead and send the protection details," Drury told Grayson.

"All right… Wait, hold on a second."

Even though there wasn't any alarm in Grayson's voice, Drury went on instant alert. Caitlyn, too. And they waited for several long moments before Grayson finally came back on the line.

"This is apparently the day for surprises," Grayson said. "The cops just found Jeremy."

THE DAY FOR SURPRISES.

Caitlyn hoped Grayson's comment didn't come true in a bad sort of way. It sickened her to think of leaving the baby, even for a short period of time, but that wasn't even her biggest concern.

There could be another attack.

Not only on her, either, but someone could go after the baby while the protection detail was taking her back to the ranch. She hoped they were keeping watch as well as Drury was right now. Though Drury's and her ride was only a short distance, and the ranch was miles away.

"My cousins will protect the baby with their lives," Drury reminded her.

It was the right thing to say, and she believed him. The Rylands might not like her, but they were good lawmen and would do their jobs. Still, that didn't mean the worst couldn't happen, and besides, the visit could all be for nothing. Caitlyn was past the point of having second thoughts about this and had moved on to fourth and fifth thoughts and doubts. That didn't just apply to Melanie.

But to Jeremy.

She listened as Drury got a phone update on the man, and apparently Jeremy had wandered into San Antonio PD with a story about escaping from his kidnappers. Whether that was true or not remained to be seen, but at least now that the cops knew where he was, maybe they could keep an eye on him to make sure he wasn't planning another attack.

"Was Jeremy hurt?" she asked when Drury finished his call.

"Not a scratch on him, but his clothes were disheveled."

Which he could have easily done himself. "How did he *escape*?"

Drury shook his head. "SAPD's questioning him now, and after they're done, they'll send us a copy of the report. In the meantime, we'll deal with Melanie and then head back to the ranch."

That couldn't come soon enough for her. "I'm not even sure why Melanie wants to see me," she said. "If she's really got something dirty on Helen, why wouldn't she just give it to Grayson?"

It was a question she'd already asked herself a dozen times, and she still didn't have an answer.

"Maybe Melanie wants to bargain with you about something," Drury suggested.

She shook her head, not able to imagine what that would be.

"If the baby is Grant's," Drury continued, "maybe she thinks she can convince you to turn the child over to her."

Caitlyn hadn't intended to curse, but the profanity just came out. "No way would I give that woman a baby, any baby."

He lifted his shoulder, continued to glance around as they approached the front of the sheriff's office. "Melanie probably doesn't think too highly of you so she might think she can buy the baby from you."

"She doesn't think much of me, and the feeling's mutual." Caitlyn huffed. "But it does sound like Melanie believes I'd do something that despicable."

The deputy pulled to a stop directly in front of the door to the sheriff's office, and Drury quickly got her inside. He didn't stay at the front with her but rather headed past reception and straight to Grayson's office. Grayson was there, seated at his desk, and he tipped his head to the room across the hall.

"Melanie's in there. Brace yourself," Grayson warned them. "She's a piece of work."

Caitlyn had firsthand knowledge of that, and she tried to look a lot more confident about this meeting than she felt. She wanted only to finish it so she could get back to the baby and complete the plans for a safe house and bodyguards.

When Drury and she walked in, Melanie was seated,

her attention on her phone screen, and she barely spared them a glance before continuing to read a text.

"You took your time," Melanie grumbled.

The other times she'd crossed paths with Melanie, the woman had been wearing some high-end outfit suitable for the runway, but today she was wearing skintight jeans and a red top. The heels of her stilettos were no thicker than pencils.

"What did you have to say to me?" Caitlyn asked, and she didn't bother to sound friendly. "I understand you have something on Helen?"

Melanie glanced at her again. A disapproving glance, and as if she had all the time in the world, she got to her feet. With those heels and her height, she towered over Caitlyn and could practically meet Drury eye to eye.

"This is how this will work," Melanie said. "I'll give you some information, and in exchange you'll give me what I want."

Drury's hands went on his hips. "And what exactly is it you want?"

"To do a DNA test on the baby that Caitlyn believes is Grant's and hers."

So, this was about the baby. But Caitlyn certainly hadn't expected Melanie to demand a DNA test.

"What's this about?" Caitlyn pressed.

"It's about giving me a DNA test." She spoke slowly as if Caitlyn were mentally deficient.

Caitlyn had to stop herself from rolling her eyes. "Why don't you explain what you mean?" she asked at the same moment Drury had his own question.

"How did you know about the baby?"

Judging from Melanie's hesitation, that wasn't something she wanted to answer, but she must have felt she couldn't sidestep it. Not with Drury glaring at her like that.

"Helen," Melanie finally said. "She told me. But it doesn't matter how I found out. This is about what went on at Conceptions." Again, the tone was an attempt to make Caitlyn feel like an idiot. She didn't feel like one, but she was confused. "Helen went to Conceptions to stop Grant and you from having a baby."

"Old news." Caitlyn hoped her own tone made Melanie feel like an idiot. "Helen already admitted that."

Judging from the brief widening of Melanie's eyes, she hadn't expected that. "Did she also tell you that she succeeded, that she did stop it?"

"I stopped it," Caitlyn clarified. "When I filed for a divorce."

"But you think someone else started it again." Melanie wasn't smiling exactly, but it was close. The expression of a woman who had a secret. "Well, you're wrong. No one started it the way you think."

"What the hell are you talking about?" Drury snarled.

With that sly half smile on her face, Melanie sank down onto the chair. "I went to Conceptions, too. Not to stop Caitlyn and Grant's procedure. Grant had already promised me that he would put a stop to that."

Drury glanced at Caitlyn, no doubt to see if that was true, but she had to shrug. It possibly was. Near the end of their marriage, things hadn't been exactly rosy between Grant and her. Of course, Grant could have lied to his mistress, too.

"I didn't go to Conceptions until after Grant died," Melanie continued. "And I went there to have my eggs harvested. I paid them to use Grant's semen."

"That's illegal," Caitlyn pointed out, but just as quickly, she waved it off. It wouldn't have mattered to Melanie if it was illegal or not. Heck, judging from everything that'd happened at Conceptions, it wouldn't have mattered to them, either.

"I wanted Grant's baby," Melanie said as if that justified everything. "Not yours and his baby. Mine and his."

It took a moment for Caitlyn to find the breath to speak. "Are you saying you think the baby I rescued is yours?"

"Absolutely," Melanie answered without hesitation. "I paid Conceptions to implant mine and Grant's embryo into a surrogate. That's why I'm demanding a DNA test."

Caitlyn felt Drury slip his arm around her waist, and only then did she realize that she wasn't too steady on her feet. "Melanie could be lying," Drury reminded her.

Yes, she could be, but Melanie's smile made Caitlyn think otherwise.

"Why would you use a surrogate?" Drury asked the woman. "Why not just do artificial insemination and carry the baby yourself?"

"Because I have female problems. Not that it's any of your business. Besides, I don't handle pain very well and didn't want to go through childbirth."

And she probably didn't want to risk stretch marks and such on her model-thin figure. In that moment, Caitlyn hated Grant for bringing Melanie into their lives. Hated even more that all of this could be true.

"What's the name of the surrogate?" Drury snapped.

"I don't know. I don't," Melanie repeated when that intensified Drury's glare. "The person at Conceptions told me that had to be kept confidential."

That didn't surprise Caitlyn. Some surrogates would have wanted to keep their identities a secret.

"Even if you paid Conceptions to do the procedure," Drury said, "there are no guarantees that they carried through on it. They were into all sorts of illegal activities and could have just taken your money."

"But there's a baby," Melanie argued.

"A baby that could just as easily be Caitlyn's. After all, the kidnappers contacted her for a ransom. Why wouldn't they have gone to you?"

The smile faded, and Melanie glanced away. "Probably because I'm not loaded like Caitlyn. She's the one who inherited all Grant's money. I didn't get a penny of it."

Yes, and Melanie was just as bitter about that as Helen was. "Did you use your own child to get ransom money from me?" Caitlyn came out and asked.

"No," Melanie practically shouted. But the volume and emotion did nothing to convince Caitlyn that it was true.

God, it could be true.

The baby might not be hers after all. Her stomach knotted and twisted until she felt as if she might throw up.

Drury stared at Melanie. "Let me guess. You think if you have Grant's child that Helen will pony up lots of cash to get shared custody. Or maybe you plan to charge her for visitation rights?"

"That's none of your business. I have my DNA on file at several labs in San Antonio," Melanie went on. "But I don't trust you to tell me the truth. That's why I want you to bring the baby here so I can watch someone do the test."

"The baby is in protective custody because someone's trying to take her," Drury snapped. "A real mother wouldn't want to put the child in danger by demanding that she be brought here."

That caused Melanie's shoulders to snap back, and she opened her mouth, no doubt ready to argue. But she must have realized just how that would make her look—like the cold, calculating person she was. Plus, if Drury was right about Melanie using the baby to get money from Helen, she wouldn't want to risk her investment being harmed.

"My lawyer will be in touch to schedule that DNA test," Melanie said. "With witnesses. I don't want Caitlyn or any of your cowboy cops trying to pull a fast one on me."

With that accusation, Melanie waltzed out.

Drury kept his arm around her waist, and Caitlyn was thankful for it. Thankful, too, that he'd refused to bring in the baby for testing. Of course, he might not be able to refuse for long. If Melanie had any proof whatsoever that she was the child's mother, then she might be able to get a court order.

"I'll give you two a minute," Grayson said, stepping out and closing the door.

Caitlyn thought she might need more than a minute.

"You okay?" Drury asked her. "Dumb question, I know, but I'm in that gray area where anything I say could make it worse."

She could only shake her head. "Until the kidnapper called me with a ransom demand, it'd been a long time since I'd thought about having a baby. Now, it crushes me to think that I might lose her."

"Yeah." Without taking his arm from her, he stepped in front of her, reached out and touched her cheek. Except he was wiping away a tear. Caitlyn hadn't even realized she was crying until he'd done that.

"Just know that everything Melanie said could be a lie," he continued. "Her story doesn't make sense. She claims she doesn't have money, but she would have needed plenty of cash to bribe someone at Conceptions, plus pay for a surrogate. It's more likely that she tried to get Conceptions to go along with her stupid plan but didn't have the money to put the plan into action."

Caitlyn latched onto that like a lifeline. "Thanks for that."

He nodded but didn't move. Drury stayed put right in front of her. Too close. Well, too close for him anyway, but she wished he would pull her into his arms.

And that's what he did.

Caitlyn stiffened for just a moment from the surprise, but then she felt herself melting right into him. He seemed to do the same against her, and just like that, the memories returned. Good memories, and she had so few of those in her life that it was almost impossible to push them away.

She certainly didn't push Drury away.

Nor did he do any pushing.

He lifted his head a little, their gazes connecting. He was so close to her that she could see the swirls of blue and gray in his eyes. Could see the muscles stirring in his jaw. Drury seemed to be having a fierce debate with himself about something, but Caitlyn didn't know what exactly.

Not until he kissed her, that is.

It barely qualified as a kiss. His mouth just brushed over hers, but his warm breath certainly made her feel as if she'd been kissed.

Now, he stepped back. Cursed. And shook his head. "I just complicated the hell out of this."

"It was already complicated," she assured him.

She figured that wouldn't get any better, either. Drury and she would always have this attraction between them, and because of the past, they would always feel the need to fight it.

"We should get back to the ranch." He didn't wait. Drury headed into the hall but then came to a dead stop.

That's when Caitlyn heard a too-familiar voice.

Jeremy.

He was in the reception area where one of the deputies

was frisking him, and the moment she stepped into the squad room, her former brother-in-law spotted her.

"I figured you'd be here," Jeremy snapped. He pointed his finger at Caitlyn. "You want to explain to me why you had me kidnapped?"

Chapter Eight

Drury did not want to have to deal with this now, and he was pretty sure that Caitlyn felt the same way. However, it was clear they were going to have to at least address the stupid accusation Jeremy had just thrown at her.

First, though, Drury had his own issue to address. "Why are you here? Shouldn't you be at San Antonio PD?"

"Not that it's any of your business, but I walked out."

Grayson groaned and took out his phone. No doubt to call his brother Nate, who worked at SAPD, to find out what was going on.

Jeremy flung another pointed finger at Caitlyn. "Now, why did you have me kidnapped?"

"I didn't," Caitlyn answered. "And what makes you think I did?"

Jeremy gave her an annoyed look. "Because one of the kidnappers said you'd hired them."

Caitlyn gave him the look right back. "I didn't hire them, and why would you believe them? They're kidnappers."

"Well, someone kidnapped me, and since whatever's happening seems to be centered on you, that made it easier to believe. That and you hate my guts."

Caitlyn certainly didn't deny the hate part, but she looked at Drury, gave a weary sigh. "Can we leave now?"

Drury nodded and looked at Gage. "Could you bring the car around to the back?" That way, they wouldn't have to go past Jeremy.

Gage returned the nod and headed out of the building. It wouldn't be a fast process, though, because Gage would have to check and make sure no one had planted any kind of tracking device on the vehicle.

"You're not leaving," Jeremy said to Caitlyn. "Not until you tell me who came after me and why."

Caitlyn gave another sigh. "I don't know. The man who tried to kill Drury and me escaped or maybe was taken from the hospital, so I don't have any more answers than you do."

Jeremy disputed that with some ripe profanity. "Then why was that idiot Melanie just here?"

"To be interviewed," Drury stated. He didn't give Jeremy any more info, something that caused his eyes to narrow.

"Did Melanie have me kidnapped?" Jeremy snarled.

"Maybe. With your personality, I'm surprised half the state doesn't want to kidnap you. Or just shut you up. Now, why would you think Caitlin is involved?" Drury demanded. "And if you're going to make any accusation, I'd like some facts and proof to go along with it."

"She's a gold digger. What more proof do you need?"

"Something that'll hold up in court," Drury flatly answered.

"Something like phone records," Grayson added the moment he ended his call. Drury hadn't heard Grayson's conversation, but apparently he'd learned something. Judging from Jeremy's expression, it wasn't anything good, either.

Grayson turned to Drury. "SAPD examined Jeremy's

phone records and discovered four calls from our missing kidnapper, Ronnie."

Yeah, definitely not good for Jeremy. "Want to explain those calls?" Drury demanded.

"I didn't know who he was, all right?" The volume of Jeremy's voice went up a notch. "He said he was interested in investing in one of my business ventures. I had no idea he was into anything illegal."

Maybe, but Drury wasn't going to take the man's word for it. "Did SAPD get anything else?" Drury asked Grayson.

"Only that Jeremy was uncooperative and unable to give any details whatsoever about the people he claimed kidnapped him."

"They wore ski masks!" Not only did his voice get louder, the muscles in his face had turned to iron.

Obviously, Jeremy had a temper, and he wasn't saying or doing a thing to convince Drury that he hadn't been the one to orchestrate this plan to ransom the baby and attack Caitlyn and him. Of course, Melanie and Helen were still on his suspect list, too, and the three were going to stay there until the person responsible was caught.

"Did you have anything to do with what went on at Conceptions Clinic?" Caitlyn asked Jeremy.

Jeremy threw his hands up in the air. "So, now you're accusing me of that, too?"

"Did you?" she pressed.

"Of course not." He spat out some more profanity. "From what I've heard, Grant could have a kid out there because of the mess at Conceptions. You really think I'd have any part in creating an heir?"

"No," Caitlyn agreed. "But you might have had a part in trying to make sure that heir didn't exist."

Jeremy's eyes narrowed. "I'm sick and tired of you making me out to be the devil in all of this. Why don't you go after my mother?"

"You'd love that, wouldn't you? Because with your mother behind bars, you'd control the estate."

Jeremy shrugged, clearly not denying that.

Drury had seen and heard more than enough from this clown, and the timing was perfect because Gage came in through the back exit. "The car's ready," Gage said.

That was all Drury needed. Apparently Caitlyn, too, since they both got moving.

"That's it?" Jeremy called out to them. He tried to follow them, but one of the deputies blocked his path.

Drury ignored him. "Is someone else going with us?" he asked Gage.

Gage nodded. "Someone I found in the parking lot." He opened the door, and that's when Drury saw Lucas in the front seat.

"Worried about me?" Drury joked when Caitlyn and he got into the backseat. Gage took the wheel. The moment they were all buckled up, he took off, heading onto Main Street.

Lucas glanced at him. Then at Caitlyn. Even though there was no way Lucas could have known about that near kiss earlier, his brother could no doubt see that the attraction was still there.

"Yeah, I am worried about you," Lucas admitted, but he didn't spell out what that worry included. However, Drury figured Caitlyn was part of that concern.

Lucas took out a photo from his pocket and handed it to Drury. "Either of you recognize her?"

Caitlyn leaned closer to Drury to have a look. Drury studied it, too. A young woman in her early to midtwenties. Brunette hair and slight build.

Drury and Caitlyn shook their heads at the same time. "Who is she?" Caitlyn asked.

"Nicole Aston."

Drury repeated the name under his breath to see if it would trigger any kind of recollection, but it didn't. "Should we know her?"

Lucas flexed his eyebrows. "I think she might have been the surrogate."

That certainly got Drury's attention. Caitlyn's, too. "How do you know that?" she asked.

"I ran a search on recent female missing persons in the state and found out that Ms. Aston was a college student. According to her friends, she was a surrogate. And she disappeared a week ago."

Bingo.

Caitlyn studied the photo a moment longer before she handed it back to Lucas. "I don't think I've ever seen her before. But I doubt Conceptions or whoever's behind this would have wanted me to cross paths with the surrogate."

Lucas made a sound to indicate he agreed with that. "I just thought maybe she would try to get in touch with you. Especially if she suspected anything illegal was going on at Conceptions. Of course, maybe the powers that be made sure she didn't get suspicious."

Even though this conversation was important, Drury continued to keep watch around them. So did Lucas and Gage. Now that they were out of town, it was a little easier since there weren't many buildings. Just some ranches and a lot of open farm road.

"Do Nicole's friends and family have any idea where she could be?" Caitlyn asked.

Lucas shook his head. "Both her parents are dead. No boyfriend. Her *friends* are pretty much just her classmates who said she kept to herself a lot."

Which might have explained why Conceptions would have wanted her for a surrogate. Still, there was another possibility. "Nicole could have given birth and then changed her mind about giving up the baby. She could be in hiding."

Lucas agreed fast enough that Drury knew that he had already considered it. "Her bank account hasn't been touched in a week, though. Prior to that, there were monthly deposits of fifteen hundred dollars. I've put a tracer on the deposits, but it was wired in, probably from an offshore account."

In other words, the tracer was a long shot. It also meant someone had tried to cover their tracks. Most people who hired a surrogate didn't need to have their tracks covered like that.

Drury was so caught up in what Lucas had just told him that he hadn't realized some of the color had drained from Caitlyn's face. "Someone could have killed her to silence her."

Yeah. Drury decided not to confirm that out loud. Besides, Gage made a sound that had his attention shifting in that direction.

"What the hell?" Gage grumbled.

Drury followed his gaze and asked himself the same thing. There was something on the road just ahead.

Gage slammed on the brakes, and Lucas and Drury automatically drew their weapons. That's because they got a better look.

That *something* was a body.

CAITLYN DIDN'T GET a long look at the person in the middle of the road. Drury had pushed her down onto the seat. All three lawmen kept their guns ready, obviously bracing for some kind of attack.

But nothing happened.

"I'll call Grayson," Lucas volunteered, and a moment later she heard him doing that.

The car also started to move again. Slowly. Gage was no doubt trying to get even closer to see if the person was truly dead or if this was some kind of ruse. After everything that had happened in the past twenty-four hours, none of them was in a trusting sort of mood, and Drury's gaze was firing all around them. No doubt searching for anyone who might be lying in wait.

"Blood," Drury said under his breath. "Anyone recognize him?"

Caitlyn lifted her head, just long enough to have a look at the man. He was belly down on the pavement, his face turned toward the car, and while his eyes were open, they were lifeless. Fixed in a blank stare.

For a moment she thought it was Ronnie since the man had the same hair color and a similar build, but it wasn't him.

She also glanced around at their surroundings. There were no houses. No other vehicles, either. Just miles of flat pastures stretching out on each side of them. Thankfully, there were only a few trees, and the ones that were nearby weren't wide enough to hide a gunman.

"Grayson's sending an ambulance and some deputies," Lucas relayed when he finished his call. "He'll be here in less than ten minutes." He tipped his head to the body. "Anyone else thinking it'd be a really bad idea to go out there and make sure the guy's dead?"

"Agreed," Drury and Gage said in unison.

"As soon as the deputies arrive to secure the scene, we're out of here," Drury told her. Then he turned back to Gage and Lucas. "Keep an eye on the ditches," he added.

Caitlyn's heart was already racing, and that certainly

didn't help. Some of the ditches could be quite deep on the farm roads. Deep enough for someone to use to launch another attack.

The seconds crawled by, and it felt like an eternity. An eternity where Caitlyn had too much time to think, and her thoughts didn't go in a good place.

Oh, God.

"This could be a diversion so kidnappers can go after the baby," she blurted out.

None of them dismissed that, which only caused her to panic even more, and Drury took out his phone. "I'll call the ranch," he said.

Even though she was close to both Drury and his phone, Caitlyn couldn't hear what he said to the person who answered. That's because her heartbeat was crashing in her ears now, but she watched for any signs on Drury's face that he'd just gotten bad news.

More of the long moments crawled by before he finally said, "Everything's okay there. The place is on lockdown. Two of the deputies are with the baby, and the ranch hands are all armed."

Good. Of course, that didn't mean all those measures wouldn't keep the kidnappers from trying to take her again.

"Someone's coming," Lucas said, getting their attention.

Caitlyn had another glimpse over the front seat, and she saw the red truck approaching from the opposite direction. It wasn't a new model, and it appeared to be scabbed with rust. It definitely didn't look like the sort of vehicle that their attackers would use. Plus, this road led to several ranches, so it could be someone just headed into town.

Lucas, Gage and Drury lifted their guns anyway.

The truck slowed as it neared the body and their car, but because of the angle of the sun and the tinted windshield, Caitlyn wasn't able to see who was inside. She especially wasn't able to see when Drury pushed her back down on the seat.

Not a second too soon, either.

She got just a glimpse of the passenger in the truck. He threw open the door and aimed an Uzi at them.

A hail of bullets slammed into the car.

The sound was deafening, and the front windshield was suddenly pocked with the shots. The glass held. For now. But this wasn't just ordinary gunfire. The rounds were spraying all over the car, and even though it was bullet resistant, that didn't mean the shots wouldn't eventually get through.

"Hold on!" Gage told them.

That was the only warning they got before he threw the car into Reverse and hit the accelerator. The tires squealed against the asphalt as he peeled away.

The shots didn't stop, though. The gunman continued to fire into the car, and it didn't sound as if he was getting farther away. Because he wasn't. She glanced out again and saw that the driver of the truck was coming after them. The shooter was leaning out the window to fire at them.

Gage cursed and sped up, but he was driving backward, and the shots had taken off his side mirror.

"Stay down," Drury warned her.

She did, but Caitlyn wished she had a weapon. Judging from the last glimpse she'd gotten of the truck, it was going fast, and if it was reinforced in some way, the driver could ram into them and send them into the ditch. If so, they'd be sitting ducks.

"Backup's on the way," Drury reminded her. Probably because she looked terrified. And she was.

But Caitlyn was also furious with the gunmen and with herself. Here, once again, she'd put Drury and his family in danger, and she still didn't know who was responsible for this.

Jeremy and Melanie both knew Drury and she had been at the sheriff's office, and it wasn't much of a stretch for them to figure out that they'd be heading to the ranch. Of course, Helen could have known that, too. Any of the three could have sent these thugs to try to kill them.

And there was no doubt that's exactly what they were trying to do.

This wasn't a kidnapping attempt. No. Those bullets were coming one right behind the other, each of them tearing into the car and windshield.

"Enough of this," Gage growled.

He hit the brakes, and for several heart-stopping moments, Caitlyn thought he was going to get out and make a stand. However, he backed the car into a narrow side road. In the same motion, he maneuvered the steering wheel to get them turned around. He darted out right in front of the truck. So close that it nearly collided with them.

Gage sped off.

"We'll lead them straight into backup," Drury said. He took out his phone, no doubt to let Grayson know. "We need to take them alive," he reminded the others.

Yes, because it was the fastest way for them to get answers.

"Hell," Drury mumbled.

She wasn't sure why he'd said that, but the shots suddenly stopped. Caitlyn followed his gaze, and he was looking back at the truck. She lifted her head just a fraction and peered over the seat to see that the truck was turning around.

Mercy.

They were going to try to get away.

She could only watch as the truck U-turned in the road. And that's when she got a look at the driver. It was someone she recognized.

Ronnie.

Chapter Nine

Drury figured he should be feeling some relief right about now. After all, he had Caitlyn safely back at the ranch, and other than the unmarked car being shot to pieces, there'd been no other damage.

Well, not to Caitlyn, him or his family.

But a man was dead. They didn't have an ID on the guy yet, but he'd almost certainly been murdered to get them to stop in the road so they could be gunned down. It was a high price to pay.

Caitlyn was paying a high price, too. She wasn't crying or falling apart. Not on the outside anyway. However, she had the baby in her arms and was rocking her as if that were the cure for everything. It had certainly soothed the baby. She was sacked out, and maybe just holding the little girl would soothe Caitlyn, too.

As much as she could be soothed considering she'd come close to dying.

"Grayson will question all of our suspects again," Drury reminded her. He was at the front window, volleying glances between Caitlyn and Lucas. His brother was outside the guesthouse and was pacing across the porch while he talked on the phone.

No doubt pushing to get any updates on the attack.

Drury was thankful for his help because he didn't exactly want to have those phone conversations in front of Caitlyn. Not with that shell-shocked glaze in her eyes.

"Ronnie," she said under her breath.

She didn't add any profanity, but Drury certainly had whenever the man's name came up. He'd never believed Ronnie's story that he was the baby's father and innocent in all of this, but the attack proved it. Ronnie had definitely been behind the wheel of that truck.

So, who'd hired him?

Drury checked his laptop to see if there'd been any breaks on finding a money trail. Breaks on anything else for that matter. But nothing.

"There's an APB out on Ronnie," Drury told her. "Everyone will be looking for him."

That wasn't a guarantee that they'd find him, but the APB was a start.

She nodded, and he thought the shell-shocked look got even worse. He also noticed that not all the rocking was actually rocking. Caitlyn was trembling. Probably feeling pretty unsteady, too, because she eased the baby into the carrier that was on the coffee table directly across from her.

Drury glanced out the window again. In addition to Lucas, two other armed ranch hands were out there. The front gate was locked, and the perimeter security system was on. That meant things were as safe as they could possibly be, so he left the window, went to the sofa and sank down beside her.

Caitlyn squeezed her eyes shut a moment. Groaned softly. And she eased against him, her head dropping onto his shoulder.

"I can still hear the gunshots," she said.

Yeah, so could he. He didn't want to tell her that she would hear them for the rest of her life. But she would.

So would he. And he would remember that look of terror on her face.

There wasn't really a way to comfort her right now, so Drury just slipped his arm around her and hoped that helped. It seemed to do that. For a couple of long moments anyway. Until she lifted her head, and her eyes met his.

Any chance of comforting her vanished. A lot of things vanished. Like common sense because just like that, Drury felt the old attraction.

"I don't know how to stop this," she said. Her voice was a whisper, filled with her thin breath.

She wasn't talking about the danger now.

It would have been safer if she had been.

Before he could talk himself out of it or remember this was something he shouldn't be doing, Drury lowered his head and kissed her. There it was. That kick. He'd kissed her plenty of times, but he always felt it. As if this was something he'd never tasted before.

And wanted.

He hated that want. Hated the kick. Hell, in the moment he hated her and himself. But that didn't stop him from continuing the kiss.

This would have been a good time for Caitlyn to pull away from him and remind him just how much of a bad idea this was. She didn't. She moaned, a sound of pleasure, and she slipped her hand around the back of his neck to pull him even closer.

She succeeded.

The kiss deepened. So did the body-to-body contact, and her breasts landed against his chest. He felt another kick. Stronger than the first one, and even though he knew it would just keep getting stronger and stronger, he kept kissing her.

It didn't take long for things to rev up even more, and if

Drury hadn't heard the sound, the heat might have taken over. But the sound was the front door opening, and that caused Caitlyn and Drury to fly apart as if they'd been caught doing something wrong.

Which they had been.

Kissing Caitlyn not only complicated things, but once again he'd lost focus.

Drury reached for his gun, but it wasn't necessary. Lucas came in, and yes, he'd seen at least a portion of the kiss. Or maybe he'd just caught the guilty look on Drury's face.

Lucas spared them both a glance, but his attention settled on the baby. He went closer, looking down at her, and he brushed his fingers over her toes that were peeking out from her pink gown.

His brother was certainly a lot more comfortable with the baby than Drury was. With good reason. Lucas was a father himself to a two-month-old son, and he was raising him alone since the baby's mother was in a coma.

Bittersweet.

Much the way Drury felt about this baby. He'd been protecting Caitlyn and the little girl, so that created a bond between them. But the old wounds were still there. Always would be.

"Grayson got an ID on the dead guy," Lucas said, sitting on the coffee table next to the baby. "His name was Morgan Sotelo. A druggie with a long record. No known family or address."

Which was probably why he'd been killed. No one would have missed him. Drury doubted the guy was actually involved in the attacks, and that sickened Drury. He'd been killed so that Ronnie and his henchmen could kill again.

"Nothing on Ronnie?" Caitlyn asked.

Lucas shook his head. "But the dashcam on the car recorded the whole attack, so we might be able to get an ID on the shooter since he wasn't wearing a mask. Sometimes, an ID leads to an address and friends or neighbors who might rat out his location."

A location that wouldn't be easy to find because the snake had no doubt gone into hiding. Temporarily, anyway. If Ronnie and the thug got another chance to attack, they would.

"Why do they want me dead?" she asked. "And why do they want her after I paid them the ransom?"

Drury had been giving that a lot of thought, and it wasn't a theory Caitlyn would like hearing. "If Melanie's behind this, she could want you out of the way, and then she could sell the baby to Helen."

Caitlyn's forehead bunched up and she nodded. "And the same could be true for Jeremy. Neither one of them would care if they put the child in danger, either, but Helen… Why would she risk something like that?"

"Maybe she hadn't. That still doesn't mean I'm taking her off the suspect list, though. After all, the men who attacked us are low-life scum. Even if Helen gave them orders to keep the child safe, that doesn't mean they followed those orders."

There was also a fourth possibility. That the low-life scum had gone rogue and were trying to cash in on a much bigger chunk of the money. After all, if they killed Caitlyn, Helen would rightfully be granted custody, and they could possibly milk a huge ransom from Grant's mother.

The baby whimpered, snagging their attention, and even though she did that a lot, this time she didn't go right back to sleep.

"She probably needs to be changed." Caitlyn got to her

feet and lifted her out of the carrier so she could head to the bedroom.

She gave Drury a glance, and even though she didn't say anything, he saw the fresh concern in her eyes. Not for the attack this time. But because Lucas had witnessed that kiss.

Lucas watched her leave, no doubt waiting to discuss a subject that Drury didn't want to discuss. However, his brother didn't start that unwanted discussion. He just sat there, staring at Drury. Waiting. This was a brother's game of chicken.

"What?" Drury finally snapped.

Lucas kept staring. "I didn't say anything."

"You don't have to speak to say something."

The corner of Lucas's mouth lifted for just a second. The smile faded fast. "If you stay, you'll have to forgive her."

In the grand scheme of things, forgiving her would be the easy part. "Caitlyn told me right from the beginning that she didn't want to get involved with a lawman."

Lucas nodded. "Because of her dad." He paused. "Last I checked, you're still a lawman."

"Yeah. The badge didn't stop us from landing in bed four years ago."

"And it won't stop you now," Lucas reminded him. "But maybe the notion of a heart-stomping will. You really intend to go through that again?"

Now, here was why he wished he could avoid this discussion. Because the answer was obvious. He didn't want to go through that again. Coming on the coattails of losing Lily, it had nearly broken him. And that's why somehow, some way he had to stop it. That started with finding the sick jerk who was behind the attacks.

He stood, ready to head to his laptop and get to work.

That would also cue his brother that it was not only the end of this chat but also that he should be getting back to whatever he was supposed to be doing. However, before Drury could even take a step, his phone buzzed.

Grayson again. Since this could be an important update on the case, Drury answered it on the first ring.

"The lab just called," Grayson greeted. And he paused. "They put a rush on the test and got the DNA results for the baby."

CAITLYN TOOK HER time changing the baby so that Lucas and Drury would be able to have the talk that she could tell Lucas was itching to have. Lucas was no doubt out there right now lecturing Drury about the kiss he'd witnessed.

She was lecturing herself about it, too.

Of course, it wouldn't help. For whatever reason, she seemed to be mindless whenever she got within twenty feet of Drury. Just the sight of him could break down the barriers she'd spent a lifetime building. The trick would be continuing to build them, and that wouldn't be easy to do as long as Drury and she were under the same roof.

There was a knock at the door. A second later it opened, and she saw Drury standing there.

"What happened?" she asked, getting to her feet. She left the baby lying on the center of the bed. "Did Lucas chew you out for kissing me?"

When Drury didn't jump to confirm or deny that, she knew that this wasn't about his brother but that there was some kind of new information about the case.

"The baby's DNA results are back," he said.

Caitlyn sucked in her breath so fast that she nearly choked. "This soon?"

He nodded. "The baby is yours and Grant's."

Even though Caitlyn didn't have any trouble hearing

what Drury had said, his words just seemed to freeze there in her head. For several seconds anyway. Then the relief came.

Sweet heaven.

This was her daughter.

She wasn't Melanie's. Not Ronnie's, either. Her child.

Drury went closer, took her by the arm and had her sit. Good thing, too, because the emotions came flooding through her. So fast and hard. The shock, yes. But there was something much, much deeper.

The love.

Caitlyn had felt the love the instant she'd seen the baby, but it seemed much stronger now. And complete. She was the mother of a child she'd always wanted.

Even though the baby had gone back to sleep, Caitlyn scooped her up and kissed her. She woke up, fussing and squirming a little, but Caitlyn continued to hold her. This time, though, she looked at her through a mother's eyes.

Yes, the love was overwhelming.

"Are you okay?" Drury asked.

Caitlyn managed a nod. She was more than okay. For a couple of seconds anyway, and then she remembered the danger. That was suddenly overwhelming, too, now that she knew someone had not only created her baby, they wanted to steal her back.

Drury sank down on the edge of the bed next to her. Not so that he was touching her, though, but it was still close enough to get the baby's attention. The little girl opened her eyes, and she stared at him as if trying to figure out who he was. The corner of her mouth hitched up in a little smile.

Caitlyn had read enough of the baby books to know that the smile wasn't a real one, but it certainly felt real. It must have to Drury as well because he returned the smile before his attention went back to Caitlyn.

"Grayson is letting Child Protective Services know so they'll stop pursuing temporary custody," Drury explained.

Good. That was one less thing on her list of worries. "And what about Melanie?"

"Grayson will let her know, too. Since no one has contacted her with a ransom demand, I think it's safe to say that Grant and she don't have a child."

Caitlyn had to agree. "The more I think about it, Melanie's baby claim made even less sense. The only thing Grant and I had stored at Conceptions was the embryo. There wasn't any of his semen for them to create an embryo for Melanie."

Drury nodded, and since he didn't seem surprised, maybe he'd already considered that.

"What about the safe house?" she added. Because it suddenly seemed more critical than ever to get her out of harm's way.

"It's ready."

She immediately heard the *but* in his tone.

"After what happened on the road earlier, I'm not sure it's a good idea to take her off the ranch," Drury continued. "It's next to impossible to secure all the farm roads and ranch trails, but we've got security measures in place here at the ranch."

Even though it was hard to concentrate, Caitlyn went through the pros and cons of that. Yes. And as much as she hated to admit it, the ranch was the safer option. For now. However, staying didn't accomplish one thing—putting some distance between Drury and her.

But she had to put the baby first.

Drury must have understood because he didn't try to

keep selling her on the idea of staying put. He did look at the baby again, though.

"You'll have to name her," he said.

Yes. Caitlyn had held off on doing that because in her mind it would have made it harder to give her up if the DNA test had proved this wasn't her child. Now that she was certain, she couldn't just keep calling her "the baby."

"I did a list a long time ago and wanted Elizabeth for a girl and Samuel for a boy." She looked down at the baby, as well. "But Elizabeth doesn't seem to fit her, does it?"

Drury lifted his shoulder, maybe trying to dismiss any part in this, but then he made a sound of agreement. "What was your second choice?"

"Caroline." It had been her grandmother's name.

He tested it out by repeating it a couple of times and nodded. It was silly to be happy over his approval, but she was.

"Caroline," she verified.

The moment seemed too intimate. Something that parents would do together. And they definitely weren't parents.

Drury must have sensed that as well because he eased away from her. "Too bad Grant died not knowing he would become a father."

Caitlyn figured she should just give a blanket agreement to that and end the discussion. But she didn't.

"Grant didn't actually want a child," she confessed. "I was the one who pushed him to go to Conceptions. He wasn't sold on the idea. In fact, he told me if I had a child that he or she would be just *my* child."

That brought Drury's gaze back to hers, and he cursed. "And you went through with the egg harvesting anyway?"

"I thought he'd change his mind." She paused, shook her head. "*Hoped* he would. And I reasoned that even if he didn't, I'd still have a child." Caitlyn gave a nervous laugh. Definitely not from humor. "Now you know just how desperate I was."

He stayed quiet a moment. "But you didn't stay desperate for long after you found out he was cheating on you."

"No," Caitlyn had to admit. "I decided it'd be better to have him completely out of my life. That included using the embryo at Conceptions. In fact, I was looking into adopting a child right before all of this happened."

This baby was a miracle for her. A miracle that she prayed she could keep safe.

Caitlyn heard the footsteps a few seconds before Lucas appeared in the doorway of the bedroom. At least this time Drury and she weren't in a lip-lock, but that still wasn't an approving look on Lucas's face. Except she thought maybe the look wasn't for her since Lucas was putting away his phone. He'd likely just finished another of the calls he'd been taking and making since they'd arrived at the guesthouse.

"The FBI found a money trail for Ronnie," Lucas explained. "Payments, big ones, that were wired to his account. The surrogate, Nicole Aston, was paid from the same account."

So, it was all connected. Not that Caitlyn had thought otherwise, but it was chilling to hear it spelled out like that. The same person responsible for arranging for her baby to be brought into the world had also arranged for Caitlyn to be killed.

Drury slowly got to his feet, his attention focused solely on his brother. "And did the FBI learn who owned that account?"

Lucas shook his head. "Not yet. It's offshore and buried under layers of false information. But that trail wasn't the only one they uncovered. The FBI found out who received the ransom money."

Caitlyn got to her feet, too. "Who?" she asked.

Lucas looked at Caitlyn. "You."

Chapter Ten

Drury hated every part of what was happening. Caitlyn being accused of orchestrating her baby's kidnapping. Having to take her to the sheriff's office to be questioned by an FBI agent. Having her out in the open again so someone could attack her. But Drury thought all those were a drop in the bucket compared with the final thing about this that he hated.

That Caitlyn was having to leave her daughter after learning the child was actually hers.

Of course, the baby was well protected with two deputies and the ranch hands, but this should be a time for her to savor an hour or two of getting to be with her child instead of being interrogated for something Drury knew she hadn't done.

And his faith in her innocence had nothing to do with the kiss or the attraction between them. This was common sense.

"We'll get this all straightened out," Drury assured her the moment Lucas pulled to a stop in front of the sheriff's office.

Caitlyn looked at him, and he could see the weariness in her eyes. "I didn't do this," she said.

It wasn't necessary for her to tell him that. Drury knew.

No way would she have intentionally put a child, any child, in danger.

As they'd done with their previous visit, the moment Lucas pulled to a stop in front of the sheriff's office, Drury got Caitlyn out of the car and inside. Away from the windows, too. And he immediately spotted someone he recognized.

"You know him?" Caitlyn asked.

"Yeah. FBI Agent Seth Calder."

Seth did his own introductions with Caitlyn. It didn't surprise Drury that they wouldn't want him or one of his cousins to do this interview with Caitlyn. No way could they be impartial, but at least the Bureau had someone whom Drury considered decent and fair.

"Good to see you again, Drury," Seth said before shifting his attention to Caitlyn. "Wish this were under different circumstances, though." He motioned for them to follow him to one of the interview rooms.

Both Grayson and Gage stayed back, following protocol, but it'd take a lot more than protocol to keep Drury out of the room. Thankfully, Seth didn't turn him away when he ushered Caitlyn down the hall.

When they passed in front of one of the other rooms, that's when Drury noticed it wasn't empty. Helen was in there, and she was having a whispered chat with a man who was probably her lawyer.

"Yes, she's here," Seth volunteered. "I'm interviewing her next. Then I'm bringing in Jeremy. He should already be on his way over."

Drury wouldn't have minded talking to Jeremy, but maybe they could dodge the man for Caitlyn's sake. Of course, there was no dodging Helen.

"I want to talk to you," Helen snarled when her attention landed on Caitlyn.

"It'll have to wait," Seth snarled right back.

Seth ushered Drury and Caitlyn into the other interview room. "Arrest Helen if she tries to come in here," Seth told Grayson.

Since Helen had already started to do just that, apparently ready to continue the confrontation, it was a timely order. It got the woman to stop even though she shot a glare at Caitlyn.

Drury glared back at her, and he closed the door behind him as he went into the room with Seth and Caitlyn.

"I'm innocent," Caitlyn said right off the bat.

"Someone is setting her up," Drury added.

Seth didn't refute either of those claims, and once they were seated, he slid some papers toward her. It was a report on the money trail. The one that seemingly led straight to Caitlyn.

Her mouth tightened as she read it. "Why would I take money from Grant's estate to pay myself?"

"Trust me, I had to think long and hard to figure out some possibilities. Maybe so that Grant's family wouldn't try to challenge it, or despise you for having it?"

"They'll always despise me. And Grant's will was written so that they can't challenge it. The money is mine. *Was* mine," Caitlyn corrected. "I used almost all of it to pay for the ransom."

"The ransom that's in an offshore account with your name on it."

"I didn't know anything about that account," she insisted.

Again, Seth didn't dispute that, but he did pause a long time. "I believe you."

Caitlyn released her breath as if she'd been holding it a long time.

"Someone did this to try to get you in legal hot water,"

he went on. "Not just for this but for the baby itself. The agreement you signed at Conceptions was that neither you nor Grant could use the embryo you stored without the other's written permission."

She nodded. "I did that so he wouldn't be able to use the embryos after we divorced. He wasn't especially thrilled with the notion of fatherhood, not then anyway, but I didn't know if he would change his mind years later."

Seth made a sound of agreement. "Someone in Grant's family could file a civil suit against you, though, if they could prove you took the embryo illegally."

Drury was about to say there was no proof for that, but maybe that's what the bank account was about. If Caitlyn had the money, then she would look guilty.

Well, maybe.

"Even if she had stolen the embryo," Drury said, "why go through with a fake kidnapping and ransom?"

"I'm sure a lawyer could argue that it was to gain sympathy. Or that maybe she has some kind of need for attention."

Caitlyn cursed. A rarity for her. "The only thing I need right now is for my daughter, Drury and his family to be safe."

Drury silently added Caitlyn's name to that list. He didn't want her daughter to be an orphan, and that was just one of the reasons he had to keep her alive.

"Someone else could have access to this bank account," Drury pointed out.

"Yes," Seth readily admitted. "Unfortunately, if someone else did this, I can't tell who. That's where I need Caitlyn's help. The person who created this bank account had access to her personal info. Her Social Security number, for example. That's the password for the account."

"Either Grant's mother or brother could have gotten

that," Caitlyn insisted. "For that matter, Melanie could have, too."

Another sound of agreement. "They made it too obvious, though. I mean, why would you open an offshore account using your own name and Social Security number? Yes, it was buried under dummy corporation accounts, but it didn't have nearly enough layers for someone who was genuinely trying to hide dirty money."

Now it was Drury who was breathing easier. He'd known all along that she was innocent, but it was good to hear a fellow agent spell it out. That, however, led him to something else.

"Why did you want to bring Caitlyn in if you knew it was a setup?" Drury asked Seth.

"Because of this." He passed another piece of paper their way. "I didn't want to get into this over the phone, but this was in the memo section of the account. Most people with legit accounts just type in things like what the payment was for. What do you think it is?"

Drury and Caitlyn looked at the paper together. It was the letters *N* and *A* and the word *Samuel*.

"'*N, A,*'" Drury read aloud. Since there wasn't a slash between the letters, it probably didn't mean *not applicable*. He went through all the info they'd collected during this investigation.

Bingo.

"Nicole Aston," Drury and Caitlyn said in unison.

"She's the woman we believe was the surrogate," Drury added to Seth.

Seth nodded. "And who's Samuel?"

Drury started to shake his head, and then he remembered something Caitlyn had told him. "You said if you had a son, you'd name him Samuel. Would Helen, Jeremy or Melanie have known that?"

She stayed quiet a moment, giving that some thought. "Maybe." And she paused again. "But it could be a place. Helen owns an apartment complex, and it's on Samuel Street in San Antonio. I remember because when I first told Grant about my name choice for a baby, he mentioned it."

"Nicole could be there," Drury quickly pointed out. "But if she is, the apartment's not in her name."

Seth was already taking out his phone, and he made a call to get someone to look for her. The moment he was done, he stood.

"You can watch through the observation mirror when I question Helen," Seth said. "For now, I'd rather both of you stay back, but she's clearly got a temper. If she doesn't spill anything useful, I might try to spark that temper by bringing you in to confront her."

Caitlyn and Drury nodded. He wanted Helen to spill all. However, he hated that once again, Caitlyn was going to have to be put through something like this, especially coming on the heels of being accused of having set all of this up.

Drury took her to the observation room and moved her away from the door just in case Helen came barreling out of the interview with plans to confront Caitlyn again. He doubted, though, that Seth would let that happen. Seth wasn't the sort to let Helen ride roughshod over him.

"If the attackers end up killing me," Caitlyn said, "please don't let Helen get custody of the baby. I know it's a lot to ask," she quickly added. "But I don't have anyone else to turn to."

Yes, it was a lot to ask, but there was no way Drury would refuse. No way he'd let Helen get her hands on the baby.

"You wouldn't have to raise her yourself," Caitlyn went on. "Just make sure she has a good home."

That was it. Drury stopped the gloom and doom with a kiss. All in all, it was a stupid way to stop it, but he didn't want Caitlyn going on about being killed. Even if someone had already tried to do just that.

Drury had intended the kiss to be a quick peck, but it turned into something that fell more into the scalding-hot range. It left them both breathless, flustered and wanting more.

It also distracted them.

Seth's interrogation could turn up something critical, and here he was complicating the hell out of things by kissing Caitlyn again.

Drury forced his attention back on Helen, and he both heard and saw her deny whatever Seth had just asked. Her shoulders were stiff. Eyes, narrowed. And she was volleying glares between Seth and the observation window where she no doubt knew Caitlyn and Drury were watching.

"I didn't arrange to have my granddaughter born," Helen snapped. She jumped up and got right in Seth's face. "But I will be part of her life. A *big* part, without anyone interfering." That was obviously aimed at Caitlyn. "You won't stop that, and neither will my former daughter-in-law."

Seth had his own version of a glare going on, but it had a dangerous edge to it. "You should restrain your client before I do," Seth told her lawyer. His voice was edged with danger, as well.

And it worked. The lawyer took hold of Helen's arm and put her back in the seat. He whispered something to her, probably a reminder that it wouldn't help her case if she managed to get herself arrested.

"Tell me about your bank account in the Cayman Islands," Seth threw out there while he glanced through the papers he was holding.

Of course, there was no proof that it was indeed Helen's account, but the woman didn't know that. Well, if she was guilty, she didn't.

"I have no idea what you're talking about," Helen insisted, but before she could continue, her lawyer leaned in and whispered something else to her. "I have accounts in many places, so you'll have to be more specific."

"The account you used to orchestrate the birth of your granddaughter and the attacks on Caitlyn. You know which attacks I mean. The ones meant to kill her so she wouldn't be in your way." Seth leaned in closer. "On a scale of one to ten, just how upset are you that Caitlyn inherited all your son's money? I'm guessing a ten."

Judging from the way Helen's mouth tightened, she was about to deny the bank account and blast Seth for accusing her of attempted murder. However, Drury missed whatever she said because he heard the commotion in the squad room. Several people were shouting, and one of those people was Grayson.

"Put down the gun now," Grayson ordered.

That got Drury's heart pumping, and he automatically pushed Caitlyn behind him and drew his gun. "Wait here," he told her.

With his gun ready, Drury leaned out from the door, not sure what he would see. After all, who was stupid enough to come into a sheriff's office while brandishing a weapon? And the person did indeed have a gun.

Melanie.

She was in front of the reception desk. Not alone, either. She had a man directly in front of her.

Ronnie.

And Melanie had a gun pressed to his head.

"Melanie," Drury called out.

Caitlyn didn't release the breath she'd been holding. Not yet anyway, but she'd braced herself for an attack. Of course, that would be exactly what this was, though it wasn't Melanie's style to do the dirty work herself.

"Gun down on the floor now," Grayson demanded.

Caitlyn peered out the door for just a glimpse, and she saw a lot in those couple of seconds. It appeared that Melanie had taken Ronnie captive.

Appeared.

But maybe this was the start of an attack after all.

"Be careful," Caitlyn warned Drury when he stepped farther into the hall. He had his gun pointed in the direction where she'd seen Melanie.

"I can't," Melanie insisted. "This is a dangerous snake, and I don't want him to escape."

"We won't let that happen," Drury assured her and went even closer.

Caitlyn had no choice but to stand there and wait. Pray, too. Because if Melanie started shooting, she might try to take out Drury first.

There was a shuffling sound, followed by some profanity from Ronnie.

"This crazy idiot tried to kill me," Ronnie accused.

"Obviously Melanie didn't succeed," Drury answered, and judging from his footsteps, he went closer to assist Grayson in containing whatever the heck this was.

When Caitlyn glanced around the jamb again, she saw that Melanie had been disarmed and that Grayson was cuffing Ronnie. Good. But she still didn't breathe any easier, not with Helen on one side of the building and now Melanie on the other. Plus, according to what Seth had told them, Jeremy was on his way to the station.

Soon, all their suspects would be under the same roof

along with the thug Ronnie, whom one of them had no doubt hired.

"I did your job for you," Melanie bragged. "I found Ronnie and brought him here."

"I'll want to hear a lot more to go along with that explanation," Drury insisted.

"She sneaked up on me and clubbed me on the head," Ronnie jumped to say. It was possible that had happened, but with Ronnie's other injuries from the car accident, it was hard to tell.

"Yes, I clubbed him," Melanie admitted. Her gaze shifted to Caitlyn when she stepped out of the interview room and into the hall. "Still think I'm behind this?" Melanie challenged.

Caitlyn shook her head. "I'm not sure what to think." And she didn't. This could all be some kind of ruse to make Melanie look innocent.

Or to distract them.

Obviously Drury felt the same way because he motioned for her to stay back.

"She had no right to club me like that," Ronnie protested.

No one in the squad room gave him a look of even marginal sympathy. "You're a fugitive," Grayson pointed out, "and you tried to commit murder."

"But I didn't." Ronnie didn't shout exactly, but it was close. "I've been framed. I didn't escape, either. I was dragged at gunpoint from the hospital."

Caitlyn had had enough. "You were in the same vehicle with the person who tried to kill us."

"Because he forced me to be there! Just like this bimbo."

Melanie didn't go after the man for the name-calling, but she shot him a glare that could have melted a glacier.

"I'm not saying another word until my lawyer gets here," Ronnie added.

Gage stepped forward and handed Grayson a piece of paper, and he took over with Ronnie. "I'll put him in a cell," Gage offered.

Grayson nodded, his attention on whatever was on that paper. He didn't turn back to Melanie until he'd finished it.

"Now, explain to me how you found Ronnie?" Grayson prompted the woman.

"I did your job," she snapped.

Drury went to stand by Grayson's side, and the pair just stared at her, waiting for her to continue.

"I had some PI friends looking for him," Melanie went on. "When they spotted him, they called me."

"And why didn't you call the police?" Grayson asked, sounding very much like the lawman that he was.

"Because you let him get away once, and I wasn't going to let that happen again. Make sure this time you keep him under lock and key. I don't want Ronnie out on the streets where he'll have a chance to kill me."

Drury and Caitlyn exchanged glances. "Why would Ronnie want you dead?" Caitlyn pressed.

Melanie threw her hands in the air. "I don't know. But someone's been following me, spying on me," she quickly added. "And what with the attacks, I figured Ronnie had his sights set on me next."

Caitlyn had to shake her head. "That doesn't make sense. There's no reason for Ronnie to want you dead."

"There is if Helen wants to silence me. She knows I'm not going to just let this drop. She stole from Conceptions Clinic to create a child Grant didn't want. He's not around to fight for what's right, so I'll do it for him."

Caitlyn huffed. "Didn't you try to do the same thing? Or else you claimed to do it."

Melanie pulled back her shoulders. "What do you mean—*claimed*?"

"I got the DNA results. The child is mine and Grant's. Not yours. Not Ronnie's, either. And with only one viable embryo, there's no way Conceptions could have used a surrogate to carry yours and Grant's child."

Melanie opened her mouth, closed it, then opened it again. She seemed genuinely stunned. "Those people at Conceptions duped me," she finally managed to say. But then in a flash the fire returned to her eyes. "Or you're lying. That's it, isn't it? You're lying and so is Helen. She wants me dead."

Caitlyn wasn't sure if the woman was plain delusional or truly believed Helen had a motive to kill her. Either way, Caitlyn didn't have time to press her on the issue because she saw a man making his way to the sheriff's office.

Jeremy.

Drury obviously believed this could be the start of another attack because he stepped in front of her again. "Go back to the observation room," he whispered to Caitlyn.

She hated that once again Drury might have to fight a battle for her, but Caitlyn didn't think this was the time to stand her ground. Especially since it could be a distraction for Drury and Grayson. She hurried back to the room but stayed in the doorway so she could watch what was happening.

"Are you the one who hired Ronnie to come after me?" Melanie asked Jeremy before he'd fully gotten inside.

He drew in a long breath, huffed and shifted his attention to Drury. "Has Melanie been telling you lies about me?"

"I'm not sure," Drury answered. "Did you hire Ronnie?"

Unlike his mother, he didn't have a flash of temper. Not

on the outside anyway, but Caitlyn knew the anger was simmering just below the surface.

"No," Jeremy answered after several long moments. He reached into his pocket, prompting Grayson and Drury to go for their guns. "I'm just getting this." He pulled out a USB drive and handed it to Drury. "You'll want to go over what's on there."

"Why?" Drury asked. He passed it to one of the deputies.

"Because it's got everything you need to convict her of these crimes." Jeremy tipped his head to Melanie.

The woman howled out a protest, and she bolted forward as if she were about to rip the storage device from the deputy's hand. Drury blocked her path and turned toward Jeremy. "What's on there?"

"Lies," Melanie insisted.

"Transcripts of conversations that I had with Melanie."

This time Grayson had to physically restrain the woman. "You're a pig!" she shouted, the insult aimed at Jeremy.

Jeremy certainly didn't deny that. "Melanie and I had an affair. A short one," he emphasized. "I recorded our conversations, and in several of them, she says outright that she wants Caitlyn dead."

Melanie called him more names, punctuating it with plenty of ripe curse words. "You'll pay for this, Jeremy. Just wait. You'll pay."

It was hard to hear over Melanie's screeching, and Grayson must have gotten fed up with it because he handed Melanie off to the deputy. "Put her in a holding cell until she calms down."

The deputy carried her away while Melanie shouted obscenities and threats.

"Do you always record conversations with your lovers?" Drury asked once the room was quiet again.

"Always." He tipped his head to the USB drive that the deputy had put on the table. "Somewhere around page thirty, Melanie says she wants to steal the embryo from Conceptions so she could use the baby to get Grant's money from Caitlyn."

Caitlyn's stomach twisted. Was that what this was really all about? A way for Grant's mistress to get his money?

"You said it was transcripts," Caitlyn said, going closer now. "Those can be easily faked. The only way we'd know if it was true would be to listen to what Melanie actually said."

"The recordings were accidentally erased." Jeremy waited until after both Grayson and Drury had finished groaning. "But Melanie mentions a bank account. Offshore. There could be something to help you identify where the account is and if it's the one used to pay off men like Ronnie."

Maybe it was the same account that Seth had found. Of course, maybe Jeremy was just doing this to take suspicion off himself. If so, it wasn't working. Jeremy would stay on her list of suspects.

"Go ahead." Jeremy tipped his head to the storage device. "Read what's on there."

Grayson shook his head. "It could contain a virus to corrupt our files. I'd rather have the FBI check it out. Plus, it could be a waste of my time. And if it is, if you're trying to manipulate this investigation, I can see if obstruction of justice charges apply here."

Judging from the way Jeremy pulled back his shoulders, he didn't like that one bit. Maybe this was an attempt to destroy some evidence by corrupting the computer system. If so, then Grayson would definitely have some charges to file against the man. Too bad those charges wouldn't put Jeremy in jail for long, though.

"Why would you sleep with Melanie?" Caitlyn asked him. "You knew what she was."

He lifted a shoulder. "I blame it on sibling rivalry. I never liked Grant having something I didn't."

It surprised her a little that he admitted it, but then Caitlyn remembered that Jeremy had once hit on her. She'd refused, and she had always thought that was one of the reasons he hated her so much. But maybe it was simply a case of him hating what he couldn't have.

"How did the recordings get *accidentally* erased?" Grayson asked.

Jeremy huffed. "Obviously I'm wasting my time here when I was just trying to do you a favor."

"A favor like Melanie bringing in Ronnie?" Drury didn't wait for an answer. "The only favor we need from either of you is concrete proof to stop these attacks. You got that kind of proof?"

"No," Jeremy said after a long pause and a glare. "But you have to consider that Caitlyn brought this on herself."

Caitlyn tried not to react to that, but she flinched anyway. The memories of the attacks were still too fresh in her mind. Always would be. "I didn't bring this on myself," she managed to say.

Jeremy made a *whatever* sound. "You knew what Grant was before you got involved with him."

It felt as if he'd slapped her. Because it was true.

Jeremy turned as if to leave, but Grayson stopped him. He motioned for a deputy to come closer. "Make sure Mr. Denson isn't armed and then take him to the interview room."

"What?" Jeremy howled. "You're still questioning me even after I bought you the dirt on Melanie?"

"Yes," Grayson said.

Despite Jeremy's protests, the deputy frisked him. No weapons so the deputy led him through the squad room and to the interview room directly across the hall from his mother.

"Jeremy's right," Caitlyn said under her breath. "I should have seen that Grant wasn't who he was pretending to be."

"He's not right," Drury snapped, and he slid his arm around her waist. "Everything Jeremy says and does could be to cover his tracks."

Caitlyn knew that, but it still didn't rid her of some guilt in this. If she'd never gotten involved with Grant, none of this would be happening.

"You wouldn't have your daughter if you hadn't been with him," Drury said as if reading her mind.

It was the perfect thing to say, and it eased some of the tension that had settled hard and cold in her chest. At least it eased it until she noticed that Grayson was looking at the paper that Gage had given him right before Jeremy had shown up.

"Bad news?" she asked.

Grayson didn't hesitate. He nodded. "SAPD sent someone to Samuel Street to find out if Nicole was staying there."

That got Caitlyn's attention. "Was she?"

Another nod. "The super ID'd her from a photo. The lease wasn't in her name but rather a corporation. One of the dummy companies on the offshore account."

That didn't surprise Caitlyn since Nicole—and Ronnie—had been paid from that same account.

"Nicole wasn't there," Grayson went on, and he handed the report to Drury. "The place had been ransacked, and there was some evidence of a struggle."

Oh, mercy.

"What kind of evidence?" Caitlyn pressed when Grayson didn't continue.

Grayson met her gaze. "Blood."

Chapter Eleven

Blood. Definitely not a good sign.

Especially this kind of blood.

According to the report Grayson had given Drury to read, SAPD had found high-velocity blood spatter on the wall of the living room in the apartment where Nicole had been staying. That meant there'd probably been some blunt-force trauma.

Reading that was enough to make the skin crawl on the back of his neck, but there was more. Much more. And that more was something Drury wasn't sure he wanted Caitlyn to know.

"They killed her," Caitlyn said.

That's when Drury realized the color had drained from her face. She also didn't look as if she could stand on her own, so Drury tightened his grip on her.

"We don't know for certain that Nicole's even dead," Drury insisted, and Grayson gave a variation of the same before he went to the cooler to get Caitlyn a drink of water.

"If they didn't kill her, that means they hurt her," Caitlyn amended.

"Not necessarily. It might not be her blood," Drury tried again, though that was reaching.

After all, the person who'd hired her to be a surrogate

could want her murdered to tie up any loose ends. Nicole wouldn't be able to ID anyone if she was dead.

Caitlyn's hand was shaking when she took the paper cup of water from Grayson. Her voice shook, too, when she thanked him. That's when Drury knew he needed to get her out of the squad room. Away from the other officers. And especially away from the windows. After all, they had their three suspects under the same roof, and it was possible hired thugs were also nearby.

With the report still in his hand, Drury took her to the break room at the end of the hall, and he shut the door. With Helen and Jeremy just a few yards away, he didn't want Caitlyn to have another encounter with them. Not until she'd steadied her nerves anyway. As much as Drury hated it, sooner or later she'd cross paths not only with Helen and Jeremy but also with Melanie.

"I have to get back to the ranch," she said. "I need to see my baby."

Drury understood that, but the timing wasn't good. "Grayson, Gage and the other deputies are tied up right now. Just hold on a little while longer until we've got someone to drive back with us."

She looked up at him. Nodded. But he could tell the only place she wanted to be right now was with her daughter.

And that would happen.

However, Drury kept going back to the idea that there were probably hired guns nearby, and he didn't want those guns taking shots at them. That meant clearing the area before he took Caitlyn from the building.

Caitlyn shook her head as if she might argue with that, but then the tears sprang to her eyes. "I'm so sorry about putting you in the middle of all of this trouble."

Drury wanted to snap at her for the apology. It was an insult to a lawman since the only reason he had a job was *because* of trouble. But considering he'd also kissed Caitlyn blind, it was a different kind of insult.

Of course, he shouldn't have been kissing her, either, so he wasn't exactly blameless in the insult department.

She looked at him, their gazes connecting, and even though he hadn't mentioned those kisses out loud, she was likely remembering them.

Feeling them, too.

Drury sure was.

The moment seemed to freeze or something. Well, they did anyway, but it didn't stop the old familiar heat from firing up inside him. Kissing her now would be the biggest mistake of all what with this emotion zinging between them, so he forced himself to look away, and his attention landed back on the report Grayson had given him.

It was several pages stapled together, and Drury made the mistake of flipping to the second page. To the picture that was there. Now the blood spatter was there for him to see.

And for Caitlyn to see, as well.

It'd been easy to sugarcoat the possibility of what had happened, but it was hard to sugarcoat something right in their faces. Along with the blood on the stark white wall, the coffee table and chairs had been tossed over. A lamp was on the floor.

So was a baby carrier. Next to the carrier was a diaper bag filled with supplies.

"Mercy," Caitlyn said, her voice filled with breath. "That's where she must have been holding Caroline."

"Maybe." But inside, Drury had to admit that the answer to that was *probably*. He only hoped the thugs had taken the baby to safety before they'd gone after the woman who'd given birth to her.

"Does the report say how long the blood had been there?" she asked.

Drury glanced through it, hoping that it was recent, as in the past hour or so. That way, it could mean the baby hadn't been around for whatever had gone on. Since there wasn't a body in the apartment, it could also mean that Nicole had escaped and was out there injured but alive. Or better yet, that she'd managed to bludgeon someone who'd tried to attack her.

But no.

"The CSIs will need to test it," Drury explained, "but it appears to have been there for several days." Maybe even as long as a week. That meshed with what her neighbors were saying—that they hadn't seen her in days.

Caitlyn blinked back tears, obviously processing what he was saying. It didn't process well. Because it meant the baby could have been there in the living room when the attack occurred. Caroline hadn't been hurt, but it sickened him to think that she could have been.

"Did anyone hear a disturbance in the apartment? Screams? Anything?" Caitlyn added.

"No." That didn't mean someone hadn't heard, though. The apartment wasn't in the best part of town. It was the kind of place where a lot of people would have turned a blind eye.

Caitlyn took the report from him, glancing through it, and he saw the exact moment her attention landed on what he wasn't sure he wanted her to see. Her gaze skirted across the lines, gobbling up details that were probably giving her another slam of adrenaline.

"Nicole gave birth in the apartment," she said, her voice thin.

"The cops on the scene are only guessing about that."

But it was a darn good guess considering the blood they'd found in the bedroom and adjoining bath.

There'd been evidence of a home delivery, including some kind of clamp that was used for umbilical cords. Other evidence, too, that Nicole hadn't been planning on staying put. They'd also found a plane ticket to California.

"She was taking the baby," Caitlyn whispered.

Everything was certainly pointing in that direction, especially since Nicole had already packed a diaper bag with baby supplies. Her wallet was missing, but Drury was betting she'd had enough cash to live on, for a while anyway.

"Nicole might have found out what was going on at Conceptions," Drury explained. "If she gave birth to the baby before her due date, she might have thought she could escape."

Of course, that meant the woman might have been trying to escape with Caitlyn's daughter, but Nicole might have believed this was the only way to keep the child safe. At least that's what Drury hoped she had in mind. There were cases of surrogates getting so attached to the babies they were carrying that they fled with the infants. No way, though, would the person behind this have allowed that to happen.

Not with a million-dollar ransom at stake.

Obviously, Caitlyn didn't have any trouble piecing together that theory, either, and because Drury thought they could both use it, he pulled her into his arms. She didn't resist even though they both knew this was only going to make things harder when this investigation was over. Still, with that reminder, Drury stayed put and probably would have upped the mistake by kissing her if there hadn't been a knock. Before Drury could untangle himself from her, the door opened.

Because every inch of him was still on high alert, Drury automatically reached for his gun again.

But it was just Grayson.

Like the other time he'd seen Drury close to Caitlyn, Grayson didn't react. He hitched his thumb in the direction of the interview rooms. "You'll want to come out for this," he said. "I think all hell's about to break loose."

"Not another attack?" Drury quickly asked.

Grayson shook his head and motioned for them to follow him. They did with Drury keeping Caitlyn behind him, and they stopped along with Grayson in the door of the interview room. Drury hadn't been sure what he would see once he looked inside. Jeremy was there as expected, but so was Helen, her lawyer and Melanie. It wasn't standard procedure to get suspects together for a joint interrogation, so Drury had no idea what was going on.

Seth was standing at the back of the room, his back against the wall, and he was eyeing their trio of suspects as if they were all rattlesnakes ready to strike.

"You're making a huge mistake," Jeremy said like a warning, and his comment was directed at Melanie.

Drury figured this was just a continuation of the verbal altercation they'd had in the reception area, but then he saw the photo on the phone screen in the center of the table.

"I don't even know why I'm in here," Helen grumbled. "I had nothing to do with that."

Drury went closer with Caitlyn following right behind him.

"That's Jeremy," Melanie announced.

Yes, it was, and the man was in some kind of waiting room. Drury looked at Grayson for an explanation, but Melanie continued before he could say anything.

"That's Jeremy at Conceptions. He was there to try to steal the embryo so he could destroy it."

Drury expected Jeremy to jump to deny that. He didn't.

"Tell them how you got those photos," Jeremy countered.

Melanie hiked up her chin. "I hired a PI to keep an eye on Conceptions. Because I was worried that someone would try to do something dirty. What I did isn't against the law."

"It's not against the law for Jeremy to have been there, either," Helen pointed out.

"Don't defend me," Jeremy snapped.

"I wasn't." Helen's voice was filled with just as much venom as her son's. "I was about to explain that Melanie could have hired that PI to steal the embryo, as well. But these pictures aren't proof that either of you committed a crime."

Everyone turned to the woman. Because that didn't sound like some kind of general statement. It sounded as if she had firsthand knowledge.

"You know something about this?" Grayson pressed.

"I don't know anything," she insisted, "but common sense tells me it didn't have to be Melanie or Jeremy who took the embryo. Caitlyn has a much stronger motive than either of them. And she couldn't have legally gotten her hands on them because she wouldn't have been able to get permission from Grant."

"That's true," Caitlyn admitted. "But I didn't steal them." She looked at Jeremy. "Did you?"

Jeremy took his time answering. "No." A muscle flickered in his jaw. "But I considered it. Briefly," he quickly added. "And I dismissed the idea just as fast. Frankly, I didn't think you'd want to have Grant's baby, not when you've obviously still got a thing for the cowboy here."

Caitlyn opened her mouth, probably to deny what Jeremy was saying, but since Drury and she had nearly just kissed again, she didn't voice her denial.

"So, if you thought I wouldn't want Grant's baby," Caitlyn continued a moment later, "then why consider stealing the embryo?"

Jeremy gave her a flat look. "You're not the only player in this sick game, Caitlyn. Mommy wants a grandbaby. I think she has hopes of getting it right this time, since she screwed up with Grant and me. But personally I'd like to make sure she doesn't get another chance at motherhood."

Jeremy sounded convincing enough. And maybe he was telling the truth. That didn't mean, though, that he hadn't created an heir to use as some kind of blackmail for his mother and Caitlyn.

"I did the best I could with the likes of you," Helen snapped. "You've always been an ungrateful son."

Jeremy faked a yawn. "Unstable mothers produce ungrateful sons. Am I done here?" he asked Grayson.

"No, he's not done!" Melanie howled. "You need to arrest him."

Grayson huffed. "And I'm sure Jeremy will claim I need to arrest you for what's on those transcripts." He looked at Helen. "You probably want me to arrest both of them."

"I do," Helen verified. "And Caitlyn. I know she had something to do with all of this."

Caitlyn went closer, practically getting right in the woman's face. "I would never do anything that would put my child in harm's way."

Helen stared at her a moment, then shifted her attention to Drury. "Are you the baby's father?"

Well, he sure hadn't seen that question coming. "No." Though he hated to dignify it with an answer.

Helen's stare turned to a glare. "I want to see the baby's DNA results."

"Get a court order," Drury tossed back at her. "If you can."

And he doubted she could since Caitlyn wasn't using the baby to make any kind of claim on Helen's estate. Of course, that wouldn't stop Helen from trying to get those visitation rights or even custody of the baby.

"Am I free to go?" Jeremy repeated.

Grayson didn't jump to answer. He made Jeremy wait several long moments. "Yeah, you can go. Not you two, though." He pointed first to Helen and then Melanie.

Obviously neither woman liked that. Both started to protest, and again Helen's lawyer had to restrain her. That's when Drury decided it was time to get Caitlyn out of there. Seth stepped up to take Helen and her lawyer back to the interview room across the hall. Grayson went in with Melanie, and he shut the door. Jeremy walked out the front of the sheriff's office without even sparing them a glance.

Drury kept his eyes on Jeremy until he was out of sight. "How deep do you think he's into this?"

Caitlyn shook her head. "I don't know, but I just hope they're not all working together."

Drury agreed, though he doubted they trusted each other enough for that, and he was certain there was plenty they weren't telling him.

"We can't leave yet, can we?" Caitlyn asked. He could hear the weariness in her voice and see it in her eyes.

Not with Grayson and the deputies still tied up, but maybe Drury could get some outside help. He took out his phone to call Lucas. Maybe his brother could arrange to bring a couple of the ranch hands with him. Drury definitely didn't want Caitlyn out of the building until he had some security measures in place. However, before Drury could even press his brother's number, he spotted Gage coming toward him. Fast.

"You've got a call through nine-one-one," Gage said, sounding a little out of breath. "The caller says she's Nicole Aston."

Chapter Twelve

Caitlyn tried not to get her hopes up, but that was impossible to do. After everything she'd just read in the report of Nicole's apartment, she had thought the surrogate was likely dead.

And she might be.

This call could be a hoax, designed to make the cops think a murder hadn't occurred. After all, it wasn't as if Drury or she would actually recognize Nicole's voice. Still, this was a thread of hope that didn't exist a couple of minutes ago.

She followed Drury to Gage's desk. The call had come in through the landline, and Gage put it on speaker.

"Nicole?" Drury asked. "I'm Agent Ryland. Where are you?"

"Is Caitlyn Denson with you?" the woman immediately said. Clearly, she was ignoring Drury's question.

"I'm here," Caitlyn answered. "Are you the surrogate who carried my daughter?"

"I am." A hoarse sob tore from her mouth. Too bad Caitlyn couldn't see the woman's face so she could try to figure out if she was faking that agony. "I swear I didn't know what was going on. Not until it was too late."

"Where are you?" Drury pressed.

"I can't say. Not yet. Not until I'm sure I can trust you."

"You can trust us," Drury assured her. "But the real question is—can we trust you?"

"Yes," she said without hesitation. "I had no part in anything that happened. Like I said, I didn't know what was going on until shortly before I gave birth."

"How did you find out what was *going on*?" Drury again.

This time there was some hesitation. Several long seconds of it. "I overheard some things, and I was able to piece together what was happening."

Drury huffed. "I'm going to need a lot more information than that. First, though, I have to make sure you're safe."

It sounded as if Nicole laughed, but it wasn't a laugh of humor. "I'm definitely not safe. Someone tried to kill me in my apartment."

"Yeah, I saw the photos. SAPD is there now. Is that your blood on the wall?"

"No. I hit one of the men who attacked me." Another pause. "God, I was just trying to protect the baby."

Hearing that robbed Caitlyn of her breath. Her daughter had been there with all that violence going on. Well, she had been if Nicole was telling the truth. Caitlyn had so many questions.

So many doubts, too.

"How do I know you're really the surrogate?" Caitlyn asked her.

More silence. "The baby I delivered had a small birthmark on her right ankle."

Bingo.

"She could be lying," Drury whispered to her. "She could have just seen the baby, that's all. Or could have been told about the birthmark."

Yes, and it didn't take Caitlyn long to realize why this woman would lie about something like that. She could be trying to gain their sympathy. Their trust. So she could use that connection to draw them out or find the location of the baby.

"How did you know the baby you were carrying was my daughter?" Caitlyn had so many more questions for the woman, but this might be the start to helping her understand the big picture of what had gone on at Conceptions.

"I knew something was wrong with the surrogacy arrangement," Nicole said. "Too much secrecy, and they were paying me in cash. Each month a man would show up with the money, and sometimes he would move me to a different place."

Yes, definitely secrecy.

"Then about two weeks ago I heard the man talking on the phone," Nicole went on, "and he mentioned your name. I did an internet search. Internet searches on Conceptions, too. All the mess that went on there."

There had indeed been a *mess*. Other babies born just like her own daughter, and all for the sake of collecting a huge ransom.

"Why are you calling exactly?" Drury came out and asked her. "Do you want me to arrange protection for you?"

"I want you to arrest the men who attacked me. Until they're caught, I'm not safe. None of us are safe."

That was the truth. Because even if Nicole was working for the person who'd orchestrated this, it didn't mean her boss would keep her alive. If the attack in her apartment was real, then Nicole would have realized she was a target.

"Give me some information so I can arrest them," Drury insisted.

Nicole sobbed again. "I can give you physical descriptions, but I don't know who they are, and they were both wearing ski masks."

"And they're the ones who took the baby?" Caitlyn

asked, though she wasn't sure she actually wanted to hear the answer.

"They did." Another sob. "I swear, I tried to stop them, but I knew if I stayed there and fought them, I'd lose. I'd just delivered the baby, and I was weak."

Drury and Caitlyn exchanged glances, and she saw the skepticism in his eyes. There were holes in what Nicole was telling them. Because if she was indeed so weak, how had she managed to fight off two hired guns.

"What about the blood in my apartment?" Nicole continued. "There must have been blood. Was there a DNA match?"

"Not yet. The CSIs haven't had time to do that. But they will."

"Good. Maybe that'll help you find them."

"You could help with that, too," Drury went on. "You need to tell me where you are so I can send someone to get you."

"No! I can't risk that. Those men could have tapped the phone lines."

"This line is secure," Drury assured her.

"Nothing is secure right now."

Caitlyn couldn't be certain, but it sounded as if the woman was crying. Maybe for a good reason—because it was indeed possible that nothing was secure.

"Nicole, you can't stay in hiding," Drury continued. "I can arrange protective custody for you with a team I trust. A team you can trust," he emphasized. "All you have to do is tell me where you are."

Silence. For a long time. "All right," Nicole finally said.

The relief Caitlyn felt faded as fast as it'd come when Nicole added, "But I'll do this under my own terms."

"What terms?" Drury snapped. "Because meeting you

had better not involve Caitlyn going out in the open so someone can shoot at her again."

More silence from Nicole. "No. I won't involve Caitlyn. She's as much of a target as I am. Maybe more."

"How do you know that?" Caitlyn couldn't ask fast enough.

"I heard one of the thugs mention you by name. I heard a lot of things I shouldn't have," Nicole said in a whisper.

"What things?" Drury demanded.

"I'll tell you all about it when we're face-to-face. Let me find a meeting place. Once I'm sure I'm safe, I'll call you."

Drury groaned. "How long will it take you to set this up?"

"I'll need some time. It probably won't be until tomorrow. I'll call you when I have things in place."

Drury opened his mouth, no doubt to demand some of that info now, but Nicole had already hung up.

"Were you able to trace the call?" Drury immediately asked Gage.

"She was using a burner cell."

Drury cursed, and Caitlyn knew why. There was no way to trace a burner or disposable cell. Obviously, Nicole knew that. It could mean the woman truly was in danger, or it could all be part of a ruse to make them think that.

"You want me to assemble a protection detail?" Gage offered.

Drury shook his head. "I'll get Lucas to do it. You're already spread too thin here."

Gage didn't dispute that, and he stepped away when one of the other deputies motioned for him to go into the hall that led to the holding cells.

"I don't want you to have to wait around here any longer," Drury said, taking out his phone. He fired off a text. "Once Lucas gets here, he can escort us back to the ranch.

You can stay there with Caroline while I meet with Nicole. If Nicole calls back, that is."

Yes, Caitlyn was skeptical, too. Even though the woman had reached out to them, it didn't mean she would cooperate.

"Nicole could be part of the dirty dealings that went on at Conceptions," Caitlyn threw out there.

Drury quickly agreed, and he led her back to the break room. Caitlyn was thankful to be away from Melanie and Helen, but she didn't like that troubled look in Drury's eyes.

"Nicole could have also called to pinpoint our location," Drury said.

Oh, mercy. Caitlyn hadn't even considered that.

"We'll just take some extra precautions," he assured her. But she must not have looked very assured because Drury hooked his arm around her waist and led her to the sofa. "I asked Lucas to bring a couple of the ranch hands with him."

"But you'll all still be in danger," she quickly pointed out.

He made another sound of agreement. "It might not be any safer to stay put."

Drury was right. Yes, this was the sheriff's office, but there'd been attacks here before, and the office was right on Main Street, sandwiched between other buildings and businesses.

"Are we safe anywhere?" she asked, but then Caitlyn waved off her question. She already knew the answer. They weren't.

The only silver lining was that, whoever was behind this, they seemed to be after her and not the baby. For now anyway. That could change if and when she was out of the way.

Caitlyn hadn't realized just how close Drury and she were sitting until she turned to look at him again. Too close. Practically mouth to mouth. She glanced away but not before she saw something else in his eyes. Not just worry and concern.

But the attraction, too.

And maybe even something else. Because his forehead was bunched up.

"Are you okay?" she asked, automatically slipping her hand over his.

"I've been having flashbacks," he finally said.

That wasn't what Caitlyn had expected him to say, but she should have. Of course, this would have triggered the horrific memories of his wife's death.

"The sooner you can distance yourself from me, the better," Caitlyn reminded him.

A new emotion went through his eyes. Anger, maybe, but it didn't seem to be directed at her. Judging from the way he groaned, he was aiming it at himself.

"Lily died right in front of me." His voice was a ragged whisper. "Did you know that?"

She nodded and hated that her own flashbacks came. She had seen a man die. Her father. And those were images she'd never forget. It had to be even harder for Drury because Lily had been pregnant. He'd lost his wife and baby with one bullet from a robber's gun.

"Yeah," he grumbled as if he knew exactly what she was thinking. "We've both got plenty of emotional baggage."

They did, and that seemed to be a caution to remind her that neither of them were emotionally ready to have a relationship. And they weren't. That's why she was so surprised when his mouth came to hers.

There it was. That instant slam of heat. The one that could chase away the flashbacks. But that heat could also

cloud her mind and body. Definitely not something she
needed right now, but Caitlyn didn't stop him. Nor did
she stop Drury when he upped the contact and deepened
the kiss.

He slipped his arm around the back of her neck, easing
her closer and closer. She didn't resist. Couldn't. Drury
certainly wasn't the first man she'd ever kissed, but no
man had ever drawn her in the way he did.

Caitlyn slid her arm around him, making the contact
complete when her breasts landed against his chest. Now
she got memories of a different kind. No flashbacks of violence but rather of the times they'd been together.

In bed.

Like his kisses, Drury had her number when it came
to sex. She doubted that had changed, but she didn't want
this need she felt for him. Didn't want the ache to build
inside her. It complicated things and would only lead to
a broken heart.

That didn't stop her, though.

She melted into the kiss. Melted into Drury until they
were pressed against each other. Until the fire sent them
in search of something *more*. And more wasn't something
they could have. Not right now anyway.

Drury pulled back, and as if starved for air, he gulped
in a deep breath before going right back to her again. This
kiss wasn't as deep, but she could still feel the emotion.
Could still sense the fierce battle going on inside him.

"I should regret that," he said with his lips still against
hers. "I want to regret it," he amended.

"Same here." But she didn't, and judging from the way
he groaned, neither did he.

"The baby," he added a moment later.

Caitlyn braced herself for Drury to tell her that he
couldn't get involved with her because of the baby. Be-

cause Caroline would always trigger memories of his own child that he'd lost. Plus, Caroline would always be Grant's daughter, which would give Drury another dose of memories that he didn't want.

But he didn't get a chance to add more because Grayson opened the door.

"A problem?" Drury immediately asked, and he got to his feet.

"Possibly a solution. Ronnie just said he wants to cut a deal. Information in exchange for reduced charges."

Of all the things that Caitlyn had thought the sheriff might say, that wasn't one of them. "Why the change of heart?"

Grayson lifted his shoulder. "Maybe he thought his thug cronies wouldn't be able to break him out of jail as easily as they got him out of the hospital."

True, but she was still suspicious, and she definitely didn't like the idea of a man who'd tried to kill them getting a lighter sentence. She wanted him behind bars for a long time.

"What's he offering?" Drury wanted to know.

"The name of the person who hired him."

There it was. Probably the only thing Ronnie could have put on the table that would have made this impossible to turn down.

"Of course, we can't begin to start working out a deal like that until his lawyer gets here," Grayson went on. "And the DA will have to be the one who approves it." He paused. "It could still fall through."

And it could take time. In fact, Ronnie could drag this out so long that there could be another attack. And this time, it might succeed in killing them.

Drury's phone dinged to indicate he had a text message. "It's Lucas," he said, glancing at the screen. "He's just out the back door with Kade. Two ranch hands are behind them in a truck."

Kade was another Ryland cousin. An FBI agent, and while Caitlyn was glad about having three lawmen for protection, that meant less security at the ranch.

"We can hurry," Drury told her as if he knew exactly what her concern was. He stood, helping her to her feet.

"I'll call you with any updates," Grayson assured them while he punched in the security code to disarm the alarm on the back door.

Drury thanked him and got her moving. Of course, he was in front of her and had his gun drawn when he cracked open the door and looked out. Lucas was indeed there, behind the wheel of what appeared to be an unmarked car. Caitlyn hoped it was bulletproof.

"Move fast," Drury reminded her.

He took a single step forward and then stopped cold. For a second anyway. Then he moved them to the side and peered out around the jamb.

Caitlyn couldn't see what had caused him to do that, but Lucas reacted, as well. He, too, drew his gun, and their attention shifted to the park area just behind the sheriff's office. There were clusters of trees and trails back there. Plenty of places for someone to hide, too.

"What's wrong?" Grayson also pulled his gun and joined Drury at the door.

"Someone's out there," Drury said.

Those three words caused Caitlyn's heart to slam against her chest. Please, no. Not another attack.

There were security lights on the back of the sheriff's office. Lights on the trails as well, but there wasn't enough illumination to see the whole area. Even though it wasn't pitch-dark yet because the sun was still setting, it would be easy for an attacker to use that dimness to his advantage.

"Don't shoot," someone called out.

A woman. And it was a voice that Caitlyn thought she recognized.

Nicole.

Chapter Thirteen

Hell. This was not how Drury wanted this to play out. He'd wanted to get Caitlyn out of there before something bad happened. And maybe this wasn't bad, but since it was unexpected, it had the potential to take a nasty turn.

Drury glanced at Caitlyn to make sure she was okay. She wasn't. Her breathing was already way too fast, and it was obvious she was getting another slam of adrenaline. His body was also gearing up for a fight.

A fight that he hoped wouldn't be necessary.

"Please don't shoot," the woman repeated. That voice sure sounded like Nicole's, but that call could have come from someone pretending to be the surrogate.

"Step out so I can get a good look at you," Drury demanded. "And put your hands in the air."

Even though she was probably a good twenty feet away, he could still hear her gasp. "I'm not armed."

"Then prove it. Put your hands in the air." Drury didn't bother to tone down his lawman's voice. Better to be safe than sorry, and he wanted to make it clear to this woman that he would shoot her if she tried to attack them.

"Tell the other men to go away," Nicole bargained. "I don't trust them. And I want to see Caitlyn."

"That's not going to happen," Drury assured her. "Not until I know you're who you say you are. Step out now."

Drury wasn't sure she would. Not with four lawmen's guns trained on her. He figured the ranch hands in the truck behind the car had their weapons drawn, too.

"I don't want to die," Nicole said, her words punctuated with sobs.

"Then come out so I can help you," Drury offered. "You can come inside, and we'll put you in protective custody."

"No. That man is in there."

Drury had to think about that for a few seconds. "You mean Ronnie?"

"Yes."

He waited for Nicole to add more to that, and when she didn't, he asked, "How do you know Ronnie?"

A few seconds crawled by. "He's the one who moved me into the apartment. He works for the people behind all of this, and if he gets the chance, he'll kill me."

Drury had no doubts about that. Well, no doubts if Nicole was telling the truth that is. But she didn't mention Ronnie in their other conversation. Only the two thugs who'd attacked her after she delivered the baby.

"I need to see your face," Drury tried again. "I need to make sure you're really Nicole Aston."

Just as when she was on the phone, there was a long silence. So long that Drury thought the woman might turn and run. He hoped that didn't happen because it could be part of a ruse to divide and conquer. Because at least two of them would have to go after her since she could have critical information to spare Caitlyn from yet another attack.

Just when Drury was about to give up, there was some movement. Not from the trees but rather from some shrubs.

"Stay back," Drury reminded Caitlyn. He wished there

was time to move her to another part of the building, but he didn't want her out of his sight. Besides, there could be gunmen at the front of the building by now.

More movement in the shrubs, and finally the woman lifted her head. Not her hands, though.

"I want to make sure you aren't armed," Drury ordered.

She lifted her hands, slowly. No gun. Not one that was visible anyway, but that didn't mean she didn't have one nearby.

Drury picked through the dim light to study the woman's features. She looked like the Nicole Aston in the driver's license photo.

"I told you I wasn't carrying a weapon," Nicole said. "I came to you for help, but if you don't trust me, I'll have to go elsewhere."

"Someone's trying to kill Caitlyn. Maybe trying to take the baby, too. I have to be suspicious of everyone who might be connected to Conceptions."

And Nicole was definitely connected. The question was, just how deep was her involvement?

"Come in so we can talk," Drury tried again.

No hesitation from her that time. She quickly shook her head. "I want to see Caitlyn."

"I can't risk that," Drury said at the same time Caitlyn said, "I'm here."

Drury shot her a glare. He hadn't wanted Nicole to know Caitlyn's position, but then it was highly likely that Nicole had caught a glimpse of her the moment Drury opened the door.

"You need to do as Drury says," Caitlyn called out to the woman. "Come inside. It's not safe out there."

"I know," Nicole answered.

Apparently, she meant that because her gaze was firing

all around them. She appeared to be as much on edge as the rest of them because Lucas, Kade and Grayson were doing the same thing. Drury was trying to do that while keeping watch on Nicole. He still wasn't convinced that she wasn't about to pull out a gun.

Tired of this standoff, Drury decided to put an end to it. "Tell me what you came here to say, or else I'm shutting this door."

"I don't want to go to jail," Nicole said.

Once again, she'd surprised him. "For what?"

"I signed a lot of papers when I became a surrogate. A couple of months ago when I heard on the news about what had gone on at Conceptions, I got worried."

She was right to have worried. There'd been a lot of illegal things going on at the clinic.

"When Ronnie came by to give me my monthly payment," she continued, "I told him I wanted out of the deal. I was afraid what they might do to the baby. He said the papers I signed were like a confession. That if I went to the cops that they could use those papers to put me in jail. But I swear, I didn't have anything to do with stealing any embryo."

"I'll want to take a look at those papers," Drury insisted.

She shook her head. "The men who attacked me took them."

Maybe just more tying up of loose ends, but they also might have taken them because they could implicate their boss.

"That's why I need to talk to Caitlyn," Nicole went on. "Ronnie said the baby's mother could be arrested, too, because she's the one who helped with the plan."

"I didn't," Caitlyn quickly said. "I had no idea what was going on until I got the ransom demand."

"So, Ronnie lied."

Nicole's voice was so soft that Drury barely heard her. But there was something in her tone. Something in the way she said Ronnie's name. Maybe it was nothing, but it seemed as if Nicole might know more about him than she was admitting. Drury really needed to sit her down for an interview. There was no telling what she would reveal when questioned.

"Come inside," Drury pressed. "Caitlyn is in here, and the two of you can talk."

Nicole was shaking her head. Until he added the last part. Obviously, Nicole was very interested in seeing Caitlyn because she stopped shaking her head and made another of those nervous glances around her.

"All right," Nicole finally agreed. "But don't point your gun at me when I come out. I have panic attacks, and I don't want to trigger one."

A panic attack seemed the least of her concerns right now, but Drury glanced at Grayson. Grayson understood exactly what Drury wanted him to do because he stepped to the side, out of Nicole's line of sight.

And he kept his gun ready.

Drury lowered his to his side.

Even though Kade and Lucas were still armed, that didn't seem to bother Nicole. Perhaps because they were inside the car. Or maybe she wasn't able to see through the tinted glass. Either way, she pushed the shrubs aside and started toward them.

She didn't get far.

Nicole made it only a couple of steps before the shot blasted through the air.

THE SOUND OF the shot was so loud and seemed so close that Caitlyn thought for a moment that Drury had been shot.

She caught onto him, pulling him out of the doorway, but he was already headed her direction.

Grayson scrambled to the other side.

It wasn't a second too soon because the next shot slammed into the jamb only inches from where they'd both been standing.

Outside, Caitlyn heard a scream. Nicole. Mercy, had the woman been shot?

Even though she wasn't certain she could trust Nicole and that she'd told them the truth about everything, Caitlyn didn't want her hurt. Or worse. Someone could be murdering her right now in front of them.

She fought the flashbacks of her own father's murder. Fought the fear, too, but that was hard to do. The adrenaline was already sky-high, and her heartbeat was crashing in her ears, making it hard to hear. Hard to hear Nicole anyway.

Caitlyn had no trouble hearing the next shot.

It, too, slammed into the doorjamb.

Drury cursed, pulled her to the floor and covered her body with his. Protecting her. Again. She wished she had a gun or some kind of weapon so she could help him, and while she was wishing, she added for the shots to stop.

They didn't.

Two more slammed into the building.

"Can you see the shooter?" Grayson asked Drury.

Drury shook his head. "But I think he's in one of the trees in the park. Somewhere around your ten o'clock."

That didn't help steady her nerves. Because that meant the shooter was in a position to keep firing. Which he did.

"What about Lucas and Kade?" Caitlyn had gotten only a glimpse of them before Drury had pulled her away.

"Still in the car. They won't be able to get out."

No. Because they'd be gunned down. That also meant they would have a hard time returning fire. But at least they were safe. However, she knew that shots could get through a bullet-resistant car.

"What about Nicole?" Caitlyn managed to say.

Another headshake from Drury. "I can't see her, either. I hope to hell she stays down."

Maybe that meant Nicole was still alive. Of course, she wouldn't be for long if they couldn't get her out of the path of the shooter.

Except the gunman wasn't firing at her.

"All the shots are coming into the building," Caitlyn said under her breath.

"Yeah," Drury verified. "It could mean Nicole's in on this. Or…"

He didn't finish that because another shot came at them. One that caused Drury to curse again. And she knew why. Because the angle of the shot had changed. Either the gunman had moved or there were two shooters.

Drury reached up, slapped off the lights and moved her even farther away from the door. Two deputies came in from the squad room, but Grayson motioned for them to get back. Good thing, too, because the shots went in their direction. Clearly, the shooter was pinpointing their moves, and with the lights off it could mean he was using some kind of infrared device.

"The walls and windows of the sheriff's office are all reinforced," Drury said to her. Perhaps he gave her that reminder because she was trembling now and cursing as well with each new shot.

Caitlyn wasn't sure how many rounds were fired, but it seemed to last an eternity. And then it stopped.

Silence.

That was more unnerving than the shots because she knew it could mean the gunmen were closing in on them.

"Stay down," Drury warned her.

He reached in the slide holster of his jeans and handed her his backup weapon. Caitlyn took it, but she had no idea what he had in mind. Not until he started to inch away from her.

Toward the door.

She wanted to pull him back, to try to keep him out of harm's way, but there was no safe place in the room right now. Because if those gunmen got closer, they could start picking them off.

Grayson moved, as well. Both Drury and he stayed low on the floor, but they made their way to the door. Drury lifted his head, listening, and his gaze was firing all around the area. She suspected Kade and Lucas were doing the same thing.

"You can't let them take me," Nicole called out.

Caitlyn had no trouble hearing the terror in the woman's voice, and she instinctively moved to help her. She didn't move far, though, because Drury motioned for her to stay down.

"It could be a trap," he whispered.

She almost hoped it was. Because a trap like that would fail, and it would mean Nicole wasn't out there with hired killers. Of course, if it was a trap, it meant they had a very dangerous woman on their hands.

After long moments of silence, the sound of the next gunshot caused Caitlyn to gasp. And it didn't stay a single gunshot.

"I see him," Drury said to Grayson a split second before he leaned out and fired.

Caitlyn hadn't thought the shots could get any more

deafening, but she'd been wrong. Because Grayson began to fire, as well. And the shooters outside didn't stop. However, even with all the noise, Caitlyn heard Nicole scream.

"No!" she shouted. "Please, no."

Mercy, did that mean she'd been hit?

Caitlyn lifted her head just a fraction so she could peer out the door, but the angle was wrong for her to see Nicole.

However, she saw something else.

She got just a glimpse of a man wearing dark clothes and a ski mask. Obviously one of the shooters. He took aim at Drury.

"Watch out!" Caitlyn warned him.

But no warning was necessary. Drury had already seen the man, and he fired two shots, both of them slamming into the shooter's chest. He made a sharp sound of pain and dropped to the ground.

"I think he's wearing Kevlar," Drury said to Grayson.

If so, then the guy might not be dead after all. He could just have gotten the wind knocked out of him, and once he regained his breath, he could try to kill them again.

"You see the other gunman?" Grayson asked.

"No."

Caitlyn figured it was too much to hope that he'd run away. And she soon got confirmation that he hadn't.

"Hell, he's going after Nicole," Drury spat out.

He scrambled to an even closer position by the door, and he took aim, but Drury didn't fire. Neither did Grayson nor the deputies.

"Please, no," Nicole repeated. Caitlyn hadn't thought it possible, but the woman sounded even more terrified than before.

"You want her dead?" someone called out. It was a man, but Caitlyn didn't recognize his voice.

"I want you to let her go," Drury answered.

"No can do. But if you shoot now, the bullet will go into her. Is that a risk you want to take?"

That meant this thug was using Nicole as a human shield, and Caitlyn got a glimpse of that when the gunman moved into her line of sight.

Yes, he had Nicole all right.

The man had his left arm hooked around Nicole's neck. His gun was pressed to her head. And he was backing away from the building. Caitlyn also saw something else.

Another gunman.

The second guy was to the thug's right, and he had a rifle aimed at Drury and the others.

As terrifying as that was, this could also be a different kind of terror for Drury. Because this was almost identical to the way his wife had been murdered.

"What will it take for you to let her go?" Drury tried to bargain with the man. "She's innocent in all of this."

"I don't care. Just following orders, Agent Ryland. You really don't want to watch another woman die, do you?"

So the gunman knew who Drury was. And he knew about Drury's past. Not exactly a surprise, but she had to wonder why the gunmen had made such a bold attack. Plain and simple, it was risky because they'd fired those shots into a building filled with lawmen.

"Why do you want Nicole?" Caitlyn shouted.

That earned her another glare from Drury. Probably because he didn't want the gunman's attention on her and also because he figured the gunman wouldn't answer.

But he did.

"Nicole'll get a chance to tell you all about that," he said. "We'll be in touch soon."

"Don't let him take me!" Nicole shouted.

However, they had no choice but to let the gunman do just that. With his gun still against her head and with his armed partner leading the way, the man took off running, dragging Nicole with him.

Chapter Fourteen

We'll be in touch soon.

The gunman's words kept playing in Drury's head. The words of a kidnapper, not a hired killer. At least it didn't seem as if the guy had plans to kill Nicole. Not yet anyway.

But what did the gunman and his boss hope to gain from this?

Money was the obvious answer. Maybe since they didn't get an additional ransom from Caitlyn, this was a way of making up for that. Of course, this could be some kind of sick bargaining plan to get Caitlyn out in the open.

That wasn't going to happen.

She'd already come too close to being killed, and Drury had to put a stop to it. He also had to put a stop to the other images that kept going through his head.

Yeah, the flashbacks had come at the worst possible moment.

Thank God he hadn't frozen, but that's because he'd had to fight those old images by reminding himself that other lives were at stake. He couldn't go back in time and save Lily.

Hell, he hadn't saved Nicole, either, because the surrogate was in the hands of hired killers.

Drury nearly jumped when he felt the soft touch on his arm. He'd been in such deep thought what with wrestling his demons that he hadn't heard Caitlyn walk up behind him in Grayson's office.

"I wish it were something stronger," she said when she handed him a bottle of water.

Yeah, they both could have probably used something stronger, but it would have to do. Especially since they couldn't go anywhere. The break room was closed off, now essentially a crime scene, and the building was on lockdown until Lucas and the other deputies made sure the area was clear.

"I called the ranch," she added, "and talked to the nanny who's staying with Caroline. Everything seems to be okay there."

By *okay* she meant *safe*, but it wasn't truly okay because Caitlyn wanted to be there with her daughter. At least Caroline was in good hands. There were several nannies at the ranch, including this nanny, Tillie Palmer, along with plenty of cousins to help take care of her.

"We shouldn't have to be here much longer," he told her. Hoped that was true. And because he thought it would help, he brushed a kiss on her cheek.

It didn't help.

That look was still in her eyes. The look of a woman who'd just been through hell and back. Hell that wasn't over now that Nicole was a hostage and two of the gunmen had escaped.

The third was dying.

At least that was what the medic said when they'd whisked him away in an ambulance. The guy hadn't been wearing Kevlar after all, and both of the bullets Drury fired had gone into the man's chest. He was in surgery, but it wasn't looking good.

"Your family has really stepped up to help me," she said. "I won't forget that."

Yes, they had stepped up, and Drury wouldn't forget it, either. He, his brothers and cousins had a strong bond, and they didn't forgive easily when one of them was wronged. In their minds, Caitlyn had wronged him, but that hadn't stopped them from doing the right thing.

"You two okay?" Grayson asked from the doorway. He had his hands bracketed on the jamb.

Both Caitlyn and Drury settled for nods. Of course, they were lying, but at least they were alive, and none of his cousins or the other deputies had been hurt in this latest attack. It could have been much, much worse. It sickened Drury to think that Caroline could have been with them.

"Helen and Melanie are still whining about leaving," Grayson went on. "If they keep annoying me, I just might let them."

Of course, if it was one of them who'd hired the gunmen, then that person would be safe. The other could be toast.

"Any news?" Drury asked.

"Nothing on the wounded shooter or Nicole, but Gage just loaded the security footage." Grayson tipped his head to the laptop on his desk. "Kade's going through it, too, but it wouldn't hurt to have another pair of eyes on it."

Drury welcomed the task. Anything to get his mind off the flashbacks and that haunting look in Caitlyn's eyes. She must have welcomed it, too, because she joined him at the desk. Not exactly a good idea, though.

"You don't have to see this," he reminded her.

She dragged in a deep breath. "I have to do something."

He understood. Standing around with too much time to think was the worst way to deal with raw nerves. That said, he didn't want her to watch the actual shooting. Hell, he wasn't sure he wanted to watch that part, either.

Grayson left them, probably to go another round with

Helen and Melanie, and Drury had Caitlyn sit at the desk. He stood behind her and pressed the keys to load the security footage. There were four cameras, one on each side of the building, and the screen had the feed from all four. Drury focused on the one at the back.

He fast-forwarded through the footage, not really seeing much until Lucas and Kade pulled to a stop next to the rear exit. No sign of Nicole or the gunmen, though, so he froze the frame and zoomed in on the area where he'd shot the man.

Still nothing.

It took a few more tries before he finally spotted the gunman in the tree. He was well hidden behind a thick live oak branch, and it didn't help that his dark clothes and ski mask camouflaged him.

"I only see the one gunman," Caitlyn said. "You?"

He was about to agree, but then Drury saw the slight movement on the camera that faced the parking lot. It covered just the edge of the park, and he finally saw the second and third gunmen come into view.

And he also saw Nicole.

She was coming from the other side. No car. She was on foot, but it was possible she'd parked a vehicle somewhere nearby. If so, the deputies would find it, and it could be processed for evidence.

Drury continued to watch as Nicole moved closer to the spot where she'd called out to them. She was staying low, looking all around her. Definitely the way a frightened person would be acting, but that didn't mean this wasn't all just that—an act. Especially since Nicole was clearly staying out of Lucas's and Kade's line of sight. In fact, so were the gunmen. That meant they must have scoped out the place beforehand and knew just where to position themselves.

Nicole ducked behind those shrubs, and Drury tried to calculate the angle of the gunmen. The guy in the tree would have definitely seen her. Probably the other two as well, but they hadn't tried to take or shoot her. So, why wait?

Drury didn't like the answer that came to mind, and it twisted at his gut.

Because maybe the thugs were waiting for Nicole to lure Caitlyn out of hiding.

It was less than a minute before Drury saw when he'd opened the door. There was no audio on the feed, but he could tell from their reactions as Nicole had called out for them not to shoot. Seconds later, the shots had started, and Grayson, Caitlyn and he had been pinned down.

"What is that?" Caitlyn asked, pointing to the camera feed from the right side of the building.

Drury had been so focused on the gunmen and all the shooting that he'd missed it. But he didn't miss it now. It was just a glimpse of a man, and like the others he was dressed in black and wearing a ski mask. Skulking along just at the edge of the parking lot, he aimed something at the camera. The screen flickered, and not just a little motion, either. The man had jammed it so that the images were clouded with static.

"Why would he have done that?" Caitlyn looked up at Drury for answers.

Answers he didn't have. It didn't make sense to jam the camera on that side, not when the other camera was capturing the shooters and Nicole.

Drury leaned in, hoping to pick through all the static to catch sight of the man. And he did. Fragments that he had to piece together. The man was on all fours, crawling toward the back door of the sheriff's office.

Maybe.

If he'd come at them from that angle, they wouldn't have been able to see him. Neither would Kade or Lucas. So, why hadn't he attacked?

"He took something from his pocket," Caitlyn said at the exact moment that Drury caught the motion.

It was small enough to fit in the palm of his hand, and it wasn't a gun. Nor was it the same device he'd pointed at the camera. A few seconds later, Drury saw what the man did with it.

He placed it beneath the rear of the car and then scurried back to the side of the building before he stood and took off running. Not toward them. But away from the sheriff's office.

"You think it's a tracking device?" Caitlyn asked.

No. Something worse. "I think it's a bomb."

Caitlyn didn't have much color in her face, and that didn't help. "Stay here," he warned her.

Drury hurried out of the office and made a beeline for the back exit just off the break room. The door was slightly ajar, and Lucas and Kade were back there with a CSI team. So was the car. It was still parked right where his brother had left it when they'd come inside after the attack.

"I think there's an explosive device on the car," Drury warned them.

Lucas cursed, and he quickly relayed the warning to the CSIs. All of them scrambled inside the break room and then toward the front of the building just as soon as Lucas kicked the door shut.

"I'll call the bomb squad," Lucas volunteered.

While his brother did that, they all got as far away from the car as they could while remaining inside.

Hell. Drury thought this was over, and it was possible that it was just beginning. If it was indeed a bomb, it could blast through the building.

Gage went out front, no doubt to make sure the area stayed clear. Both the building and the parking lot were roped off with crime scene tape, but they had to make sure gawkers weren't too close just in case the device detonated.

Caitlyn and Drury went back into Grayson's office and shut the door. Not only in case of a possible explosion but also because Helen was peering out of the interview room. And she was cursing them because she was in danger.

"The gunmen probably intended to set it off once we were in the car," Caitlyn said.

He couldn't disagree with that. But there was an even worse possibility. It could have been timed to go off once they arrived back at the ranch. If so, the baby could have been hurt. Hell, a lot of people could have been hurt.

If that was the intention, then that led him right back to Jeremy.

Jeremy was the only one of their suspects with a strong motive to get rid of his brother's heir. Of course, Melanie might not be too thrilled about it, either. Still, it didn't rule out Helen simply because the bomb might have been rigged to have another go at murdering Caitlyn.

And that meant they were back to square one.

Well, they were unless the wounded gunman somehow managed to stay alive. Then there was Ronnie. Once the bomb threat was taken care of, Grayson would no doubt figure out if Ronnie was blowing smoke or if he truly had something to make a deal.

All of those thoughts were racing through Drury's mind, but he hadn't forgotten about Caitlyn. Now that the adrenaline was wearing off, it wouldn't be long before she crashed. There was an apartment on the second floor. More of a flop room, really, but if they ended up being stuck here for a while, he might be able to coax her into getting some rest.

Alone.

With all the energy still zinging between them, it definitely wouldn't be a good idea for him to get close to her right now. Caitlyn had a different notion about that, though. She stood, slipping right into his arms, and she dropped her head against his shoulder.

"Don't you dare apologize," Drury warned her. "Because none of this is your fault."

"This is my fault," she argued, and Caitlyn glanced at the now-close contact between them.

Yes, it was, but that still didn't cause Drury to back away from her. No way could he do that because this was soothing his nerves as much as he hoped it was soothing hers. It wouldn't last, of course. Because he knew the comfort would turn into so much more.

Even now he wanted her.

Hell, he always wanted her, and he couldn't seem to get it through his thick skull that being with her could complicate his life in the worst possible way. Drury wasn't sure how long they stood there, but the sound of his phone buzzing had him finally breaking the contact. He expected to see his brother's name on the screen, but his chest tightened when he saw that the caller had blocked his identity and number.

Caitlyn saw it, too, and she sucked in her breath. "Put it on speaker," she insisted.

Drury did, but he would have preferred to buffer any bad news, and he figured this would fall into the bad news category. He hit the answer button but waited for the caller to speak first.

"Agent Ryland?" a man said. Drury couldn't be sure, but it sounded like the same person who'd fired shots at them. The one who'd taken Nicole at gunpoint.

"Where's Nicole?" Drury snapped.

"Alive for now. If you want her to stay that way, then I'll be needing some cash. Lots of it. I know she's not Ryland kin. Hell, she's probably not even someone you're sure you can trust, but hear this, I will kill her if you don't pay up."

The caller was right about Drury not being certain that he could trust Nicole, but there was something in this guy's voice. Something to let Drury know that he would indeed kill the surrogate.

"How much?" Drury asked.

"I'm lettin' you off cheap. A quarter of a million. Chump change for folks like you and Caitlyn."

"Caitlyn's already drained her accounts paying the ransom for the baby. And why should I pay? The surrogate is nothing to me."

It was a bluff, of course. She was something to him. Not just because she was a human being who probably needed protection, but also because Nicole could perhaps give them answers that would put this thug and his boss in jail for the rest of their miserable lives.

"You'll pay," the man answered, "because you're one of the good guys. A real cowboy cop with a code of honor and junk like that. I, however, have no such code. Start scraping together the money, and I'll call you back with instructions on how this drop will happen."

"I want to talk to Nicole. I want to make sure she's all right," Drury countered.

"She's all right," the guy snapped.

"Then prove it," Drury snapped right back.

The guy cursed, and a few seconds dragged by before Drury heard something he didn't want to hear.

Nicole.

Screaming.

Chapter Fifteen

No matter how much she tried to shut it out, Caitlyn couldn't stop Nicole's scream from replaying in her head. Couldn't stop the fears she had about the woman's safety, either.

She could be dead.

They had no way of knowing because right after that scream, the kidnapper had ended the call. It was possible that he'd killed her on the spot, but Caitlyn was praying that he'd only frightened Nicole into making that bloodcurdling sound. After all, if Nicole was dead, he wouldn't get the quarter-of-a-million-dollar ransom. Maybe that alone would be enough for him to keep her alive.

She sank down onto the bed of the small second-floor apartment where Drury had told her to wait. It was definitely bare bones, a place for the cops to rest when pulling long shifts.

Like now.

All the Silver Creek lawmen, including Drury, were scrambling to remedy this nightmare, and she figured they wouldn't be doing much sleeping until they made an arrest.

Whenever that would be.

She finished the sandwich that Drury had brought her earlier. Not because she was hungry. She wasn't, and her stomach was still in knots. But she didn't want to give him anything else to worry about since he'd insisted that she eat something.

The bone-weary fatigue was catching up with her fast, so Caitlyn went to the small bathroom and splashed some water on her face. It didn't help, but nothing would at this point. Well, nothing other than the person behind this being caught so everyone could try to get on with their normal lives.

For her, though, it'd be a new normal.

Since Grant's death, she'd been working again as a CPA and had a full list of clients. That would have to change since she wanted to spend as much time as she could with Caroline. She was looking forward to that.

Not looking forward, though, to dealing with the fall-out from Drury.

And there would be fallout. Caitlyn wasn't sure how she was going to get over this broken heart. Nor was she sure she could stop herself from falling in love with him. Talk about stupid. But it was as if she had no choice in any of this.

She wiped away a fresh set of tears when she heard someone coming up the steps that led to the apartment. As Drury had instructed, she'd locked the door, and she didn't jump to open it. Not until she heard Drury's voice, that is.

"It's me," he said, and he relocked it as soon as she let him in. It was just a precaution, he'd assured her, but Caitlyn knew he had to be concerned about another attack. She certainly was.

"Bad news?" she asked.

He shook his head. "Nothing from the kidnapper anyway. But the bomb's been disarmed. No one was hurt."

Good. There'd been enough people hurt. "Was the bomb on a timer?"

"No, it was rigged with a remote control, and there

weren't enough explosives to blow up the car, only to disable it."

It took Caitlyn a moment to process that. "You think they wanted us stranded on the road?"

"That's my guess. That's why Grayson's having all the roads and ditches checked between here and the ranch. It might take a while, though." He paused. "That means we might have to stay here all night."

Part of her had already figured that out, but it didn't hurt any less.

He brushed a kiss on her cheek, got the laptop from the desk and brought it to her. He sat down on the bed next to her. "I thought maybe you'd like to see the baby. Tillie is setting up the video feed. It should be ready any second now."

Drury had managed to make her feel as if she were melting when he kissed her, but this was a melting feeling of a different kind. Caitlyn was so touched that she kissed him even before she knew she was going to do it.

It was a good thing that the movement on the screen stopped the kiss before it had a chance to catch fire. A good thing, too, because Caitlyn soon saw her precious baby on the screen.

"She had a bottle about ten minutes ago," Tillie said. She wasn't on camera. Only Caroline, who was sleeping in the bassinet that one of the Ryland brothers had brought over, was.

"Has she cried much?" Caitlyn asked.

"Hardly at all. And she's got such a sweet disposition. So calm. Unlike Mason's boys. Those two can run you ragged pretty fast."

"They can," Drury agreed. "Max and Matt. When they team up with Gage's boy, Dustin, all the nannies at Silver Creek Ranch have to join forces just to keep them out of trouble."

Caitlyn smiled through the happy tears. The conversation was something that families had all the time, and since she'd lost both her parents when she was young, she'd missed this. Missed having the support system that Gage and Mason clearly had.

Drury, too.

"Thank you for watching her," Caitlyn said. "I know you have plenty of other things you could be doing."

Tillie went to the side of the bassinet so that Caitlyn could see her. "She's no trouble at all. Besides, we're in between newborns at the ranch right now. A rarity, I can tell you, and newborns are my favorite."

Caitlyn was thankful for that, but she still wished she was the one there taking care of her.

"Soon," Drury whispered, slipping his hand over hers.

Caitlyn wasn't sure if Tillie could see the gesture, but she smiled. "Lynette's coming over to get some cuddle time and to spend the night," she went on. "That's Gage's wife."

"Yes, I remember her." She owned the town's newspaper. "Uh, is it safe for her to be outside, though?"

"The ranch is under heavy guard right now. Mason even hired some private security to patrol the fence. Don't worry, Lynette will be careful. We'll all be careful," Tillie added.

Caroline squirmed and made a face, and Caitlyn watched as the nanny scooped her up in her arms. "I think it's time for a diaper change. Tell you what, if you're still stuck in town come morning, we'll have another computer chat over her morning bottle."

Caitlyn thanked the woman again, blew her daughter a kiss and watched until the screen went blank. Almost immediately, she felt the loss. Mercy, these were the moments she should be spending with her daughter.

"I'm sorry," Drury said, putting the laptop aside. "I thought it might make you feel better."

"It did." She wiped away the tears. "Seeing her helped."

"You're sure about that?" He used his thumb to brush away a tear on her cheek that she'd missed.

She tried to force a smile. Was sure she failed. Was also sure she shouldn't start this conversation, but Caitlyn did anyway.

"Do you think of Lily when you see the baby?" she asked.

Drury looked away, dodging her gaze for a couple of seconds, and she was certain the answer was yes. It cut her to the core to think what this was doing to him.

"No," he said.

Oh. And she added another "oh" when their eyes met again. That wasn't the look of a man dealing with the old memories.

"Sometimes, it'd be easier if I did think of her," he added. "Because then I wouldn't feel this guilt that I'm forgetting her."

"You'll never forget her," Caitlyn assured him.

He made a sound that could have meant anything and then groaned softly. Caitlyn was sure he would find an excuse to leave so he could deal with these feelings that were causing chaos inside him.

But he didn't leave.

Drury stared at her. "If you're going to stop this, stop it now."

She knew exactly what he meant by *this*. Sex. They'd been skirting around it for days. Heck, for years. Now the fire was burning even hotter than ever, and the walls they'd built between them were crumbling fast.

Caitlyn shook her head, almost afraid to trust her voice. "I'm not stopping it."

She couldn't tell if that pleased Drury or not. But he must have accepted it because he slid his hand around the back of her neck and pulled her to him.

DRURY DIDN'T ALLOW himself to consider that this was a mistake. Everything he did with Caitlyn seemed to fall into that category, and he was tired of fighting this attraction. This need. Tired of fighting with himself, too.

Apparently, Caitlyn felt the same way because she moved right into the kiss. Before his mouth touched her, all Drury had felt was the spent adrenaline and the bitter taste of what would be regret.

The kiss erased them both.

Caitlyn somehow managed to rid him of the remaining doubts along with heating up every inch of his body. He didn't believe in magic or miracles, but she could weave some kind of spell around him. She'd always been able to do that.

She slipped her arms around him and pulled him closer. Not that she had to urge him to do that. Drury was already heading in that direction anyway. And he continued moving, continued kissing her until there was no way for them to get any closer. Well, not with their clothes on anyway.

"Don't stop," Caitlyn warned him.

A good man would have. Or at least a sensible one would have. But Drury wasn't in a good, sensible place right now. He was in an apartment, the door was locked, and even though they could get interrupted, he'd go with this and try to put out this raging fire they'd started.

He took the kisses to her neck and got the exact reaction he wanted. Caitlyn made that silky sound of pleasure. He knew there were other places where he could get the same reaction from her, and Drury wished he had time to rediscover them all. But there wouldn't be much time for foreplay tonight.

Maybe next time.

That thought didn't give him much comfort. Because there might not be a next time, and even if there was, next times came with even more complications. Sex couldn't be just sex with Caitlyn.

He shoved up her top and went even lower with his next round of kisses. To the tops of her breasts. She repeated the sound, kicking the heat into overdrive. Apparently kicking up her own need, too, because Caitlyn kissed him right back. On his neck. His chest.

That sure didn't slow things down.

Along with the raging need, Drury could feel everything speeding up. Not just for him but for Caitlyn. Her hands were trembling, hurried, when she took off his shoulder holster. Drury helped. Helped with his shirt, too, though he didn't manage to get it off, only unbuttoned.

Because Caitlyn went after his zipper.

"Please tell me you have a condom," she said.

"Wallet," he managed to answer.

She rummaged around for that while Drury pulled off her top. Then her bra. No way could he pass up her breasts, so he dropped some kisses there despite the fact that Caitlyn seemed hell-bent on finishing this off now.

Drury hated that this felt like some kind of race. Hated that it would only cool the fire temporarily. But that hate vanished in a split second when Caitlyn peeled off her jeans and underwear. Then his. Seeing her naked was a way to rid him of any doubts he had about this. A way to rid him of every thought that had been in his head.

He took her.

Drury pulled her back onto the bed with him with only one thought in mind. Finish this. So that's what he did.

Their bodies automatically adjusted, and he eased into her. He had to take a moment, to rein in his body. To settle himself. But he also took a moment just to enjoy the feel of her. Always pleasure.

Always something more.

The *more* fueled him. Not that he needed anything else now. He had plenty of motivation.

The years melted away, and they fell right into the old rhythm. The one that would end all of this much too soon. Drury tried to hold on to each sensation, each sound that she made. The taste of her.

Each moment.

He kissed her when she shattered and gathered her close. That was all he needed.

Just Caitlyn.

Drury held on to her and shattered right along with her.

Chapter Sixteen

Caitlyn had been certain that she wouldn't be able to sleep. Not with the insanity that had been going on. And especially not with Drury in the bed with her. But when she woke up and looked at the clock, she realized it was already past midnight.

Four hours of sleep might not sound like much, but it was the most rest she'd gotten since this whole ordeal had started.

She could thank Drury in part for that.

The sex had calmed her nerves along with giving her the pleasure that she knew Drury was plenty capable of giving. The trouble was she wanted more of that pleasure. She wanted more of him.

He was still next to her in the small bed. A surprise. Though he was no longer naked. Sometime after she'd fallen asleep, he'd gotten dressed. Probably because the building was full of Ryland lawmen. That reminder was her cue to get dressed as well.

Caitlyn tried not to make a sound, but the moment she moved, Drury's eyes flew open.

"They'll knock first before they try the door," he said, sounding very wide-awake. "And the door is locked."

Yes, she knew that. "If they knock, I don't want them to hear me scrambling around in here for my clothes."

Of course, she also didn't want to climb out of the bed naked and dress with Drury watching her.

"They'll know we've had sex," Drury added. "I don't know how they'll know, but they will."

Caitlyn didn't doubt that. There seemed to be a deep connection between Drury and his cousins and brothers. She'd witnessed many instances where unspoken things had passed between them with just simple glances.

She nodded, and despite the being-naked part, she got up anyway, gathered up her clothes and took them to the bathroom so she could freshen up and dress. Caitlyn figured she was in there only five minutes or less, but when she came back out, Drury was not only up, he was making a fresh pot of coffee and was looking at something on the laptop.

"Did something happen?" she asked.

The corner of his mouth lifted for just a moment, and Drury glanced at the bed.

"Did something happen other than the obvious?" Caitlyn amended. "I know what went on there."

Now Drury's gaze came to hers. "Do you? Because I'm still trying to figure it out."

This seemed like much too deep of a post-sex question, so she went to the coffeepot and poured them both a cup.

"I, uh, don't want you to think this means something," she said. "I mean, it does mean something. To me." Mercy, she was babbling. "I just don't expect you to have to feel the same way. In fact, you don't have to feel any way at all."

Yes, definite babbling.

Drury's expression didn't change even though he was staring at her, and just when Caitlyn thought he was going to sit there and let her keep talking, he stood, brushed a kiss on her mouth.

A kiss so hot that it could have melted chrome.

"It meant something to me, too," he said in that hot and cowboy way that only Drury could have managed.

But she didn't get a chance to ask him what he meant by that because there was a knock at the door. When Drury opened the door, she saw Mason standing there. Since he was only a reserve deputy these days, it meant Grayson had to be plenty busy to call him out, and Mason didn't look very happy about it. Of course, Mason wasn't the looking-happy-about-anything sort.

"The roads are clear," Mason greeted. "No guarantees, of course, but there are no signs of the kidnappers or idiot clowns who want to shoot at you. That means you can head back to the ranch, unless you're busy…" He glanced at the unmade bed. Then he turned those glances on Drury and her.

Yes, Mason knew all right.

"You ready to leave?" Drury asked her.

"More than ready. I want to see my daughter."

"I figured you would." Mason started down the stairs, and they followed him. "Gage had to leave. Lynette's having labor pains. Somebody's always having labor pains at the ranch," he added, though he didn't seem upset that it had caused him to be called into work.

However, Drury's forehead bunched up. "Isn't it a little early for Lynette to be having the babies?"

Mason shrugged. "The doc said twins can come early."

Drury didn't exactly seem comforted by that. Maybe because it brought back memories of Lily. The sex upstairs wouldn't have helped with that, either, and Caitlyn suspected it wouldn't be long before he would feel guilty. Almost as if he'd cheated on his wife.

"Is Lynette having boys, girls or one of each?" Caitlyn asked.

"Boys," Mason answered. "No shortage of those at Silver Creek Ranch." He looked back at her. "Having your little girl there is a nice change. Not just for Drury but for all of us."

Caitlyn couldn't be sure, but she thought maybe that was some kind of hint that she was welcome there. Or maybe even more than that. Was he matchmaking?

No, she had to be wrong about that.

When they made it to the squad room, Caitlyn immediately spotted the car parked right outside the front door. "It's not a cop car," Drury explained. "It's one of Mason's."

"Is it bullet resistant?" she quickly asked.

He nodded. "Mason had it modified, and I'm hoping that since it doesn't look like a cop car, we won't be followed."

She hoped that, as well.

Drury didn't have to tell her to move fast. Every second out in the open was a second they could be gunned down, so she hurried into the backseat of the car with Drury following.

However, Mason didn't join them. Deputy Kara Duggan was behind the wheel, and Dade was riding shotgun. The moment Drury and she were inside, Kara took off.

"We need to take the long way," Dade informed them. "Just to make sure no one is following us."

As much as Caitlyn hated spending any more time away from Caroline, this precaution was one she welcomed. She definitely didn't want to lead those armed thugs back to the ranch.

Dade glanced back at Drury. "The safe house is finally ready. Just as you requested, first thing in the morning the Rangers will be taking over the protection detail for Caitlyn and the baby."

That brought on an uncomfortable silence. Drury had made those arrangements before, well, *before*, and maybe he wasn't regretting them now. Or not. He could want some space so he could sort through everything that'd happened.

"Of course, I can cancel the Rangers if you'd rather keep them in your protective custody," Dade added.

Even in the darkness, Caitlyn had no trouble seeing Dade's half smile. So maybe he wasn't totally opposed to Drury being with her. But that didn't mean the Rylands would welcome her with open arms. Heck, it didn't mean Drury would, either.

"Was there some kind of family meeting about Caitlyn?" Drury came out and asked.

"Some things were mentioned," Dade admitted. "The wives got involved."

And with that cryptic comment, Dade turned in the seat to look at her. "They seem to think we've all been too rough on you. Of course, there's the part about you drop-kicking Drury's heart, but the *suggestion* I got was that everyone deserves a fresh start."

Drury opened his mouth but didn't get a chance to answer because his phone buzzed. Caitlyn was close enough to see the blocked caller on the screen, and her stomach dropped. No. Not another call from the kidnappers.

"I'll record it," Dade offered, and he pressed the button on his phone to do that just as Drury took the call and put it on speaker.

"Drury?" she heard the caller say.

It was Nicole.

"Are you okay?" Drury immediately asked.

"For now. I escaped, and I stole the kidnapper's phone so I could call you. You have to help me, Drury. You have to help me now."

Drury groaned softly. Not because he wasn't relieved that Nicole was alive, but because he didn't want to do this with her in the car.

"Where are you?" Drury demanded.

"Nearby. Pull over right now."

Caitlyn glanced around. They were at the end of Main Street where there was only a handful of businesses. All closed for the night.

"Should I stop?" Kara asked.

She could practically see the debate going on inside Drury and Dade, and like her, they were trying to pick through the dimly lit street.

And Caitlyn finally saw her.

Sweet heaven.

Nicole staggered out from between two buildings, and Caitlyn got just a glimpse of the woman's bloody, battered face before Nicole collapsed onto the ground.

"Don't you dare get out of the car," Drury warned Caitlyn when she reached for the door handle.

She was probably running on pure instinct to help an injured woman, but it was possible that Nicole wasn't even hurt.

Or if she really was hurt, she could be bait.

Either scenario wasn't good because it meant someone was going to try to ambush them.

"I'll call Grayson so we can get some help out here," Dade said, taking out his phone.

"Please help me," Nicole begged. At least she sounded as if she were begging, but Drury wasn't about to trust any of this.

"Where are the men who kidnapped you?" he asked.

Nicole didn't answer right away. All he could hear was her ragged breath, and she lifted her head, only for it to drop back down again. It twisted at him to think she could be truly injured and that he was just sitting there. But he didn't have a lot of options here.

"I ran from them," Nicole finally said. "They were going to kill me after they got the ransom. I heard them say it. They were going to kill both Caitlyn and me."

"Why Caitlyn?" Drury pressed.

Nicole lifted her head again. Shook it. "I don't know, but I think they want the baby. Please don't let them have the baby."

"I won't," Caitlyn quickly assured her. That's when Drury realized she was trembling. Of course, she had a good reason to do that since she'd just heard that someone was out to kill her. If they were to believe Nicole, that is.

"Grayson's on the way," Dade relayed when he ended the call.

Both Kara and he already had their guns drawn. Drury, too. And they had them aimed at Nicole. Like the others, Drury also continued to look around to make sure no one was trying to sneak up on them. As soon as backup arrived, he wanted to get Caitlyn out of there.

"Watch the tops of the buildings," Drury told Dade, and Drury turned his attention back to Nicole. "How bad are you hurt?"

"Bad. I think one of the thugs broke some of my ribs. I'm in a lot of pain." She moaned again.

"Why did they only hit you?" Drury pressed. "If they wanted to kill you, they could have just shot you." He heard his own words and mentally cringed. Definitely not kid-glove treatment, but he had to treat her like a suspect until he was positive that she wasn't.

"They were holding me just a few blocks from here, and I ran when they stepped away to make a phone call. They caught up with me, and the big guy tackled me. Then he punched me. He would have killed me, but I kicked him between his legs and ran. I came here because I need you to help me."

Yeah, she'd made that clear. "Help is on the way."

She lifted her head, looked at him. He expected her to demand that he allow her in the car. Something that would give her or those thugs easy access to Caitlyn. But she didn't.

"Thank you," Nicole said, and she lay her head back down.

Dade's phone rang, the shrill sound shooting through the car and causing Caitlyn to gasp. Obviously she was as much on edge as he was. Dade didn't put the call on speaker, maybe because he didn't want the call to drown out any sounds they might need to hear.

Like footsteps.

But only a few seconds into the conversation, Dade cursed, and Drury knew they had more trouble on their hands.

"Grayson said someone set fires on Main Street," Dade told them, and now he pressed the speaker button so they could hear the rest from Grayson himself.

"It's a wall of flames right now in both directions," Grayson went on. "I have no way of reaching you, except on foot."

Hell. That was not what Drury wanted to hear. It meant backup couldn't get to them, and he figured that wasn't an accident. No. This was all part of someone's sick plan to get to Caitlyn.

"My advice is to get out of there," Grayson went on. "Fast. I'll get to Nicole as soon as I can."

Which might not be very soon. Or in time. Because if she was truly innocent in all of this, she would be easy prey for the kidnappers to finish off.

"Someone's on the roof," Kara said, and she pointed to the building across the street. "And he's got a gun."

"Get down on the seat," Drury told Caitlyn.

Because of his position, he had to lean down to see the

shooter on the roof. He was in the shadows, but Drury had no trouble figuring out where the guy was aiming. Not at the car.

But rather at Nicole.

Oh, man. This thug was going to gun her down. Nicole must have seen him, too, because she managed a strangled scream and got to her feet. She staggered toward the car.

There was no time for Drury to debate what he had to do. No time for anything because the first shot rang out and blasted into the sidewalk, just a few inches from Nicole.

Nicole kept coming toward the car. Kept screaming for help, too. And knowing it was a decision that he could instantly regret, Drury opened the door. He took hold of Nicole's arm and pulled her inside.

"Go now!" Drury shouted to Kara.

The deputy sped off as the bullets slammed into the car.

Chapter Seventeen

Caitlyn's heart went into overdrive, but she figured she wasn't the only one in the cruiser with that reaction. The bullets were coming right at them, and it was possible they'd just let one of their attackers into the car.

"Go faster," Nicole insisted. "They'll kill us all."

Nicole certainly sounded terrified. Looked it, too. Caitlyn peered around Drury so she could see the woman. And she saw her all right. Nicole's face was a bloody mess, and judging from her ragged breath and wincing, she was in a lot of pain.

Kara did hit the accelerator, and the tires of the cruiser squealed as the deputy turned off Main Street. Caitlyn couldn't tell where she was going, but she prayed they could outrun whoever was attacking them.

"I have to frisk you," Drury told Nicole. "Put your hands on your head and don't make any sudden moves."

The woman didn't object. Nicole just nodded and did as he'd instructed. Drury kept himself positioned between Nicole and her while he checked the surrogate for weapons.

"She's not armed," Drury told them after he'd finished.

Caitlyn released the breath she'd been holding, but she didn't feel much relief. Since Nicole wasn't armed and she was injured, it meant she'd likely been telling the truth. It also meant she needed medical attention.

"Call the hospital," Drury told Dade. "If the shooter isn't tailing us, we'll take Nicole to the ER."

It was necessary, but Caitlyn knew it wouldn't necessarily be safe. For any of them. After all, an armed thug had gotten into the hospital to take Ronnie, and while that particular kidnapping had been fake, it was a reminder of just how easy it would be for a gunman to get inside.

If one wasn't already there.

In fact, those thugs could have injured Nicole as a way to lure them all into a trap.

Caitlyn looked at Drury to tell him that, but judging from his expression, he already knew.

"We've got a tail," Kara warned them.

Even though Drury pushed both Nicole and her lower on the seat, Caitlyn managed to get a glimpse of the SUV that was coming up fast behind them. It was too much to hope that it was someone from the sheriff's office who'd made it through that fiery roadblock.

"Something's wrong with my phone," Dade said. "I'm not getting a signal."

Caitlyn hoped it was just a matter of them being in a dead zone. There were some places in Texas where you couldn't use a cell phone, but they were just outside town where that shouldn't have been a problem.

While still volleying his attention between Nicole and that SUV, Drury took out his phone and handed it to Caitlyn. "See if I've got any bars."

Her stomach sank when she saw no signal on the screen. She shook her head. "Nothing."

Several seconds later, Kara verified the same.

No. Now they had no way to get in touch with Grayson and the others to tell them where they were heading. Once they knew where they were heading, that is. Right now, their only goal was to escape before this attack escalated.

"Maybe the SUV's got some kind of jamming device aimed at us," Dade suggested.

That didn't help with her nerves. "Is that even possible?"

A muscle flickered in Drury's jaw. "Yeah. I've seen devices that can shut down services for up to a mile. Any chance you can put some distance between us and the SUV?" he asked Kara.

"I'll try." She slowed, only so she could make another turn, and gunned the engine again.

The problem with getting away from the SUV, though, was that they were heading farther and farther away from town. And they couldn't go to the ranch. Not with possible gunmen in pursuit. At least the men weren't shooting at them.

Not now anyway.

But Caitlyn figured that probably wouldn't last. Added to that, the men probably had their own backup all over the area. There weren't that many roads in this part of the county, and they could have someone stashed on each one of them. Of course, that meant those *someones* had stayed hidden when Mason and the others had been checking the roads.

Drury glanced at Nicole again. "Did the men who kidnapped you have you in that SUV?"

She dragged in a long breath and looked back at the vehicle. "I think so, yes. But I didn't see any kind of equipment in it that could jam phones. They had a lot of guns, though."

"Think hard," Drury pressed. "Is there anything about them that will help us out of this situation?"

She started shaking her head again but then stopped. "One of them is injured. He fell when they were chasing me, and he hurt his shoulder."

It wasn't much, but maybe it would be enough if it came

down to a face-to-face showdown. Of course, maybe there were more than two men in that SUV.

Drury tipped his head to his phone that Caitlyn was still holding. "Keep checking the phone to see if we get a signal, but stay down."

The words had no sooner left his mouth when Caitlyn heard a sound she definitely didn't want to hear.

A gunshot.

The bullet crashed into the back windshield. The glass held, but it cracked and webbed.

Another shot.

Then another.

Both tore into the glass even more, and Caitlyn knew it wouldn't be long before the bullets made it through.

"Hold on," Kara said a split second before she slammed on the brakes so she could take another turn.

Caitlyn was wearing her seat belt, but she still slammed against Drury, and Nicole hit the window and door, causing her to make a sharp sound of pain. She obviously needed to get to the hospital, but that couldn't happen until they lost the goons behind them.

"Still no phone signal," Caitlyn relayed to them after she checked the screen again. She'd hoped that the turn Kara had made would have been enough to lose the jammer. But no such luck.

She got proof of that when the next shot bashed into the window.

"The shooter's leaning out the passenger's-side door," Dade said, looking in the mirror. "Let me see if I can do something to stop him."

"Be careful," Drury warned him, and he looked at Nicole. "I need you to move next to Caitlyn so I can try to take out the driver from this window. So help me, you'd better be an innocent victim in all of this."

"I am. I swear, I am."

Drury apparently didn't take that as gospel because he took out his backup weapon and handed it to Caitlyn. "Watch her," he said.

Caitlyn would, along with keeping an eye on the phone screen, but now she had a new distraction. Drury was putting himself right in the path of those bullets, and there wouldn't be any glass to protect him.

Drury maneuvered himself around Nicole, putting the woman in the middle of the seat, and he lowered the window. Leaned out. And fired.

From the other side of the car Dade did the same.

Both got off several shots, and that seemed to do the trick of stopping the gunman from continuing to fire. Now if they could just get away from them and regroup.

"Hell." Drury added more profanity to that. So did Dade. Both of them quit shooting and dropped back in their seats.

And Caitlyn soon figured out why.

The SUV rammed into the rear of their car.

DRURY HAD SEEN the impact coming. Had tried to stop it from hurting Caitlyn and Nicole, but he failed. The jolt slung them around like rag dolls, and even though Caitlyn was wearing a seat belt, her body still snapped forward.

Nicole yelped in pain. Heaven knew what this was doing to her if she truly did have broken ribs. An impact like that could puncture a lung.

And worse, it didn't stop.

The driver of the SUV plowed into them again. Then again.

Drury glanced back, hoping like the devil that the collisions were tearing up the front of the SUV, but it must have been reinforced because he couldn't see any damage at all.

Unlike their car.

The back end was bashed in, and the windows were holding by a thread. The SUV and the bullets were tearing the vehicle apart. Which was no doubt the plan. After that, these thugs could pick them off one by one.

"Still no signal on the phone," Caitlyn said, though he wasn't sure how she managed to speak. Especially not when the SUV rammed into them again.

This was obviously a well-thought-out plan, and they'd been waiting for Caitlyn and him to leave the sheriff's office. In hindsight, that was a mistake. Of course, there could be an attack going on there, too. With Ronnie in the building, his comrades might try to break him out of jail.

"I'm turning on Millington Road," Kara told them. She was fighting with the steering wheel, doing her best to keep them out of the ditch—where the SUV driver was apparently trying to force them to go.

Just when Drury thought it couldn't get any worse, it did.

After the SUV rammed them again, the shots returned. The shooter was barely leaning out of the window, and he started sending a spray of bullets into the back windshield.

"Oh, God," Kara said.

Drury's gaze whipped in her direction to see what'd caused that reaction, and he soon saw it. A fire just ahead. And it stretched across the entire width of the farm road. Drury hadn't seen the fires that Grayson had described near the sheriff's office, but he suspected this one was identical to those.

Set by the same people.

People who clearly wanted them dead.

Kara slammed on the brakes, and even though they were still a good forty feet from the fire, the wind was whipping the smoke in their direction. They couldn't see far enough to know how deep those flames extended, which meant they were now officially sitting ducks.

The SUV braked, too, but it wasn't nearly enough. It slammed into them again. The hardest impact of all, and this time it didn't just send them flying around. The car jolted.

Because it wound up in a ditch.

The car immediately tilted, the tires on the passenger's side sinking deep into the ditch. Drury figured these thugs weren't just going to drive off and leave them there. They also had help nearby because after all, someone had set that fire.

"Keep watch around us," Drury warned them.

They did. Caitlyn, too. She still had his phone in her left hand and continued to check it for a signal. Which they likely weren't going to get out here. No jamming equipment needed since this spot was far away from any houses and not close enough to the tower for them to have service.

Part of this sick plan, no doubt.

But the question was—how would they get out of this?

They were probably outnumbered, but there were two cops and an FBI agent in the car. Plus, Caitlyn was armed, though he hoped it didn't come down to her having to shoot.

However, the men in the SUV didn't get out.

Maybe Nicole had been right about one of them being hurt. Or they could be just waiting for the rest of their thug crew to arrive.

"We can't just sit here," Drury said, talking more to himself than the others.

He looked around to try to figure out how to do this, but there weren't many options. They couldn't get out on the driver's side because that would mean they'd be on the road. With the SUV right there, they'd be gunned down the moment they stepped from the car.

That left the ditch.

Both doors were blocked on the passenger's side because of the way the car was wedged in, but there was another way out.

"We can crawl out the windows," Drury suggested. "Once we're out, we can use the ditch for cover." Actually, it was more than a suggestion. It was their only option.

Caitlyn and Dade didn't waste any time lowering the windows, but while Drury kept watch of the SUV, he scrambled across Nicole and her. No way did he want them going out there first. He snaked his way through the window but didn't go toward the front of the car that he could use for cover. Instead, he needed to provide some cover for Caitlyn and Nicole.

Dade got out as well, and he moved back to make room for Caitlyn. Once she was out, Dade hurried her to the front.

Of course, there were no guarantees that there weren't other gunmen on that side, but at least they wouldn't be coming up the road that way because of the fire. Unfortunately, there was plenty of pasture and even some woods for killers to hide.

Kara got out, helping him with Nicole. He could tell from her labored breathing that each movement only caused her pain to spike, but there was nothing he could do about that now. This was their best chance of making it out of here alive.

Drury kept volleying glances back at the SUV, and he tried to steel himself for the bullets to start flying. But the goons didn't shoot.

Why?

Maybe because they wanted at least one of them alive? But again, he had to ask himself why.

There was a cluster of huge trees only about fifteen feet away from the ditch. Close but that would mean plenty of time out in the open. Still, if they could make it there, they could perhaps then go into the woods. The creek was less than a quarter of a mile away, and they could follow it either to the ranch or back into town.

"We could just wait here and see what they decide to do," Kara said.

"Or we could make it to those trees and use them for cover," Drury countered. The darkness and smoke would help some with that. Still, it was risky. Everything was at this point.

"Hell," Dade spat out. "We've got to move now."

Drury glanced back at the SUV, and he, too, cursed. The passenger's-side window was down now, but it wasn't a gun that the thug had aimed at them. It was some kind of launcher. Drury didn't know if it held a grenade or a firebomb, and he didn't want to find out.

"Stay low and move fast," Drury ordered. "Get to those trees." He fired a shot at the SUV with the hopes of getting the guy to duck back inside the vehicle.

It worked, but he knew their luck wouldn't hold out for long.

Caitlyn crawled out of the ditch, dragging Nicole with her. Kara helped, and while they scrambled toward the trees, Dade and Drury continued to send some rounds in the SUV. The bullets weren't making their way through the windshield, but they were holding the guy with the launcher at bay.

At first anyway.

But then the barrel of the launcher came out again. Not

the shooter, though. He stayed protected behind the reinforced glass.

And Drury knew Dade and he didn't have much time.

"Run!" he shouted to Dade.

They did. They took off, heading for the trees. Not a
second too soon.

Because the firebomb ripped through the car.

Chapter Eighteen

The sound of the blast roared through her, but Caitlyn didn't look back. She tightened her grip on Nicole and just kept moving as fast as she could.

She prayed, though, that Dade and Drury hadn't been hurt.

They'd stayed back, to protect the rest of them, but that could have cost them their lives. Still, Caitlyn tried not to think about that, tried not to give in to the fear that had her by the throat.

With Kara on one side of Nicole and Caitlyn on the other, they made it to the trees and ducked behind them. Caitlyn got her first good look at the effects of the explosion then.

There was nothing left of the car.

It was nothing but a ball of fire.

Of course, it created even more smoke, and this was thick and black, and it took her several heart-stopping moments to look through it and spot Drury and Dade.

Alive.

Thank heaven.

They were running toward the trees, and just when Caitlyn thought they might make it, she saw something else. Something that caused her fear to spike even more.

The thug who'd launched that firebomb was leaning out the window again, and this time, he had a gun.

"Watch out!" she shouted to Drury and Dade.

But it was too late. The shot slammed through the air.

The scream wouldn't make it past her throat. It was jammed there, stalling her breath, causing the panic to rise. It didn't help when the thug fired off another round of shots.

Caitlyn couldn't tell if either had been hit, but she couldn't just hide there and watch them get gunned down. She leaned out from the tree, took aim with the backup weapon Drury had given her.

And she pulled the trigger.

She wasn't sure where the shot landed, but it must have been close enough to the shooter that it got him to duck back inside. From the side of another tree, Kara fired off a shot as well, pinning down the gunman enough so that Dade and Drury could scramble in beside them.

"Stay down," Drury immediately snapped, and he pushed her out of the line of sight of the thug in the SUV.

Not a second too soon.

Because he fired off more rounds, each of them slamming into the spot where she'd just been. It stunned her for a second. Then terrified her. Because those bullets could have hit Drury, too.

"Keep watch all around us," Drury instructed, and he glanced at Nicole. "How's she doing?"

Nicole managed to nod, though she was holding her hands over her stomach and chest. "Just stop these monsters, *please*."

Caitlyn knew that Drury and the others would try to do that. So would she. But they didn't know what they were up against.

She glanced around at their surroundings. The night.

The smoke. And way too many places for backup thugs to hide and ambush them. It sickened her to think that Drury, Kara and Dade were in grave danger because of her. These men were clearly after her. Probably Nicole, too, since she might have witnessed something while captive that could be used to identify them.

Nicole moaned, drawing Caitlyn's attention back to her. She knelt down beside her and tried to see if there was anything she could do to help her. There was a gash on her forehead that was bleeding, but it wasn't enough to be life threatening. However, the woman could have internal injuries.

"Caitlyn?" someone called out. It was the man in the SUV. The one who'd been shooting at them. "You can make this easy on your boyfriend and the cops if you just give yourself up."

"That's not going to happen," Drury shouted before she could say anything. "It's not," he repeated to her.

Caitlyn knew that Drury wasn't going to want to hear this, but she had to try anyway. "You could use me to draw them out. Then we could maybe take the SUV and get Nicole to the hospital."

As expected, Drury was shaking his head before she even finished. "They'll gun you down the second you step out into the opening."

"Maybe. But they might want to take me to the person who hired them."

Drury cursed. "That isn't helping to convince me. In fact, nothing will convince me to let you go out there."

Caitlyn went closer to him. "It could save you. It could save the others. At least consider it."

Drury's next round of profanity was much worse. "You're not going out there. Do you want to make your daughter an orphan, huh?"

It felt as if he'd slapped her. No, she didn't want that, and going out there could indeed get her killed. It ate away at her to think of her baby growing up without a parent, but this was eating away at her, too.

"We'll find another way out of this," Drury insisted. He tipped his head to the phone. "Keep checking for a signal." Before she could continue the argument, he switched his attention to Kara. "You keep watch on your right. Dade, look for anything coming up from behind. Caitlyn will make sure the left side stays clear."

Judging from the way Drury barked out those orders, there wouldn't be any compromises or debates. The glare he shot her only verified that. He knelt down by the side of the tree and pinned his attention to the SUV, so Caitlyn did the same. Except she looked in the area he'd assigned to her.

Nothing.

Well, nothing that she could see anyway. There was another cluster of trees about only ten yards away, and it was plenty thick enough for someone to be hiding there.

"Caitlyn?" the thug called out again. "Maybe this will convince you that it'll be a good idea to come with us."

The barrel of a rifle came out from the SUV, and the shots started. A string of them. The bullets slammed into the tree and sent a spray of splinters all over them. Caitlyn and the others had to shelter their eyes. Worse, the wind shifted, and the smoke started drifting their way. It wouldn't kill them, but it would be hard to aim if they were coughing.

Even though the bullets were deafening, Caitlyn volleyed her attention between the phone and the area to their left. At least she did until a slash of light caught her attention. Not coming from the trees but rather the road.

Mercy, had Grayson or the deputies found them?

She held on to that hope for several seconds. Until she heard Drury curse again. Caitlyn glanced at the SUV and saw the black car pull to a stop behind it. Since the thugs weren't shooting at the vehicle, it meant this was probably more hired killers.

"What the hell are they doing?" Dade asked.

Drury shook his head, and Caitlyn tried to follow his gaze to see what had caused that reaction. Someone stepped from the car. Yes, definitely another thug. He was dressed in all dark clothes and was wearing a ski mask.

He also had the launcher aimed at them. It wasn't the same size as the other one had used. This one was much smaller.

Caitlyn's heart slammed against her ribs because she thought it might be a grenade or another firebomb, but when it hit the ground, there wasn't a blast. Instead, it began to spew out a thick cloud of smoke.

"Are they trying to get us to run?" Kara asked.

Neither Dade nor Drury answered. They continued to keep watch. Not just on the smoke but all around them.

With everything going on, it was a miracle that Caitlyn remembered to glance down at the phone, but when she did, she saw a welcome sight.

"We have a signal," she said. "It's a weak one, but I can try to text Grayson."

"Do it," Drury insisted.

Caitlyn's hands were shaking, and it took her a few seconds to steady them. However, she'd barely gotten the message started when Drury caught onto her arm and pulled her to her feet. He immediately pivoted and took aim in the direction of the SUV.

"Run!" Drury shouted.

Dade picked up Nicole and started running, too, with

Kara racing right along behind him. Caitlyn glanced back but all she saw was the milky smoke.

At first anyway.

Then she saw the man. Maybe the same one who'd fired at them from the SUV, and he had the big launcher. And he fired.

The firebomb came right at them.

CHAOS.

That one word kept repeating through Drury's head.

He fired two shots at the goon with that launcher, but couldn't stop him in time. Now, all hell was breaking loose.

"Run!" Drury repeated to the others, and he hoped like the devil they were doing that.

He ran, too, toward the other cluster of trees that was nearest to them, but he also pulled up, pivoted and fired at their attacker. Maybe, just maybe, Drury could stop him from shooting another firebomb. Or even regular shots. At this range, the gunman would be able to pick them off.

It didn't take long, mere seconds, for the smoke to get so thick that Drury couldn't see. Plus, there was the heat from the fire.

He couldn't stay put, not out in the open like this, because those gunmen could come from that wall of smoke at any second. He also didn't want to leave the others alone any longer than necessary since they'd probably already made it to the trees. That twisting feeling in his gut let him know that this could get even uglier than it already was.

"Get behind cover now and stay down," Dade called out to them.

Drury tried to do just that, and he hoped Dade had eyes on whoever was coming after them. Drury raced to those trees, dropped down and took aim. He immediately saw one of the thugs who was positioning himself to shoot what appeared to be another firebomb.

Right at them.

Drury double-tapped the trigger, sending two shots into the guy's chest. He fell, but Drury couldn't tell if he was dead or not. He hoped so because he didn't want the idiot to get another chance to use those bombs. Of course, that didn't mean there wasn't someone else ready to take the downed thug's place.

The seconds crawled by while Drury waited for someone else to come at them. There could be a half dozen or more in the SUV and car. Heck, there could be more in these woods, and that's why Drury glanced around to get his bearings and to make sure they weren't about to be ambushed.

Kara was about three yards behind him, watching their backs. Dade had taken up position two trees over, and he was looking all around them. Nicole was flat on her back and moaning in pain.

Drury hated that he couldn't do anything to help the woman, but maybe Caitlyn had managed to send that text to Grayson so that he would have their position. Grayson wouldn't be able to get an ambulance in here, not with the possibility of shots still being fired, but he and the other deputies could help them deal with the attackers.

He glanced around to ask Caitlyn about that text.

And his breath stalled in his throat.

She wasn't there. He frantically looked around while also trying to keep watch for the attackers, but there was no sign of her.

"Where's Caitlyn?" he asked Dade and Kara.

They, too, glanced around, and Drury could tell they didn't have a clue. His first instinct was to call out to her, but that would give away their position, so he dropped back and began to search behind every tree. Hard to do that, though, with the thick underbrush covering the ground and the smoke. It was getting even thicker now.

Hell, was Caitlyn hurt?

That revved up Drury's pulse a significant notch. In all the mayhem of them running for cover, one of the thugs could have shot her. Or maybe she hadn't made it out at all.

With his stomach twisting, Drury looked back at the other set of trees. The ones that were on fire now. If she was in the middle of that, then… But he didn't even want to go there.

Caitlyn couldn't be dead.

He heard the sound to his left. A snap of a twig maybe, and the relief flooded through him.

But not for long.

It was Caitlyn all right, but she wasn't alone. Nor was she all right. There was someone behind her. One of the ski mask–wearing goons. And he had his left arm clamped around her throat in a choke hold.

He also had a gun pointed at her head.

"Surprised to see me?" the man taunted.

That immediately caused both Dade and Kara to pivot in his direction, and they took aim just as Drury already had. But none of them had a clean shot. The man had ducked down and was using Caitlyn as a human shield.

"I'm sorry," Caitlyn said. "I didn't see him in time."

Drury hated that she felt the need to apologize. Hated, too, that look in her eyes. Fear, not just for herself but for all of them.

"You probably know what you have to do next," the man continued. "You gotta all put down your guns just like Caitlyn did."

"I didn't put mine down," she snapped. "He knocked it from my hand."

"Just doing my job, and my job includes killing her right here, right now if you don't put down those guns. Same for the bimbo on the ground. My friend wants me to give her a little payback for hurting him. Of course, she won't like my version of payback."

Drury didn't recognize the guy's voice, and it definitely wasn't one of their suspects. However, it was obvious he was connected to the men who'd taken Nicole from the back of the sheriff's office.

"Who are you working for?" Drury demanded.

The man tightened his grip on Caitlyn's throat. "What part of my order didn't you understand? I mean, it was simple enough. Guns on the ground now!"

Drury hated to surrender his weapon because he didn't have a backup. He'd given it to Caitlyn. But Kara and Dade almost certainly had some other weapon stashed away. Weapons they would no doubt need to get all of them out of this alive.

Dade was the first to drop his gun. Then Kara. Drury finally did, too, while he continued to fire glances around them. It would be a good time for other attackers to swarm in and take them all, and if that happened, their chances of survival would drop considerably.

"Now kick the guns away so you can't get to them," the man ordered.

They did, but Drury kicked his in Nicole's direction. It was a risk since there was a slim chance she could be working with these clowns. But he doubted it. And even though she was clearly in a lot of pain, maybe she'd be able to use his gun if it came down to it.

"So, what now?" Drury asked the goon when he just stood there.

"Waiting for the boss. Shouldn't be long now."

Drury doubted the boss had anything good in mind for Caitlyn. For any of them really.

The moments crawled by, and when the wind shifted, Drury saw someone walking through the smoke. Not just one person but three. Two men both dressed in black and wearing ski masks. They were armed.

But not the person in the middle.

Hell.

So, this was the *boss*.

Chapter Nineteen

Because of the way the goon had her standing, Caitlyn couldn't see the reason Drury had cursed. But she figured it couldn't be good.

Nothing about this was good, and they'd need plenty of luck to get out of it alive.

Since Dade, Kara, Drury and even the thug holding her now had their attention focused in the direction of the road, Caitlyn considered trying something. Maybe like elbowing the guy or dropping to the ground. It might cause him to shoot, but at least his gun was still aimed at her.

Mercy, she didn't want to die. But she doubted whoever was coming would spare any of them. This way, there might be a scuffle. One that Dade, Kara and Drury could maybe win.

But why hadn't the goon already killed her?

That was the question racing through her head when Caitlyn finally saw the people making their way toward them. Two more hired guns.

And Melanie.

The woman wasn't a hostage, either. Dressed as if ready to attend a business meeting, she was walking beside the men, and even though she wasn't armed, she didn't need a gun. Not with those two hired killers.

"I got her just like you said," the goon holding Caitlyn relayed to Melanie.

"Good." Melanie barely spared the others a glance. Instead, she kept her stare on Caitlyn.

Except it was a glare.

Even in the near darkness, Caitlyn had no trouble seeing it. Melanie hated her, and while she hadn't exactly kept that hatred under wraps while they were at the sheriff's office, this was pure venom that she was now aiming at Caitlyn.

Melanie's glare was still in place when she made a sweeping glance around them. "Couldn't get your lover out of this, huh?" she directed at Drury.

"The night's not over," he countered, matching her glare for glare.

Melanie smiled as if all of this were a done deal. It wasn't. Somehow they had to fight their way out of this because if Melanie and those hired killers eliminated them, they might go to the ranch next.

"Is she still alive?" Melanie asked when she looked at Nicole.

"Yeah," the goon behind Caitlyn verified. "Wasn't sure if you wanted her kept alive or not."

"No. She's worthless to me now that I can't get any money for her."

There it was—Melanie's motive all spelled out for them. Well, her partial motive anyway. She wanted Grant's money.

"Is that why my baby was born, because you wanted me to pay for her?" Caitlyn asked. She didn't bother to contain the anger in her voice and wished she could blast this idiot to smithereens.

"Of course," Melanie readily admitted. She glanced at the others again. "And I guess you know that means it's bad news for all of you. Well, bad news for everyone but Caitlyn."

Caitlyn replayed the words to make sure she'd heard her correctly. "Why would you keep me alive?" But she immediately thought of the answer. "You want me to drain all my bank accounts and give the money to you. There isn't much left."

"I want every penny of it." Caitlyn hadn't thought Melanie's venom could get any worse, but it had. Melanie fanned her hand over the thugs. "Grant's money paid for all of this."

"And you put that money in an offshore account with my name on it," Caitlyn snapped.

Melanie shrugged. "It seemed the easiest way to cover my tracks, and there's no way you could have gotten your hands on it because you didn't know the security code I set up."

And by covering her tracks, Melanie had also tried to make Caitlyn look guilty. It hadn't worked, but she hadn't needed it to work since she had the upper hand here.

"Grant's money will pay for a whole lot more since there are some loose ends that need to be tied up," Melanie added. "And what it doesn't cover, Helen will pay for. My personal living expenses, nannies and private schools for the baby."

Everything inside Caitlyn went still. "Are you talking about nannies and private schools for my daughter?"

"She's Grant's daughter, too, and I plan to raise her as my own. That way I'll have a part of Grant. If Helen cooperates with me, then she'll get to see the child. Not here, of course. I won't be able to live here."

If the thug hadn't held her back, Caitlyn would have gone after her. "You're not getting my child."

Melanie shrugged. "We'll see about that, and I'm sure

Helen will pay up when she realizes I have her grand-daughter."

"Is Helen in on this?" Drury asked.

Melanie made a you've-got-to-be-kidding sound. "No, this was my plan and my plan only, but since you didn't take the bait when I planted evidence against Jeremy and her, it means you sealed everyone's fate."

Drury shook his head. "What did you do?"

Melanie actually smiled. "Jeremy deserves what he gets. Do you know he killed Grant?"

"Got any proof of that?" Drury countered.

"Jeremy talks in his sleep," Melanie said under her breath. "No way could I let him get away without being punished." She motioned toward the goon holding Caitlyn. "Come on. Bring her to the car. Kill the rest," she added to the other two. "No need to do a cleanup. I'll have the kid and will be out of the country before any of these Silver Creek lawmen figure out it's me. They'll be too busy chasing Jeremy."

She'd obviously set him up somehow, but Caitlyn didn't care about that. "How do you think you're going to get my baby?"

Melanie tipped her head to the fires. "Plenty of those. In comparison to the rest of this, firebombs don't cost much at all, and I figure if we land enough of them on the Silver Creek Ranch, the Rylands will give her up to save their own."

Clearly, she didn't know the Rylands. They'd never give up the baby. But that didn't mean plenty of them wouldn't die or get hurt trying.

It felt as if someone had clamped onto her heart and was squeezing it hard. The rage bashed at her like a violent storm, building and building until Caitlyn knew where she needed to aim that rage.

At Melanie.

Melanie turned to walk away, and the goon started moving, dragging Caitlyn along with him. Leading her to where she would no doubt be tortured and eventually killed. Of course, Drury and the others would be targets long before that. They'd die within seconds if Caitlyn didn't do something now.

She latched onto all that rage she was feeling and let it and the adrenaline fuel her. Caitlyn bashed the back of her head against the goon's face, as hard as she could. So hard that she could have sworn she saw stars. She pushed aside the pain, though, and dropped to the ground. The goon didn't drop with her, nor did he let go of the gun. He was cursing her now and latched onto her hair.

That's when all hell broke loose.

Drury lunged at the thug. Dade went after the other two, and Kara scooped up Drury's gun off the ground. She probably didn't have a clean shot, but at least one of them was armed, and maybe she could stop Melanie from getting away.

"Kill them!" Melanie screamed.

Her thugs were certainly trying to do just that. Caitlyn's attacker still had hold of her hair and was using his fierce grip to sling her around to block Drury from slugging him. Drury didn't give up, though, and he finally managed to bash the guy right in the face.

It was enough to get him to stagger back and let go of her hair.

Drury pushed her away and went after the guy, plowing right into him and sending him to the ground. Caitlyn frantically looked around for the goon's gun, and her breath stalled in her throat when she saw that he still had hold of it. Worse, he was trying to aim it at Drury.

"Do your jobs and kill them." Melanie's voice was a

screech, followed by some ripe profanity. She sounded insane. And probably was.

Since Melanie wasn't armed and wasn't running, Caitlyn tuned her out for a moment and tried to help Drury.

"Stay back," Drury warned her.

He probably didn't want her to be anywhere near that gun, but she wasn't just going to let him fight this alone. Caitlyn kicked at the goon's legs. And she continued to kick until the sound of the shot stopped her cold.

Oh, mercy.

Had Drury been shot?

It seemed as if time slowed to a crawl, and the sounds in her head were a series of loud echoes. She couldn't lose Drury. Especially not like this, while he'd been trying to protect her.

Caitlyn clawed at the goon, hitting any part of him that she could reach, but that's when she realized Drury hadn't been hit. The bullet had come from behind her.

Kara.

The deputy had put a bullet in one of the thug's heads. Lifeless, he dropped to the ground.

One down, but Dade and Drury were still battling the other two attackers. She couldn't tell if either was winning, but at least Kara had a gun, and the deputy hurried closer, waiting for a shot that Caitlyn was sure she would take if she got the chance. Maybe they'd actually get out of this alive.

But that's when Caitlyn saw something she didn't want to see.

Melanie was running. Getting away. And if she reached the car or SUV, she could escape. Maybe she would even try to get to the Silver Creek Ranch and try to take Caroline.

Caitlyn went after her.

It wasn't easy. She'd burned a lot of energy hitting the thug, and the smoke didn't help. It wasn't as thick as it had been, but it cut her breath. Still, that didn't stop her. Nothing would at this point. Not even Drury shouting out to her.

"Caitlyn, come back."

He was probably concerned that there were other hired killers who would come to Melanie's aid. And maybe they would, but Caitlyn couldn't let Melanie make it to the road.

Behind her, there were two shots. She hoped they'd come from Kara or that maybe Dade and Drury had managed to get hold of a weapon. Part of her wanted to go back and see, but she had to stop Melanie.

Melanie was running a lot faster than Caitlyn thought she could, and she made it all the way to the thug whom Drury had shot before Caitlyn caught up with her. Caitlyn dived at her, catching onto Melanie's waist and dragging her to the ground.

That's when Caitlyn saw the gun.

Melanie must have grabbed it from the dead guy, but she lifted her hand, taking aim at Caitlyn.

Caitlyn didn't think. She only reacted. She hit Melanie's hand just as the woman pulled the trigger.

The shot roared through the air.

Caitlyn couldn't tell where the bullet had gone, but she prayed it hadn't hit Drury or the others. Prayed, too, that she could stop Melanie from firing again. She latched onto the woman's wrist, and even though Melanie outsized her by a good thirty pounds, Caitlyn had something to fight for.

Her daughter.

If the woman escaped, there was no telling what she might do.

Behind her, there were more shots. Caitlyn had no trouble hearing them, but she couldn't look back and see if Drury was okay.

Melanie cursed her, calling her vile names while she fought like a wildcat. She kicked and dug her fingernails into Caitlyn's hand. She drew blood, but Caitlyn drew blood, too, when she rammed her forearm against Melanie's face.

She howled in pain, cursed even more and tried to bash Caitlyn against the head with the gun. Caitlyn dodged it and dropped her weight onto the woman, pinning her arms to the ground. That didn't stop Melanie from screaming and fighting, and just when Caitlyn wasn't sure how much longer she could hold her, she heard the movement behind her.

Since she hadn't been able to look back and see what was going on, Caitlyn didn't know if this was friend or foe approaching her. Worse, there was nothing she could do because if she let go of Melanie, she would pull the trigger.

The fear rose inside Caitlyn as the hurried footsteps got closer and closer, but she tried to steel herself for whatever might happen.

"It's all right," someone said.

Drury.

The relief nearly caused Caitlyn to go limp. Temporary relief, anyway. She still wasn't sure he was okay.

He wrenched the gun from Melanie's hands and moved Caitlyn off her so he could flip Melanie onto her stomach. He restrained her with some plastic cuffs that he took from his pocket.

Caitlyn pulled in her breath and held it. Until Drury finally turned and looked at her. He had some blood on his face. No doubt from the fistfight with the hired gun, but he was all right.

"You shouldn't have done that," he said, his breath gusting. "She could have killed you."

"She didn't," Caitlyn managed to say, but she could see from the stark look in Drury's eyes that this had almost certainly triggered some flashbacks of Lily's death.

Even though Drury didn't exactly have a welcoming expression, Caitlyn leaned in and kissed him. A very quick one because his attention went back to where she'd last seen Dade, Kara, Nicole and those other goons.

Caitlyn snapped in that direction, too, and she spotted Dade hurrying toward them. He had Nicole in his arms. Kara was right behind him, and she was still keeping watch all around them.

"What happened to the gunmen?" Caitlyn asked.

Kara shook her head. "All dead."

It was hard to feel any grief over the deaths of hired killers, but Caitlyn also knew that if they'd managed to keep at least one of them alive, then he could perhaps spill details they might not get from Melanie.

"You think this is over?" Melanie snarled when Drury hauled her to her feet. She looked back at Caitlyn, and the raw hatred was all over the woman's face. "It's not over. You'll never see your daughter again."

Chapter Twenty

"Hurry," Caitlyn insisted.

Though she really didn't have to remind Drury to do that. He already was in the "get there fast" mode and hadn't even waited for backup to arrive. Instead, Caitlyn and he had taken the car that Melanie and her thugs had used. It was a risk since there could be some kind of tracking device on the vehicle, but Drury weighed that risk against an even greater one.

Not getting to the baby before there was an attack at the ranch.

"Do you have a signal yet?" he asked, tipping his head to the cell phone she was holding.

Caitlyn shook her head. Cursed. It was frustrating, all right, but they'd be out of the dead zone soon, and she should be able to call the ranch. And Grayson. Drury had no idea what was going on with him, and it was entirely possible that Melanie had had another team of attackers go after the lawmen in the sheriff's office.

As Drury continued to do, Caitlyn glanced all around them. Watching for more of those hired guns. He was certain that Kara and Dade were doing the same thing. They'd taken the SUV so they could get Melanie to jail and Nicole to the hospital.

The surrogate was yet another concern.

Her injuries could be life threatening. Of course, Melanie was high on his list of worries, too, because she could have arranged for more gunmen to be positioned on the road. He didn't know how many hired killers that the million dollars of ransom money would buy, and Drury didn't want to find out.

"What do you think Melanie did to Jeremy?" Caitlyn asked.

Drury hadn't had time to give it much thought, but he didn't need a lot of thinking time to know that it probably wasn't something good. Melanie had been plenty riled over Jeremy's rejection and betrayal, and she'd no doubt set him up somehow to take the blame for all of this.

He took another turn onto a farm road, heading toward the ranch, but they were still a good ten minutes out. Drury figured it would seem more like an hour before they got there.

"Finally," Caitlyn said, looking at the phone screen. Her hands were shaking when she pressed Grayson's number.

Drury hoped that his cousin would answer on the first ring. And he did.

"You two okay?" Grayson immediately asked.

"Yeah, but Melanie might have sent someone to attack—"

"I just got off the phone with Dade, and he told me. I've alerted the ranch hands, and Nate, Mason and our cousin Sawyer are heading down to the road now to make sure no one is there."

Caitlyn's breath rushed out from relief. They weren't out of the woods yet, but there was no way his cousins would let Melanie's thugs get close enough to do any real damage.

"I told Ronnie that we had Melanie in custody," Grayson went on, "and he's ready to spill all for a plea deal."

Drury had to shake his head. "If Ronnie was working for Melanie, why did she bring him at gunpoint to the jail?"

"Ronnie says that's the plan they worked out. That she'd pretend to turn him in, and that he'd take the fall in exchange for his kids getting a ton of money. He figures there won't be a payoff now that Melanie's being arrested."

No, there wouldn't be. In fact, Melanie's accounts would be frozen, and Caitlyn would get back any portion of the ransom money that Melanie hadn't spent on these attacks. Of course, that was probably the last thing on Caitlyn's mind right now. She just wanted to see her baby and make sure she was all right.

"Let me call you back after I've finished talking with the DA," Grayson continued. "Oh, and be careful when you make it to the ranch."

Drury would be, but he doubted he was going to be able to hold Caitlyn back. She had such a grip on his phone that she would probably have bruises. Bruises to go with the ones on her face.

It turned his stomach to see them. To know just how close he'd come to losing her.

"After this is done," he said, "I intend to chew you out for going after Melanie like that."

"You would have done the same thing if you'd been me."

He would have. "But I'm an FBI agent trained to do things like that." He paused, huffed. "That doesn't trump motherhood, though."

She made a sound of agreement. Followed by a helpless moan. "Please just hurry," Caitlyn repeated.

Drury did, taking the final turn. When the ranch finally came into view, he saw something that had him hitting the brakes.

There were men clustered around the cattle gate at the start of the ranch road, and someone was on the ground.

Hell.

Drury hoped he hadn't driven Caitlyn into the middle of another attack. Just in case, he turned off the headlights and eased closer. While he was trying to get a better look at what was going on, his phone buzzed, and he saw Mason's name on the screen.

"Is that Caitlyn and you in the car?" Mason growled.

Drury felt some of the tightness ease up in his chest. If Mason could call them, then he was okay. Well, maybe.

"Yes. What happened?" Drury asked.

"This dirthead we've got on the ground thought it would be a good idea to try to shoot something at the ranch. Trust me, he knows now it wasn't a good idea. We're about to haul him off to jail."

"Is Caroline okay?" Caitlyn asked.

"She's fine. Josh and Bree are with the nanny and her."

Josh, his other cousin, and Bree, who was Kade's wife and had once been in law enforcement. Caroline was in good hands. Better yet, she was safe.

Caitlyn's breath rushed out again. And the tears came. Tears of relief, no doubt. The happy tears would come once she had her baby in her arms.

"Was the hired gun alone?" Caitlyn asked.

"He was," Mason verified. "But we've got the hands patrolling the area just in case. They found the clown's car just up the road, and there are no signs that anyone else was in it."

Maybe because Melanie had thought one firebomb shooter was enough. Or perhaps the woman had just wanted to save a little money.

"The gate and the fences are all armed, though," Mason went on. "So the alarm will sound if there are any stragglers who try to get onto the grounds. Someone's also monitoring the security cameras."

Good. It was a lot of security, but it had obviously worked since they'd caught this guy before he'd managed to do any damage.

He watched as Nate and Sawyer got the hired gun to his feet and started moving him toward a car that was nearby.

"Is it okay for me to drive Caitlyn to the guesthouse?" Drury asked Mason.

Mason kept his glare on the man being arrested. "Yeah, because if this dirthead moves even an eyelash, he's going to pay and pay hard. It's too late to be testing my patience."

Drury wondered if it was ever a good time to test Mason's patience, but he didn't say that to his cousin. He drove onto the ranch.

"By the way," Mason said just as Drury was about to end the call. "Have you fixed things with Caitlyn yet?"

Since they were on speaker, Drury hesitated before he said anything. "Fix things?" he settled for asking.

Mason cursed. "Have you told her you're in love with her? And no, the question isn't for me. It's because I know when I get back home, Abbie will ask me how the personal stuff worked out for you two."

Drury glanced at Caitlyn, who seemed a little shell-shocked. Maybe because of the whole ordeal she'd just been through. Maybe in part because of Mason's *you're in love with her* comment.

"I'll keep you posted," Drury answered, and he didn't bother to take out the sarcasm.

There was a ranch hand at the main entry gate, and he ushered Drury in, closing the gate behind them. Yet another security measure that Drury appreciated.

When Drury approached the guesthouse, he parked as close to the front porch as possible, and the moment he stopped, Caitlyn hurried out. He didn't try to stop her. No chance of doing that. So, he just raced in after her.

With all the chaos that'd gone on, being in the quiet room seemed a little surreal. The baby was asleep in her bassinet. Josh was sitting next to her, guarding her, and Bree was at the kitchen table quietly looking at the feed from the cameras.

"She's okay," Bree assured Caitlyn. Maybe because Bree was a mother herself, she no doubt figured Caitlyn would want to hear that right off.

"Thank you," Caitlyn said, and she repeated it several more times while she scooped up the baby. She pressed a flurry of kisses on her cheeks and held her close. Drury wondered if she'd ever let Caroline out of her sight again.

"She's a quiet baby," Josh added. "Unlike mine and most of the others on the ranch."

That was true. There were several contenders for the loudest Ryland kid, and Josh's was one of them.

"You think you two will be okay without us?" Bree asked. "Lynette had the twins, and I'd like to go to the hospital to see her. If Kade will let me off the grounds, that is."

Kade probably wouldn't allow that for a while, not until they were positive all was well.

"Are Lynette and the babies all right?" Caitlyn asked.

Bree nodded. "Gage sounded downright giddy when he called and said that the C-section went well. The boys are little, only four pounds each, but otherwise healthy. I could hear them crying in the background."

Great. More criers. More kids. But Drury found himself smiling at that thought. He'd never wanted to live on a quiet ranch anyway, and there was something comforting about knowing there'd be another generation of Rylands to run the ranch. Some of them might even follow in their footsteps and become cops.

"We'll be fine here," Drury assured Bree. Then he looked at Josh. "You can head home, too. The thug that

Mason and the others caught is on his way to jail. Melanie, too." In fact, she was probably already there.

Caitlyn and Drury thanked them both again. Josh and Bree gathered up their things, both of them kissing the baby before they headed out. Drury locked the door behind them and armed the security system.

"It's just a precaution," Drury said when he saw the renewed concern in Caitlyn's eyes.

"Good. I don't want to take any more chances."

That sounded a little unnerving, as if she weren't just talking about security now. Maybe she wasn't ready or willing to take a chance on, well, him.

He eased down next to her on the sofa and was prepared to tell her how sorry he was that all of this had happened. But he didn't get a chance. That's because Caitlyn leaned over and kissed him. It wasn't a peck, either. This was an honest-to-goodness kiss, not of relief, either. This felt more like foreplay.

"The adrenaline," he said, ready to offer an excuse so she'd have an out. If she wanted an out, that is.

Apparently she didn't.

"I didn't kiss you because of the adrenaline," she insisted. "Or because we were nearly just killed." She paused. "Okay, maybe it did have a little to do with nearly dying, but things got crystal clear for me tonight when I thought I'd lost you."

Drury had experienced some of that clarity himself. "Yes," he settled for saying.

She stared at him, maybe waiting for more, and since Drury wasn't sure what more to say, he just kissed her right back. At first he thought she might be disappointed that they hadn't continued what could be the start of a promising conversation, but she moved right into the kiss. As much as she could anyway, considering that she still had the baby in her arms.

"You're very good at that," she said with her mouth still against his.

"I think it's just because we're good at it together."

Caitlyn eased back, met his gaze, and again she seemed to be waiting for him to say something important. Something that didn't have anything to do with what had just happened.

Drury finally managed to gather some words that he hoped made sense. "I realized tonight that life's short. And there are no certainties."

She frowned but nodded. "You're talking about Lily now."

It was Drury's turn to frown. "No." And he wasn't. "I was talking about us." He had to stop and try to figure out how to say this. "I don't want you to leave. I want Caroline and you in my life."

At least she didn't frown, but Caitlyn did continue to stare at him. That wasn't the response he wanted, so Drury kissed her again, and he kept on kissing her until they were both breathless.

When they finally broke for air, she looked down at the baby. "She'll always be Grant's biological daughter."

He lifted his shoulder. In the grand scheme of things, DNA didn't seem important. "She'll always be *your* daughter. And I get what you're saying. Or maybe it's what you're asking. Can I accept her? Can I accept any of this?"

Caitlyn nodded.

Drury nodded, too. He could definitely accept it if Caitlyn was willing to stay and give them a chance. However, he didn't have time to spell that all out for her because his phone buzzed, and he saw Grayson's name on the screen.

Hell, he hoped something bad hadn't happened.

"Put it on speaker," Caitlyn insisted, and she eased the baby back into the bassinet as if preparing herself for one more round of the nightmare that they'd thought was finished.

"Are you two all right?" Grayson asked the moment Drury answered.

"Yes," they both answered cautiously. It was Drury who continued. "Did something else go wrong?"

"Not here. Why? Did something go wrong there?"

"No." Drury looked at Caitlyn. But everything wasn't all right just yet. He still needed to tell her so many things. First, though, he had to get through this call with Grayson.

"Dade just called me from the hospital," Grayson explained a moment later. "Nicole is being examined now, but the doctor doesn't think her injuries are life threatening."

Drury could see the relief in Caitlyn's eyes. Could hear it also in the slow breath she released.

"I've already got the approval from the DA for a plea deal with Ronnie," Grayson went on. "Don't worry, he'll still get plenty of jail time, but in exchange for testifying against Melanie, he won't be charged with murder."

"Murder?" Drury and Caitlyn asked at the same time.

Grayson paused. "Jeremy's dead. I've only spent about ten minutes with Ronnie, but according to him, Melanie set it up to look like a suicide, and in the note he confessed to killing Caitlyn and you. Grant, too."

"Melanie said Jeremy did murder Grant," Drury explained. "No proof, of course. And at this point we might never know for sure since Jeremy's dead."

"You're right. And I don't believe everything in this fake note. In it, he claims that Helen is responsible for stealing the embryo from Conceptions."

"But she didn't?" Caitlyn said under her breath.

"No, it was all Melanie, and Ronnie even has some

proof. Guess he didn't completely trust his boss because he recorded some conversations that he says will prove Melanie was scheming to get both the baby and the ransom money. The recordings won't be admissible in court, but Ronnie can testify against everything on them."

That would tie everything up. Well, except for Helen and Jeremy. Jeremy was dead, and Helen had lost another son. Even though they obviously weren't close as most mothers and sons, Drury figured she'd still feel that loss. That didn't mean he had much sympathy for the woman.

"Helen's not getting Caroline," Drury insisted.

Caitlyn had a new look in her eyes now, one of thanks for backing her up. Drury intended much more than playing backup for her, though.

"Can't see how Helen would have a claim," Grayson agreed. "Caitlyn doesn't have as much as a parking ticket, and none of what happened was her fault. When I tell Helen about Jeremy, I'll remind her that if she ever wants to see her granddaughter, then she'd better try to mend fences with Caitlyn."

That might work, and if it didn't, Drury would have a chat with the woman. After everything that Caitlyn had been through, he didn't want her to have to deal with the likes of Helen.

"What about Nicole?" Caitlyn asked. "Other than being the surrogate, please tell me she didn't have any part in this nightmare."

"According to Ronnie she didn't. I asked. He said Nicole didn't have a clue what was going on, not even after Melanie decided to have her kidnapped and held hostage. I'm sure Ronnie will give us a lot more info on how that all went down."

Yes, it sounded that way. Which was a good thing considering Melanie's other hired guns were all dead and wouldn't be able to spill their guts the way Ronnie was doing.

"Guess you heard that Lynette had the babies?" Grayson continued a moment later.

"Bree told us," Drury answered. "She said Lynette and the babies were doing okay."

"They are. Gage maybe not so much. He's crazy happy, but I figure it'll soon sink in that he's not going to get much sleep for the next few years what with twin boys in the house. By the way, has anyone mentioned that the females are seriously outnumbered on the ranch?"

Drury was instantly suspicious. "Mason said something about that. Any reason you're bringing it up?"

"You're a smart man. You figure it out." And with that, Grayson hung up.

This was Grayson's attempt at matchmaking, and he sucked at it. He was about as subtle as all the Ryland kids piled into the same room.

He put away his phone, checked the baby to make sure she was okay. She was. Then he looked at Caitlyn.

Not okay.

She was frowning again, and after all the good news they'd just gotten, that expression shouldn't be on her face. Especially since the frown was paired with a determined look in her eyes.

"I'm in love with you," she said as if it were a declaration of war. "I know that's probably not what you want to hear, but I can't undo my feelings for you. That doesn't mean you owe me anything—"

Drury stopped her with a kiss, one of those long ones that did more than rob them of their breaths. The heat slid right through him.

"I don't want you to undo your feelings for me," he assured her. "And having you say you love me is exactly what I want to hear."

She blinked. "Really?"

"Oh, yeah. Because I'm in love with you, too."

Finally, that got the frown off her face and erased the doubt in her eyes. She smiled. Kissed him until he was certain if they kept kissing, it was going to lead them straight to the bed.

Or the sofa.

Smiling in between the kisses, Caitlyn eased him back until his head was against the sofa's armrest. She didn't stop there, thank goodness. She slid her body on top of his.

"So, where do we go from here?" Caitlyn asked, glancing down at their new position.

Drury didn't think she was just talking about sex, and neither was he. "Everywhere. I love you, Caitlyn."

"And I love you," she repeated, pulling him to her.

* * * * *

Don't miss the final book in USA TODAY
bestselling author Delores Fossen's
THE LAWMEN OF SILVER CREEK RANCH
series when LUCAS *goes on sale next month.*
*You'll find it wherever Mills & Boon Intrigue
books are sold!*

"You're the new agent?"

Emir's words were heavy with disbelief. "You're the one Adam recommended?"

"Yes," Kate said. "I'm K.J...."

"This won't work."

"By this, you mean me?" She took a step forward. Now she was in his face.

"That's what you meant, wasn't it? I'm not a man so..." She left the remainder of the sentence hanging.

"You need to get on the first flight home," he said through clenched teeth.

"Give me a chance."

"It's not me that's the problem."

"I know," she interrupted. "It's the customs, the tribes outside the city, the..."

"It won't work."

"Look, I know what I'm getting into. I'm qualified. I specialized in Middle Eastern studies—an exchange student. I'll help you find your sister. You just need to trust me."

SHEIKH'S RULE

BY
RYSHIA KENNIE

MILLS &
BOON

First Published in Great Britain 2017
By Mills & Boon, an imprint of HarperCollins*Publishers*
1 London Bridge Street, London, SE1 9GF

© 2017 Patricia Detta

ISBN: 978-0-263-92874-7

46-0417

Printed and bound in Spain
by CPI, Barcelona

Ryshia Kennie has received a writing award from the City of Regina, Saskatchewan, and was also a semifinalist in the Kindle Book Awards. She finds that there's never a lack of places to set an edge-of-the-seat suspense, as prairie winters find her dreaming of warmer places for heart-stopping stories. They are places where deadly villains threaten intrepid heroes and heroines who battle for their right to live or even to love. For more, visit www.ryshiakennie.com.

For Rourke, who was dedicated to the art of fun.
The "Wookie Man" would have loved to
rip this book to shreds, while enjoying
every word and every moment of it.

Chapter One

Marrakech, Morocco
Monday, September 14, 5:54 a.m.

The first haunting notes of the call to prayer seemed
troubled, almost off-key, when usually the melodious
sound wove through the predawn stillness, beckoning
with an easy allure not unlike the nimble fingers of
the weavers in the casbah who wove the many rugs
sold to the tourists. Like the rugs, the ancient chant
was as much part of the rhythm of life and the fabric
of Marrakech as was the still night-shrouded skyline.
But today, in a mansion hidden in the depths of palatial
grounds and secured by the most current technology
and the best in security guards, the simple power of the
timeless notes not only felt off, they were lost in the gut-
tural roar that sounded more wounded beast than man.

Emir Al-Nassar crushed the pen in his right hand.
On the desk, the smartphone lay where he had thrown
it, the blue protective cover fractured, the crack running through the Blue Jays' baseball emblem. A thin
line of ink ran down his arm and dripped onto the thick

Persian carpet. Like blood, he thought, and wondered how much more blood would be spilled before she was safe once again.

"I won't lose her, too," he muttered thickly, his voice choked. The emotion that had welled up only seconds earlier had taken everything he had. "None of us will."

But, despite his words, the unthinkable had happened. His sister had been kidnapped.

He couldn't fathom how frightened she might be. And at this particular moment there was nothing he could do. He was at the whim of the demands of others. But inaction was not in him, no matter what they had ordered.

His mind was already jumping through a series of options. Most importantly, what action would not increase the danger that already threatened Tara and what would ultimately bring her home where she belonged. He needed to think logically, think that it was someone else's sister, that it was not Tara. It was the only way he could give everything to her rescue without the emotion he knew would only cloud his judgment.

He dropped the broken pen, not caring about the stain that might ruin the ancient carpet. He took a step away from the desk as the last notes of the call to prayer died away. He turned slowly, as if facing an executioner. Through the open blinds, the city lights shone a warm glow across Marrakech's still-shadowed beauty. It was a view he never got tired of. But today he could have been anywhere in the world for he saw none of it.

A door slammed somewhere in the hallway and suddenly the room was full of unleashed testosterone as two of his brothers, Talib and Zafir, entered the room.

"Emir, what's going on?" Talib began. "Your Jays are done and the Yankees don't play for another hour, even with the time difference, so—"

"Shut up about bloody baseball, Talib," Zafir interrupted as he looked at Emir and the silent awareness that had always run between the twins jumped like a living coil across the space that separated them. "No one cares about your fave team or even Emir's for that matter. He wouldn't call us here, at this hour of the morning, unless—" He broke off, looking to Emir for confirmation, his eyes troubled, as if expecting the worst.

"Tara's been kidnapped," Emir said with no emotion. His back was to them and he was still facing the window that allowed a view of the grounds his sister loved so much. He turned to face his brothers, schooling his features, reining in his thoughts. It was difficult, for he couldn't believe how foolish his sister had been.

"Kidnapped," Zafir repeated, a frown slicing his handsome face, his jaw clenched, his eyes blazing.

"Impossible!" Talib said as his fist smacked the palm of his hand and disbelief laced through the word. "We have one of the best security teams in the country. How?"

The word reverberated for a second, then two, as Talib and Zafir processed what this meant, how the impossible had become possible.

"She was on a night out with the girls. But, at the end of the night, she left her girlfriends behind and, it appears, her security, too. Fortunately her team caught

up with her. The reports say she was with her security team just outside the gates. The evidence is in the
signs of a scuffle and the fact that they left one of them
dead." Emir said the words reluctantly, as if it had been
his fault. "I can't imagine how they got so close to the
compound—how they got her—unless security was distracted. They were two of our best." It wasn't an excuse
and he still couldn't believe it had happened.

Zafir clenched his fist, his jaw tight. "She's alive?"
And while it sounded like a question, they all knew it
was really a command or, more accurately, a demand
that she was alive or there would be hell to pay.

"As far as I know," Emir said, his voice devoid of
emotion. He glared at Zafir for flirting with the reality
he hadn't dared consider—that Tara was hurt, or worse.
"She was taken just outside the grounds."

"She dodged her security?" Talib repeated as if not
believing the possibility. "She knew the risks. She…"
His voice broke and he turned away.

"When we find her, she'll be grounded for the rest
of her life," Zafir snarled as if anger at her would somehow ensure his sister's safety.

"She's twenty years old," Emir reminded him. The
words came almost by rote, meaningless considering the
scope of what had happened. But sometimes it was difficult to remember that his sister was officially an adult.
He thought of her as his little sister in need of protection. And the fact that, physically, her petite size made
her almost doll-like only accentuated those thoughts.
But Tara's personality was another story. It was as forward and brash as her physical being was delicate. Emir

prayed that her larger-than-life personality and piercing intelligence that could challenge and often match him in many a game of chess would see her through.

"Her security tracked her, apparently found her immediately before the kidnapping," Emir continued. "The kidnappers used knives. Ahmed lived..." he said, referring to one of the men assigned to Tara. He took a breath, as if that would put reason into the insanity they faced. "He's in rough shape. It's touch and go right now. He's not able to give any information but when he is..."

"I'm on it." Zafir's jaw clenched as he said it and at the same time Talib's open palm slammed against a vase that, at best guess, had been created over three centuries ago. The vase crashed to the floor and none of the brothers bothered to look as pieces flew across the room. Instead they stood poised like predatory animals, unmoving, contemplating the unfathomable.

Normally, Emir would have been all over Talib and his well-known temper for breaking the vase. He was the one who cared about the irreplaceable items that foretold a long and venerable heritage. But now, in a crappy and equally frightening situation, he knew Talib's anger was more than justified.

He'd felt the helpless rage himself and, as much as he hated the emotions that had rolled through him in the minutes since he'd learned the incomprehensible truth, he couldn't stop them. He'd been at the kidnappers' mercy. And, without consultation with his siblings, he'd given in to their first demand in the hope of buying time and knowing what they asked was small enough to assure a second request, possibly even a third. That's what he told himself. The truth was that he wasn't sure what to expect or even what to do in this situation. The only thing he wanted to do was to kill the men who held his sister, if he only knew where or who they were. Kidnapping was neither his nor his brothers' expertise.

"We'll need guns and—"

"No," Emir growled as he cut Talib off. He turned to Zafir. "I need you to take my phone. Not now," he said as Zafir held out his hand. "Later. That's how they'll contact us." Their voices were similar and, as identical twins, one could easily imitate the other. "When I get an idea of where they might have gone, I'm going after her—alone, at least without the two of you. All of us moving in a pack would alert the perps to what we're doing. Therefore, we all can't go. Someone—" he looked pointedly at Zafir "—has to be available for their demands. Let them believe we're waiting, getting funds together—playing the game as they want."

"There's already been a request," Zafir said quietly as he put a hand on Emir's shoulder. It was not a question; as twins there were things each had always known about the other.

"It was small. There'll be more," Emir confirmed.

Although he was by no means a kidnapping expert, he knew the pattern with other kidnappings of strangers, people he had not known or loved—people who were not his sister. And, while they weren't following the M.O. of an average kidnapper—sadly there was such a thing—he suspected they weren't unique. He moved away, slipping from his twin's abbreviated touch.

Zafir nodded. "And you've paid it."

"You think that will get Tara back?" Anger was tight in Talib's voice. He was a gifted member of their team but, of all of them, Talib had the least control over his emotions, especially now.

As always, his twin was on the same wavelength, he knew that as he saw the look of approval in Zafir's eyes. He was the one who would most likely hold his emotions in check and who could make it look like Emir was doing exactly what the kidnappers wanted—waiting and complying.

"No. They'll want more. But for now we look cooperative, and that's good for Tara," Zafir said.

"Hopefully we'll have bought enough time to get some help," Emir said.

Talib paced, his fists clenched and his jaw set. "We can't do nothing," he growled.

"Agreed." Emir paused, considering the options. He met Zafir's eyes. Although Zafir was younger by only minutes, there was never dissention because of birth order; they were usually in agreement. The slight tilt of Zafir's head told him they were in agreement in this situation, as well. His gaze went to Talib—of the three of them, the one most likely to act impulsively, more likely to insist, as he already had, that they go at the kidnappers en masse with guns blazing. He didn't blame him. They all felt the pain, the shock and the anger. For it was their baby sister they were talking about.

"For now, we act like nothing has happened," Emir said.

"No." Talib's fist clenched and he brought it down on the desk, making a trio of pens jump. His eyes met Emir's, passion blazing as his jaw clenched. His shoulder-length hair did not hide the strength in his jaw or the anger in his flashing brown eyes. "I'll kill…"

"We'll kill…" Zafir corrected. "When the time comes. First we get Tara home in the safest way possible. Too many of us would be an obvious and threatening action to the kidnappers, which will only endanger Tara. And that's one thing we will not do."

For it was not just them, Emir knew. There was their youngest brother, Faisal, whom he had yet to contact. He feared that Faisal would be on the first plane from Jackson, Wyoming, to Marrakech as soon as he heard. It was why he'd contacted their second-in-command at their Wyoming branch first, for Emir hadn't thought of a way to forestall his brother once he was aware of the situation. "Faisal…" he began as if his thoughts and his voice were one.

"I'll speak to Faisal." Zafir cut him off. "There's no need for him here. Not yet."

Emir nodded. He worried that it might take both of them to keep Faisal in the States and not jumping on the first plane. He hoped Faisal's common sense would do the job when he heard what was in place to ensure Tara's safe return.

"I spoke to Adam," Emir admitted. It was one of the first things he'd done when he'd received that devastating call just before 4:00 a.m.

Adam Whitman had been a good friend from his college days at Wyoming State and was now second-in-command in the Wyoming branch of their security agency. He was one of the few people outside the family Emir could trust. They had always had each other's back, even though, through the years, there'd been long lapses where neither one had contacted the other.

"And?" Zafir prodded.

"Adam's concerned that our family is high-profile, too well known. If this is a straight kidnapping case, that's one thing, but if there's some sort of revenge on the family…" He paused, collecting his thoughts.

"Revenge?" Talib's fist clenched and Zafir looked worried.

"We don't know, but fresh eyes… Adam might have something. The agent he's assigned will be looking at it from a different angle, without any preconceived ideas."

"He might see something we'll miss because of familiarity," Talib said.

"Exactly," Emir agreed and Zafir nodded.

"The other thing…the man he's recommending is an amazing profiler. Exactly what we need and the first thing I mentioned when I called Adam. We want nothing less than the best." He looked at his brothers, saw the pained expression on both their faces and, still, determination radiated from them. They wouldn't be beaten. He felt hope just being surrounded by them and he knew he in turn gave them hope. That was the way it had always been.

"Who is it?" Talib asked. "There've been a number of new hires in the Wyoming branch."

Emir shrugged. He'd get the name when he gave Adam the update after his brothers left. For now, names were irrelevant; he trusted Adam's judgment. "He's new, but Adam claims he's good."

Silence seemed to steep like an uneasy brew through the room as every instinct urged them to surge forward, armed-dangerous, potentially lethal as they plowed over the threat. But they were hobbled by a threat that had intelligence they weren't privy to; it knew exactly where they were and, worse, it held what they claimed most precious.

"We have no idea where they've taken her," Emir said. "Only that they want money and their demands, I suspect, will continue to go up."

Emir's stomach clenched and he ached to see his sister's kidnappers' blood seeping into the depths of the endless desert sand. But he needed something more than revenge. He needed his baby sister safe. He looked at the ink staining the ancient rug and the cracked phone, both evidence that he had lost control.

"Here's what we will do…" He motioned his brothers to sit and he laid out what had and would be done in the hours that followed.

"I don't like it, but it makes sense," Talib said ten minutes later.

"Forty-eight hours, Emir. No more," Zafir interrupted as he clapped his hand on Emir's shoulder.

"Or less if we're needed," Talib said.

"Or if you lose contact," Zafir said.

"Agreed. But if there's progress, that may change." Emir had explained his conditions and knew it was a shaky agreement. With their sister's life in jeopardy, he was surprised his brothers had agreed to that much. But they knew how delicate a situation like this was. No one had to be reminded of what they stood to lose.

Tara, the only girl in the family, with none of the brothers in a steady relationship, was all that was soft and feminine in the family. Without her, Emir knew that the niceties in life would disappear as easily as that beautiful vase beneath Talib's fist. She organized family celebrations and get-togethers, remembered family traditions. Only last month she'd gotten them all together on Skype for a toast to his and Zafir's birthday. Without her... He wouldn't think of it, couldn't.

Twenty minutes later, as his brothers exited the room, he picked up the phone. Fortunately its case was the only thing that had cracked in his initial rage. He punched the number of the Wyoming branch of their security agency. Adam picked up on the second ring.

Emir laid out what had transpired since they'd last spoken.

"Don't do anything more until K.J. gets there. Promise me." Adam's voice held an edge of concern.

Eight hours. It was a long time—it was forever. "I don't know if I can do it," he said.

"I don't know what more to say, Emir. K.J.'s already en route."

Emir sucked in a relieved breath at that.

"As we agreed, I'm sending the best. And despite the fact that I'm not coming over—this agent is better than either me or, for that matter, Faisal. It took a bit of work at this end, had to rearrange a few cases, but you're not going after these perps without the best at your side."

"I appreciate it," Emir said, and the call ended seconds later. There was nothing more to say.

For now, all he could do was wait. He began to pace.

Somewhere over the Atlantic
Monday, September 14, 9:00 a.m. GMT

K. J. GELINSKY'S LONG legs were stretched in front of her and a cup of coffee sat at her elbow. Jackson, Wyoming, was a long way away and yet only days ago she'd been admiring the view from her apartment window, still in awe of the mountain peaks that cradled the city. Now the only view was the blind that covered the jet's window and hid the endless expanse of the Atlantic. At another time she would have soaked up the luxury of flying on such a plane, the decadence of being the only passenger with a flight attendant just a call-bell away. She'd been with Nassar Security for a little over a month and their use of private jets was still a novelty.

No expense had been spared to get her on a jet and flown over the Atlantic at a moment's notice. Briefly, she considered the resources of the men who owned both the agency in Wyoming and in Marrakech.

She'd met only Faisal and then only briefly. But she'd liked him immediately. His youth had surprised her. But, at twenty-five, only the snowboard he'd carried under his arm when she'd met him unexpectedly in the parking lot had indicated anything other than what he was: a serious business owner. He'd welcomed her to the team and put the snowboard down to shake her hand with the cordiality she'd later heard he offered to all his employees.

Faisal was approachable, friendly—the opposite of what she'd heard of his oldest brother who was rarely seen, at least by the Wyoming branch of the agency.

With only hours before wheels to the ground in Marrakech, she was anxious to get started, intrigued by the assignment and more than curious to meet Emir Al-Nassar. The head of the Moroccan branch of the agency, Emir, and his twin, Zafir, were the reason the agency had expanded as rapidly as it had. Emir was a friend to the man she directly reported to, which was interesting in itself, as were Adam's words as she'd prepared to leave. "He is one of the few people on earth I would trust completely."

This assignment was a coup for any agent. She'd been lucky that both her skill set and the fact that she'd been in New York on the last day of a training session had placed her as not only the logical choice but four hours closer than she'd normally have been.

She pulled her thoughts back to the case. The fact that she would be working with Emir and what kind of man he might be was irrelevant. What recognition she might get from her employers, the potential boost to her career, also moot points that only clouded her thinking. And yet they were very valid moot points. This case would—could, she amended—be career-making. She emptied her mind, bringing herself into a state of meditation for a few minutes.

Fifteen minutes later she was centered and focused on one thing: finding Sheikka Tahriha Al-Nassar.

On the tray in front of her was everything she knew and everything she might need to know about the case. She'd been through much of it already. Now she scrolled through the pictures Adam had just sent her. She memorized the features of the kidnapped sister, but it was the picture of her oldest brother that wouldn't leave her mind. Despite the fact that he was the president of the company, she'd never before seen a picture of him. She'd known that he and his brother Zafir were twins, but she hadn't known they were identical. She'd never seen either of them in person. Adam had provided her with a picture of each of them, for although it was Emir she'd be working with, they were all in Marrakech awaiting her arrival.

She clicked on Emir's picture, noting the difference that ran deeper than the length of their hair—Emir's shorter than his brother's, clipped above his ears. The difference was in the depth of his piercing brown eyes. She kept going back to his picture and told herself it was part of this assignment to know who she was meeting at the other end. But that was only part of the truth. Emir had an aura about him, a powerful sense of confidence that seemed to emanate from the picture.

K.J. closed her eyes. Despite her mind-focusing meditation, a nap would help her hit the ground running. But that wasn't an option. There was more to be done. She needed to know everything they had on the Al-Nassar family.

Despite working in the office headed by Faisal, she'd had little contact with him or his family, and now it was critical to fill in those gaps, along with learning everything about today's Marrakech. The last time she'd been in Morocco had been five years ago. She needed to familiarize herself with not only present-day Marrakech but also with the surrounding area if she was to get Sheikka Tahriha safely home.

She remembered the conversation just before she had taken off.

"There's been a payment," Adam had said in his usual, abbreviated, no-intro sort of way. "Hopefully that will hold them off."

"You've advised that no more payments are to be made."

"Emir is well aware of that." Adam paused, clearing his throat. "One other thing. Be careful. A woman in rural Morocco—" he shook his head "—I'm taking a chance on this."

"I know. Don't worry, Adam," K.J. had said with a confidence she hadn't felt. It might be the twenty-first century, but this was the land of sheiks where ancient traditions and strict religious laws governed much of day-to-day life, especially in the rural areas where it was highly possible the kidnappers had fled to. She'd considered that and brought tops with long sleeves, and long pants. She'd also be sure to secure her long hair before she landed so that it was away from her face. Still, she knew it wasn't enough. But it was the best she could do. Her knowledge of the area would be her best defense. And if they wanted the best, she thought with more self-awareness than conceit, they would have to take her as she was.

She scrolled through the additional information. Then, she set down the tablet and lifted the paper report and skimmed through the pages. The report didn't give her a lot of hope. The kidnappers weren't sophisticated, judging from the trail of evidence. Thugs were more difficult to reason with. In some instances, thugs couldn't be reasoned with at all. She feared that, in this situation, that might be the case.

Chapter Two

Emir glanced at his watch. Adam's last text told him that the investigator was thirty minutes away from landing. It was 2:30 p.m. and, according to the evidence, Tara had been missing for over twelve hours. Time was slipping away and yet there was nothing he could do beyond what he already had. Now, he waited, and only his iron-clad will kept him from taking charge of this case alone. That, and the knowledge that emotion had already colored his judgment.

The airport was crowded with people and luggage as commercial airline queues filled up and passengers waited for their flights, oblivious to his inner turmoil or to the fact that his family was in dire straits.

Emir strode through the crush of incoming passengers emerging from one flight and into a back room where few were admitted, to the security area where the pulse of the airport was monitored on a second-by-second basis.

"How much longer, Sihr?" he asked the man who had first become familiar to him in the aftermath of the horror of the car crash that had killed both his parents six years ago. It had been here where an emergency crew had taken off in the hope of airlifting survivors from the isolated mountain road, and this man who had facilitated the quick takeoff. Emir ran a hand over his chin as if that would dispel the memory of a tragedy that had changed everything. Instead, all he felt was stubble and a reminder that time was slipping away.

He went over the expected time of arrival in his mind juxtaposed against weather conditions. As an amateur pilot he knew that, despite Adam's report fifteen minutes ago, flight conditions could easily have changed the plane's arrival time. "Early?"

Sihr gave him a brief nod. "It's landing now." The lean, middle-aged man swept his arm toward the back of the small office. "We can go out this way and meet them at the gate."

Emir was three steps ahead of the smaller man as he strode down a narrow corridor that turned into a common area used only by security. They were in an area that was off-limits to the average passenger, but not to Emir. Despite the fact that he had come to know Sihr during one tragedy where rules had been bent, despite the fact that his family employed Sihr's brother, being allowed into the security area wasn't a favor, at least not one in the traditional sense. It was how things were done for him, his family and those around him. It was how it had always been.

As they made their way through the bustling security area and Sihr opened a door that led directly to the runway, a small breeze hit him. That was immediately overlaid by the smell of jet fuel and the roar of a commercial airliner taking off that erased the chance of any conversation even if Emir had felt like starting one. He did not. He had nothing to say and nothing that Sihr needed to know.

To the left, a Gulfstream jet had just landed and was taxiing toward them.

"Security will clear them on the tarmac. Barring anything unexpected, you should be able to go straight through," Sihr said in his brisk, business-first manner.

Emir nodded. That bit of information was unprecedented for a foreign-origin aircraft and he knew it was Adam's doing. Their investigators traveled the world, sometimes disguised as normal tourists, and each time clearance was negotiated before the jet took off.

One passenger got off the jet. He waited. No one else appeared. He frowned, unsure of what was going on and yet sensing something wasn't right. His gaze traveled back to the passenger. She was a good-looking woman. He could tell that even from this distance. She was blond, her hair short or pulled up and away from her face, it was hard to determine which and none of it mattered. Still, he continued to watch as a security agent ran a wand down one side of her, skimming shoulder to ankle. Emir's gaze shifted away, uninterested—waiting for the investigator K. J. Gelinsky.

Minutes passed and then she was in front of him. She only had to tip her head slightly to catch his eye; a tall woman with a forward attitude. He took a step back, taking her out of his personal space.

"Mr. Al-Nassar," she said, holding out a slim hand. "I'm K. J. Gelinsky."

"Emir," he said almost by rote for "mister" had been his father and that era had ended in tragedy over half a decade ago. But even as he responded, the thoughts were shoved to the background as the reality of what she had said hit him.

"K.J.," he repeated as if he needed the repetition to commit the initials to memory. Something inside froze as he realized what Adam had done—what he would have said if Adam had told him the sex of the investigator beforehand. Adam would have known how he would have reacted. He would have known that this meeting would never have happened. He didn't offer her his hand. He couldn't.

"You're the new agent?" he asked, the words heavy with disbelief. "You're the one Adam recommended?"

"Yes," she said brightly. "I'm K.J.—"

"This won't work," he said. His thoughts were clouded with anger at the thought of what Adam had done, of how much time might be wasted, and of Tara whose life would be further endangered now that there was no help forthcoming.

Her wide, smoky-blue eyes narrowed. "By 'this,'" she said slowly, "you mean me?" She took a step forward. Now she was in his face.

He frowned. If she were a man that would have been a mistake. But she was no man.

"That's what you were meaning, wasn't it? I'm not a man so…" She let the remainder of the sentence hang.

He paused long enough to take a breath to control the anger that made him want to lash out at someone, anyone. "You need to get on the first flight home," he said through clenched teeth.

"Give me a chance." There was no hesitation in her voice or in her stance as she faced off with him, her head up, her eyes sparking as if enjoying the challenge.

"It's not me that's the problem or needs to give you a chance," he said. All he could feel was the pressure of an invisible clock ticking and the betrayal of a friend thousands of miles away. Adam knew the customs, the inherent sexism that still wove through the ancient traditions of the desert tribes. He knew it all and, still, he had sent her.

"I know," she interjected. "It's the customs, the tribes outside the city, the—"

"It won't work," he interrupted, thinking of the desert and where he suspected Tara's kidnappers were hiding. He'd always been an equal opportunity employer and supported his sister, Tara, in her fight for change. It was a man's world. It didn't matter how much he disliked the fact, it was a truth that, for now, wouldn't change.

"Look, I know what I'm getting into. I'm qualified," she said, her bag swinging from her shoulder, her eyes bright with passion. "I specialized in Middle Eastern studies—an exchange student." She waved one delicate, well-manicured hand at him.

Just looking at that hand confirmed every doubt he had. It wasn't just about customs, she was female and because of that and so many other things, she was the wrong person for the job.

"I'll help you find your sister. You just need to trust me."

"No!" The word came out with all the pent-up fury that had built since the fateful call from Tara's kidnappers and now the full impact of it sparked in his eyes as his temple pounded and his fists clenched.

"No," he said with less edge but with no room for negotiation. He was wasting time, had wasted time, first waiting and now in a senseless airport run. "I don't care what you specialized in. You're a woman and because of that you're going home," he said bluntly. "I've wasted enough time. I'll speak to the pilot and we'll get you out of here."

"You're not being fair."

"I'm not being fair," he repeated, emphasizing each word. If she'd been a man he would have had her by the collar up against the wall, his face in hers. But she wasn't and that was the problem. "You're useless to me. I'd have to watch out for both you and me. That's a distraction. Look at you—you couldn't swing a punch or..."

One minute he was seething, glaring at her, and the next he was flat on his back.

"You bloody flipped me," he snarled, leaping to his feet.

"As you can see, I know martial arts as well as being an excellent marksman."

"Do that again," he said in a slow, measured tone, "and you'll wish you hadn't."

"That's it?" she asked, one eyebrow quirked. "That's all you've got?"

"This isn't going to work. None of it matters. Whatever your skill set, it comes down to you're a woman. Useless to me in this environment."

"You don't have a choice. It's me or no one," she said and glared at him.

His jaw clenched.

"Oh, and by the way, your attitude about women sucks. I feel for your sister."

"Keep Tara out of this," he snapped, realizing it was a ridiculous thing to say when it was all about Tara.

"This might not just be about money. I think you already suspect that."

He held his surprise back. He hadn't expected that; it was an idea he and Adam had only briefly touched on.

"Adam told you."

She shook her head. "Tara is the heart of your family. Without her, it's broken."

She was bang on and he wished she wasn't for it changed everything, including his decision to send her home.

"These could be men with a grudge against the House of Al-Nassar. After all, your family has a long and deep history in Morocco. Someone has more than likely been hurt along the way. What better opportunity than a chance to bring you down by taking the sister you and your brothers adore and bleeding you for some cash." She shrugged. "Simplistic, I know, but not improbable."

"Don't make me sorry," he said, hoping that by not escorting her back to the plane he wasn't making the biggest mistake of his life.

"There's no time to waste," K.J. said, swinging around and striding ahead of him. She didn't stop talking and her comments trailed behind her.

With no choice but to follow, he did, even as his eyes drifted downward and he found, in spite of the situation, that he couldn't take his eyes off the endless length of her legs, which were enticing despite the fact they were covered by faded, beige-cotton pants. That and the generous curve of a hip only confirmed that in no way could she be mistaken for the man he had only minutes ago hoped she was. He pulled his gaze away. He was engaging in exactly the kind of behavior he abhorred and the behavior his sister, Tara, would have berated him for. No playful calls of "it's a guy thing" would ever quiet her criticisms and attempts to get him and his brothers to toe the line. But all of those looks and comments in regard to the opposite sex, at least in Tara's presence, had only been made in jest, brotherly teasing of a sister they all adored.

"The first twenty-four hours are critical," K.J. said over her shoulder, as if telling him something he didn't know. She stopped, pivoted on one heel and faced him with more determination on her face than he'd seen on anyone in a long time. "You know that time is a luxury you don't have and I'm a problem you didn't factor. That's why you're angry, and I don't blame you."

The admission and her logical, calm attitude in the face of what he knew had been insulting, even contentious words, surprised him.

"Whether you want me or not, I'm here. There's no time to get a replacement and I have knowledge you don't have and objectivity that you desperately need. I believe that's why you made the call to bring me here. Am I right?"

"What do you know about the Middle East other than your studies?" The words revealed all the disdain and upset he was feeling. "What experience do you have?" Her education meant nothing. It wasn't experience and therefore, to him, not real. "You grew up—" He was going to say in Midwestern America; the truth was in the way she said certain words.

"Morocco." She cut him off and he guessed she was being deliberately vague. He could hear the edge in her voice.

"Really?" he said and didn't soften the sarcasm that laced the word.

"Really," she repeated and turned to face him. "At least, a few years anyway. Six years total—as a child and then a number of years in my last years of high school." She seemed to draw herself taller. "My father was an economic counselor in the American Embassy in Rabat. A few years later he returned, accepting another position in the Moroccan Embassy." She eyed him with a challenge in her eyes. "Are you done?"

His jaw tightened. She was right, there was nothing more to say.

"Good," she said and began to walk away then stopped. "By the way. Call me Kate." She threw that over her shoulder as if it were an afterthought. "One phone call?"

"So far."

She stopped.

"So the call came in shortly before 4:00 a.m.?"

"Correct. I alerted Adam immediately and got a plan in place. Apparently that was a mistake."

His phone beeped. He pulled it from his pocket and looked at it for just a split second as dread roiled through him.

"Yeah?" he snapped and then his hand stilled as his pulse seemed to speed up. He couldn't believe their audacity and knew it didn't bode well for them to have contacted him twice in such a short period. They weren't following a normal pattern. "You've been paid, release…"

Kate shook her head, mouthing something at him. He didn't know what it was, didn't care. He needed to focus on this, on what the kidnappers wanted and on how to get his sister out of their clutches.

"Put him off," she mouthed.

He gave her a brief nod. It wasn't anything he didn't know but at least it was confirmation they were on the same page. "I can't get it together right away."

The call ended shortly after and somehow during that brief time he and K.J. had formed a shaky alliance. "This time they want a quarter million," he said to her. It was double what they had first asked for and it was nothing in the scope of what his family was worth.

"By when?"

"Forty-eight hours or they'll kill her. There was no drop information."

"This is their second request and you paid them once."

He stopped, surprised, and then realized that Adam would have told her.

"You negotiated with them successfully." She nodded approval. "That's promising. I suspect they're a fragmented group but, even so, they're testing your limits, prodding you, making you more vulnerable by not giving you the drop site, making you worry."

"Making me react emotionally."

She nodded, as if his response were normal. "The next contact should give us a drop. They have their initial demand, still I doubt if they'll chance playing it out any longer. And that call? They were tormenting you—nothing more."

He thought of what he had done in those first desperate hours when he'd heard his sister was missing and what his first thought had been to do now, but there'd been no drop site and Kate was right. She knew her stuff. It was clear in her perception and instant analysis of what had transpired in the short time in which they had been together.

"Surprised?" she asked with a smile that was more a lifting of her lips as no emotion showed in her beautiful yet deadly, intelligent eyes. "Small. Unorganized." She wiped a strand of hair that had escaped her ponytail from her face. "Not so much unorganized as brought together temporarily for a common goal. What I mean is…"

"This isn't what they do regularly. They have no cause."

"Exactly. I would say that they're rough men needing money. Colleagues of some sort…"

"And none of that matters."

"All of it matters. We need their profile to get in their heads, find out who they are, to ultimately find Tara and get her out safely."

She was right and he didn't want to admit it. Yet he

was beginning to believe that, despite his doubts, what she had in her head, the profiling ability she spoke of, would be invaluable in finding Tara.

"Satisfied?"

He nodded, his mouth set. "But you do what I say, especially if this takes us, like I suspect, into the desert."

"Thanks," she said pertly, an edge to her voice.

He had no idea if that was a yes or a no. The only thing he was certain of was that she was staying.

"Let's get going," she said briskly. "I need to be briefed on everything that's happened since you last spoke to Adam and anything you might not have told him." She looked at him with eyes that seemed to rip through the protective layers that shielded his emotion from the world. "I need everything."

But as she said those words they emerged into the crowded main area of the airport and nothing was said as they made their way past a queue of passengers dressed in everything from blue jeans to sundresses and burkas. The crowd thinned near the doors leading to the outside, where the air was thick with the scent of the heated rubber of airplane tires and exhaust fumes.

The driver had them loaded and they were leaving the airport within minutes, but it was as they exited the airport and a few miles away that chaos erupted.

Chapter Three

"Dell," Emir said to the driver of his Hummer. He put his hand on his shoulder. "This is K. J. Gelinsky, she's here to help us get Tara back." He turned to Kate. "Dell's a good friend. He's had my back more times than I can count." He knew that didn't explain everything to Kate but it gave her a reason to trust this newcomer.

The big, blond, broad-shouldered man had a grim look that, combined with his size, made most people back away. But despite that, his unsmiling face and rather utilitarian brush cut, there was a warmth about him few people except his close friends ever saw. His distinctive look with his bleached-blond hair was a striking contrast to his swarthy complexion, but no one would dare comment on the look, for Dell's size intimidated most people. Emir knew Dell could be deadly but he also had a soft spot for women, children and cats. In fact, he'd seen the big man stroke a tabby, murmuring to it like it was a baby.

"K.J.?" Dell asked her as if hinting there should be more to her name than just initials.

"K.J.," she agreed with an easy smile and a "don't mess with me" look in her eye.

Emir bet there were few people who called her Kate. It wasn't anything she had said but rather the way she owned the initials and the odd way she had looked when he'd called her Kate despite her having given him permission. He wondered why she'd allowed him the privilege. Was it merely because he was her boss or...? Whatever the reason, it was irrelevant under the circumstances.

He still had reservations about her. There was no proof of her abilities other than an expertise in martial arts and what Adam had said. Despite that, he had to admit there was something in her demeanor, a confident air, that took the edge off his doubts. She acted like someone who knew the Moroccan culture, exactly as she had claimed, and she moved with the fluid ease of a local, regardless of her foreign look. None of it mattered. The only thing that did was that she could do the job and that, with her, they could bring Tara home.

But something was off. Oddly, it wasn't doubts about Kate that had him on edge. It was something else and he knew she felt it, too. The ease he had felt radiate from her in the airport and even just now, when she'd met Dell, was gone. Now she was tense, her attention taking in her surroundings.

As he looked at her, a silent communication leaped between them. Yet there was nothing tangible, no action to take, and he didn't feel comfortable with that. He could see that she was equally as disconcerted. Her brow was furrowed and her hand was on the seat in

front of her, the other on the holster of her gun. He suspected that she, too, was considering the possibilities
of a threat that might not yet be visible.

He leaned forward.

"What's going on?"

Dell shook his head. His attention was focused on
the road but a tendon in his neck stood out and his grip
on the wheel was tighter than required for the driving conditions of a low-traffic road bordering the out-
skirts of the city. Tension seemed to run through the
vehicle. "I don't like that Rover," he grumbled. "Don't
ask me why."

The Land Rover was the only vehicle besides theirs
on the road. It was ahead of them, having turned in from
a side road only minutes ago. From the moment it had
moved in front of them there seemed to be an instinctive
reaction by everyone in the Hummer. It was a feeling
that was common in the field, one he'd discussed with
his brothers and one they had all agreed had validity.
Instinct was what many modern men ignored and one
in which the Al-Nassar brothers and their associates had
committed to never sweeping aside. In fact, it was what
had been the difference between success and tragedy
on a number of occasions.

Other than the fact that it was moving slowly along
the road, there was nothing overtly threatening about
the Rover. The back window was tinted and they
couldn't see inside. That fact alone had Emir moving
his hand to the shoulder strap beneath his jacket and
the reassuring feel of gunmetal.

He looked at Kate. She didn't look at him, but instead

her attention was riveted on the steel-gray Land Rover. Something was off and he didn't like it.

"Why in Allah's name are they moving so slow?" Dell asked, his voice troubled.

"Something's not right." Kate pulled her Colt from its holster.

"I'm going to pull back," Dell said as the Land Rover maintained its rather slow speed, as if taunting them to pass.

In the Hummer the tension had just moved into overdrive, everyone poised for a threat that had yet to be determined.

The silence in the Hummer was thick. Emir glanced at Kate. There was no give in her posture and her jawline and lips were tight, her eyes focused ahead, her gun in her hand. Tension seemed to tick between them like a bomb about to explode. His finger twitched. Behind them was a stretch of empty road, but that could change at any moment.

Without warning the Rover stopped and Dell had no choice but to hit the brakes or go around. Without a backward glance to see if they were on board with the decision, Dell put the Hummer in reverse, taking them away from the Land Rover.

Emir's instinct sent prickles down his spine. None of this made sense. His eyes were fixed on the vehicle ahead of them that was now flipped around so that it blocked the road.

"What the...?" Dell reached for his gun and the driver's door almost at the same time as their vehicle stopped. "They're blocking us."

He had no worries about Dell, who, as a former soldier in the Moroccan military, knew how to not only take care of others but how to take care of himself. It was the guidelines Emir had used to hire many of his security and why it had been such a shock to hear of Tara's kidnapping. He'd surrounded her with the best.

His hand was on the door handle and his other pulling his gun from its holster when a shot was fired from someone in the Rover. It narrowly missed Dell. They'd been right to suspect trouble, but they hadn't been quick enough to avoid ambush.

Kate flung her door open almost simultaneously with Emir as he leaped to the ground on the other side, using the door for cover.

Out of the corner of his eye he saw her crouch before she jumped to the pavement and fired, taking out the Land Rover's left rear tire, crippling it.

Emir moved forward, keeping his head down as he used their vehicle for cover. Ahead of them, the passenger door of the Land Rover hung open. He peered over the edge of the hood of the Hummer and saw what looked like a hand, the black metal of a gun gleaming over the door. He fired, one shot and then two, and ducked down.

Silence.

He glanced behind him, mindful of their proximity to the airport. There was the possibility that at any moment innocent travelers could be heading out of the airport and directly into the line of fire. And almost as bad, possibly worse, there could be police. They didn't need the confusion or the procedures of police involvement complicating the situation and taking valuable time away from the search for Tara. This was their business and no one else's. He gripped his gun grimly, determined to end this and end it soon. Whoever these renegades were, they were obviously out of sync with what was going on and, more obviously, by the law of coincidence, somehow involved with Tara's kidnappers.

He took in the scene in front of him, the threat and the results of the threat that still remained. Twenty-five feet ahead and to the left was a body. He dove, taking cover as gunshot sprayed over the pavement. A glare from the passenger side momentarily blinded him as sunlight sparked off the metal of the opposing weapon and confirmed that someone was still alive.

"We want at least one of them alive," Kate said. She had moved around to his side and behind him. "I've counted two. Not giving us good odds," she muttered, "that we don't easily kill them both."

It was the ideal situation but it was also hard to control. The most they could ask for was that he, Kate and Dell came out alive. That was mandatory. Emir refused to accept anything else. He set the bar high when it came to keeping his employees safe.

Another shot was fired. This time it was clear that the weapon was different. It was a handgun. He'd seen the glint of the short barrel and then nothing—a single shot and silence. It was hard to tell how many there were. He wasn't as sure as Kate that there were only two. No more than three, he suspected, but they were keeping down, out of sight. So far there was no visual, so he couldn't pinpoint it.

A shot from the passenger side and then another and as he raised his gun. It was obvious that the choice to keep one of their attackers alive might not be theirs to make.

Emir fired and the man's gun clattered to the pavement, but no body followed. Instead the passenger managed to fling himself into the driver's seat even as Kate fired again and again. The Land Rover peeled away, veering right then left as the smell of burned rubber and gunpowder knifed through the air before the Rover careened to a stop about four hundred feet away from them. The vehicle listed slightly to the left with one tire flat and its right side jammed against an embankment of dirt and discarded cement.

"Stay here," Emir said to Kate.

He nodded to Dell. "Cover me."

But as he came up to the vehicle, there was no movement. The Rover had pitched on its side. The smell of gas permeated the air. Emir moved to the right, away from the driver. Everything was still. He inched along the driver's side where the man was slumped. Dead, unconscious or feigning—it wasn't clear. The only thing that was clear was that he wasn't moving and that, for now, he didn't pose a threat. Still, one couldn't be sure. Emir held his gun in one hand and pulled the driver's door open as he jumped back, both hands on his gun.

Nothing.

He moved forward, jammed the gun in the man's ribs and took a closer look.

"Dead," he muttered.

"Bad luck," Kate said as she came up behind him.

"Or not." She held her handgun in one hand, her other free. "He probably wouldn't have given you anything, anyway, whether he knew where she was or not. You know that. It was all a long shot," she said matter-of-factly.

Emir looked at her. He wasn't surprised that she was there. Somehow, despite his command to stay, he had known she would back him up. In an odd way, it both infuriated and pleased him. The thought ran through his head even as he assessed the truth of what she'd said. It was clear that, somehow, in some way, these men were connected with his sister's disappearance. Otherwise, none of it made sense. Now it was possible they might never know how they were involved or, more importantly, what they might know.

She moved past him, poking her head into the vehicle, looking at the corpse, her movements quick and decisive as she went through his pockets.

He went up beside her. "Any ID?"

She shook her head.

"We don't have a lot of time and we don't want to get caught up in the bureaucracy of airport security." He looked back to where their vehicle sat and then above, where the roar of an approaching plane reminded them of the nearness of the airport.

Over two hundred feet away the man who had been on the passenger side lay sprawled on the pavement. With no thought to Kate, assuming only that she'd follow, he sprinted back the way they had come, his long legs easily covering the distance between the two vehicles. He heard Kate behind him, her breath coming in short puffs, and whether she could keep up or not—for now, it was not a consideration.

He stopped by the body, bending to get a closer look, but it lay facedown. He turned it over—male, he already knew that, and there was nothing unique about his clothing. The passenger had been thirty or so, and was dressed to blend in, in brown cotton trousers and boots. Like the man they had just killed, his T-shirt was brown, as well, and it, too, had no identifying markings. There was nothing but a slim gold ring on his right hand that might be used to identify him.

Emir eased the corpse down after a quick check of his pockets and gave him a final once-over, this time only with his eyes, looking for clues they might have missed. He stood. He hadn't expected answers but he had hoped that there would have been something—one clue that might bring him closer to finding Tara.

"Who are they? It makes no sense that they would attack us."

"You're assuming this is connected?"

"Aren't you?" She looked at him as he grimly nodded agreement.

Kate bent and pulled something from the man's shirt. She held it up. "Camel hair. This guy's been outside the city, and recently."

He took the small wad of coarse hair from her. It was more than likely camel—the texture, length and color was right—but what did that mean in a country where camels were common? "There are camels in Marrakech. Camels everywhere—this is Morocco," he said as if it was a fact that needed pointing out.

He wasn't making fun of her or, for that matter, even contradicting her. The blood seemed to roar in his ears. He wasn't thinking straight, hadn't been since Tara disappeared. He had to get it together and, in an odd way, despite their initial meeting, he was counting on Kate. His eyes met hers and he could see something troubling in their depths. He knew she was considering what he had said and more.

"True," Kate said. "But he's not the type to own one." She lifted a hand and turned it palm-up. She ran a thumb along the tips of his fingers. "Too soft. There's no evidence he worked with his hands, other than with firearms." She laid the arm across the decedent's chest and straightened as she pointed to his boots. "Knock-off Ralph Lauren boots." She grimaced. "Not something a camel owner would have, but maybe someone who had been near one recently. Sand on his boots." She turned the sole of the boot sideways. "Not much, but I think he came from somewhere out there. Look, the leather is scraped, like he was walking on rough terrain, not city sidewalks." Her arm swept in the direction of the mighty Sahara Desert. "What brought him here?"

She glanced in the direction of the airport. "We need to get out of here before the police show up."

"You're right." He gave the scene a final once-over. These men weren't professionals and he'd bet neither were those who held Tara. The burning question was whether the two of them were connected and, if so, why had they targeted him? It seemed improbable. Why kill him and jeopardize a ransom? He glanced at Dell, who had been quietly listening to what they had to say.

In the distance the sirens from approaching emergency vehicles began to wail. They all headed back to the Hummer.

"Trouble. Let's get moving," Dell said as he motioned for them to get in.

Emir opened the rear passenger door and Kate slipped inside.

"None of this makes sense," Emir said as he sat beside Kate.

"Or it makes complete sense," she said softly.

They were silent for the next few minutes as the Hummer sped away, leaving the mayhem behind for the authorities.

Emir's attention was now on Marrakech's sprawling yet oddly elegant skyline as the vehicle turned from the rural landscape and headed back to the heart of the city.

THE SILENCE WAS thick over the next few minutes as the miles dropped behind them and distance separated them from the recent mayhem. While Kate appreciated the opportunity to mull over her theory without questions, she suspected that Emir, too, had theories with no solid answers and, like her, was mulling them over, trying to piece it all together, to make sense of it.

She looked at him, at the seemingly unfeeling line of his lips and yet she knew, from the little he'd said, that he had to be worried sick. He cared for his sister, and he'd do anything to get her back. That he'd give his life—that he'd said and she was here to make sure that didn't happen.

Everything was still, quiet between them.

She noticed little things. His hands were thick, sun-bronzed, yet he had long fingers. His hands were like those of an artist mixed with those of a laborer. But none of what was in his hands matched the aristocratic planes of his face or... Her heart pounded just a beat faster—and her mind wrestled with distance, with control. This was not about lust or even like but about life and death. She was here to do a job.

"We need to do this silently and quietly. That means as few people involved or in the know as possible." She glanced at Dell. In the heat of battle Dell been a good addition. But finding Tara was a different matter. They had to be subtle and more people created noise, figuratively speaking, and could alert the kidnappers. Besides, she knew nothing of Dell. She didn't know if she could trust him, even though Emir did, or if she wanted to.

"Dell's ex-military," Emir said as he watched her attention turn to Dell. "We served together. He's going to help while he can. Don't question that or anything else I decide," he said, practically ordering her not to question him.

She didn't say anything. She didn't like it, but she'd see how it played out for now.

"I'll show you what we think is ground zero," he said as if that were the reward not for her success in the field but for her silence.

She looked at the tense way Emir gripped his handgun and the tight line of his jaw and saw pain, a strong man who was fighting not to break. He needed help and not just someone who wielded a gun, not just muscle—

he needed someone who could think clearly, unaffected by the emotion he refused to admit. Emir, whether he knew it or not, needed her.

"Where they took Tara," he said.

And it was with those words that she found herself locked into the reality of going back in time with the dark and silently brooding Sheik Emir Al-Nassar.

Emir, she corrected, for she couldn't think of him as "Sheik." Sheik didn't fit the persona of the young and brash man beside her. He was a man she imagined could easily steal a woman's heart even after annoying her as deeply and maddeningly as he had her. He was also a man in the midst of a tragedy that, she'd instinctively thought from the moment she'd seen his name, would eventually lead her to the hinterlands of the Sahara Desert.

But it was the man, not the desert, that caused her to pause. There was something about Emir, a passion and an intensity that was different from any man she had ever known. And that scared her more than anything else.

Chapter Four

Monday, September 14, 5:00 p.m.

"I need a vehicle registration search," Emir said as he spoke to his contact. It was standard procedure, a first link to who or what these men had been—dead bodies didn't talk.

"Stolen vehicle," he said to Kate after he ended the call.

"Not what either of us hoped for."

He shrugged. "Did you expect anything else?"

She paused as if pondering the information. "It fits. Definitely not best case, but not a surprise, either. The vehicle makes sense but the attack itself seems like a piece that just doesn't fit. If the men who attacked us at the airport were originally with the kidnappers, why would they leave the group, come back and try to kill us?" She rubbed her thumb along the inside of her wrist, as if doing so would somehow provide answers. "They won't get money from a body. It makes no sense."

Emir looked at her. "I have three brothers."

She frowned. "They can still negotiate with one of

your brothers." Her eyes met his. "Were they trying to kill you to ensure the others paid?"

"Maybe. I don't know."

As the Hummer slowed, Emir pulled out his phone and punched a series of numbers. The massive bronze gates leading to his home slipped smoothly open and Dell maneuvered the vehicle inside.

Emir slid the passenger window down.

"Heard anything?" A middle-aged man with a Beretta strapped to his waist and an AK-47 over his shoulder asked as he stepped out of the one-room stucco cabin that functioned as a guardhouse. Lines of worry etched his forehead and his lips were compressed in an angry line.

"I'm sorry, no," Emir said, his eyes on the guard as if some silent communication were passing between the two.

He could feel Kate's eyes on him and knew that it might seem odd to apologize about his sister's disappearance to his staff. It certainly wasn't the norm, but then, nothing about this estate had been the norm since they'd lost both a matriarch and a patriarch on the same day. After that, the rules of running a large estate had changed.

Many of his employees were also friends, especially of Tara. Tara was a favorite among the estate's staff and he knew they were worried sick about her. She had the ability to touch the heart of everyone she met. Little things mattered to her, like knowing the birthdays of each employee. She could ask each of them about their families, the smallest details of their lives and call their children by name. Considering the number of staff in their employ, Emir had never been sure how she did it.

The guard's hand moved to the Beretta at his side, touching it almost reverently in an unspoken acknowledgment of solidarity.

"Rashad, this is K. J. Gelinsky. She'll be working with me to get Tara back."

Rashad gave a solemn salute and a nod.

"Pleased to meet you," Kate said.

"Been with the family twenty years," Emir said as the vehicle moved on.

"He has an alibi?"

Emir tensed. "Rashad is devastated by what happened to Tara."

"But he was questioned?" she persisted.

"He was at home with his family when it happened. There're a half dozen men who work with him, all of them with airtight alibis. Zafir questioned everyone, not just security."

"I'd like to see where she was taken."

"Of course…" Emir said, and couldn't help but admire the way she remained focused and calm no matter what was thrown at her. "On the outside, away from the main gate."

"We need to go back," she said.

"You're surprised I didn't stop there right away?" he asked at the slightly puzzled look on her face.

"No." She shook her head. "You were testing me." She looked at him, her eyes sweeping his face. "And, yes, I need to see where Tara was taken."

Dell's phone buzzed. A minute later he turned around

with a troubled expression. "My mother just texted me. My father doesn't have long."

"Dell, I'm sorry..." Emir began.

Dell had offered to drive him as a favor between friends. Even with his father in hospital and the family gathered for those last moments, Dell had insisted on at least taking him to the airport. He suspected that Dell had sensed something off—and, as usual, that instinct, which had saved them a number of times on previous assignments, had been right.

"Don't be," Dell said as he opened the door and got out.

Emir got out of the backseat. Dell was obviously anxious to go as he handed the vehicle's keys to him. He looked over to see Kate slip out the other side and grab the small canvas travel bag that Emir remembered tossing into the backset at the airport, which seemed like a million years ago. He turned his attention back to Dell. It was a difficult situation and he wished that he could change things for his old friend.

Instead, he could only take the keys Dell handed him.

"Dad's had seventy good years. Meantime, you need to find Tara. If you need me, you know..."

"I know, man. No worries," Emir replied. Dell had been there with him not only today but after his parents' deaths, and while he and his brothers raised a sister who at the time had been a young teen.

Emir watched as Dell turned with a nod and headed toward a battered-looking Jeep at the edge of the long drive that led to the entrance of the property. He could feel Kate's presence beside him but he didn't look at her. He needed a minute to let his emotions settle. There'd been too much tragedy in too short a period of time.

The sky was cloudy and the temperature was in the high sixties, much lower than average. Somehow the air seemed even cooler. He looked over as Kate shivered.

"You all right?" Emir asked as he looked at her with more concern for her comfort than he knew he'd shown since she arrived.

"It's been a long day," she admitted. "I'm tired and just a little chilled," she said as she pulled a lightweight jacket out of her bag, the soft smell of coconut wafting around her.

If she'd been a man he wouldn't have worried about her comfort. Another reason why she shouldn't be here.

The masonry wall that surrounded the compound stretched out in front of them. They'd retraced their way on foot to the entrance of the compound, stopping seventy-five feet outside of it to a spot where Emir had been told his sister had been taken. Behind them, it was dusty and flat, a field that stretched into nothingness. Behind that, a public road ran about three hundred feet perpendicular to where they were. It was close enough that, had there been any traffic, the noise would have been disturbing. Ahead of them, rows of palm trees announced the entrance to the Al-Nassar compound.

"They took her with little fight," Kate said minutes later.

"How do you know that?" he asked. It wasn't something anyone else had seen. In fact, with one man dead and another in the hospital, it seemed rather a ludicrous pronouncement. A movement behind him had him turning around. On the public road, a thin, sun-bronzed man in T-shirt and faded jeans peddled past on a bike that pulled a small cart. Around them Marrakech spread out on both sides, the city seeming to glow as a result of the rich red clay that defined many if its buildings, whether the towers of a mosque or the walls of the city.

"Do you have the kidnappers' original message?" she asked.

"I don't know where you're going with this."

"Trust me," she said, holding out her hand.

He pulled his phone from his pocket, punched in a code and handed it to her.

She took the phone, listened and then hit Replay immediately after it ended.

"What do you think?"

"The voice isn't distinctive. It's male, but beyond that there's nothing. Midrange. No accent of any sort. Odd."

"Exactly what I thought," he said.

"Too bad we couldn't listen to the second. Compare."

"They were different. I'm sure of it," he said. Unfortunately there'd been no time to record that message.

She handed the phone to him.

"They used a knife," she said. She didn't wait for him to answer for they both knew that had been in the report. "Interesting choice of weapon. Silent, but it also takes surprise or strength, ideally both, to be effective. At least to do it quietly with little struggle."

"It was dark, past midnight. She was almost home and her security was taken by surprise."

"Will he make it?" she asked, referring to the man who was now in the hospital.

"I went to see him. He's critical." His fist clenched. "Ahmed was a good man—is," he amended. "He tried to help, to stop them. That's what I assume from how it all ended. He wouldn't have done otherwise." The thought of one of his employees so close to death was gut-wrenching. There wasn't anything about this case that wasn't. He cleared his throat. "And then he tried to help me, give me information…but he's in such rough shape."

Emir's voice was tight even to his own ears and he could still feel the pain of seeing someone he'd known for years struggling to live and yet still wanting to help. "Ahmed would do anything for Tara." He took a breath as if controlled breathing would somehow change how he felt. "It will kill her to find out what has happened to him." He stopped for a moment, trying to regain control of his emotions.

"He said something?" She looked at him with eyes alight at this new piece of information. "That wasn't in the report. You spoke to him after," she said, confirming what was already clear. "What did he say?"

He knew that she was anxious for a clue that would get this investigation on the road. They both were.

"He said 'desert' and then, the irony of it all is that the next words weren't clear, but it sounded like a name—Davar. I don't know what Ahmed was trying to tell me. He coded almost immediately after." He clenched his fists, his gaze somewhere over her shoulder, his mind back to that hospital room. "They were working on him when I left."

If what he'd heard and what he now suspected was right, the desert was where they needed to go. But the Sahara was a big place—it was like saying they were going to Europe.

"Emir."

Her voice was like a caress and he took a step away. His jaw tightened and he fought not to send her home then and there.

"I've never heard of it as a place. I imagine you ran a check of local surnames?"

"Nothing," he said. "Maybe I heard wrong. He was half mouthing—could barely speak." He shook his head.

"It will be sunset soon. We can't be heading out, not in the dark and with no idea where we're going."

"Agreed." But she didn't move. Instead she stood there, considering. "Was it a name—place name, I mean? And if so could it have been something close— not exactly what you heard?"

"I don't know. There hasn't been much time to examine the possibilities."

"You had to pick me up and then there was the small shoot-out," she said.

"Exactly," he said with a slight smile. "Thanks."

"For what?" She frowned.

"For at least an attempt at humor. Oddly, it helps." There was more that helped, but he feared it also distracted—her lithe figure for one…and most of all her sharp intelligence and quick wit. He was still going to tear a strip off Adam, but he felt slightly more confident than he had an hour ago.

"Can I see her quarters?"

"There was nothing—"

She cut him off. "Trust me."

"THIS WAY," HE SAID.

Kate noticed that he didn't temper his pace. At six-one, he was only three inches taller than her, yet his legs covered distances quickly.

She strode beside him, thankful for long legs that sometimes made finding jeans a challenge. This time, they were a gift that allowed her to keep up as they headed toward the sprawling mansion that was a mix of old and new. The size and opulence was like nothing she'd seen in the working-class neighborhood of Detroit where, except for the stint in the Middle East, she'd grown up, or like Jackson, Wyoming, where she now lived. Her gaze swept the area, focusing on security details, potential breaches, rather than the opulence of the building and the grounds.

"There are sensors on the wall that monitor activity inside and out."

His arm swept the five-acre square where as far as she could see, a cream-colored masonry fence surrounded the complex's grounds.

"The cameras are on twenty-four-seven."

If Kate hadn't spent years immersed in Moroccan culture and, as a result, been aware of what "rich" in Morocco meant, she would have been pie-eyed with disbelief. This wasn't the wealth of royalty, and by no means a palace, but it was more than 90 percent of the population of Morocco would ever see.

She could understand why the security was as intense as it was and why Tara had been taken. The estate's opulence combined with their business, Nassar Security, added to riches that could be hugely tempting to anyone with a criminal bent. She knew the history of the company, knew that the twins had begun it and then, with the inclusion of their brothers, built a business that had taken on more high-profile cases than any other security company of its kind in either the western United States or Northern Africa.

"Interesting—about the security I mean." Her gaze met his. "And yet they took her at a place near where the cameras didn't reach."

His jaw clenched. "I'd planned to add security cameras there, too. But somehow it felt like overkill. Now, it's a glaring error."

"Cameras wouldn't have stopped—"

"No," he interrupted. "But alarms and—"

"You couldn't have known," she interjected as she tried to reassure him.

But the anger that emanated from him made it clear he didn't want reassurance.

"One of Tara's security is dead and the other, the only witness, is fighting for his life," Emir said. "It was an unforgivable lack of judgment on my part. I should have…" His voice dropped off as if he couldn't, or didn't, want to finish.

"What? Known? Are you psychic?"

"No, I don't believe…" He stopped and turned to

look at her, his brow furrowed. "You were being facetious."

"The man who lived. He was knifed in the chest. I'd guess that he was defending her."

Emir shook his head. "He shouldn't have been there. Ahmed was estate security. He volunteered to go with Tara that night. It wasn't his usual job but one of our regulars called in sick."

"That wasn't in the file," she said.

"Like I said, some of the details weren't available, at least not then. I wanted an agent on the first flight here. I couldn't wait to fill in the blanks."

Nor could he wait to ensure the sex of the agent, either, she thought dryly, admonishing herself.

To be fair, after the opposition at the airport, he now seemed to have accepted her for what she could do and had at least stopped talking about sending her back because of her sex. It appeared that she was the only one who had yet to get over that faux pas, but in her mind it had been a big error. Enough, she told herself. She needed to focus on the key elements of the case.

"The security seems airtight. Explains why they didn't take her here," Kate said as they walked through the massive entrance that led to the Al-Nassar family home.

She glanced at Emir as he ran a hand down the dark stubble that covered his chin and jaw. He was an extremely good-looking man, but then, she'd known that. Now he looked agonized, worry lines creasing his forehead. She wanted to say something to comfort him but there was nothing that would help until his sister was home—safe. No matter what he thought, it hadn't been his error. It had been Tara's. His sister had made an error by ditching her security and that could cost her her life.

Still over a quarter of a mile away, she took in the scope of the house, more aptly a mansion, and its surrounding grounds and thought there was some irony in its sweeping size when only half the family lived here at any given time. She knew the majority of the family spent a great deal of time overseas. On most days she imagined that Emir was vastly outnumbered, not by family, but by the staff necessary to maintain such an estate.

"Emir?"

He looked at her as if he had been somewhere else. And she imagined he was fighting his own fear—fear for his sister's well-being and for her very life. He was too close emotionally and that was why he needed her. Her ability to move ahead without emotional attachment to the victim, his sister, whom she'd never met, was critical.

"And yet none of this security kept Tara safe," Emir said and both of them could hear the irony in his voice.

"You couldn't protect her night and day." She touched the back of his arm, the heat of his skin seeming oddly intimate. He tensed and she dropped her hand. "She's a grown woman."

From the corner of her eye she saw Rashad approaching.

"I'll run you up to the main house," Rashad said as he walked with them the remaining few feet to the guardhouse. He opened the door to the Hummer that

Dell had so recently left, for Kate. His dark eyes were full of questions and yet he asked nothing.

Within minutes they were driving around a circular drive that had been hidden behind massive palm trees. They skirted a white-marble fountain that was devoid of water.

"Maintenance issues?" she asked Emir. "Your estate is immaculate and yet the fountain isn't working?"

"The plumber was called but I put the repair on hold."

She turned. "Anyone else who's been here recently? Aside from staff, I mean."

"No one, except the plumber two days ago," he said.

"Was Tara around when the plumber was here?"

"Yes, I believe she was. I don't remember her coming out of her quarters, though," Emir said. "The plumber had done work for me on numerous occasions. We've contracted him for years—in fact, I believe he worked for my father, too. Anyway, he didn't stay long. I decided against the repair. I hadn't planned to be here for this long."

"By here, you mean Marrakech?"

"Morocco, actually," he said. "If all this hadn't happened, I might have met you in Wyoming. I'd planned to go there. A recent case involving the Wyoming secretary of state's brother piqued my interest."

"Faisal will have his hands full. It's high-profile," Kate said. "So, plumbing is minor considering everything that's come down in the last week."

"You could say that." He shrugged as if it were all of no consequence while the tension around his eyes and mouth made him look almost feral, like a man who would protect anyone or anything whose heart belonged to him. She had to force her thoughts back to what he was saying.

"I promised Tara that when she was home for summer vacation, I'd have the fountain up and working. She finds it soothing."

"Was anything else happening that day or any day after?"

"Nothing out of the ordinary."

The Hummer stopped in front of the mansion with its huge columns and sprawling white-tiled front entrance.

She glanced back at Emir as she stepped out. She wondered if he felt like he'd been interrogated, for, without meaning to, she knew that was what she had done.

He stepped ahead of her to open the massive wood-and-brass door. In the seconds that it took, her gaze ran the length of his muscular back and she had to pull her eyes away from the lush, seductive curl of his dark hair as it flirted with the edge of his collar.

Get a grip, she told herself as she walked past him and into a vast tile-and-marble area that stretched beyond the colossal entrance doors, eclipsing them in opulence. For a moment her reason for being here was clouded by her feeling of disbelief. Her life, her two-bedroom apartment, compared to this? The juxtaposition of the two realities wasn't even fathomable. This was a fantasyland, a different world that she'd known of but of which she couldn't have imagined until now. It was laughable, really, eight hundred square feet that she lived in compared to this. The comparison was as unstoppable as it was fleeting, rather like looking at a magazine rack and seeing one on budget travel lined up beside another that was geared to luxury resorts.

She pushed the thoughts out of her mind and instead considered everything this wealth brought—including the case she was now assigned to. She knew fortune such as this did not come without responsibilities. She also knew there were expectations here and duties Emir had inherited from his father, and even from his grandfather—a responsibility to the people, to give back. She knew Emir took his responsibilities seriously; she'd heard Adam speak of it. It explained why Emir seemed so contained, controlled—older than the thirty-one years she knew him to be.

She looked around, taking in the length and width of the area even from the entrance. The hallway seemed to stretch indefinitely and, rather than the chill one would expect from such a large space, the air was warm.

As they moved down the corridor she couldn't get over the size. The estate was massive, more imposing than she'd expected, both inside and out. There had been no available pictures, even of the grounds; nothing she could get from the internet. Oddly, even the area outside the gates hadn't been Google-mapped. She guessed that had been Emir's doing.

But it was the pictures some yards from the entrance that made her pause; they were the only decor in the hallway that stretched easily a half a city block. She stopped for a minute as she looked at a picture of a man and a woman, middle-aged—the woman looking younger and very much like the photos she'd seen of his sister, Tara.

It was odd that the pictures were here in this luxurious but barren corridor with the only other decor, the oval, brass entranceway doors facing them not ten feet away. "These are your parents?"

"Yes, taken only months before their accident. Of course," he added, "that was a long time ago."

Six years wasn't a long time ago. Was he distancing himself from the trauma of the loss? She supposed it didn't matter either way. What was important were the facts. She'd read about the traffic accident on a treacherous, isolated mountain road and the resulting fire that had tragically taken both Emir's parents.

"Tara looks very much like her mother." Kate stared at the picture as if the answer to saving Tara was somehow in the dark eyes of the beautiful woman who stared back at her.

For a moment she was caught by the woman's image. Her eyes reflected the same rich ebony as her eldest son. Her smile was the same as Tara's picture in the file she carried. But whatever answers or secrets those eyes might hold wouldn't be forthcoming from a picture.

"Kate."

Her name was a command as he waited for her to catch up. She was reminded of how few people called her that. Allowing Emir to call her by her given name had surprised even her. She'd gone by her initials since she was a child. She couldn't tell when or why it had begun, but the initials had served her well in the profession she'd chosen as an adult. Now, K.J. just was and it was odd that Emir had become one of the exceptions. At another time she'd have analyzed what that might mean.

She walked beside him, her pace matching his. White columns ran from the tiled floor to a ceiling that soared over twenty feet above them. Their footsteps echoed on the ceramic tile as they turned left and into another corridor as vast as the first. This one brought them to within fifty feet of another massive door not quite as large as the entrance and this time without the brass. Instead these doors were wooden with gold glittering in a heart design over both panels.

"Tara's apartment," Emir announced. "This was the women's area centuries ago," Emir said as if he'd seen the disbelief in her look and wanted to confirm what she already knew. "Tara thought it laughable to claim for herself this area that, a hundred or so years ago, was a harem." He shook his head. "She's always about being contrary."

"Contrary?" Kate frowned.

"I didn't mean that," Emir said. "We are all more Western in our thoughts—the family, I mean—but Tara wanted to change the thinking, the old ways, that exist elsewhere. Chauvinism that still hasn't disappeared. She wasn't content to let modern ideas remain within the walls of this compound or within the boundaries of Marrakech, for that matter."

The pain in his voice was palpable.

"We'll get her home." She met the troubled look in his eyes and hesitated, feeling the need to comfort. She dropped the thought when she saw the anger in his eyes. Anger was not something she could change with simple words or a touch and, at this stage, she suspected it would be unwelcome.

As they entered Tara's quarters, it was as if facts were his safety net as he commentated as they walked. "Built almost two hundred years ago, this area is pretty much impenetrable to outsiders. Always has been. We've upgraded, of course. This section was built in the mid-1800s. We've put in a computer-monitored surveillance system in the last few years, added motion detectors and thermal laser-heat detectors. It was all we needed without going overboard. At least, so we thought…" He shook his head, lines bracketing his mouth.

"You couldn't have known."

"Don't placate me," he growled. "I should have known. It was my job to know."

The security keypad was imbedded in a teak panel arched into a design that looked rather like a small pseudo door set alongside the door frame.

Emir punched in a code.

The doors in front of them opened with the whir of a hidden motor, leading to a smaller teak doorway and a wooden door that, while arched like the first set of doors, was smaller, singular and, as a result, much less imposing than the first set. Emir unlocked the door, flicked on the light and stood aside for Kate to enter first. Inside was the sleek metal lines and modernity of a penthouse apartment without the extravagantly opulent touches of the entranceway.

His hand was on the small of her back as she hesitated, taking it all in. Her heart beat just a little faster as his hand rested there for just a few seconds longer before the intimate touch was gone and it was as if it had never happened.

She was being ridiculous and, worse, unprofessional, she chastised herself, dragging her thoughts to what was important—learning about Tara and finding anything that might help to bring her home, safely, to her family.

"Tara detests the old look. It reminds her of the old ways and the customs that still impact women. She left some of the original touches, the original door and entranceway, because they amused or maybe, more aptly, intrigued her."

Kate walked the length of the cool, ivory tile that matched the rest of the mansion and straight through a kitchen and sitting area to a bank of windows that looked out to a gleaming infinity pool surrounded by palm trees. She turned back to Emir.

"If she wasn't so smart, this wouldn't have happened. She wouldn't have pushed the rules, tested her limits," Emir protested. "She'd have been inside and safe." His lips were taut, his eyes dark and troubled. Kate held back the urge to put a hand on his shoulder, to offer what little comfort she could.

"You can't turn back the clock," she said softly.

Her gaze went to the sofa as she walked over to the bookcase. "She's very serious," she said, her eyes skimming the titles. "And yet she has a lighter side, fun-loving." There were characteristics of Tara that were obvious in her choice of furnishings. The sleek, butter-yellow leather sofa hinted at a lighter side. The heavy, teak desk with generations of wear marring the surface and the three volumes of Wells's *The Outline of His-*

tory leaning against an economic text were testament to her seriousness.

Kate glanced at a collection of graphic novels but picked up an archeological magazine from a pile and thumbed through it. It was a unique collection for a young woman whose major was computer science with a minor in psychology. She put the magazine back on the stack that seemed to cover the prior year.

"Did she just read about archeology or had she gone on a dig?"

"What does it matter?" he asked.

"Anything you remember could help, you know that."

He nodded. "You're right. She wanted to go check out a new find. It was a day trip into the desert and another back."

"And you told her no?" Kate guessed and got her answer from his silence. "That must have been hard for her to take. Maybe impossible, considering she's legally an adult. Is it possible that she planned to go anyway, that maybe…?"

"No!" A minute of silence hung between them before he spoke again. "What are you implying?"

Tara picked up another magazine and thumbed through the pages, deliberately putting off her answer. It was best that he knew now, before this investigation went any further, that she wouldn't be intimidated. She also knew he was a hard man to convince, considering a gunfight hadn't done it.

She would have laughed if the situation hadn't been so serious. Instead she continued her perusal of Tara's living space, finding bits of information that would give her insight the file and Emir hadn't. Finally, after a minute had passed, and then two, she looked up, met his gaze and saw a hint of what might be admiration.

It was vital that she had his full attention. What she had to say could be very important to who, at least, some of the perpetrators might be. She didn't expect him to take what she was about to imply well, but it had to be said. "Is it possible that days or even weeks ago, she made first contact, made the culprits aware of her vulnerability?"

This time his look was thunderous as he turned away from her. The tension between them was thick and bleak before he turned back. Now his eyes glimmered with anger, agony—maybe a combination of the two, it was impossible to tell.

"Is that so unbelievable? I'm not saying it was her fault but only that…" She paused.

"Yes, it's possible. But I don't know anything more than I've already told you and what was in the report."

"What about that night? What wasn't in the report, Emir?"

"She was celebrating the beginning of the school year, getting together with some old school pals on a few days' jaunt home before going back to the States. And…" His full lips thinned and his jaw tensed, and she could see he was struggling with something.

"Sit," she offered with a wave of her hand to the chair opposite her.

He sat.

"I admit the report is missing some information. It wasn't all known. I learned it after your plane took off and—" he wasn't looking at her "—I've filled in all the blanks." He opened his mouth as if to say more.

She cut him off. "I need to know what Tara was doing last night—all of it."

"I…"

She met his rich, dark eyes, saw the trouble, the doubt, that lurked deep within them, and still she didn't back down.

"She left the restaurant alone with her security. She managed to ditch them shortly after—no one knows why." He blinked, as if that would change the words she knew, for whatever reason, he didn't want to admit.

"It won't help to hold anything back."

Silence ticked between them.

"The only thing that matters now is having all the information so we can figure this thing out and find her. What aren't you telling me?"

"She'd been drinking," he admitted. "That's what her friends said."

"What else did her friends say?" she asked softly.

"I didn't want this in the report, it…"

"Could ruin her reputation." She paused. "Look, Emir, we've all gone there. A youthful mistake—a bit too much to drink. It happens. Usually it turns out well—we luck out. Let's make this turn out well. Tell me what happened. Everything you know, including what you screened from the report."

She looked at him as if he were no different from any other witness.

"You knew this before I left the States and you left the fact that she'd been drinking out of the report. You did that on purpose, thinking it didn't matter. It wouldn't change anything or help us find her."

She sank onto the luxurious softness of the leather couch and thought how she'd love such a piece for her small apartment. Then she turned her focus on Emir. "That's where you're wrong—and you know it. Everything matters, every piece of evidence."

He ran his hand along his brow and his gaze dodged hers. "I've never known her to overindulge. Her friends admitted it happened rarely." He looked at her as if daring her to say otherwise.

"A mistake that many of us have made at one time or another."

He shook his head.

"Where are they, her friends?"

"I've already spoken to them. They left her, from what I can determine, over an hour before she was taken. They didn't see her after that. That part is in the report."

"I read it," Kate admitted as she got up and went over to the window. She didn't remind him of what hadn't been in the report. Her fingers skimmed the window frame. "Bulletproof." She glanced at the door. She'd noted the hinges earlier; the door swung out rather than in, difficult for a man to break down. Not that it mattered. The crime had happened elsewhere.

"Let's go back to the airport and the attack," she said. "There's a connection, but what is it?"

He stood, pacing along the couch to the window and back, and then stopping a few feet from her.

"So we have two bodies and one gives us some

clues," she said when she was met by silence. "Camel hair and his boots—the sand on them, it was caked, not something you get hanging around the city. I'd say he'd recently been in the desert. What better place to get lost in or to request a ransom and remain out of reach of detection? Even the best technology can fail against the might of the Sahara." She looked away as if regretting having to speak the words they both knew. Extracting Tara was not going to be easy.

"I can't argue with any of that," he said in his distinctly low voice. "It kills me to think of her frightened or in pain." He ran a hand through his dark hair that, despite the short cut, curled wildly and only succeeded in giving his sun-bronzed, chiseled good looks a rakish edge.

This was a difficult case, fraught with emotion and involving the man who was effectively her boss. And yet it was hard to think of him like that when, from the first moment she'd seen him, there had been a connection, an unseen emotion that seemed to pulse between them. She shoved the ridiculous thought from her mind. For now, he was her assigned partner and client rolled into one—nothing else.

Chapter Five

"So far the name Tara's injured guard gave you—Davar—doesn't exist. Not as a surname and a given name would be impossible to track. Even in the state he's in, Ahmed would have known that. No, he was giving us something we could find," Kate said. "I know we did an initial check, but I've gone beyond that search and been through everything. I've had the records of anyone who had a vaccination, a driver's license or even stepped foot in Morocco scoured. Nothing."

She ran one hand through her hair, bunching it in her hand and pulling the long, silken mass back and away from her face.

"Are you sure that was exactly right? He was mouthing the word, you said. Could you have misunderstood?"

"It's possible, but it's all I can get for now and, if it's not exact, it's close. He's in and out of consciousness," Emir said as a nerve caused his jaw to twitch. Time was wasting and there was nothing they could do but wait and speculate.

"So we use what we have. Both time and evidence," Kate said as she perched on the edge of the massive rosewood desk that had been his father's. They'd left Tara's apartment and entered his office an hour ago.

He knew she was going over the possibilities of that one word, the name the injured guard had provided—Davar. Yet his attention went to her long legs that hung over his desk and the creamy satin of her neck as she leaned her head back against the filing cabinet that butted up to the desk. She had beautiful skin and, for a second, he imagined what it would be like to caress it.

And, as if she read his mind, Kate looked at him with determined eyes and lips that were soft, kissable. His thoughts were out of line, inappropriate and unproductive. But he couldn't seem to dodge them for, despite his outrage that Adam had sent a woman, he'd been drawn to her since the first moment he'd met her.

"We'll get her, Emir. We'll get Tara out and home safe. I promise." There was grit in her words. It was as though her saying them somehow made them true. He only wished it was going to be that easy.

He strode over to the window. The city sprawled out in front of him. It was the place where he'd been born and where he'd grown up—the city he'd thought to escape in his young adult years and the city that now seemed to promise the secret to saving his family.

The second call had been long enough to be tracked by their office team to within a twenty-five-mile radius of Marrakech. They'd received that information almost immediately after the call had ended. It wasn't enough. They were still looking for a needle in a haystack.

Kate was now pacing the room, a pensive look on her face. He knew they both felt the passage of time and the frustration of their current inertia, but there was no getting around it. Kidnap victims had died because of ill-prepared rescue attempts. He was determined that Tara would not be one of them. Behind them the office clock ticked, the dull beat of time a passing reminder of everything they could not do.

She looked at him, her eyes seeming to reach out to console, but he couldn't help noticing instead the long wisp of blond hair that had again escaped the elastic band and curled down her face, caressing her chin, bringing his attention to the soft, seductive rise of her breasts—

What was he doing? He needed to remain focused. His sister's life was at stake and he was letting a beautiful woman distract him. Again, he was reminded why a woman should not be there, why he should have held firm, why...

"No woman will voluntarily go with a man she doesn't know. Especially at night, in the dark," Kate said softly, interrupting his thoughts as he found she was apt to do. This time it had been a good thing.

Kate pressed her forefinger to her lips. "To take someone that quickly and easily, I believe there are only two scenarios that might work."

"She knew her captor," he said grimly.

"Exactly. Or she was tricked. A stray animal, a child needing help—another woman."

"I don't think anyone we knew would have done this," he said.

"You mean you don't want to believe that someone you know would do this."

She'd called him out again. He met her eyes, saw rock-solid determination, and knew she had his back.

"No matter, Emir. We have to consider all possibilities."

"You're right," he agreed. She was everything Adam had said she would be, except she wasn't a man. He was beginning to wonder if that mattered.

"I still think she knew them, was at least familiar with them," Kate persisted in a voice meant to get a man's attention and a mind that challenged him to keep up.

He pushed the distracting thoughts back and focused on what she had said. It was interesting she'd said "they" instead of "he." It was another possibility for which he had no answers. He turned to the window, squinting as the setting sun shone across the square, bounced off a distant, copper-topped bell tower and created a glare that was almost impossible to see against. Dusk was fast approaching and soon the call to prayer would taunt them, remind them of passing time. Normally patience was what he was good at, yet patience was what he found impossible to implement in the one case that mattered more than any other.

"Her guards were easily disposed of," Emir said.

"She might not have seen the violence. They might have been attacked without her even knowing. Then the perpetrator comes up to her, lures her, and she's not suspicious because she knows who it is."

The fact that Tara might have known the perpetrator, that someone he had given his trust to, could have betrayed him in the worst way possible almost took him out at the knees, even though the possibility was something Kate had alluded to earlier and one he'd considered himself. Now, for the first time, he was able to entertain an idea that had the potential to make this case, if that were possible, even more gut-wrenching.

"Emir?"

Kate's voice was calm yet husky in a completely feminine way. She'd taken him out, literally flipping him onto his back, but it was her voice he knew could be his undoing. Now it was all he needed to bring him from his thoughts and into her presence.

"When was the last time you spoke to Tara?"

"Yesterday afternoon. It was a quick call. She told me that she planned to meet some friends—she mentioned the local nightclub. That was it." He shook his head, his eyes not meeting hers. He didn't need that distraction, that allure—he needed to focus and she was making it difficult. "All I told her to do was have fun. Instead, I should have…"

"Should have what, Emir?" Kate interrupted. "You're not psychic. You did what you could—better than most. She's a grown woman. She made her own decision and, unfortunately, the consequences were nothing anyone could anticipate. The only thing we can do now is get her home safe."

She was right. He needed to quit thinking in the past unless it was something that would help. Although Kate hadn't said any of that, he could read it in her tight stance, the accusing spark in her eye and the set of her chin. She wasn't putting up with any emotional swaying on his part. She was making him toe the line—and it was exactly what he needed. Ironically, he was the most unemotional of his brothers, the least likely to act on emotion despite the circumstances.

But the thoughts wouldn't be stilled as he contemplated the horrible thought that Tara knew her attacker. That the perpetrator who had planned this crime knew his sister. That he had her trust. It seemed more and more likely that that was the only thing that made sense.

Four questions—who, why, what and where—and no one had the answers.

He glanced at his watch. If his calculations were right, Tara had been gone for over fourteen hours.

They'd hypothesized enough. Time was running out.

AT THE SOUND of his voice, Tara cringed and pulled her knees up to her chest, as if making herself smaller would make her invisible. She pushed her back against the sand-crusted cliff.

"I should have never listened to him. Cousin or not, he's an idiot," the man said, continuing his one-person tirade.

She made herself look at him, at the horrid scar that brutalized one side of his face, at the dark hair slicked with gray—at the person who threatened her very life. She needed to find out everything she could to help her brothers get her out. She'd known since the beginning that this man was in charge. What was frightening was that he was no stranger to her. But he wasn't the man she remembered, either.

She watched as he wiped the back of his hand across his stubbled chin as another man, slimmer and taller, walked past. He muttered something and the man she had come to loathe, and who led them all, cuffed him across the back of the head.

"Stop that," he snarled. He spoke in his native Berber and it was unclear to Tara, and she suspected to the man he had just accosted, what it was he should stop.

Silence settled for a few seconds in the small oasis that had become her nightmare. She looked around, conscious that he was sensitive even to her silent scrutiny. She was doing as little as possible to draw attention to herself. The thought of her brothers is what kept her strong and would get her through this. But the leader's next words frightened her like no others could.

"I'll bring the bloody house of Al-Nassar to its knees." He chuckled, the sound as dry as the endless sand that swept around them, flirting with the boundaries of the only greenery for miles. "Soon I will be a rich man."

He turned so that he partially faced her as he coughed and scowled.

"What are you staring at?" he snarled.

"Nothing," she said with oomph in her voice. For the one thing she'd learned since her kidnapping was that the man she would now think of only as *he*, detested weakness.

She stared at him before he finally turned his back to her.

The word he snarled as he stormed away was as evil as all the others he'd cursed at her. She knew the anger wasn't directed at her but at the house of Al-Nassar and everything he thought it stood for. He'd made that clear in the first miserable hours when they'd taken her and all the hours since.

Tara breathed a sigh of relief and prayed, for she didn't know how much longer she could keep the evil at bay.

Chapter Six

Monday, September 14, 7:00 p.m.

They had agreed that there was nothing they could do until daylight. The Sahara wasn't welcoming during the day, never mind at night. There was no need to push the limits, especially as there had been no further communication from the kidnappers.

That worried Emir.

"The airport attack had to be tied to the kidnappers. But why?" Kate asked. "Something doesn't fit."

He paced and tried to ignore the pulsing headache. He'd already popped a couple of aspirin and an hour ago he'd admitted to himself that there was no hope for it, the headache was there until Tara was brought home unscathed.

"We should have gotten a final demand by now. None of this makes sense," he said, knowing it could make perfect sense. But maybe it all made sense and it was that last, unspoken option he didn't want to contemplate.

"Could their plans have gone somewhat awry?" Kate mused. "We were attacked at the airport by men who we believe were part of Tara's kidnappers, but why attack us?" She shoved her hands into her pockets as she paced the room. "They've got to be connected—the kidnappers and the airport attackers. And they had to have a motive for the attack. Is it possible they're working at odds with each other?"

Emir heard the reluctance to believe her own theory in her voice. Like him, she knew that if she was right, if there were problems among the kidnappers, that could only mean problems for Tara. It wasn't the usual kidnapping pattern, but for every norm there was the deviant. These kidnappers were obviously true deviants. And that only made him angry and fearful at the same time, fearful that they wouldn't find Tara alive.

"She'll be fine, Emir. We'll make sure of it."

He took a breath, focusing on what could be done now.

He had to think about practical things. Things that needed to be done by morning—gathering supplies that would see them through a journey into the desert. He'd already set staff to complete that task. But there were other things. They needed to eat, rest and prepare for what lay ahead.

Whether they heard from the kidnappers or not, whether her abductors returned Tara voluntarily or not, they would face justice and Emir would be the one leading that charge.

His stomach rumbled, reminding him of a more immediate problem. But already that problem was also on the edge of resolution. He'd sent word to the kitchen and ordered Moroccan omelets for both of them. It was a light meal enhanced with the subtle tastes of various herbs, tomato and onion, perfect for not making one so satiated that lethargy set in. They couldn't afford that.

There was movement in the doorway, followed by a hesitant knock.

He looked up and saw Baz, the son of one of his estate security. The teenager hesitated in the doorway as he held a tray of food Emir had ordered less than twenty minutes ago.

"On the desk would be fine, thanks." He eyed the boy. "You're off duty soon?"

The slight yet gangly, dark-haired youth nodded. "I'm sorry about Tara, I…" He dropped his head and backed up, his hands behind his back. "Can I help? Find her, I mean."

For the first time in hours, Emir had a faint urge to smile. It was a fairly public secret that the boy had a crush on Tara. But, at only seventeen, his youth combined with his current status in life—son of a guard—might mean that life wasn't going to throw him a chance at his sister's affections. Too bad. In a few years Emir thought it was a good guess that the boy would mature into a man who could make a woman proud. His jaw tightened. He wanted Tara to live to have the choice. He pushed the thoughts away and met the boy's concerned gaze.

"No. You don't want to intimidate them with too big a show of force," he said, flattering the boy. "We'll find her," he assured him as Baz nodded and left.

They ate their meal quickly and in silence. It was sustenance only and, oddly, a moment to collect their thoughts individually before they began brainstorming all over again.

"We've still got nothing but assumptions as to where they've taken her. For all we know, she could still be in the city, she might never have left," Emir said as he picked up their plates and utensils and set them on a tray Baz had left on a table by the entrance.

"I'm not so sure," Kate said.

She looked young and too fresh and pretty to have wielded a gun as efficiently as she did. He'd read in the file that she was twenty-eight years old.

"The evidence on the man in the airport seemed to indicate desert or rural. And Tara's security indicated the same. That's what we'll have to stick to, barring further evidence."

Emir scowled. "So far it's the best we have."

"Exactly," she agreed.

He watched as she stood, walked into the hallway and over to a white-marble pillar that was just one of many lining the length of the two-hundred-foot hallway. He knew she wouldn't find any answers there. Only space.

As familiar as he was with all of it, he still, at times, felt the overpowering opulence of the office walls. He'd seen her look of surprise when he'd first brought her into his office. He imagined she thought he'd decorated it to suit his personality rather than realizing what it was: a tribute to the generations that had come before him.

If it were up to him, the office would be simpler, less elegant. The rosewood desk was opulent enough to stand alone. Sitting on a richly vibrant, deep, brown-and-blue Persian rug that covered the majority of the floor made it even more so. And yet neither the opulence of the desk nor the richness of the rug or the elegance of the other accessories fit with the pictures on the office wall. Pictures of his brothers and his sister in various locations—a ski hill, a beach—and at all different ages, and then a picture of all of them together. He knew that it all appeared as if he'd moved into someone else's home and never added anything to his own liking, except, possibly, the pictures. And it didn't matter to him. This was his family's history and he honored it. The decor meant nothing more than that.

He knew she was back, he could sense her before he looked up and saw her. She took a step past the doorway, facing him but not looking at him, obviously focused on her thoughts. He imagined from the expression on her face that she might be replaying in her mind what had been done so far. He waited as minutes passed silently between them before she spoke.

"At least if the tower dump info you requested on the first call would come in…" She walked toward him. "What range are they using?"

"I kept it fairly simple. The city limits and thirty miles out. Fortunately the call came in early in the morning. The traffic was light. There were only a little over six hundred," he said. "With Barb, we've got the best on it. We can't do more."

The tower dump had requested cell phone companies in the area to reveal records of users during a specific time frame. It was an invasion of privacy implemented only at the request of law enforcement and, in situations like this, where Nassar Security had pull and reach.

She frowned at him.

"Sorry, you've never met Barb Alamy."

"Not officially," she agreed. "I'm just curious. Western given name…"

"She's an American who came to Morocco on vacation. Long story short, she's been here over a decade, married a local man. Now she's the office tech guru and has since taken over research."

"I don't know how you found her, but Barb's definitely a tech guru."

"She found us," he admitted of his recent addition. "And now we have her working in both offices."

"She'll be busy on this one."

A minute later she yawned. "We should get some sleep. Or at least try," she said.

She was right. He'd woken this morning into a nightmare and hadn't had time or thought to even run a comb through his hair. His only consideration for the last fourteen hours had been Tara and he knew she would be his purpose until she was home safe. Yet, as he met the blue smoke of Kate's eyes, he felt oddly connected, calm.

Minutes seemed to tick by like hours. She yawned again and stretched out on one of two leather sofas that rested against opposing corners of the sprawling office. He got up and brought a blanket to her, laying it gently over her.

"You should get some sleep, too," she suggested.

But fifteen minutes later he knew she wasn't going to sleep, either. He could hear her turn this way and that. He stood at the window, the thought of sleep an impossibility. He leaned against the ledge. There was nothing for them to do and nowhere for them to go, and it was killing him.

Suddenly her phone buzzed a warning for an incoming text message. He turned around and switched on a nearby light as she sat up, the blanket spilling around her waist, and pulled her phone from her pocket. There was something oddly erotic at seeing her in that state, sleepy, although she hadn't slept, her hair mussed, as if she'd just had a passionate... He bit back the thought.

"I didn't know that you left my number for the tower dump info," she said.

"My phone stays here," he said, his voice husky with conflicting emotion, fear for Tara, desire for Kate. Only one of those emotions was acceptable and it seemed he could control neither. "I'll take the satellite phone."

"I suppose I should have assumed that as we're not taking your phone with us."

"Right. Zafir will be acting in my stead. Pretending to be me."

She paused as she read the message. She frowned. "The location changed slightly. Barb says the original call came from thirty miles southeast of Marrakech." She scrolled down and then looked up.

"We head out at first light exactly as we planned, nothing changes," he said. "Anything else?"

"I'd suggest we leave earlier. We could be going deep into the desert or not." She shrugged. "It's a crap shoot at this point and we don't know what we might encounter. We can make up time on the highway at night, head in the general direction of that call. That way, if anything goes wrong or changes—we're already on the road. I'd feel better about that. I'm sure you would, too."

Minutes passed and turned into an hour. The silence was becoming unbearable.

Then Emir's phone rang and he pulled it from his pocket and looked at the caller ID.

"Faisal."

He was surprised, and yet oddly not, to see that it was his brother. Faisal was the only one in the family who hadn't known about Tara. He guessed that was no longer the case.

"Yeah," he answered, thinking how few telephone conversations he had with Faisal except on a business level. They usually communicated by text. That fact alone told him that Faisal knew what had happened.

"I heard about Tara, man." There was tension and worry straining Faisal's voice.

Emir gripped the phone, wishing he had news, something to give his brother, hope for all of them. Faisal was close to Tara in ways neither he nor the rest of his brothers were. For Zafir and Emir, and even Talib, she had been the child they had raised. For Faisal, who was nearest in age, she was his childhood playmate and friend, and even now, as adults, they were close to each other. That was one of the key reasons why Emir didn't trust Faisal not to go off on a mission to kill those who had taken his sister. As a result, they had delayed telling him.

He'd meant to call in the minutes before he put together what was needed to take him and Kate safely into the desert, but Faisal had beat him to it. "How'd you find out?"

"When were you going to tell me?"

"Soon. I didn't want…"

"I had a right to know."

"I know and I would have…" He stopped. He'd waited too long. But what was done couldn't be un-done and justification wouldn't change anything. "Who told you?"

"Talib called."

"Talib," he said, and his voice held little inflection as he fought a red cloud of anger. At another time he would have torn a strip off Talib for going against his wishes. But this was an emotional time for all of them. Faisal needed to be told. Emir had just wanted to ensure that the way Faisal heard wouldn't set him off.

"Where are you?" he asked, afraid to hear the answer, knowing that Faisal could be impulsive when it came to something this serious, especially if it involved Tara. His fist clenched and his temple pounded, and he didn't want to hear the answer. His brother could be on a flight to Morocco for all Emir knew. That was the last thing they needed. Too many people looking and Tara could pay with her life. He turned, startled as a gentle hand touched his arm, and he was looking into blue eyes that reminded him of an azure sea. He took a step back, looked away from her mesmerizing eyes, unsure what to make of Kate's touch, but her intent was clear. Calm down.

"At home." Faisal's voice was strained. "But I'm de-bating if that's smart, if…"

Relief flooded through him that Faisal hadn't boarded a plane and wasn't halfway across the Atlan-tic on his way there. Hearing his voice…for a moment it was like Tara was in this room, like everything was right. But that wasn't the case. She was still missing. But Faisal was cooperating, for now. "Stay there. We don't need—"

"Me flying over there." Faisal cut him off. "And killing the creeps who did this and anyone else who stands in my way?" Anger and sarcasm laced his words. "Don't worry. I'm not coming over. Not yet. I know we need calm heads to find them and get Tara back, but once that's done..." His words trailed off.

"We're doing everything necessary—"

"Stop!" Faisal warned. "I know you're on this. Adam's already briefed me. No worries," he said before Emir could add anything to that. "Adam will be kicking butt if I make a move to go over there. But, man, I can't do nothing. At least, I'm having a hard time doing it." He laughed. A dry, humorless sound that seemed to make fun of his words more than anything else. "Can you find her? Will you be enough, you and K.J.?"

"We have to be. We need you in Wyoming," Emir reiterated, knowing it was a fact Faisal was well aware of and, despite what he'd said, probably the one reason he was still there. They'd acquired a number of high-profile cases over the last months and Emir only expected more. And, like Faisal, Talib was also occupied with managing their office here, at least until Tara was found. The only difference was that Talib could still be involved, if necessary, for he could be here on a minute's notice, unlike Faisal. He knew that would be tough for Faisal to take, but it was how it had to be.

"Yeah, I know," he said, an edge to his voice that

wasn't normally there. "Damn. I just hope she's not frightened."

Frightened. It was a word that hung thick and dark between them. They'd rather have Tara pissed than frightened, but reality danced and darted unspoken between them.

"We'll find her." Emir felt like he was repeating a phrase he'd committed to in blind faith. But this couldn't end any other way than the way he wanted it to end—with Tara, at home laughing with them and at them, as she always did.

"You're still at the compound?" Faisal asked.

"Yeah," Emir said. "But not for long. I'll fill you in soon. Kate and I—"

"Kate?" Despite the gravity of the situation, there was an amused edge to Faisal's voice that made Emir feel oddly defensive.

"K.J.," he said, shifting to the initials that it seemed everyone else used, and yet she'd asked him to call her Kate. But it was more than that. To him, she was Kate, not K.J. He shifted the phone from his left ear to his right, as if that would change the fact that his brother had just hinted there might be something in his feelings for Kate that was more than employer and employee. Utterly ridiculous. He liked her. They were partners in this case, nothing else. "We're heading out just before dawn. We're trying to play it low-key, not look like we're doing anything more than waiting."

"So what do you have on them?"

"Not much. We think there might be two groups, un-organized, possibly not working together. We'll track them to the last phone call and from there, after what Ahmed said, we think they might be heading into the Sahara." He hesitated. What they had was so little—nothing to go on. "Zafir will handle negotiating with them going forward." He didn't mention the fiasco at the airport. None of that was relevant, not now, at least not to Faisal, and could only convince him that he was needed. Right now, giving him less information was for the best, as was involving less people.

"Exactly what I would have done," Faisal said shortly, the frustration evident in his voice.

"Look, I'll be in touch." Emir hesitated again. "If you have any…"

"Ideas. Yeah, you bet I'll call. And, by the way, about K.J.—Kate," he corrected, that infuriating hint of amusement back in his voice. "You might only have known her for a short time, but I believe our father fell for Mother in the space of twenty-four hours." He chuckled at his dig.

"We'll find her," Faisal said, the humor replaced by an edgy determination.

"We will," Emir repeated and clicked off. So far he'd managed to ensure that Faisal was staying put, for now. He sank back in the rich leather chair that had been his father's, put his elbows on the massive desk and lowered his head to his arms.

"Bloody lie," he muttered, for, despite his words, in his heart he was very afraid there was the possibility of failing, of losing Tara. It was a possibility he'd refused to admit but it was a fear that had harbored like a thorny intruder in his heart since the beginning.

Chapter Seven

Kate looked at her watch. "I feel like we should have something substantial to move on but yet if it were like any other case…" Her voice trailed off.

"But it's not," he said. "Especially the way it's been going. They're not following a norm. Two demands for money. You know that's not normal or, at least, standard behavior."

"They're not rushed. They feel like they have time. That's a good thing."

He didn't reply as he stood at the window, the same one he'd stood at all those hours ago after he'd first received the news of Tara and while he'd waited for his brothers. He was pulled to the window, and had been throughout the evening, to the lights of Marrakech that seemed to lead him beyond and to the outside of the city. But there was no promise of answers. All he could see was a memory, Tara's face—smiling, happy. But all that had vanished. Instead she was in jeopardy. He tried to focus on the city, on taking his mind elsewhere and in that way relaxing enough to possibly come up with another angle—an idea that had yet to be considered.

He turned, looked to the right at the lights of the more modern city center and business hub. Then his gaze moved to where the ancient beginnings of Marrakech lay, taking in the labyrinth of tight streets and passageways, where businesses and residences hid behind ancient walls and where tourism and local shopping blended easily with snake charmers and tattoo artists.

The art and culture that crowded the narrow streets came from a heritage they all shared, from beginnings somewhere deep in the heart of the wind and sun-carved desert. It was a place of mystery and charm and one that hid the good as easily as it hid the bad.

His grip tightened on the window ledge. This was doing no good at all. For it was from the country's heart that Tara had been taken.

"Emir? What is it?"

Kate's voice had that caress, subtle, unintentional, but it reached to the heart of who he was, to places he hadn't let anyone in, in a very long time.

He couldn't look at her. He couldn't bear the sympathy he told himself he knew she was feeling. She didn't understand—couldn't—for, no matter how well intentioned, to her, Tara was just a case. She couldn't be anything else, for Kate didn't know her. They'd never met. "Nothing. Get some sleep while you can."

"I already tried that, didn't work."

He could hear her moving quietly in the darkness. Only the wafting scent of coconut combining oddly with the faint scent of myrrh alerted him that she was near. He didn't know how it had come to be, that the scents of his homeland seemed such a part of her.

And then she was beside him. "It's beautiful even at night."

He said nothing. There was nothing to say.

"She's not just a case," she said as the moments of silence turned into minutes. "Not to me. Not like you think."

He started. How had she read his mind? She lay a hand over his where it rested on the ledge. She'd done that before, but this time heat seemed to run through his core, connecting them in a way he was unable to analyze, wanting him to turn to her to...he pulled his hand away.

He was torn. Worry for Tara, fury at her captors and now the conflicted feelings toward Kate. He had to get it together and that meant focusing on something completely different.

There were hours before they could move into action but, in the meantime, they needed to set safeguards in place. He picked his phone up and turned it over. "It's our only contact with them—the pigs who have Tara." He put the phone down. "I don't like the idea of leaving it...of trusting..."

"Zafir will be fine," Kate assured him. "They'll never know it's not you. And we'll be in touch." She looked at her watch. It was only 7:55 p.m.

"How do you know he won't slip? That—"

"You're not giving him credit."

He shook his head. "Zafir's good, but this is Tara

we're talking about. Any one of us could break under the pressure. We—"

"Stop." Her shoulder brushed against his. "I'd work with any of you in a heartbeat. And in a case like this, the most important one you'll ever work, no one's going to mess up." She looked at him and he knew she could see the doubt in his face. He couldn't hide it. He'd never doubted any of their abilities before, but it had never mattered so much.

"Zafir is good," she repeated. "You know that. And I can vouch for him. I've read some of the cases he was involved in." She smiled. "Despite the talk—he's good."

Emir turned to face her. She'd taken the elastic out of her hair and now her long, straight, blond locks hung loose and soft, framing her face and skimming well past her shoulders.

"Interesting, your brother."

"What do you mean?"

"The rumor is that he's always got a romance going. Most recently a model. Gorgeous redhead." She laughed.

"Office talk?" He frowned. He abhorred gossip.

"I'm sorry," she murmured. "I was trying to lighten the mood. Inappropriate, I know…"

He glanced down and saw that she wove her fingers together—long, delicate fingers. Sensitive fingers, Tara might have said, but Tara had always been an intuitive sort. *Is*, he reminded himself. They'd find her.

"Emir, listen."

She shifted, her hair gleaming in the gentle, low light of the reading lamps. Again the delicate scent, the combination that was so uniquely her, wafted from her and seemed to overwhelm him, to make him more aware of her than he wanted or needed to be.

"I'm listening," he said.

She looked up at him. "I feel like there's something eluding us."

"So let's go over it again—what we know," he said with relief to be doing something.

She leaned against the desk.

He leaned back against the window ledge. "I don't know what we could have missed. She was taken by one, maybe two, men outside the gates, but we know there were others involved."

"If two of them died this afternoon, how many are left?" Kate asked as if the attack had been no more traumatic than a trip to the grocery store.

"What are you suggesting?"

"That there are no others." She shrugged. "I know that sounds unrealistic, impossible even, but we have to explore every option."

"That isn't an angle we've even considered."

"There hasn't been a demand in hours. Since the attack…" Her words hung in the silence between them, which seemed dark and treacherous now that the disturbing alternative had been presented.

"I don't think it's possible." The truth was that he didn't want to think it was possible since it brought forth so many other options. But that wasn't who he was; he had to go there—to explore possibilities that were difficult to consider.

"That she's out there in the night…" His voice threatened to break. He took a deep swallow and breathed out the last word, and it almost broke him. "Alone."

He pushed away from the window and began pacing the room. He stopped as he faced the window again, his thoughts focused on the terror of that one thought. It was more horrific than anything that had come before. A shudder ran through him, deep and agonizing. He couldn't imagine his baby sister alone, possibly terrified.

"She's tough," Kate said. "That was clear in everything I've read. And, truly, what I said earlier, I'm sorry. I've only added more worry by introducing the possibility."

"Don't be." He cut her off, hearing the gravel edge of emotion in his voice.

"I doubt very much if it's true. There'll be another demand. Those men might be a splinter group or part of the main group who wanted you out of the picture for whatever reason, and me, as well. I think both those explanations hold more validity than my other theory."

"We can't discount anything."

"And definitely not the fact that they're going to be demanding more money. Three hundred and fifty thousand, considering what your family is worth, isn't a lot for all the trouble they're going to. They seem to know you won't call the authorities." She cleared her throat. "And having said that, ignore my last hypothesis—that there are no others. It doesn't fly."

"You're right." He took a breath. "But why are they taking their sweet time to demand more?"

"To put you on edge. Which will obviously give them

an advantage. You are kept guessing, the stress of waiting, of inertia, wears you down."

He knew she was right about everything but the thought of Tara alone, left in the desert to find her own way out or die. Once that idea had been introduced, he knew it would be almost impossible to dispel.

"I think our original theory that they are a group who, for some reason, started acting against each other is far more plausible," Kate said. "Forget my earlier musings. I was thinking aloud, exploring possibilities."

There was something intuitive about her; a calming presence that put him off balance and made him want to take her in his arms and kiss her.

"Emir?"

He pushed the inappropriate thought from his mind and gave her his full attention.

"It was a theory that probably isn't very plausible. Hopefully we'll have more information, a direction, before we hit the road. If not, we get moving, anyway. With any luck, by this time tomorrow, this will be over—or..." She hesitated. "Or at least close."

Silence hung between them for a minute then two.

"Do you think they meant to keep you from leaving Marrakech and following them?" Kate asked as she mulled over the profiles of the deceased pair of attackers.

"By attempting to kill me or, more appropriately, us?" He could hear the amusement in his voice. If it hadn't been about Tara, he would have enjoyed sparring with her—going over the theories, discounting them, coming up with new ones.

"I don't think they expected me or Dell. And when they realized you weren't alone, it all fell apart." She stood, paced the length of the office.

"So, opening fire at the edge of airport property was to threaten the family."

"Exactly. You were the one who would go after them. They knew that."

"And Faisal or any of the others wouldn't?"

"Faisal is an ocean away. Zafir is more apt to play their game and, of course, Talib will agree with Zafir. He usually does." She smiled. "Not that Talib doesn't have his own mind, but he tends to think much like Zafir." She looked at him. "Whereas you? You will play to a point but it won't stop you from going after her. You're more like Faisal than you know." She smiled. "You're wondering how I know that."

"Am I?"

"I've studied many of the agency's past cases and I've spoken to Adam. I might not be completely right, but I think I'm close. As far as Talib is concerned?" She put a finger to her chin as if considering. "Middle child. I filled in the blanks—classic."

"Assumption," he said with a pained attempt at a smile. "But impressive."

"And you? Oldest child, responsibility of raising a younger sibling foisted on you at a young age. Serious. Determined. In charge. Textbook."

"So this was all about getting me out of the way?" he asked and couldn't kill the sarcasm in his voice. "The theory must seem like overkill, even to you."

"Maybe. Or maybe not," she said. "Think about it."

There were so many different angles in any kidnapping case and because it was Tara, there seemed even more. The silence since the last call they'd received from the kidnappers terrified him, not for himself but for Tara. She was everything and it was up to him to make sure she came back, for their family was nothing without her.

"Emir..." Kate began, her hand reaching for his.

He shook his head. He couldn't remember a time in his life when he'd felt any lower, any more desperate. It was an out-of-control feeling that terrified him and he knew he had to get it together.

He looked at Kate and wished that he hadn't. He couldn't handle the compassion in her beautiful eyes. Her lips were slightly parted and seemed to offer the only chance at hope he had in this dark and dreadful night.

He leaned down and, as his lips met hers, he felt the power of what the two of them were and had proved only a few hours ago. Now he felt a different power, the power of where her soft lips could take him, where the taste of her could lead, where... He drew back, leaving the kiss as only a sweet meeting, a gentle caress, leaving the potential behind.

"I'm..." He wasn't sure what he'd been about to say. His emotions were playing with his logic and all he wanted to do was to kiss her again. He shoved the feeling back. The life-and-death adrenaline rush had awoken another primitive need, nothing more.

But as he turned his back to her and faced the city, the haunting tones of the call to prayer began. The ancient notes pierced the silence and taunted the occupants of that one room in the Al-Nassar compound with the reminder of how life was so much more important than the moments that defined it.

And worse, that time was slipping away.

Chapter Eight

Monday, September 14, 8:15 p.m.

Emir's phone beeped just as the call to prayer ended, as if the solemnity of the one had somehow influenced the other. He pulled the phone out of his pocket as his eyes met Kate's and he knew they were on the same page. She connected with him like no one, no woman, ever had. It was different than how he connected with Zafir, for this connection felt intimate. It was another thought he didn't want to consider. All he wanted to consider right now was that they were back in business.

"Zafir," he said for Kate's benefit. He'd known without looking at his phone, with an instinct that they'd had since birth, that it was his twin. "What do you have?" he asked. He nodded at Kate's look and pressed the speaker button as he alerted his twin, "You're on speaker."

"An ID on one of your attackers. Unfortunately we couldn't find anything on the other. But the one we did find…well, he's got an interesting trajectory."

Emir looked up and met the full impact of Kate's thoughtful yet intense look. She was leaning forward, her chin in the palm of one hand and her phone in the other. He started when he realized she was recording the call. She was good, proving once again that she was one step ahead of him.

For a minute it was as if neither he nor Kate breathed. It was the news they were looking for, hopefully a lead. Emir gritted his teeth. He was almost afraid to ask but he hadn't succeeded in life by being afraid or by clinging to superstitious silence. "Who is he?" he asked, allowing for only a brief hesitation.

"Atrar Tashfin. Berber—and one would think that's simple enough but there's something a bit strange about him."

Emir choked back an impatient involuntary reaction at what he considered Zafir's theatrics. Short and simple, that's what he lived by and what he preached to his siblings. But he was cut off almost immediately by Zafir's next words.

"Here's the thing. We tagged Atrar. That's the one you thought came out of the Sahara. You know, the one with the fancy boots? The sand and camel dung—"

"Knock-off Ralph Lauren," he interrupted as if that mattered.

"Yeah, it's the same one. He belongs to a Berber village on the south edge of the Atlas Mountains. The village of Kaher. I looked it up and it's pretty remote, backs the mountains but fronts the beginnings of the Sahara. I think you need to pay it a visit. There might be answers there and it's a good place to start. It might be better than what you've been doing. So you can get moving now, rather than waiting, agreed?"

"Agreed," Emir said shortly. "Someone in that village may know something."

Kate's attention was fixed on him but there was a troubled look on her face and he knew she was already going through possibilities. He'd never lacked confidence, but with her beside him, he felt like he could have scaled Everest without equipment. No woman had ever made him feel like that. No woman had needed to, but Kate… He let the thought trail, not sure what it all meant.

"What about the other?" Emir asked, looking over as Kate nodded approval, as if he'd read her mind or, at least, as she'd showed in the short time she'd been here, that she was on the same wavelength.

"Can't get anything on him. Not yet," Zafir replied. "I'm sure the authorities will have an ID eventually, but we can't wait. So I'm giving you what I've got."

"Emir!" Kate whispered urgently.

"Just a minute," Emir said to his twin.

"We need to get there as soon as possible. Does he have the coordinates?" Kate was on her feet.

"I sent them to your email, Em," Zafir said.

"There could be more information there and a more specific area—" She broke off, a worried expression on her face.

"Exactly what I was thinking," Zafir agreed, his voice slightly distant through the speaker phone.

"Is it possible to land anywhere nearby?" Emir asked.

"There's a short landing strip. I've spoken to them and they'll have it lit for you," Zafir said.

"This confirms what we were already thinking."

Emir looked at Kate and saw the same urgency he felt, to get going, reflected in her eyes. Already he was planning their new strategy even as he saw the intense look on Kate's face, the frown that marred her normally smooth brow and knew she was considering options. None of his agents did any less than think on their feet. It was how they succeeded in some of their most difficult cases and how they protected the clients they had—how they had become number one on two continents.

"The sooner someone gets there, the better. I'd go there myself…" Zafir paused. "But apparently I'm on Emir duty."

Emir gave a half smile. It was how Zafir had always referred to the times when they had switched roles, more notably in their youth. As adults, this was the first time they'd resorted to such tactics.

"Kate and I have it covered." He looked at her with a wry smile, thinking how much his opinion of her had changed and how, only a few hours ago, he couldn't imagine himself saying that. But she'd more than proved herself in the short time they'd known each other. She'd proved her skill in the best and worst situations. She'd been willing to take a bullet for the cause. Fortunately, good marksmanship on both their parts and Dell's had prevented that from happening.

"We'll fly tonight. Hopefully we can get there soon enough to get some answers. That means you, like you said, lead this show. Tara's kidnappers have to be heading into their final act and asking for more and soon. I don't think they can play this out much longer." He looked over at Kate, who nodded agreement.

"I'm a good twenty minutes away," Zafir replied.

"We'll wait."

"That's not all I've got. I think I have a major lead, man. More than what I just told you, but you needed to know that first. There's no getting around the fact that someone has to go there. And, as we agreed, that's you and K.J.," Zafir said. "But there's something else," he repeated.

"Shoot."

"A sighting—and it's a good chance it might be Tara."

"Why didn't you say that right away?" Emir's eyes met Kate's, his heart pounding at the idea—hope and fear seeming to converge at what this might mean.

"Because I think it's more important you get to the village."

"You thought? Zaf, this isn't your case."

"She's my sister, too. You're not the only one who is torn up about it," his brother growled. "Look, this is what I have. A girl who looks like Tara was reported in Ouarazate Province by a couple of Berbers."

"When?"

"That's the problem. We received the information late. The man who reported it said they'd seen her just before noon today. At the time, they didn't know about the kidnapping. Word's gotten out since then. I think what happened may have been let out by our own staff at the compound. You know, mentioning something of our situation to friends or family. Many of them or their families have ties to the desert. Anyway, he contacted me as soon as he heard. They said they came upon the group over twelve hours ago and they were in a Jeep. There were five of them and the girl."

Emir cursed under his breath. Ouarazate, the gateway to the desert. But too much time had gone by; they could be anywhere.

"Look, I'll be there as soon as I can. There are a few things I have to clear up here and then, depending on the traffic…" Zafir paused, as if considering options. "Don't wait. You've got to get moving. There is too much that needs to be done. Too much at stake."

"You're right. Tara can't wait," Emir said.

"Get moving. Let's get our sister," Zafir said.

"Done," Emir said and clicked off.

TARA CRINGED. She hated the dark, the shadows her imagination had the uncanny ability to turn into more threats than those she already faced. Time seemed to be crawling by and the darkness was never-ending. Without the moon, the night was only broken by the few, too distant stars, and by the fire that crackled and spit over thirty feet away. There was a tent, but she preferred to sit outside it and, oddly, they'd allowed that one request.

Maybe, somewhere in the back of his mind, the leader remembered her for who she was and what she had been to him. Whatever the reason, she was grateful. Somehow it seemed safer here where there was some distance between her and them. She clutched the blanket. It was cold again tonight. She shivered and her eyes never left the fire and the men around it. It wasn't safe for her to take her eyes off them. She'd learned in the early hours of her kidnapping that they were unpredictable.

She was so tired. She couldn't help closing her eyes just for a second. A minute passed and then two before she was snapped awake by angry shouts that echoed through the small, struggling oasis.

Tara drew her knees to her chest, wrapping her arms around them as if that would make her smaller, invisible. Her eyes never left the men. Loud voices meant trouble. This time, as usual, it was the leader. It seemed he didn't like what one of the men had said and now the shouts were followed by something even more deadly. Silence. The moon slipped from behind a cloud and bathed the area in light.

She wished she could disappear but there was nowhere to go. Instead she was trapped by the frightening scene in front of her as the man pulled his rifle from his shoulder and hurled it. She watched as the smaller man, who it was meant for, lunged, missed the catch and stood. The moonlight disappeared again as the gun hit the ground and skipped twice along the battered rug she knew, even in the fickle light of the fire, lay on the desert sand.

Now the gun lay forgotten and their raised voices began to dissolve into shouts and yet another fight. It was a relief, for she knew the fights kept their attention from her.

The leader muttered a string of curses in Arabic before he launched himself into their midst, punching one and grabbing the other and throwing him to the ground. His voice was harsh and, as usual, louder than necessary. She closed her eyes and hoped they remained there—killing themselves in their fight would be ideal. But, as always, she knew this fight wouldn't last long.

She prayed he'd stay away from her. Her prayers went unanswered as minutes passed, silence ensued and then came what she had hoped wouldn't.

She could see him clearly as he approached. His face was highlighted in the moonlight. It was so familiar and yet so very strange. She dropped her gaze, not wanting to meet his eyes, hoping he would leave, change his mind. Instead the sand crunched beneath his heavy boots and he squatted beside her.

She looked up and met the odd yet gentle smile. The smile didn't match the dark look in his eyes. She dropped her gaze to the sand. She could smell the sweat of him, like he hadn't bathed in weeks or even months. He was too near and she fought not to move away for she had nowhere to go and little rope with which to do it.

She drew back, trying to make herself small. He wasn't the man she remembered.

He chuckled as he ran a knuckle along her cheek.

She fought not to cringe or to move away. Although there wasn't far to move; the rope gave her five feet of freedom.

This time she blew out a relieved breath as he stood to join the others.

"Do you know what stands between us and wealth?" she heard him ask. But it was his reply that made her cringe. "Death."

She shuddered, trying not to think of whose death he might be implying. She watched as the moonlight reflected across his face and clearly showed the disfiguring scar that covered the left side. The scar made a mockery of what had once had been a handsome face. Close up, she knew the scar appeared raw, almost painful, despite the fact that it was clear it had been from wounds long healed.

But it was then that she heard the most frightening thing of all. His promise to take down the house of Al-Nassar, to take what it held most precious and to leave nothing to remind anyone it had ever existed.

Chapter Nine

"Kaher is on the fringe of the Sahara, like Zafir said. Not well used by tourists and hikers, but that might be to our benefit." Even Kate could hear the trace of excitement in her voice. "What incredible luck that they have an airstrip."

She ran her fingers through her hair and looked at him. His dark eyes were both grim and determined. "That information certainly came out of nowhere," she added. "Let's hope someone knew this guy. Like, who he was hanging with, what he was doing…"

"And we can find out who and what they know quickly," Emir said.

"At least before first light," she agreed, grimacing. "You've flown at night? I mean, you have experience at this sort of thing?"

"You doubt me?"

"No." She shook her head. "Of course not. I was just surprised."

"I'm a qualified pilot and I've flown at night often," he assured her. "I'll get us there in one piece, if that's what you're worried about."

"Did I say I was worried?" She cocked an eyebrow at him. "Let's get moving."

But before either of them could act on those words, her phone dinged, signaling a text message. She looked at it with a frown then back up at him. "It's a blocked text—no identification." She held up her index finger, warning him to silence. "This is odd."

Outside, a siren broke the quiet; the distant sound knifing in through an open window. The flashing lights seemed to pulse through the night, as if forewarning them of something even more threatening than what they already faced.

Seconds seemed to tick away and the silence within the room wrapped around them in a thick, almost choking veil.

Her eyes met his and she pushed a button on the phone.

"It's a video."

She looked up, saw the perspiration dotting his forehead and wondered if the pressure of it all was finally getting to him. She dismissed the thought. He was strong, too strong. There were other words for men such as him... Just his nearness could take a woman's breath away. She'd bet that he'd never had a woman turn him down. She remembered how, earlier, he had been outlined in his office by the city lights as he'd stood by the window, how his well-muscled form had been clearly defined by his T-shirt.

She was always in control and now, at a completely inappropriate time, her mind was running amuck thinking of...

She frowned and clutched the phone tighter. "It might be nothing—"

"Or it might be from them," he said, cutting her off. And they both knew what he meant. Tara's kidnappers.

Her finger lifted from the phone as if that were a deal-breaker. "Maybe I should watch it without you."

"No, start it. We need to see it and see it now."

They didn't know what was on the video. It could be anything or anyone. But in this situation, with everything that had happened, the possibility that it wasn't a ransom demand in some form, that Tara wasn't involved, was slight.

"Start it," he said thickly as he leaned over her shoulder.

They watched the video begin with no prelude but, rather immediately, a woman's face dominated the screen.

"Tara," he said, an edge to his voice.

Her hands were tied and she was kneeling, looking right at them or, more aptly, at the camera or at whoever was filming her.

"Please, Emir," Tara said, her voice pleading. But the words didn't seem as panicked as they seemed forced. It was as if she wasn't saying them voluntarily but instead was being coached. She hesitated and stumbled over what she was saying, sounding reluctant.

Kate swallowed. It was tough to watch. There was a flashlight on her face and Tara blinked frequently, squinting against the light. Her dark hair was long and loose, curling wildly around her dusty face. Her faded jeans were torn, not as a fashion statement, Kate suspected, but more a result of her ordeal. Her flowered, peasant-style cotton blouse had chalk-colored streaks running through it. There were numerous thin, red scratches on her hands and across one cheek, but she met the camera with fire in her eyes despite the tears on her cheeks.

"Tara," Emir murmured. "Hang in there. I'm coming."

In the video, Tara turned slightly, as if she might have heard him.

She sat on her heels on what looked like a burgundy blanket, but it was faded with age and dusty with sand. It was hard to tell if the blanket might have some sort of ethnic origin, a clue to who she was with or where she was, but that clue was lost as the camera never went near enough to give them a clear visual.

Kate tried to remain objective as she watched an animated, if you could call it that, Tara. This was the first time she'd seen her in anything other than a still photo. She made a mental note of her mannerisms and listened to what she said as she looked for signs of coaching and for some hint of who was with her. She was fairly sure that she had a better chance of seeing any of that than Emir, who was too close to be objective.

Kate looked at Emir, who confirmed everything she had thought, as anger seemed to emanate from him in the tightness in his lips and the intense way he looked at her. She knew that any objectivity he had maintained had been lost in the moment. It wasn't surprising. Anyone in his situation would have reacted the same, although in her mind he was holding on better than most. Still, objectivity and her skill in these situations, was why she was here. But now she feared that the deeper they got into this, the closer they got to finding Tara, the more difficult it would be for Emir to keep a check on his emotion. She didn't blame him, it was natural, but she also knew it wasn't going to help the investigation one bit.

"They want it in American dollars." There was no emotion in Tara's voice.

The video blurred and garbled and then became clear again.

"Someone will tell you when and where," Tara said, her words a monotone, as if she were reading a script.

There was a sound behind her, a scuffling, and then the video blanked out and came back on. This time Tara was gone and the muffled voice of a man was saying, "Be prepared, you'll have little time."

The video clicked off.

"What kind of joke is this?" Emir stormed. "They prop her up, ask for money yet again, and don't give a drop zone, an amount, even a time—nothing?"

Kate looked at him, at the fire in his dark eyes and the pain that overrode everything, and couldn't begin to imagine how it might feel. Even if she'd had siblings, she doubted she could imagine such a nightmare. She wished she could fix it, that it wouldn't carry on any longer. That somehow she could end it.

"So they want what they asked for earlier or it's another amount. Whatever it is, will that be enough? Will they let her go?" Emir's voice was raised and tense.

Kate didn't say anything. This was about Emir regaining control. He didn't need or want anything from her right now.

Silence flooded the room.

"Get in touch with Zafir. Now," she said after a minute had passed.

She listened to the one-sided conversation as Emir laid out what had happened and what Zafir needed to do.

He put the phone down and ran splayed fingers through his hair before he looked at her. "He's already on the way."

"Let's watch that video again. Can you? Is it too much…?"

"Start it," he rasped.

They watched it through two more times before she turned it off and set the phone down.

"She was in the open. There wasn't any shelter." His words were like grim drumbeats of doom.

"Emir," she warned as she shook her head, "don't go there. None of that is relevant, not now. She's not comfortable but she's not injured and she's not—" She bit off the last words.

"Dead." He filled the word in for her. "And she's not going to be, either." He looked at his watch. "Where the hell is Zafir? It's been…"

"Two minutes," she noted. "Look, let's review that video one more time. There was something I wanted to mention but I thought it was a nervous tic, considering what was going on. Where she was, what—"

"Tell me," he broke in.

She looked at him, saw the pain in his eyes that he was struggling to contain and her heart almost broke. He was a strong man but even strong men had their limits.

"I think she's trying to tell us something."

She picked up the phone and pushed Play. The video no sooner began to run before she hit Pause. "Did you see that slight tapping of her finger on her left hand?"

He frowned. He leaned closer. "Son of a desert stray," he muttered.

He hit Rewind again and again.

"This is difficult," she said, thinking how hard it was to watch his sister being held captive like that—to see she wasn't alone but surrounded by her captors. That much was evident based on the fact they could see the boots of two men obviously milling nearby. They were boots that, this time, gave them no clue. They were clean, generic, with no sign of sand or dirt—no evidence of any kind.

Kate turned her attention back to Tara. When she'd first noticed the thumb tapping on Tara's left hand, she had thought it might be anxiety. The woman had much to be anxious about.

"I don't believe it," Emir said. "Why didn't I see that before? Morse code."

"Interesting," Kate said as she thought of the eclectic collection of books on Tara's shelves and looked closer at the video.

Emir said nothing but his presence seemed to fill the room even as his attention was on the video.

"Simplistic and yet—" Kate broke off. Tara was surprising her in ways she hadn't expected. Morse code was not something a young woman of Tara's generation would have any exposure to. "Or would she?" she asked softly.

Emir turned. There was a troubled frown on his face as he watched her, his eyes seeming to lock with hers. "What are you thinking?"

"The implausibility of this…" She remembered the bookshelf. Tara wasn't just a modern girl with an attitude, she was also a serious student and an avid reader. The books on her shelves had been everything from contemporary novels to history. But one shelf had stood out. The section filled with procedural books and one, she remembered, labeled, "Code This."

"She studied Morse code?"

Emir nodded. "Not so much studied as read some books she'd found in what had been our father's private library. Like I said, it was nothing serious—goofing around, she called it. She was only fourteen or fifteen. Back then we often practiced it together in English and French. I didn't think she remembered."

Kate looked at the video. Now she watched the subtle, yet clear when you noticed it, up-and-down movement of Tara's thumb. Because her hand was a bit behind her, it wasn't something that caught your eye, or, she suspected, the eye of the cameraman. She narrowed her eyes, watching the furtive movements, the rhythm and the pattern in the long and short gestures.

Around Tara were the canvas walls of what seemed to be a tent but the video was edited enough that what was around her wasn't clear. It could be a tent anywhere or, from what Kate could see, it could not be a tent at all. But one thing was now clear. She looked closer, but once she'd made the determination, the truth was inescapable.

Emir's attention was solely on the video. Kate frowned at the thought of the obsolete code in a time when even cursive writing was almost extinct. But there was no denying that Tara was definitely trying to tell them something. The video cut off just as her thumb lifted again.

Emir looked at Kate with a frown ridging his brows. He rubbed the back of his hand across his cheek. "T-e-n e-t-e," he said, spelling it out. "It makes no sense." He ran the video again, as if going through the series of taps would change anything. The video cut off again before any more information could be divulged and before Tara's kidnappers could see what she had done. "And there's nothing more."

The room felt suddenly close, as if there were no oxygen. Kate could feel the energy of the man beside her as the tension and fear for his sister seemed to pulse between them and something else.

"Été," he said. "French for 'summer.' What summer? Where?"

"Ten," she murmured, moving what he'd just said to memory for later consideration. "Could refer to anything, but my best guess is that it refers to something about her."

"She wasn't finished. She thought she had more time. That's why it was cut off the way it was."

"Possibly."

Kate was quiet, thinking of what it all might mean. When she met his eyes she saw the silent strength and the determination in his chiseled jaw and, for a moment, it was like she forgot to breathe.

"Do you remember she gave a victory sign at the beginning?"

He frowned. "She used to do that as a kid on the first day of summer vacation or on the announcement of a family trip."

There was silence for a moment before he spoke.

"Ten," he repeated just as she had earlier. "Could she have mixed English and French? Tara is fluent in both. She's stressed. She could have used the languages interchangeably."

"Go on," Kate encouraged.

"The year Tara was ten, the most notable thing was that that was the summer my parents took her and Faisal for a short tour of the Sahara." He stood. "Could it be that easy?"

"She wouldn't want to make it difficult, yet she didn't know how much time she'd have. Thus the cut-off words." She looked at him. Saw the hope in his eyes.

A thought came to her that, somehow, what Tara's security, now so critically wounded, and what Tara had just tried to tell them were connected. "Could what Ahmed have been trying to tell you also have been a place?" She looked at him. "Emir? Where in the Sahara did your parents take Tara that summer? What was their final destination?"

"El Dewar." He smacked his hand on the desktop. "I'd forgotten about it. I don't know how I could have."

"It was trivial detail at the time, especially since you weren't involved in the trip," Kate said. "Understandable."

"That was the farthest they went before returning home. But is that the clue?"

He was quiet for a minute, considering what she had said. "Davar. Could Ahmed been trying to name the place and now she's trying to tell us the same? That she's near El Dewar, or there's information to be had at El Dewar, the same Berber village she saw at ten?"

"It's a possibility but it's also a big stretch," Kate said. She grabbed the map. "It's a small place. I doubt if she's there now. She couldn't be hidden and there are enough people that not everyone would be complicit. So, could she be near there? Is that possible?"

He didn't answer. Instead his fists were clenched, his lips in a straight line, his mind obviously elsewhere. Fighting, she imagined, with long-forgotten memories.

"Emir!" Her voice was sharp. It was the only way to get through to him. He was ready to hit the desert without a plan, with only guns and rage, and neither of those would be successful in rescuing his sister.

He looked at Kate as if seeing her for the first time. "I'm sorry. I lost it, I shouldn't have…" He paused, as if he needed time to breathe. "You have no idea," he said.

Time seemed to beat slowly between them and, for a second, all she could do was look at the strong jaw, feel his solid presence, and wish that was all it took—a minute in his arms to make all of this right for him. She shoved the thought away.

"You're right, I don't. But what I do know is that my

decisions aren't clouded by emotion. Yours are." She took his hand in both of hers and tried not to acknowledge the irony of her words. "Listen to me." She looked at him. His rich dark eyes were pools of pain. "That's what the kidnappers want, for you to irrationally follow their demands without thought. That was more than likely part of the purpose behind that video. Maybe..." she began, thinking of the lack of ransom detail. "All of it. You falling for that ploy won't help Tara. But it might ensure that, if their plan was to kill you at the airport, that scenario will still play out. Only this time, someplace else. You've got to let me lead and help you keep a cool head. It's the only way."

This time when she met Emir's eyes, she saw that, for once, they were dark with hope rather than despair. And something else, as if he were looking at her for the first time. She looked away.

She let go of his hand as he nodded and turned away from her. The tension seemed to noticeably lift from the room as she blew out a quiet sigh of relief.

"I'm puzzled. Why did they send the video to me?" Kate murmured. "How did they know about me?"

"They've got some sort of inside information. Or maybe they contacted the others when they saw you at the airport."

"How did they find out my name?"

"I don't know," he said, looking at her in a way that had nothing to do with what she was saying.

She was unprepared when he bent and kissed her, and even more so for her own reaction, for the need and want that made her put her arms around his neck and, for a few seconds, to allow herself to sink into that kiss.

It was instinctive and so very wrong. She pushed him back, her hands on his shoulders, creating a distance between them. They were trapped in an emotional situation and it was a natural human reaction to turn from trauma to passion.

He stood there for a moment then his eyes met hers and a truth seemed to pass between them. That what had happened was real, as real as the tragedy unfolding around them. But now it was Tara who eclipsed all and they both knew it.

"She'll die if we don't get her out of there soon," he said. "Let's move."

Chapter Ten

They took off in Emir's Cessna from a runway at the back of the property that wasn't visible from the main entrance. The plane had already been loaded by staff with the supplies they'd need, and Emir had arranged for a Jeep they could use to take them from the village of Kaher into the Sahara.

Now, inside the plane's darkened cabin, they were each immersed in their own thoughts. The roar of the engine and the endless night sky seemed to wrap around them and was only broken by the occasional lights of communities and vehicles traveling on highways beneath them.

The golden blanket of lights that had been Marrakech was far behind them. Ahead, the shadowed peaks of the Atlas Mountains punctured the night sky and seemed to challenge them to enter. The steady noise of the engine was all that broke the silence in the cockpit.

Kate looked to the right, where the dark outline of the wing seemed almost alien, threatening. She shivered. The darkness sheltered many secrets.

She glanced at Emir, saw the tight grip he had on the

wheel and the set of his jaw. She looked at the map in her lap. They'd dropped technology when they'd made the decision to fly to the edge of the desert. Cell towers weren't the norm as one ventured deeper into a place that in some ways was not only off the grid but on another planet. They were also a means of tracking and that went both ways. After Kaher, they were going in electronically silent with no one able to follow their tracks, at least not easily.

Her thoughts shifted and she thought of the northern reaches of the Sahara as it penetrated Morocco. The settlements were mapped in her mind for it was there they'd determined as the most likely area the kidnappers had gone. Now they just needed something a little more specific. She glanced at Emir. She'd been aware of him the entire time the plane had been in the air and all the while she'd studied the map.

"You're all right?" he asked as he turned to her. "You've spent a lot of time studying that map."

"I did. It's calming." She didn't look at him. Even in the dark, she only saw his full lips, felt the memory of them on hers and… She couldn't think of that. It was over, a mistake.

Still, she was relieved to say even those few words for there had been silence for much of the first part of the flight. She'd rather he had spoken. The silence seemed filled with the memory of the brief intimacy they had shared.

None of that had promised anything, she told herself. She looked out the window into the night sky, saw the darkened wisps of clouds and the bulk of the mountains. She pulled her gaze away from the uncertainness of the night sky that was so like her feelings for Emir.

Emir.

She wanted none of his kisses and yet, if she were truthful, she wanted the little she'd received and more. She looked at the map, pulling her attention from the line of his jaw, his strong yet artistic hands on the wheel—imagining how they would feel...

"I've located every community within a hundred miles of Kaher, as well as between that and El Dewar," she said as she pushed her unwanted thoughts away.

"And if they've taken her farther?" There was a rough edge in the timbre of his voice. He looked at his instrument panel and adjusted something, she couldn't say what. Flying in a small plane in the co-pilot seat was not something she did often and never at night.

"The desert won't be easy," Emir said as if another reminder would somehow ease the journey. "I don't know how long it will take to find her. We may need to set up camp—overnight."

It wasn't optimism she heard so much in his voice as something else. There was something almost suggestive in the words, and a shiver ran through her. Alone in the desert with Emir, under different circumstances... She let the thought trail off. Any attraction they felt meant nothing. Danger often got emotions flaring and that led, given the opportunity, to other things. That's all their attraction meant. She should have known better.

"It's impossible to know," Kate agreed, ignoring any connotation an overnight trip might have meant or if there had been any connotation at all. "Hopefully we don't have to enter blind." But that was the point of this trip—to get more information, to be able to enter the Sahara with something more than that Tara's message was connected to a childhood trip. Too bad Tara had been cut off.

Emir glanced at her, his jaw tight, his eyes shadowed in the darkness, and yet she could imagine they were hot and full of passion, a different kind of passion. She believed it was more about finding his sister. None of that was her imagination. His raw emotion filled the cabin with an intensity that caused a shiver to snake down her spine.

Kate knew there was no outcome that was even conceivable to him other than success. All she could do was provide support, be part of the team that pulled Tara out. She reached instinctively for her handgun and felt some comfort at the bulk at her waist. But her hand shook slightly as she realized her feelings had changed. She was no longer there just to get Tara out. She was deluding herself if she thought there was nothing more to this, especially when being in his arms had felt so right.

A tick in Emir's jaw was the only sign of the tension he was under. He flew the small plane with ease, as though flying over treacherous mountains through the dark that seemed to mock them was nothing. She clutched her seat belt and watched for lights, for some sort of indication of civilization, but since they'd entered the mountain range there was nothing. She knew this area of the Atlas Mountains was sparsely settled, mostly by Berber tribes, and that all were remote and distant from each other, including their destination: the village of Kaher.

Kate's phone beeped and she looked at it, startled. "It's a text from Zafir. He wants me to call him," she said even as she punched in the number. They'd kept her phone and planned to drop it at Kaher as the mobile coverage was limited in the Sahara. To lighten what they carried and to limit the possibility of being tracked, they would take only a satellite phone.

The plane dipped slightly to the right as she gripped her seat belt with one hand.

"You're on speaker," she said.

"I didn't know if I'd catch you—" Zafir began.

"What do you have?" Emir interrupted. "We're close to landing."

"I just came from the hospital. Ahmed didn't make it."

"Bloody—" Emir broke off as he slapped his open palm against the wheel of the plane. He reached over and took Kate's free hand, squeezing it. His hand was large and warm, and she felt safe.

"It was tough. His family was there. His wife's pretty torn up."

"Make sure they have what they need," Emir said. "Funeral arrangements…and we'll talk monetary assistance later. Money is the last thing his wife needs to consider, ever."

"The usual, retirement settlement, insurance…we can't bring him back, but she'll be very comfortable."

Kate glanced at Emir, not realizing, or, she supposed, not having a need to know just how much support was available for the families of not only the home compound's employees but agents, as well. She was impressed by both their compassion and their generosity.

"He said something else before he passed," Zafir continued, breaking into her thoughts. "Ajeddig."

"A name, but who?" Emir asked.

Kate frowned.

"It's not much, I know," Zafir said. "That's it, Emir. I'll use the satellite next time. I assume you're ditching the cell."

"Turning it off after this call and dumping it at Kaher," Emir confirmed.

He looked over at Kate, who had opened the map and was running her finger over it.

"Another place name?" she muttered.

"Any luck?" Zafir chimed in as Emir looked at her with a question in his eyes.

"Nothing in Morocco by that name. So, if it's not a place name, what is it?"

"It's got no relevance, at least none that I can find that correlates to anything involving the case," Zafir said. "I'm at the compound now. Got your phone in my hand. I drove in the gate just as you were taking off. That's it, all I've got."

"Thanks, man. I'll touch base as soon as I can."

Kate clicked off just as a strand of lights appeared below. "I thought there was no electricity?"

"In Kaher, no. There's some solar power that's generated and used in parts of the village…the landing strip and a few other buildings. Nothing more."

As he arced the plane she found herself looking

straight down at the ground for a few slightly discon-
certing seconds and gripped the edge of the seat as if
that would somehow prevent the plane from sliding into
the abyss beneath them.

The plane leveled off and, as it descended, Kate
could see shadowed buildings that seemed to rise from
the ground. It was strange, for they weren't skyscrap-
ers or even remotely tall. Instead they were short and
squat and crowded into a small space where the mountains ended and the desert began. As she watched, the
buildings disappeared as the plane broke through the
low-lying cloud cover.

"I've spoken to one of the leaders in the community.
A man by the name of Yuften M'Hidi. He'll meet us,"
Emir said easily as if landing in the dark on the edge
of a mountain range was something he did every day.

She laughed. "His parents must have been optimis-
tic. Really? His name means 'the chosen'?"

He smiled as he looked at her. "Firstborn son. It's all
about expectations, my dear," he said in a bad imitation
of a Southern accent. And he reached over and took her
hand and squeezed it.

"Not funny," she said with a smile. But it was a relief
to have even a brief moment of levity. They both knew
from experience that it did wonders to keep an agent
fresh when, as they always did, a case got intense and
became a marathon of tension.

The lights on the ground were now clear and the runway stretched beneath them.

"One other thing. We'll be staying tonight at his

house. He says he has extra mats for guests. Hopefully, it won't be too grim."

"We aren't expecting luxury," she replied. "If we can get some information, even better. A few hours of sleep would just be gravy," she said with a smile.

"We're going in," he said, still holding her hand as if he knew, despite her silence, how uncomfortable flying in the night in a small plane made her.

She'd never said, but she wasn't letting go of his hand, either. After that there was only the roar of the engine, the dark heaviness of the mountains as they seemed to close in, and the small river of lights that acted as landing lights.

"Despite how I first reacted when I picked you up at the airport," Emir said glancing at her as the plane rolled to a stop, "I couldn't have a calmer, more analytical thinker by my side."

Kate's hand dropped from the seat belt she'd been clutching as the plane rolled along the narrow runway, startled by the unexpected compliment. "Thank you," she said softly.

"More beautiful, either," he added as he brought the plane to a stop.

She wasn't sure if he'd really said that or if she'd just imagined it, rather like the earlier kiss. None of it seemed like the in-charge man she knew, and yet, if she were to profile him...she wouldn't. Instead she enjoyed the instinctive rush of pleasure the compliment gave her and, just as quickly, pulled her mind back to reality. There was no time for such thoughts. Instead, there was silence as they quickly disembarked.

A slight, dark-haired man, whose gray hair glinted in the lights, waved to them as he hurried down the runway.

"Right on time," he said in heavily accented English.

"You've been waiting?" Emir asked.

The words, spoken in Berber, reminded Kate of what she had read about Emir. She knew Berber was a language he had learned as a boy. His father had ensured that he and his siblings were fluent in each of the languages of Morocco. As a result, Emir spoke Arabic, Berber, English and French. The English, he spoke flawlessly, with a hint of American colloquialism. She knew, too, that he'd gone to university in Wyoming where he'd been into all things American. Adam had told her that, along with the fact that Emir was comfortable straddling the Moroccan and American cultures, easily diving into one or the other and enjoying both depending on which country he was in. What nothing had told her was that he was a man she could not only admire but desire in a situation when all of that information was completely inappropriate.

"Good to meet you." Emir reached out a hand to Yuften, who took it with hesitation. Kate guessed the ritual was foreign to the smaller man.

Yuften took a step back, his hands linked behind the back of his navy blue windbreaker. He didn't look at Kate.

She took a step forward, ahead of Emir.

"Kate," she said and didn't offer her hand, knowing it would be an affront to what he believed.

He nodded and turned almost immediately as Emir took her hand and squeezed it before letting her go.

Yuften spoke, his back to them. "Follow me. My wife will show you where your sleeping mats are later. In the meantime, I believe you have questions," he said in English and in the precise tones of someone unused to using the language. He began to walk away, leaving them to follow as his jacket and matching blue, baggy pants flapped in the light breeze and he almost immediately seemed to fade into the night.

"I'm glad you made it when you did."

They could hear his voice but now he was only an outline in the darkness.

Kate looked at Emir. "What does he mean?" she whispered.

Before Emir could reply, their host answered the question for her.

"Their type isn't welcome here. Killers and the lot."

Time seemed to stand still and only one word echoed between them.

Killers.

Kate shook her head as she looked at Emir.

His hand went to his gun. "Whoever is responsible will die," he said through gritted teeth.

And she knew without question he spoke of Tara's kidnappers and that it was a promise he planned to keep.

Chapter Eleven

Five minutes later, as Emir and Kate followed their host, they found themselves climbing three sets of rough-hewn stairs that were surface-smooth and worn, and made more treacherous by the darkness. The steps ran between small box-like houses that looked very similar. Light, flickering from the entranceways of houses that seemed to close in on them, appeared to come from a candle or kerosene lantern, for it only faintly illuminated patches of the path.

To their left, an older man in a desert-sand-colored *aselham*, also called a djellaba, and the traditional, Berber, long-sleeved robe, led a donkey through a narrow alleyway that wound amid the squat houses and looked to go upward into the foothills and beyond.

It was pushing close to eleven o'clock and the hours before daylight stretched in front of them. The path became more narrow and steep. They navigated another set of primitive stairs as they moved higher, the darkness seeming to deepen and her breath catching as if it had become difficult to breathe. They stopped in front of one house. It was a sandstone-colored building, squat like the rest they'd passed in the last few minutes.

"Here," Yuften said as he stepped through the arched doorway. He motioned with a flick of his right hand that they should follow. Inside, the room was small with soft blue plastered walls and an arched ceiling that made the area feel slightly less cramped.

Three children stared at them. They sat shoulder-to-shoulder, their legs stretched out and their backs pressed to the wall. Kate doubted if the oldest could have been more than six. She guessed that they had been commanded to sit there, for it seemed too formal for a child. She also guessed that only the excitement of strangers visiting had them up this late.

A woman stood quietly just to the right of the doorway. Her hair was covered by a pink, embroidered veil that matched the gray and pink of her traditional robe. A strand of dark hair escaped the veil and her hands were clasped in front of her as she smiled, not looking at anyone but Yuften.

Yuften nodded to her, turned to Emir and said, "My wife, Saffiya." Then he gestured with a sweep of his arm to a solid mahogany table with stubby legs that raised it only a few feet off the floor. He took a place on one side, sitting on a thick emerald-green rug that covered much of the floor. It was clear that they were to follow.

In the corner Kate could see just one chair, a rocking chair, painted orange. She wondered how that cultural anomaly had come to be or how the clash of colors seemed vibrant rather than odd. She turned her attention quickly away, for none of that had any relevance to what they needed to know now. What they needed was information that would bring them to Tara before it was too late.

"You had questions," Yuften said, again in English.

Before they could answer, Saffiya entered the room with a silver teapot and poured them each a cup of tea.

The children giggled.

Yuften raised a hand in a flagging movement without turning around and the children were silent. On a ledge on either side of one wall, a trio of thick candles flickered, throwing shadows across the room.

"Atrar Tashfin—the man you asked about." Yuften looked at them. "He was killed at the Marrakech airport? I can't believe one of ours could be involved." He shook his head. "Of course, he'd been gone a long time, but his father…" He put his teacup down. "How did it happen?"

"A gunfight with the authorities," Emir said.

The explanation was a bit of a stretch, but they were here to get information not give it.

Yuften shook his head, a frown worrying his brow. "It's too bad." He looked at Emir. "Unless he was involved in your sister's kidnapping. Then he had it coming."

"Did you know him?" Emir asked.

Yuften shook his head. "He was here not quite yesterday. But I'd heard he'd gotten mixed up with others. Like I said earlier, thieves and murders." He shook his head. "It's all the same. One leads to the other."

Kate frowned at that as Yuften continued.

"We didn't talk long. But I have heard everything from the others he spoke to. He wanted nothing but money that we didn't have. He stole from me and others…"

"How much?" Emir asked.

"Whatever we could give, but I doubt if he got much." He shrugged. "No one is well off." When he told them the amount that had been stolen from his home, he was right. It was equal to about twenty American dollars.

Their host touched Saffiya's arm. She had sat beside him after the tea was poured. A silent exchange seemed to run between them and then Saffiya nodded and smiled. "Saffiya didn't like him," Yuften said with a nod to her.

He turned back to them. "He'd been away for a long time. Left for work before he was twenty and, when he returned, his parents were old and had died years before. He never came for their burials but he came now—for money." Yuften shrugged. "He was angry, especially after he'd been here for a few days. My boy said he shoved him aside when he ran too near. A few days ago, when he did leave, he wasn't alone. Four men arrived one day by Jeep—harassed some of our young girls—I had to step in. A few hours later I was glad to see they took him away with them."

Kate glanced at Emir. "Five," she murmured. That could mean there were only three left. Three men holding Tara. But, then again, it was only a guess.

Emir turned his attention to Yuften, who was now looking at his wife. Her lips were pinched.

"Saffiya thinks I should mind my own business.

But…" Yuften hesitated. "You have come for information and I have promised you that."

Saffiya shook her head, as if contradicting him, and leaned over to whisper something to him.

"She says that it could be one of our daughters, and that is true. Despite being Berber, he and the others are up to no good. There were rumors later that some of them had killed. Who or what, I don't know. But I fear for the girl."

"What are you saying?" Kate leaned forward, her shoulder brushing Emir's and heat seemed to radiate between them as neither moved, neither pulled away.

"They had a woman with them. Her head and face were covered by a veil."

He stopped and no one said anything, for a veil was not unusual.

"I didn't get close but she didn't seem to belong with them. Her clothes were different. She wasn't one of us. She—" he said with a nod over his shoulder to Saffiya who, despite having stood, hovered by his side, as if to ensure that everything he said met with her approval "—has an eye for clothes. 'City clothes' she called them."

It was clear that while Yuften was acting as if he was in charge of the household, Saffiya was the silent voice of command in this house. She nodded, her eyes gleaming with approval.

Kate leaned forward, her attention on their host. "How did they act toward her?"

Yuften frowned. "I don't know what you mean." He turned to Emir. "They left almost immediately. I didn't have a good feeling about it, but there was nothing illegal, nothing…"

"Did the woman with them seem upset or distressed?" Kate asked.

Yuften shook his head and was about to speak when Saffiya interrupted him.

"This. Here." Her English was fractured and unsure. "She said nothing but…" Saffiya pulled a colorful, beaded bracelet from her pocket. The bracelet was thin, the beads small, a combination of yellow, emerald-green and red, delicate and obviously old. "She dropped." She whispered something to Yuften, who nodded.

"The woman tossed the bracelet to her."

The expression on Emir's face would have frightened Kate if she hadn't come to know him in the intense hours they'd been together. His lips were tight and his dark eyes seemed to gleam with anger.

Yuften's wife nodded as she clasped her hands and moved closer to him.

"It belonged to Tara," Emir said, his lips tightening and his dark eyes pools of pain as he sat still for a minute. No one spoke. Finally he reached to take the bracelet. "She's worn that bracelet since the day she received it. It was our mother's and Tara took it after she died. It was small enough, the strand of beads, to go with any other piece of jewelry. She never took it off. I normally wouldn't remember such a thing but Tara spoke of it often. She always said how it reminded her of Mother. It was as if in doing so she was making sure not just we, but she, never forgot." He shook his head. "As if I ever could."

"Do you know what direction they went?" Kate stepped in, purposely changing the subject as she sensed that what Emir had just heard and then revealed had been emotionally overwhelming.

"South. I heard one of them mention Ajeddig as a place they were going to. They did not know I was close," Yuften said.

Saffiya nodded.

"It means nothing to me. I know no one and nothing of that name." He shrugged. "Flower. What is that?"

A place name again was the first thought that ran through Kate's mind for the word was the same one that Tara's guard, Ahmed, had spoken the last time he'd been able to reveal anything. And yet the map in the plane had revealed nothing. She needed to look at it again. There had to have been something she missed.

"We need the map," she said.

"Come—" Saffiya gestured "—we have books."

Kate followed her as she moved into a smaller room behind the cooking area. Her slim hands lifted the edge of her traditional robe that flowed elegantly around her but threatened to dust the rough cobbles as she walked. Her yellow flip-flops snapped against the stone floor, seeming to keep time as she led Kate up a number of stairs at the back of the room and into another small room. This room seemed to be apart from the rest of the house and held two shelves, each filled with rows of books.

Kate looked around. She hadn't been expecting this. Of the few Berber homes she'd visited, none had had a room dedicated to books. But then, none had been as isolated as this. And even though there were only two shelves that were half the length of the wall they were attached to, it was still unique. In one corner was a wooden school desk similar to any that might be seen in a grade-school classroom in early twentieth-century America. On top of the desk was a metal can full of pens and pencils.

"You teach your children?"

Saffiya nodded with a smile and then pointed to the shelf. "Map," she said as she pulled out an oversize book with no dust jacket and a faded red cover.

"Thank you." Kate took the atlas but continued to scan the shelf. Like the atlas, the remaining books were mainly dust-jacket free with faded red and brown covers, each with a film of dust, despite the claims of home-schooling.

Saffiya backed up then turned and went out the door.

Kate glanced over the titles and realized that the majority of the books weren't in English and that the few that were, were history books. As she took a step back, she instinctively felt like she was no longer alone. She turned to see Emir regarding her solemnly from the doorway.

"Old schoolbooks will get us nowhere," he said.

"I'm not so sure," she said.

She opened the atlas, hoping she could find something, that the promise of a direction would somehow ease his worry, and knowing that nothing short of finding his sister ever could.

"Nineteen-oh-one," she murmured. She flipped the pages slowly and then stopped. "Africa." She walked over to the desk, where she put the open atlas down. She gingerly turned a page, exposing another seemingly frail, yellowed page to the flickering light of the candle Saffiya had left for her.

"Kate, the light is bad, the book is old, there's nothing."

Emir's hands were on her shoulders as he turned her around. She held back a shiver of pleasure as his touch evoked a memory of the earlier kiss and the truth that she wanted so much more.

"And we have nothing but time, at least tonight," she said, her voice low and husky. "Bear with me."

"I've never seen anyone so resolved," he said as his thumb skimmed along her cheek, his touch like a caress.

"Haven't you?" she replied as she met his ebony eyes with all the resolve she was feeling. Time's short but…" Her gaze went around the room. "We have no time to waste."

Chapter Twelve

Despite her earlier words, minutes passed.

Kate had taken a seat at the small desk while Emir had taken a position leaning against the wall. Her long legs were stretched out sideways, her body twisted as she bent over the book. The smell of pipe smoke wove into the room from the room below. The low murmur of voices and the high-pitched laugh of a child broke the quiet.

Another minute went by and then two before Kate turned and smiled at him and something caught in his chest. The sight of her dogged persistence made him think that anything was possible, that between the two of them they would find Tara.

Now she looked up with a troubled expression. "I think I've found it." She stood, the atlas in her hands.

He came over to her. His hands covered hers as he reached to take the atlas from her. The heat from her hands reminded him of how she'd felt in his arms, how he wanted her there again.

"No," she said, pulling the book back. "Let me show you."

His gaze followed her finger as she pointed to the oasis she was talking about.

She looked at him with the excitement of discovery in her eyes and something else he couldn't name. And the scent of her, coconut and something unidentifiable but equally enticing, would be his undoing as it seemed to call to him. He needed to focus.

"Emir?"

Her voice brought him back, for it was soft and husky, and oddly commanding.

"I think my hunch was right. Ajeddig is the name of an oasis in 1901. I don't remember seeing any such place on the current map, but here it's clear."

"An extinct oasis?" His gaze clashed with hers. It wasn't unheard of—water disappeared and, with it, the plants, animals and the people.

"What if there was still water left, not enough for a community but for a few people?" The question she posed hung for a moment between them. Outside the room, they could hear the low voices of their hosts.

"Wouldn't others know of it?"

"Not necessarily, not if it was obscure, hidden." She ran a finger over the area she'd been studying as if mapping their route. "Or maybe so small as to be of little interest."

He thought of the possibility she'd raised, but there were still so many unknowns. "We could drive miles out of our way in order to find out there's nothing. We could…"

"It used to be a good-size community from the looks of it. A village, anyway—a hundred people, roughly, on a guess." She spoke quickly, clearly excited by the discovery. "What better place to hide than an oasis that everyone believes no longer exists?"

She looked up at him and he leaned down and met her halfway. His lips roved over hers as he drew her into his arms. Her softness pressed against him, making him want so much more. Her mouth opened, inviting more. She was sweet and hot and... He pulled back. The last thing they needed was to be discovered, an unmarried couple making out in their host's library.

"I'm sorry," he said as he moved away from her.

"You'd better not be," she whispered huskily.

"Come here," she said, the atlas in her hands, and when he was again beside her she showed him something else that excited them both. "Two hundred miles east of here, but in the same direction as our extinct oasis. It can't be a coincidence."

"El Dewar," he said with a frown, trying not to notice the smell of her or the feel of her shoulder rubbing against his arm. It was as though fear and anger had merged with passion and become an unstoppable comet. He wanted to find his sister, kill her kidnappers and make love to Kate, and not necessarily in that order. He took her hand with his as he met her eyes. "Straight through the Sahara. There are no roads."

"Emir," she said in a soft tone, lower than normal, and one that hinted at other things. But what she had to say was all business. "Looking at this map, where the oasis is situated, if you wanted to go there, you'd have to drive through El Dewar or, at the least, near it. It's a tough drive, but we knew this wasn't going to be easy. I think we stop at El Dewar tomorrow, ask a few questions." Her eyes sparkled with excitement. "Maybe someone knows something."

Emir's pulse leaped at the possibilities.

But as he looked more closely at the landscape revealed on the old atlas, his heart sank. If this was where they had Tara, they were well defended. "If this is right—they'd be backing an almost-impermeable approach." His thumb traced the way the map outlined rises of rock and cliff that wound in a horseshoe around what had once been a desert paradise. "It would be almost impossible to get to them, sneak in, without climbing the hills behind them."

"Difficult," Kate corrected, "not impossible. I'm betting we could work our way in through the rock, over the hills—whatever. There's got to be a way. If, of course, this theory is even right."

Emir put his hands on her shoulders and kissed her. As his tongue met hers and her breasts pressed against him, it seemed like time stood still. But it was only seconds before he released her and before they took the atlas to show their host to ask him about the existence of the oasis.

"It has been uninhabited since before the days of my grandfather. Many of them moved here when it dried up. They hoped to get away from the desert," Yuften said solemnly. "I did not remember the name but the location is unforgettable."

Hours later they tried to get some sleep.

For Emir, it was impossible, for he was more aware of Kate with every second he spent in her presence.

He'd kissed her one too many times when he shouldn't have kissed her at all. Maybe if he hadn't, he wouldn't want her like he'd never wanted another woman. Her mat was feet from his and a curtain divider away, and it didn't matter.

The sound of her soft breathing through the remaining hours of the night had driven him crazy. Each toss and turn, every sound, alerted him to her nearness. The cool desert air had chilled him. He'd wondered if she was cold. But there was nothing he could offer her, nothing except his own body heat, and that was unacceptable, but only because of their host. She was too near and yet too far. Worry for Tara, desire for Kate—the torrent of emotion caused the earlier headache to return, but again even the usual two aspirins were unable to stop the pounding as sunlight began to threaten the night.

They were up and preparing to leave as the sun streaked pink across the eastern sky.

TARA SHIFTED. She had to use the facilities in the worst way. She never thought an everyday necessity that one usually didn't pay much attention to would become her Achilles' heel. She squirmed, shifting onto her side, taking the pressure off her full bladder. She couldn't risk drawing attention to herself. She'd seen how her captors had looked at her as the sun rose. She'd been in this hell for over twenty-four hours.

"Find me Emir, please," she whispered to the brother who, of all of them, had been her ultimate protector, even against the gentle teasing of her other brothers. He had always stood up for her. All her brothers were her heroes, but Emir stood out among even them. Maybe because he was the eldest. It didn't matter why. What mattered was that she needed him. She'd been wrong and she'd do anything to undo what she'd done, but that was impossible, she knew that. She prayed her repentance would be enough.

She pulled her knees up tight and took a deep breath, but it didn't help. Her tormentor was heading her way. His advances had become more and more intimate and she knew that the last time she'd been lucky.

She knew him and yet he was like a stranger, a frightening stranger. The man she remembered had been an average-size man with a glint to his dark eyes that indicated he loved a joke. And she'd told him many, at least when she'd been younger, before tragedy had struck.

Now he was lean to the point of skinny and the planes of his face were rough, wrinkled and almost feral. And then there was the scar. It wasn't the horrid scar that disturbed her most, but more the way those dark eyes skimmed over her in an almost hungry way that made her draw back and pull her knees even closer to her chest as if that would somehow protect her.

"What do you want?" she asked and realized that she might know exactly what he wanted. She could see the lust in his eyes. There was a time when she couldn't imagine him looking at her like that and, in fact, in all her life he never had. But he didn't always see her as Tara anymore. There were times when he had, briefly, in the beginning. She'd pointed out who she was once, but she now had a bruise on her cheekbone that ached when she touched it, to remind her to not do that again.

"I've wanted you for so long and yet you only looked at him." He frowned as his knuckle skimmed her cheek.

Who? she thought. She tried to think clearly through the confusion of his words.

"Who?" she whispered. She was both scared to engage and scared to not know what he was speaking of.

He cursed and raised his clenched fist.

She couldn't back down. She fought not to do just that.

"Your husband, of course. Who else?" He relaxed his fist and ran his hand through his grizzled, uncombed hair. He looked away from her and then turned back, a hard look in his eyes. "How did this happen?" he asked. His eyes were now, seconds later, reflecting genuine concern as he looked at the bruise on her cheekbone. It was as if he could not remember his actions from one moment to the next.

Tara fought with her control but it was so difficult to not pull away. She couldn't, not yet.

"I would have given you everything," he said, his voice soft and yet oddly hoarse. There was an edge to it that hadn't been there before. "But, no, you wanted Ruhul."

Was it possible? Ruhul Al-Nassar? Her father? Who did he think she was? Her heart was pounding so hard that she could barely think. But she knew in her gut it was critical that she was amiable and went along with whatever insane belief he had.

"Why do you shrink from me?"

She looked up at him with every ounce of willpower she had and smiled, hoping it was sweet and innocent, as her insides clenched so tight they hurt.

"I've wanted you for so long, Raja," he said gently, as if repetition would somehow get him what he wanted.

It didn't matter who she was. In the last few hours a new horror had been foisted on her. It was clear he was confused, at best. At worst, insane. She only wanted to curl up at the horror of it all. But she knew that wouldn't save her. She had to act out his obvious delusion. If he believed her to be her mother, then that was who she would be. Tara knew it was a survival tactic on her part. She'd learned that and more in a number of psychology classes.

It was a horrible role to play, a terrible thing to contemplate. She wasn't her mother.

Tara tried not to show her disgust or fear as his hand continued to stroke her cheek. She had to stop this before it was unstoppable, for he was quick this time and his hand had dropped from her cheek and was inside her blouse, under her bra. It was clear what he wanted and that this time he might not be ready to wait.

Fear combined with her full bladder and suddenly she couldn't control either. She peed her pants.

She saw his eyes look downward to the stream of urine pooling around her and saw the look of disgust on his face. He stood, took two steps back and strode back to the others.

For the first time since her horror began, Tara had the upper hand.

Hopefully her brothers would find her before her time ran out.

Chapter Thirteen

They were heading south and east with a slight wind that was causing the unseasonal light rain to lash against the windshield, turning the sand hitting the glass into a paste that slid along the window, obscuring the view. The Jeep's wipers beat a losing rhythm that wasn't enough to keep the window clear. They'd had to stop frequently to clear the clogged wipers.

The charts Kate had checked on her flight to Morocco had indicated the local weather had been unpredictable for the last few weeks. Now, that same unpredictability, the unseasonal and unusual rain, was making for slow going, and the abnormally cool daytime temperature wasn't helping.

"You're okay?" he asked. His hand ran along her wrist and the heat that ran through her at his touch made her shiver.

"Fine." She nodded, pulling her hand free and pushing a strand of hair back. It didn't help. Her nerves were on edge—and not because of the assignment but because of his nearness, because of what he made her feel. It wasn't how it was supposed to be and yet that awareness had been between them from the beginning.

The Jeep rocked as Emir made a slight turn to the right, adjusting for the ridges in the sand and the breeze that was now a buffeting wind. The vehicle slid as the tires kicked up sand chewed out of the ruts it was creating.

Her finger was on the map, marking where they were and where they were going. The journey had been slow. They'd had to adjust their direction a number of times. She reached for the grab bar with her right hand as the Jeep's back tires spun and for a moment it seemed like they might get stuck in the middle of nowhere.

She looked at the compass. They were going by latitude and longitude. It was a get-back-to-basics way to travel. Even the Jeep was basic, built for this type of expedition without tracking or mapping. It reminded her how easy Google Maps had made everything.

She glanced at Emir and saw the brutal way he clasped the vehicle's steering wheel, as if it were someone's neck.

They drove in silence and yet with the promise of hope between them.

The landscape began to change as another hour ticked by. Now the flat sand and occasional rolling dunes had become steeper and were framed by larger ridges that signaled imminent foothills. The rain was gone and the desert looked like it always had—clearly, like there'd been no rain in months.

"We're getting close," Kate said. "Maybe twenty

miles from El Dewar." So far they'd made poor time, a combination of both the terrain and the weather. "No one knows the desert like the Berbers," she added as Emir navigated a small dune. "Hopefully they know something more at El Dewar that can add to what we learned at Kaher."

"I'm betting that it won't be so much a matter of them knowing but of them telling us," he said.

The side windows were closed but still the sand seemed to seep in. She pulled a tissue from the packet on the dash and wiped the corners of her eyes.

His hands tightened on the wheel as the front tires began to dig into the sand. He turned to the right and she knew he was hoping to veer out of the rut before they got stuck.

The consistency of the sand was subject to change and dependent on so many things. In an odd way, like snow. It would take all his focus to drive and navigate the unstable conditions. The desert was a challenge to drive at any time and now, with worry, little sleep and what might be a brewing storm, it was even more so.

She was relieved as the vehicle again gained traction, but ahead of them was a new difficulty. A tall bank of sand dunes stretched out on either side, with no end in sight, and blocked much of the horizon.

"In my youth we used to drive the dunes for fun," he said, looking at her with concern. "We were lucky." Minutes later his mouth tightened as he looked ahead.

"What's wrong?" Kate asked and frowned at the dunes. "Can we go around?"

"Possibly," he said. "But that could set us back hours."

"Not an option."

"I agree, but these dunes aren't going to be a cake-walk," he said. "They're whaleback dunes."

They both knew what that meant. Whaleback dunes were dunes whose front incline was hard from being buffeted by the wind. It was the back half that could pose a problem. Depending on the direction of the wind, the sand could be crumbly and difficult to navigate.

He glanced at her. "You ready to do this?"

"I've been in since the beginning," she said simply.

And with a slight smile that was more a tightening of his full lips, he slowed the Jeep. "When we reach them, watch the horizon, if it seems quite sharp at the top, then we have problems on the other side," he said.

And she knew he meant there was the possibility of soft sand, softer than they had traveled through, and the type that could easily cause a rollover. The hope was that the sand on the other side of the dune was hard. Based on the way the wind had been buffeting them, she was sure they had a good chance of getting the latter.

He squeezed her hand and she looked down, aware of how large his hands were and, despite the gentle touch, how strong.

She pulled her hand from beneath his when all she wanted to do was to fold into his arms. There was no time for such thoughts. She forced her mind to the moment, to the challenge ahead of them.

"Let's do this," she said as if there was some chance that he wouldn't. "I'm fine," she added at the look of concern he gave her.

"You're more than fine," he said, turning his attention to the bank of dunes.

They eased over the dunes with little trouble, reaching the other side and finding the sand hard, buffeted by desert winds.

"Easier than we thought," he said.

She nodded and let go of the grab bar. It was easy driving now compared to where they had just come from. She still couldn't believe that finding Tara might be as easy as an ancient atlas and the words spoken by a dying man.

"I can see it," she said. "El Dewar."

He gripped the wheel as they recognized the first sign of something other than the endless sea of sand. A bit of green. An oasis. The place his parents had visited with Tara and Faisal on the last trip any of them had taken as a family before tragedy had intervened and changed the course of all their lives.

His lips tightened and she bet he was thinking of all that had transpired and of the urgency that felt almost crushing.

"The summer vacation we think she was referencing in that video," Kate said.

He gave a brief nod as the Jeep bounced through a sand-packed gulley that seemed to run diagonally for a few minutes before they climbed to the top and the terrain became level again.

They drove in silence now, as they could see the oasis. It was small, as was the village it supported, and because of its isolation, she imagined that it likely saw few strangers. The usual sandstone-colored, square buildings huddled close together as if trying to escape the inhospitable desert.

Within minutes they were there.

As they got out of the Jeep, Kate was almost blinded by the sun as it reached its peak in the midday sky. But, still, it was cooler than usual for the time of year. She folded her arms across her chest as a cool breeze buffeted her, the palm trees rustling ahead of them. The fronds, moving back and forth in the center of the village, seemed, in an odd way, to almost welcome them.

A man in a fawn-colored *aselham*, the long robe skimming the tops of his feet as his sandals whispered quietly on the path that was hard-packed sand, walked past, continuing to stare as he moved. Farther away a man was filling a metal trough with water as two camels waited, reins dangling on the ground. A woman with a basket full of vegetables and a toddler clinging to her robe made her way into the center of the village, glancing back at them once and then continuing on her way. A group of women watched them and an old man smoking a cigarette was avidly following their progress. Everyone they'd seen was dressed in the traditional Berber *aselham*.

"Emir Al-Nassar," Emir said, holding out his hand as a man in fawn-colored robes approached.

"Aqil," the man returned with a slight nod of his head.

Emir didn't introduce Kate and, unlike the last village, she didn't volunteer. They needed information and shaking up the local culture in regard to their views on women wasn't going to do it.

Still, she knew Emir could feel her eyes on him. She was letting him take the lead and honoring the customs of the community.

"I heard about your sister only this morning," Aqil said in careful English. "Our internet is spotty. But, as you know, your family is well known." He shrugged as the wind tugged at his clothes. He ran a hand through his gray-speckled beard. "We were lucky to have heard when we did. The wind is picking up. I doubt if we'll get a connection again today or even in the next few days. That's how it works."

"I know you usually have your ear to the ground out here," Emir said.

Aqil's attention went to Kate and he frowned.

"We can talk alone," Emir said as he followed Aqil's gaze. "Stay here," he said almost gruffly to Kate.

The command rankled her but it was Berber land and their rules. But there was one other thing she knew. It wasn't just the men who were privy to things in this isolated village; the women had a key role in society in a different way than they were used to in the West or even in the city. Knowing that, hopefully between them they would learn something.

Emir looked at her like he wanted to smile at her but didn't. Instead he let the amused smile on her face and her silence sit unacknowledged between them. But Aqil's attention had turned to a man who had just approached and Emir took the opportunity to address her.

"You'll be all right?" he asked in an undertone.

"I'll be all right," she said, although for the first time she felt slightly overwhelmed. No matter how much she'd studied, no matter her experience in Morocco, on this small tract of land they were thrown back in time and place and to the reality that she was a blond-haired American woman in Western clothing. She didn't fit in.

"Speak to the elders first," he advised and motioned to an elderly woman squatting beside an open fire. "If they accept you, the others may, too." He put a hand on her shoulder. "Kate?"

She nodded. "I'm fine." But despite her words she still felt unsure and out of her element.

She took a step away as the man who had first greeted Emir came up to him.

"Come," Aqil said as he began to lead Emir. His pace fast despite his short stature. He glanced behind as he talked, as if to ensure that Emir was indeed following him.

EMIR FOLLOWED WITH one last glance and a nod to Kate as his host led him along a beaten sand path that served as a road.

A group of small boys tossed a ball back and forth and a group of women were carrying on what seemed to be a lighthearted conversation as two of them laughed. But as the men approached, they quieted and stared.

Aqil stopped in front of a one-story, square, sandstone-colored building no different than any of the others. Inside, as in the previous home they had visited, furnishings were sparse. What was different this time was that what was there was of high quality. There was an ebony, pearl-inlaid hutch and gold-stamped figurines on various shelves throughout the room, indicating this village was doing well.

Emir removed his shoes and walked barefoot over a rug so thick he seemed to sink as he walked across it. This one was ruby red and in the middle sat an intricately carved ironwood table. A trio of men sat around the table, each with a long, thin, metal smoking stick. The smell of tobacco wove through the air and was strangely pleasant, unlike the acrid scent of cigarettes at home. Here it was a different smell, warmer, in a pleasant, rather earthy kind of way that blended with the smell of cinnamon and jasmine sifting through the air from a number of incense pots set in various corners.

He turned his attention to the man in the traditional long robe in front of them who had just joined Aqil. Unlike his first host, this man clearly wasn't interested in introductions.

"I wish we had met under better circumstances," the man said, his dark brows furrowed.

"The men you seek." He looked at Emir with a scowl that deepened, as if challenging him to contradict him. "Their group was seen not forty-eight hours ago heading west." He took a drag from his pipe, blew out a thin stream of smoke and continued. "They didn't stop for water nor did they enter our village."

Emir knew that piece of information was critical. Water was vital. No one would not stop for water in the desert when it was available, no matter if they carried a supply or not. Two scenarios played in his mind—they were heading to a place they knew had water that was relatively close, and had enough water to get there—

an oasis with enough water to keep their small group going or…someone here had met them with a supply.

"No one here helped them, or had any contact," the man said, as if he'd read Emir's mind. "And there's nothing nearby."

"Was there…?"

"There's nothing more," the man said and turned away from Emir. He whispered a few words to Aqil, making it clear from his actions and poise that he was a leader within the village.

Emir straightened. He knew he'd been dismissed, that there was nothing further to be learned in this room.

Chapter Fourteen

Left alone, Kate felt conspicuous and even more out of place. She tried to feign disinterest while furtively watching everything and everyone around her. It was impossible. She was a stranger, a foreigner in their midst, and she was center stage.

The children watched her curiously. One small boy came up to her and poked the back of her hand before giggling and taking a step back. He looked up at her. His dark, curly hair glistened in the sun as his curious brown eyes locked to hers. He opened his hand and held out a blue rubber ball.

"Are you going to play catch?" she said in Berber, but the boy only closed his hand, giggled and ran away. She was alone again, a curiosity in their midst. She saw a woman looking at her from her place by a pot over a cooking fire. Kate hesitated only a second before going over to her for she was the woman Emir had suggested she approach first.

"May I?" she asked, motioning to the stool. While she wasn't completely fluent in the language, she had a familiarity she'd gained through her time in the Middle East as a child with her parents when her father had worked for the American Embassy in Morocco, and again through her studies and her brief time as an exchange student.

The woman looked at her oddly. Her skin was a beautiful coffee color that glowed despite her wrinkles and advanced age. A black scarf with white embroidery partially covered her hair. Then she smiled and revealed missing teeth. She motioned for Kate to sit beside her. Her knotted fingers were quick and limber as she pinched spices from numerous tins beside her and stirred them into the pot. Kate had no idea what she was making but her stomach rumbled at the heady scent of the combined spices.

She glanced around. To her left, a group of women sat quietly watching her as they had since she'd arrived. The children played ball. The man had left with his two camels. Everything else remained the same. But something had changed. What?

Kate had never felt so out of place in her life. Despite everything she had studied, her familiarity with language and all her visits to Morocco, here she was the foreigner, the oddity with no commonality. Worse, this was the one language where she was not fluent, she could understand most of it, speak roughly but that was it. She looked back, searching for Emir, but there was no sign of him.

"Come." A woman in a mauve-and-gold *aselham*, the hood over her head so that her forehead was covered, approached and beckoned, motioning with one hand. What Kate could see of her face and dark hair revealed a woman in her early forties with a smooth, sun-bronzed face and eyes that seemed dark, unfathomable, as if they were full of secrets.

Intrigued, she followed the woman as she skirted behind the houses to a smaller building made of the same sandstone. A brown curtain served as a door.

Kate had to bend to follow the woman through the doorway. Inside was another woman. This one was younger and dressed similarly, except her *aselham* was worn with a matching veil that was gray with gold trim. A gold tassel dangled from either side of her veil. An older woman in a cream-colored *aselham* that showed the tops of a pair of black, high-heeled boots, her long gray hair uncovered, brought her a cup of tea. Kate knew the veil was not a cultural necessity among the Berbers but more than likely worn for protection from the unseasonable weather.

She took the tea. The cup and saucer was bone china like any you'd get at home and unlike the customary Berber cup that had no handles. She sank onto the rug that covered the floor, watched the others and emulated what they did. She held the cup with both hands, not the usual way to hold what seemed a traditional teacup. Despite her studies and everything she knew about Morocco and the Middle East, she'd never seen a tribe such as this that seemed to dance between traditional customs and ones that, she guessed, weren't acquired from popular culture but distinctly their own.

"They won't tell him the truth," the younger woman said in a soft voice. "He was paid too well."

The oldest of them clicked her tongue, an oddly loud

sound in the ensuing silence. She held up her hand. "Enough of such talk."

"It's true," the younger woman persisted. "They will not say anything."

Kate put her cup down and met the older woman's eyes. She took a chance that these women knew why they were here and they might very well know where Tara was. "Sheikka Tahriha Al-Nassar may die if we don't find her soon."

Silence hung within the room for what seemed like minutes and might have only been seconds.

Finally the woman who had led her there said, "I will say what I know but you are to tell no one what has been said within these walls until you leave this village." Her gaze was intense, serious. "This is between us. The women here and no more."

"I promise," Kate said sincerely.

"I tell you this. I will breach the will of our men only because one of our sisters is in danger," she said. The words were spoken in careful and precise English and because of that they seemed even more ominous.

Kate held back a shiver.

The woman squatted beside Kate and pulled her veil back, revealing fresh, clear skin that was much more youthful than Kate had imagined without the veil casting shadows along the sides of her face.

As she listened, Kate could feel the tension tightening in her gut and the implications of it all made her want to cry for Emir, for his family. But, first, she knew that the man who was intent on destroying the house of Al-Nassar must be stopped.

"Do you know where they were going?" Kate asked.

"No." She hung her head but when she looked up and her lips were set as if she'd made a decision. "That is all."

Kate nodded and stood.

"Thank you," she said. She wanted to shake the woman's hand but she knew that wouldn't be acceptable.

She was surprised when the woman offered her own hand. They shook and, with a nod, the woman led her outside before she disappeared down a narrow break between dwellings.

Where the woman had gone there was now only a goat, who lifted his head from a pail from which he was placidly eating and then turned back to his food as if whatever was going on was of little interest to him. Two children chased past her, their childish laughter no different from children anywhere, as dust rose up under their bare feet and the sun beat down on her as if nothing was wrong. Just behind them a shadow drifted between the buildings and she saw a young man, bearded, dressed in a brown robe. Their eyes met as if he were analyzing her. Then, as if she wasn't supposed to see him, he too disappeared.

She turned as a shudder ran through her, a combination of dread and determination. They'd find Sheikka Tahriha if it was the last thing she did. Despite everything, and maybe because of everything she'd learned, she had the feeling she was no longer welcome. She felt like there were eyes watching her. She needed to find Emir so they could get out of here—now.

Chapter Fifteen

"Emir!" Kate's voice called from behind him.

He turned from his conversation with one of the older men to see her hurrying toward him, her face pale, her hair escaping the ponytail, as usual.

A couple of small girls shadowed her footsteps, imitating her walk and her voice as they giggled. She looked back at them and then at Emir with a pained expression. He'd never seen her look so uncomfortable, so out of place.

She took his arm, her eyes pleading. "Let's go," she whispered.

He nodded at her. They were done here.

But there was something in her voice that said there was more.

"What's going on Kate?" he asked as they approached the Jeep parked just outside the oasis. He looked around. They were alone.

"Kate?"

She turned and, just like that, he felt like he was drowning in the rich blue of her eyes. They glistened with excitement, tears—he wasn't sure what. He held himself back from doing what he ached to do—take her in his arms. They might be alone but there still could be eyes that watched them and he wanted to get moving, they both did, even though it was clear something was troubling her.

He had the Jeep in gear and the village was far behind them before he asked, "What is it?"

"You may know one of the men who took Tara," she said.

The husky tone in her voice would have been alluring at another time. Again, the thought leaped at him out of nowhere, broadsiding him, enraging him with its lack of control.

"At least, that's what the woman I spoke to implied. But more than that, he knew your parents," she went on before he could say anything. "Maybe he worked for you. I don't know."

Shock ran through Emir and left him momentarily speechless.

"That's impossible," he growled. It implied betrayal of the worst kind. His head pounded and dread settled through him as if deep in his core he realized that, despite all their precautions, just like Tara's abduction, what she said was very possible.

"Is it?"

"That's crazy. We screened all our employees. They're all loyal, trustworthy, even friends." He couldn't believe it, wouldn't. In that moment he only wanted to fight the implication with everything in him.

"I know you ran a check through all the past and current employees. But, Emir, it's possible. What I find interesting is that it hasn't happened sooner. People envy wealth like yours—even those who call themselves friend."

"Who are you talking about?"

"While you were with the men, a woman took me aside. She told me about a man who had visited the village six years ago. He'd stopped for water and her husband had offered him a smoke and food. Her husband knew the man's family—they had once been from that tribe. She could only say that he was middle-aged, Arabic, and attractive in a tired kind of way. He said at the time, that the House of Al-Nassar was cursed. She wasn't privy to everything he said but she saw money change hands for their silence. What she remembers most is how he spoke with an almost rabid hatred of the House of Al-Nassar and kept repeating how someday he would bring it down. She remembers the name Raja."

"My mother's name!" The Jeep lurched and swerved.

She looked at him with concern in her eyes before continuing. "At the time she forgot about it, as much of what she'd heard made no sense. She'd thought it the crazy ranting of a nut. She'd left it up to the men to handle and, since her husband passed, she'd long forgotten about it until today. Your surname reminded her. In fact—"

The satellite phone rang, interrupting her and startling them both.

"Yeah?" Emir answered. He gripped the phone like he might never let it go. "What do you have, Zaf?" he asked as he stopped the Jeep.

"I've gone through all the past employees back five years," Zafir said.

"Not you, too." But Emir knew it was necessary. He'd known this situation had always been possible. But even the possibility had never stopped him from caring for the people he hired. Many of them had worked for his family for years. His employees were friends and sometimes even family. He couldn't imagine now—or more aptly didn't want to consider—that anyone he cared about would threaten him or anyone he loved.

"No matches," Zafir went on, unaware of his thoughts. "Not that we expected there would be."

Emir's knuckles were white.

Kate's hand settled on his wrist as if, again, that would somehow calm him. Oddly, it did, but the feel of her skin on his did other things, too, things that had no place there or with the shock of what she'd implied, still so fresh. He shook her hand off, concentrating on his phone call. But a glance at her face made him wish he hadn't done so, so thoughtlessly.

"I don't know, Zaf. And, as far as our current employees? There's no one working for us with a grudge. No one in need of money—at least, not to that extent. They're loyal to a fault. I don't know where else to take this."

Emir could feel Kate's eyes still on him.

"Just a moment."

"Nothing turned up. He went back five years," he said to Kate. Unfortunately, with the satellite phone there

was no ability to put it on speaker, so he had to juggle
two conversations and relay between Zafir and Kate.

"Can he take it back another five? We need to talk…
can you call him back?" she asked.

"You know there's no guarantee of a signal," he reminded her.

She nodded. "All right." Her lips thinned as if it
pained her to say the next words. "When was your parents' accident?"

Emir frowned. It was a subject that was too painful
to talk about and, after the police report had been filed,
the incident had been filed in his own mind, as well.
"Over six years ago." His gut clenched. He didn't like
where this was going, didn't know if he wanted to hear
it, but he had no choice. Tara's life depended on him.

"But when, exactly, and who was with them?"

"Why, Kate?"

"It wasn't the only time that man was there, at the
village. He was there the year of the accident and he was
there recently. And this time she heard his first name."

"Damn it, Kate, who was he?"

"Ed."

The barren reaches of desert stretched in front of
them and it was only that that kept his outrage contained. He didn't look in the rearview mirror, either, for
behind them was the place that had moved them to a
truth he feared might change everything he thought he
knew. He took a breath and then glanced at her.

"What's going on?" he heard Zafir ask. "K.J. was
asking about the accident?"

"Hang on, Zaf," he said into the phone.

"Get Zafir to check who was on staff the year of your parents' accident and also if there was anyone with them, or who they had contact with that day." She frowned. "I know some of that will be impossible to recollect, but if there was someone with them…"

"Ed," Emir said with no hesitation. "Their bodyguard. Simohamed Khain. We called him Ed," he said. "And the driver, of course. Ed was the only survivor," he said gravely.

Kate could see that his mind was there, in that moment on that fateful day when he'd learned his parents' fate and when everything had changed for him and his siblings.

"Run a check on Ed," she said.

He nodded grimly, his jaw tense and his dark eyes narrowed. "Zaf, did you hear?" Emir asked his brother.

"I'm missing most of this and I think it's a waste of time, Em."

"Yeah, well, she's right. We can't afford to toss anything out at this point. Call as soon as you know something," Emir said before he clicked off.

He swung around to face Kate. "What are you suggesting?"

"It's not what I was suggesting," she said. "It was what I was told."

"You think the accident that killed my parents was not accidental at all—is that what you're implying?"

"I don't know," she replied.

His jaw tightened. "It's one thing to have Zaf do a search, but to think a man who was like a brother to my father…on the basis of a name similarity."

"Wait. There's more." She turned away, likely gathering her thoughts before facing him, pain obvious in her eyes.

He didn't want her sympathy and he didn't want to hear what she had to say, either, for he knew that whatever it was might be a betrayal from which his family would never recover. He prayed he was wrong.

"So you think—"

"Wait." She held up her hand. "The woman in El Dewar said that the last time he visited, a few months ago, there was something new, a burn down the entire left side of his face." She looked at him with eyes full of compassion that almost did him in. "That's not all. She was wearing a bracelet that looked very much like the one you said Tara had inherited from your mother."

It was like he'd been sucker punched.

"I'm sorry, Emir."

He didn't want her apology. He didn't want to look at the sympathy in her eyes. He wanted to take her into his arms and make her stop talking, make her stop causing him to face possibilities that threatened everything he believed.

"There were two," he murmured. "I thought the second was destroyed in the accident. In fact, until now, I'd forgotten about it." He looked away. When he turned back to face her, he was more determined than ever to make the men who had taken Tara pay. "The woman you spoke to…"

She nodded. "Had what I think is the second bracelet. When I noticed the similarity, I asked her where she got it. She said their visitor had dropped it, and by the time she found it, he was gone. I'm almost positive it's a match." She stopped, concern on her face.

Emir's right hand was clenched in a fist. "Ed's face on the left side was burned pretty badly. He said he struggled to open Mother's door—to get her out."

"My informant was pretty sure it was a burn scar. She said she'd seen plenty in the village from the cooking pots and such."

"The woman heard him talking to himself as he was preparing to leave. She said that she would always remember the words, for they were spoken with hatred. She said he was muttering that he would make the sheikka pay."

"Make her pay? What had Tara done to him?"

"Was it Tara he was referring to?"

Shock rolled through him at what she might be implying. It made no sense. "Who else would he mean?"

She shrugged. "You said he tried to get your mother free from the vehicle. Why not your father? Why didn't he mention him? Attempt to save him?"

"What are you saying?"

"I'm not sure. I…"

"Kate…" He could hear his heart beat in anticipation of what she might say next. He wanted to put his hand over her mouth and not allow her to say the words he sensed would change everything he thought he knew.

"Did Ed act strangely around your mother? I mean, before the accident?"

"I…no, he was close to my father. My mother and he were formal with each other any time I saw them. An employee and a friend, he never crossed that line…"

"Never?"

"No." He shook his head. "But I remember Mother saying she didn't like him. She asked Father to fire him. That was just before the accident. Damn. She said he was taking liberties and by that I thought she meant treating Father as a friend…"

"When instead could it have been that Ed was making advances on her? Could he have been in love, lust, whatever, with your mother—and she knew or possibly only suspected?"

Kate's blue eyes were troubled and yet full of passion. He couldn't help but touch her cheek and press his lips to hers, in a desperate attempt to alleviate some of his pain. She sank into his kiss, her tongue meeting his, her breast soft, her nipple hard against his palm. He wanted her as much as he wanted all the pain of this new discovery to go away.

He let her go.

She gave him a slow seductive smile and then swung right back into business. "I don't think we can afford to discount this. If we know who Tara's kidnappers are, what motivates them, going in…"

"We have a better chance against them," he finished. "If this is true, what has he been doing all these years? He hasn't been in our employ since the accident." Emir frowned. "We paid him out a compensation package." His fist clenched. "How could he have hidden it…?" But he knew how criminals such as this might act. He just couldn't imagine that someone he had known and trusted…

"Biding his time," Kate replied. "And, I suspect, slowly losing his mind."

Emir raked his fingers through his hair. "Then you're saying that Tara's dealing with a madman?"

"Possibly," she said quietly.

And both of them knew they'd just hit worst-case scenario.

DESPITE THE FACT that it was still daylight, Tara was so tired she could barely keep her eyes open. But she was too afraid to sleep. It was the only reason she could think that he had been able to come up to her, to surprise her without her realizing he was there.

His thick, dark hair was curly and too long, but it framed a face that might have been handsome, had he not been either so thin or so twisted. The intent in his eyes took away from any potential beauty in his face. His mouth curved in a self-satisfied smile that sent a chill down her spine and had her shifting away from him.

"It's been a long time," he said softly.

Tara blinked, as if that would clear her vision, as if that might change the reality of the man before her. "Why? Why have you done this?"

"Why? You dare to ask that as if you didn't know— you, with your life of privilege. I will be glad to end it when it comes to that."

"But what about the money?"

"What about the money, my foolish little princess, looking down at all of us, thumbing your nose at…"

"You taught me the rules of American football.

You—" She broke off, unable to say any more. When he was so near, she tensed to the point she forgot to breath. She took a breath. He seemed to realize in this moment that she was not her mother. It was as though his reality shifted from one moment to the next.

"You were easier to deceive than your brothers, but you all came around."

She stared into a face that was barely familiar, into eyes that were filled with hate, and at a man that it was now clear she had never known. She willed herself to not shrink back, to not show weakness, for in her gut she knew he wanted that as much as he wanted the money.

He reached for her as she twisted away, but it was impossible to escape. The rope that held her only allowed her to move so far.

His knuckle ran down the side of her face. "You never wanted me, did you, despite everything? It was always him." He looked at her as he dropped back on his heels and stood. "I can keep you forever. He will never find you and I will bleed him dry." He ran a thumb along the ridge of her collarbone. His touch was chilling despite the fact that two layers of cotton fabric lay between him and her.

"My brothers…"

He looked at her with angry, confused eyes.

"You call your sons, brothers?"

Tara's sleep-deprived brain didn't have an immediate comeback. She fought not to shrink back as the horror returned and her brain made sense of what he had said. Again, he thought that she was her mother. He'd slipped back into his mad delusion where she became her mother. A chill ran down her spine and she forced herself to look at him.

"He'll never agree," she said, not giving names, meaning her brothers and especially Emir, and leaving it open to his interpretation.

"Then you, my dear, must die. Not now," he said as she looked at him with all the panic she was feeling. "I, of course, will shed tears. But there's really no other way."

She shivered as the chill of the day and the thought of the inevitable night combined with thoughts of her potential destiny, and all of it settled harsh and heavy in her heart.

Chapter Sixteen

Tuesday, September 15, 3:00 p.m.

The village of El Dewar was long gone. The clouds had moved in and the sky was ominous-looking, and the wind was again picking up.

Twenty minutes later they'd stopped for a quick break and were just about to head back to the Jeep when a billowing cloud of sand to the northwest caught Emir's attention. The buzz of an approaching engine followed and he met Kate's quizzical look.

"More than likely, a dirt bike, from the sounds of it," he said.

But it was the unmistakable sound of a gunshot and a thud of a bullet hitting metal that had them diving to the sand.

"Whoever it is, they're targeting the Jeep," Kate said in an undertone as if silence mattered.

There was nothing to say. Emir knew stopping had been a mistake. The dunes had provided camouflage and there'd been no one else around, or so he'd thought. But in trying to provide privacy for Kate he'd inadvertently made them vulnerable. There was nothing to do now but deal with the consequences.

They needed to somehow get back to the Jeep. Right now, it was too far away to be of any help. They'd have to use the small dune beside them for cover. Emir motioned with one arm but Kate was already moving that way, her gun in her hand, keeping as far down as possible as she moved. They didn't return fire, for they didn't want to alert their attacker to where they were. So far whoever it was had only fired at the Jeep. There was still a chance that whoever was shooting hadn't spotted them yet, hadn't realized they'd left their vehicle.

Emir moved forward, head down, trying to keep himself between the shooter and Kate, but she refused to be anything but an equal participant. Exactly as he'd expect from any of his agents, but as much as he hated to admit it, even to himself, Kate was different.

Another shot, this time to their left and over their heads. It was clear now that the shooter knew they weren't at the Jeep. Suddenly there was silence. Emir frowned. With both hands on the Glock, he shifted to his left, motioning Kate to follow.

They were now maybe twenty feet from the Jeep.

A bullet hit the dune just behind them and kicked up a small cloud of sand. Kate motioned with her hand that she was going to move right and along the dune.

Emir nodded as he covered her progress. But suddenly they weren't alone. The roar of the bike engine bore down on them as it flew over one dune, coming closer, only sixty feet away. He fired at it, kicking up sand and causing the biker to swerve right and away from them. Emir fired again and this time the driver lost control. The bike toppled, skidding on its side as the driver landed on his feet, his rifle in the sand behind him. They needed to get to the Jeep and they had a minute or less to do it before he was back on his bike.

Kate fired once, twice, but the angle was wrong—a dune protected him.

"Run!" Emir commanded unnecessarily as they both ran, keeping low and moving fast. They launched themselves into the Jeep.

"Go!" Kate yelled. It was another unnecessary command for he had the accelerator to the floor. The Jeep sped forward, pelting sand behind them as they flew over a dune, swerving back and forth to avoid any shots from the biker.

Kate turned and fired multiple times.

"We want him alive, if possible," Emir shouted over the roar of the engine and knew that the odds were slight that that was going to happen, especially if they both wanted to come out of this alive.

She nodded and, oddly, despite the intensity of the situation, despite the fact that their attention was fixed on their attacker, she turned and smiled at him.

Damn, he thought. She was enjoying this.

The biker was catching up. The bike swerved around them, dodging Kate's shots, and a bullet cracked the back side window. Plumes of sand kicked up from the bike and masked their attacker's identity.

Another dirt bike roared over a dune just behind them. Now there was one bike in front and one behind.

They had a fifty-foot gap between them and their assailants on either side.

Kate dropped the empty magazine, reloaded her Colt M-1911 and took aim at the second biker. She fired and a quick glance in the rearview mirror said she hadn't been lucky. The bike was still hot on their tail. The driver's face was hidden behind a red cloth that covered his face and protected him from the sand that billowed up around him.

"He's not wearing a helmet," Kate muttered. She took aim and fired once, then twice. "We'll be able to take him out that much easier."

Emir had one hand on the wheel, while with the other he held his Glock. It was almost impossible to steer and aim, but he took a shot at the first biker—at least he could keep him off balance, having to react, giving Kate a chance to line up a better shot.

The second biker was swerving now, seeming to lose control. They were still bracketed between two attackers.

"Hang on!" Emir shouted as he veered right and the Jeep sailed across the desert sand, the wind seeming to howl around them. But neither bike was stopping. Instead both bikes changed direction, one heading in a diagonal path straight at them and the other tailing them but quickly coming up on the other side.

The first biker was again ahead of them. But as he lifted his rifle to fire—the bike skidded sideways and the rider was thrown. He was up on his feet as Kate took aim and fired again. Emir fired a second shot. Sand kicked up around the biker and then he was at the bike.

He lifted the rifle, aiming at them as Kate fired, and the rifle snapped out of his hands, slewing along the sand.

"He's unarmed!" she shouted.

Emir swung in the direction of the unarmed biker, the Jeep's engine roaring, sand kicking up behind them. It was a race as to who would get to the gun first, but just as suddenly as Emir swerved, the man pulled a revolver from his belt. Kate was hanging out of the window now and all Emir wanted to do was to pull her in to safety. Instead he had to trust her.

A shot screamed off the side of the Jeep and another echoed off the hood.

"Got him!" she shouted.

The words had barely left her mouth before the remaining dirt biker came ripping over the dune, full throttle, as if he'd been waiting for this moment.

Emir swerved the Jeep, gunning the engine as much as he dared, angling, making them less of a target while Kate kept their remaining attacker busy having to swerve right and then left as he dodged her shots.

No matter her difficulty in the Berber village, here, Kate was good. It was a rogue thought and one he couldn't entertain as he veered again, shadowing the maneuvers of the biker, making them a more difficult target.

He could see Kate, both hands on her handgun, her eyes narrowed. She pulled the trigger. The bike skidded, throwing the rider as the bike rolled down a small sand dune.

"He's not moving," Emir said, looking in the rear-view mirror at the fallen biker.

He looked at Kate. Her face was flushed and there was a troubled look to her eyes as she glanced at him, and he realized the earlier smile had been all about the joy of the chase. The kill was another matter. He gripped the wheel as he turned in the direction of the first downed biker.

As they approached, and the Jeep slowed, Kate was out, crouching, her handgun raised and ready to fire. The biker lay sprawled thirty feet ahead.

Emir threw the Jeep into Park and followed Kate, his gun in both hands. But the biker still wasn't moving.

Kate looked back, nodded when she saw Emir in position just behind her and shifted to her left, carefully moving forward until she reached the body. She pushed the biker's shoulder with her foot—nothing. She squatted and turned the body over. It was a man, thin, with a scruff of dark beard, maybe thirty years old. "He was at El Dewar. I remember him standing between the houses. It was just a moment and then he vanished."

Emir could see the man's rifle was thrown five feet away and that his body lay in an awkward position. It was clear without bending to check that his neck had been broken.

"There're no more answers here," Kate said grimly. She strode over to the bike that lay eight feet away from the corpse. A worn leather bag hung over the seat. She opened it, her expression grim, and pulled out a water bottle and a cell phone. "A disposable phone," she said, turning it on. "Nothing."

Emir came up beside her. "What are you saying? That he's not one of the kidnappers?"

"I don't think so, but he's obviously not innocent. He knows something and it seems like he was trying to prevent us from going any farther."

"We're not finished here yet," Emir said grimly. "Let's go back. Maybe there're answers there." He shrugged in the direction of the other downed biker.

Five minutes later they were at the body of the second biker. Like the first, he was dead. But, unlike the first, they didn't recognize him at all and he carried nothing but his pistol, a water jug and an extra magazine for his weapon.

Kate stood and took a step back.

The wind was quickly picking up and already it was whipping at their clothes and driving sand into their faces. Emir slipped his sunglasses on and she did the same.

"We're going to have to leave him here," he said with a final look at the body. "I'll alert Zaf when the satellite connects again." The satellite had been down since they'd begun this leg of their journey.

His heart was pounding. No matter how many times he was in a gun battle, he never liked them because the outcome always meant someone was going to die. Yet, when he looked over at Kate, he saw the flush on her cheeks and a slight curve to her lips, as if she was about to smile.

As the wind whipped a strand of hair across her face and she turned to look at him with eyes that sang with excitement, he realized that, no matter how much he disliked killing, there was one thing he'd never admitted. That it was eclipsed by the heady power of the afterglow, of being the one still alive. They might have killed two men but the alternative was that they would have been killed themselves. The silent communication between them had reminded him of that and he knew in that moment he couldn't have asked for a better partner.

They drove in silence for a while. Their only goal was to get as close to the oasis undetected as they could before night came or the storm hit—whichever came first.

The ringing of the satellite phone made Kate jump. "We're back in business," she said with relief in her voice.

Emir picked up the phone before the second ring ended. "What do you have?"

"Ed hasn't been working security like he led us to believe. In fact, I'm not sure what he's been doing. I'm doing more digging. Two things. First, I think Tara's kidnappers are on to us," Zafir said. "They haven't followed up with any additional demands. I'm getting worried and I think it was a mistake to go after them."

"We didn't have a choice," Emir said and frustration wove through the words.

"Okay, look, keep your eyes open. You've got bigger trouble coming. There's a sandstorm forecasted. You need to take shelter. Weather reports look like you might have another clear hour, maybe less."

"Less. It's starting up already." Emir's tone gritted. He told Zafir what had happened and about the bodies they'd left behind.

"Give me your coordinates," Zafir growled. "I don't like any of this"

A minute later Emir turned to Kate. "We're going

to have to camp for the night." It was something they'd both known for a while now. "If we didn't suspect we were heading into a storm, Zaf's confirmed it."

The earlier excitement was gone. Kate's full lips were tight with tension. She gripped the dash, staring out over the desert with a grim look as if he'd sentenced her to life instead of one night.

And he knew her worry, knew it tenfold, for it meant his sister must spend one more night alone with her kidnappers.

His jaw tightened as he navigated a rut. The Jeep bounced and the tires spun as they hit hard, flat sand. As they came out of the dip, the wind began to whip around them. They had no choice. They didn't stand a chance in unfamiliar terrain in a sandstorm.

Emir shifted the Jeep down a gear and veered left, taking the dune that loomed ahead at an angle, as it was steeper than any of the others they had yet to encounter. Straight-on and he could visualize the rollover that would follow. They were close to the oasis. According to Kate's last coordinates, less than ten miles away.

"We need shelter!" Kate yelled five minutes later over the roar of the wind. "We can't go any farther." Sand pelted the vehicle and it was getting more and more difficult to see. But, according to the map, there were sandstone cliffs on the other side of this ridge. Before they'd been attacked, they'd been taking it slow, scouting the area—noting the weaknesses, the strengths, buying time. Now they were about to be swallowed in the storm if they didn't get to shelter quickly.

Just as that thought ran through his mind, the first shot rang out.

"What the—?" Kate bit off the rest of her comment as she swung around in the direction of the shot, her gun in her hand and crouching in her seat, taking what cover she could.

Emir swerved right then left, taking them dangerously close to a rollover. He looked over at Kate who was on her knees as she put herself in a position to defend them both. He couldn't have asked for a better person to ride shotgun.

"Go left," Kate shouted over the din of the Jeep's engine and the wind. "I think they're using that break to the right between the dunes." She glanced left. "This storm is going to be our cover pretty soon."

He couldn't agree with that assessment more, but all he could do now was get them as far away as possible.

She was firing blindly through the partially opened window, but there was only a distant shot returned and that indicated that the shooter might be on foot.

"So much for sneaking in," Emir said, his hands clenching the wheel as he realized what this could mean.

"We'll work around it, Emir." She looked at him with lips tight. She was perched on the seat as if poised to launch. They were over a mile from the first shot and, through the waves of sand and gusts of wind, he could see the rise of a hill to their right. The storm had intensified and was now driving sand so thick that there was no going much farther. They were as far away as the storm would allow.

They were so close to Tara and yet so far.

Chapter Seventeen

"There." Kate pointed as a bank of low-rise cliffs appeared to their right.

"It should work," he agreed as he fought to keep the Jeep moving in the right direction. The sand was beginning to act like water as it moved with the wind that churned it.

The visibility had rapidly decreased. Some storms could come out of nowhere, swallowing you in a sea of sand, while others were slower moving and, often, longer lasting. This one wasn't hitting them out of nowhere but it was rapidly getting worse.

Within minutes he had the Jeep angled in the direction the wind was coming from, using it to act as a barrier.

"We'll set up the tent beside the Jeep," he said. "We could stay in the Jeep if I thought this thing was going to blow over quickly, but all signs look like it might run through the night." A gust of wind hammered him from behind, pushing him forward. He looked at Kate, who was struggling to double her ponytail to keep it from whipping against her face. The scarf she'd been using had blown away minutes ago.

They wrestled with the tent to get the anchor lines secured.

Finally, inside the tent, Kate shivered, clutching her arms. "It's getting cold."

It was late afternoon but the temperature had plummeted and inside the tent it was only slightly less chilly than outside.

He tossed her a blanket. "Thanks," she said as she wrapped it around her shoulders. "One night, not too bad," she said. "Maybe the kidnappers will get in touch with Zafir by then. I don't know why they're waiting."

"Any number of reasons, but thinking of any of them isn't going to help us."

"Maybe," she said with doubt in her voice. "I don't think that last attack was planned. I mean, they shot at us twice and the second was so distant. I think whoever it was, unlike the bikers, they were shooting blind."

"As in we could have been anyone and not someone necessarily after them."

"Exactly."

"I suppose we'll soon find out once the storm is over." He knelt by the small, portable heater. "We'll get this going and it should warm up fast." He glanced at her with a smile. "Just like home."

"Home with dehydrated stew for supper," she said with a smile more poignant than humorous.

"Not even that," he said. "We have no stove. Unless you want it cold, but I'm not sure how that will work with cold water..."

"Stop," she said with a laugh.

The storm had intensified too fast and they had taken what they could from the Jeep. He'd managed to grab a bag with food supplies and she'd gotten blankets, but after that the storm had taken charge. The camp stove among a few other things had been left behind.

They had shelter and, more importantly, they were alive. They had lived and others had died.

She wasn't sure how it happened but suddenly she was in his arms and his lips were on hers. Her heart beat wildly as he held her tight against him and she could feel him hard and ready against her belly. His lips were warm and oddly soft in a demanding, masculine way as they parted hers, and her heart pounded in time with his.

She wanted to hold him tighter and demand more. And yet it all seemed too soon and too much. For the first time she had thoughts that hadn't occurred to her before. He was her boss. Her job mattered. Sex with the boss wasn't the best career plan she'd ever had.

"No." She shook her head. "I can't."

His knuckle ran along the edge of her cheek, caressing it, as his tongue tasted the edge of her lips. "What's wrong?" he asked thickly, his desire still hard between them.

"No, Emir. Not now." Why did she say that? Not ever was what she meant to say as the wind howled and the tent rocked and sand pelted against the canvas.

He caressed her breast.

She couldn't have wanted him any more than she did in that moment. Instead she pulled back, forcing him to let her go.

"You're my boss," she muttered.

His dark eyes raked her face but he said nothing.

She moved away from him but the tent wasn't large. She found herself next to the heater, a heat that was safer than the kind of heat he offered.

"We need to get some food, get some sleep and make a plan," she said.

An awkward silence seemed to descend after those words. She looked at him from beneath her lashes. His back was to her and he was going through their supplies. Apparently he wasn't fazed by rejection.

"Here's one of your demands met," he said, holding up a can. His expression was placid, like nothing had happened between them.

He tossed her a can of soup followed by a spoon and she peeled the metal lid back. Despite the fact that it was cold and, as a result, slightly congealed, it was exactly what she needed.

Ten minutes later she set the empty can aside. The storm was still going full force and as the wind pushed and pulled at the canvas, the noise was almost alarming. It was dark except for the occasional flicker of a flashlight they used to navigate the space. The wind rocked the tent and she wondered if it would hold.

"Ignore it," he advised. "We'll be fine."

But there was pain in his eyes and she knew that he thought of Tara.

"We'll all be fine," she said. "Tara, too."

He didn't say anything. Instead he handed her a tin of rice pudding.

"No." She laughed. "There's something about rice in pudding—no."

"Don't know what you're missing."

He took a spoonful of pudding that some employee had thrown into the kit and grimaced as he swallowed. He held out his spoon. "You sure?" he asked with a smile.

"From the look on your face, yes," she said with a laugh and then immediately turned serious. "We're seven miles from the oasis. That's what I got from what I saw of landmarks before the storm hit and from matching it on the map," she said thoughtfully.

He put the tin down. "We could walk in once the storm…"

"A mile of that is going to be a fairly challenging climb through the cliffs that are backing the oasis. Not wise in the dark." She paused. "I've been thinking about the kidnappers. They've been playing you, taking their time."

"And?"

"I think we buy time, make them nervous. Play the game they're playing right back at them. We put ourselves in position to move on them by nightfall." She looked at her watch. It was now only seven. "Tomorrow."

"And Tara has to spend another day and night with them. Anything could happen, they could kill…"

"They need her, Emir. I think we put her in less danger if we bide our time, make them sweat a bit more, than if we try to move in without any idea of the environment in which they're holding her. Tomorrow we'll be prepared and we can use the night to our advantage."

Hours later she slept and awoke to see that it wasn't quite as dark, that the storm had abated and that she was cold. She looked over. Emir was sitting up, his gaze thoughtful.

She sat up, too. "What's going on?"

"Not much," he replied. "Almost daylight. We've got about an hour."

"Did you get any sleep?" she asked as she blinked and rubbed her eyes.

"No." He shook his head. "You got some sleep anyway."

"I did," she replied as she ran a hand through her hair. "I must look a mess."

"No," he said softly, his eyes intense as they swept over her. "You look beautiful."

"Beautiful?" she repeated. She'd just been through a gunfight, a sandstorm—killed a man. No, two.

"They needed to die, Kate," he said as if he'd read her mind, as if he knew that despite the thrill of battle she was not a killer. "It made me sick the first time and the second. It makes me sick every time," he said.

"I threw up the first time," she admitted. "And almost quit."

"I'm glad you didn't," he said softly, meeting her eyes. His were like molten chocolate, the look in them more of that of a lover than of a friend or colleague or even boss.

"I've never met anyone like you, Kate," he said in a gravelly whisper.

She shivered.

"You're cold. The heater isn't much. Come here," he said and he could hear the edge in his voice.

He moved closer to her until he was right beside her. He lifted the blanket from his shoulders and brought it around both of them, and pulled her close to him, using his body to warm her. "Neither of us will be any use to Tara if we use all our energy trying to keep warm."

But it was only a few minutes of them sitting like that, with her pressed against his side so tight that he could feel the softer contour of her breast, that he knew it had been a mistake. Nature hadn't built enough restraint in him to hold a woman more sensual than any he'd met before and just keep her warm, or for that matter a woman he'd been attracted to since he'd first set eyes on her.

He tipped her face up and kissed her long and hard, his tongue tasting her, relishing it all; the sweet taste of the cinnamon gum she'd chewed just after awakening, the hot feel of her tongue as it mated with his, the sleek feel of her skin, all awakening a desire in him that ached to be appeased.

He took a deep breath and reminded himself of why he was there, that she was his employee, as she had reminded him—a partner for now. She couldn't be anything else. And none of that mattered. For the beat of his heart told another story.

"I want you," he whispered as if all the kisses that had come before hadn't already told her that.

"You're my boss, and my career..."

She looked at him with a desire that had him using all his willpower to hold back.

The rise of her breast seemed no more than a lover's kiss, a soft caress against his upper arm. He reached out tentatively, his palm brushing the seductive softness.

"I want to be so much more," he whispered. "The rest doesn't matter."

Her breath was a small purr of pleasure as her hand slipped under his shirt, skimmed the side of his ribs and moved down as if his words had given her permission.

His hands dropped lower, pulling her tight against him, flipping onto his back with her on top as he kissed her with every ounce of enthusiasm and feeling she gave him. His hand grazed the edge of her breast as it seductively pressed against him and his want pressed against her thigh.

She shuddered.

"You're still cold." He raised himself on an elbow, reaching for the blanket that had dropped to the side.

She took his wrist, even as she shook her head. "Don't stop."

He rolled over so that he was on top of her, blocking the cold tendrils of the breeze that seemed to find its way inside the tent. Her curves were pressed more tightly against him. His hand slid under her T-shirt, undoing the front hook of her bra, freeing her breast into his hand. One hand cupped a breast while the other pulled the T-shirt over her head, the bra followed.

She moaned as her nipple tightened beneath his fingers.

He took one nipple in his mouth, his tongue tormenting her in tiny caresses as he toyed with one and then the other. She twisted, rising up as if to meet his hardness, as if that would get them what they both wanted sooner.

"I can't wait," he said thickly as he unzipped her pants; his hand slipped under her panties to find her wet. She quivered as his fingers parted her.

Soon she was bare beneath him and her hand was reaching for his zipper.

His hand slipped between them, covering hers, stilling it.

He stood, took off his pants and was again pulling the blanket up around them, as their body heat was trapped by the blanket and combined with the heat of desire finally succeeded in warding off the desert chill.

"Now," she said as she rose to meet him and clung to him as he entered her as quickly as he'd seduced her. Yet, in the hot and cold of the desert, where life was both tenacious and fragile, somehow it felt right.

But it was only when she rolled over and took command did he wish that time was not a short commodity, because for blissful minutes the nightmare that had been over fifty hours in the making was soothed twice in the most blissful way possible.

"I'm sorry," she said when she laid by his side sometime later.

It was a strange comment and one he supposed he should have been making, but he wasn't sorry. He'd been attracted to her from the beginning—wrong place and wrong time, it didn't matter—he wanted this to happen.

"I'm not," he said and there was a hoarse edge to his voice. He sat up and snapped the top off one of their water bottles, took a long, thirsty swig and then offered it to her. "It was bound to happen."

"What do you mean by that?" she demanded as she stood, naked and unconcerned, her hair loose, caressing the edges of her breasts, her face flushed from his kisses. "I was just sorry we didn't have more time."

"Really?" Desire raced hot and wild through him. "You're damn sexy, Kate," he said. "And I think I'm falling for you. But if you don't get dressed, we'll never leave this tent."

Minutes later, dressed, she sat beside him.

"We need to focus," he said. "We're going in after Tara and I don't want to see any casualties, at least, not of anyone I care about."

Anyone I care about.

Those words seemed to hang between them, meaning so many things both spoken and not.

"I know you hate waiting," she said, trying to forget his words that had the power to change so much. "But I really don't think they have a clue what they're doing. I'm beginning to think, like we talked about last night, that we should wait until tonight. It will throw them off, which is better for us."

"If we at least get into position before nightfall, I can live with that." He stood. "Let's start getting this packed up so we're ready to move." He turned around. "And, for the record, I'd do it again," he said.

A slow smile spread across her face. "For the record—we will."

"Darn sure of yourself," he said as he leaned over to give her a chaste kiss on the cheek.

She twisted so that the kiss landed on her lips and she took it to the next level. The kiss was hot, open-mouthed, ripe with desire and the promise of more. But she pulled away as his body began demanding to take charge.

"I am very sure of myself," she replied. "Now, let's get your sister."

Chapter Eighteen

"Let's do this," Kate said as she pulled out her gun, checked the chamber and holstered it. She turned to look at him with zeal for the assignment alive in her eyes. There was a confidence about her that was all about succeeding, and that confidence was contagious.

They'd spent the earlier part of the morning scouting the terrain backing into the oasis. There had been no sign of the last man who had shot at them, but they'd been prepared if he had showed up. When they got back to the tent there was nothing to show that it had been disturbed. No footprints, no evidence that anyone, other than them, had been there.

"Looks like our guess was right. I doubt if their sniper even knew what he was shooting at. He couldn't see much in the storm," Kate said. "They know someone's here. I don't think they had a visual, but sound travels. It's clear that they had a watch."

"I think you're right," Emir agreed.

"It's rough terrain. I doubt if we'll be able to make

anywhere near the average 2.4 miles an hour. So…" She looked at her watch.

"We leave in an hour," he said as he pocketed the compass, loaded his Glock and stuffed two spare magazines into his pocket. He shifted his knapsack where she knew he had another couple of magazines, just as she did in hers. They were both prepared to hold off an army if necessary.

"Let's do it," Kate said less than an hour later.

"Kate," he said, taking her into his arms and kissing her hot, brief and full of promise.

They both knew this would be the only reference to what was growing between them. After, it would be all business.

And as if to confirm that, he let her go as quickly as he had pulled her against him. It was like they'd never been intimate. It was what they had to do, for they needed to be focused. One mistake could jeopardize everything and everyone.

For the moment it appeared they had the advantage. The kidnappers didn't know that she and Emir were out here. At least so they hoped, for just ten minutes ago Zafir had contacted them to let them know there had finally been another ransom demand, this time with specific instructions. They wanted a helicopter drop with an unarmed pilot at an oasis thirty miles to the south of the location where they now had them pinpointed. That wasn't going to happen. Now it was just a matter of getting Tara out.

Unfortunately, the kidnappers knew someone was

here, it was only a matter of time before they put the pieces together.

"If we come in from the northwest corner, there's what I believe is a crevice that leads to a tunnel through a cave and goes straight through and into the oasis, hopefully near where they're holding her. I don't know how big it is, but I know the children, when the oasis was a settlement, used to use it," Kate said with an almost breathy excitement in her voice.

"How do you know this? You have no access to internet, no…"

"At the village. El Dewar. The women had more to say than what I told you." She shrugged. "An old lady I met was born here, in these very hills, on the oasis we're heading for."

"Anything else?"

"No one uses the oasis anymore, at least, not to live. In fact, she said it was mostly forgotten. Dried up when she was a child. She thought that there was some water, enough for a traveler or two. I'd say that makes it about perfect."

He smiled and put a hand on her shoulder. "Let's go."

The valley was narrow and surrounded by low-lying sandstone hills. The oasis was on the other side of the valley and, from what she had gleaned from the atlas, backed two steep hills at the end of the chain that served to protect it from outsiders.

"From what that woman said and what I've calculated," Kate said hours later, "we should be close to the break in the rock that would take us in." They'd been moving carefully through the valley throughout the afternoon. Now, the sun was setting and spilling a vibrant orange across the valley and up into the hills that stood like ancient sentinels, protecting the valley from intruders.

"We go up from here and through the rocks there," Kate said a few minutes later as she pointed to her right and about two hundred feet up.

They began to make their way up the narrow, steep path that wound between the rocks. Within twenty-five feet the path became smooth, almost worn, making it clear that at one time it had been a well-traveled route.

"The tunnel that leads into the oasis shouldn't be much farther," she said.

The rock rose on either side as high as Emir's shoulders, then the path narrowed and he found himself occasionally clipping his shoulders against outcroppings.

"They must have used this path to get water or maybe for defense. I believe they more frequently came in from the other way," Kate said. "From the oasis."

They both knew it was irrelevant what the path had been used for. What mattered was that it was there and that they knew of its existence.

He was glad that she had been in El Dewar to listen to the musings of an old woman. Between that and the other women who had spoken to her, in the end, despite her unease, she'd succeeded. In an odd way, the women had trumped the men. He wondered what Tara would say about that and, at the thought of Tara, the old fury rolled in his gut. They were so close.

We're here, Tara, he said silently, as if his sister were privy to his thoughts.

"We'll get her out, Emir," Kate said. She stopped and took his hands in hers. "We'll get her out," she repeated and rose up on tiptoes to kiss him.

He took her in his arms and kissed her with all the emotion he was feeling. When he let her go, somehow he felt better, more centered and less angry.

That was something Kate did for him, among so many others. He felt like he'd known her forever and, as much as he wanted to find Tara, he dreaded the moment when he'd have to let Kate go. He pushed the thought out of his mind, for it was those kinds of thoughts that got one killed or worse, got one's partner killed. That would never happen. He wouldn't let it.

"Let's go," she said and they continued to make their way along the trail as it rose up and then began to go downward.

Finally they came to a dark hollow, a cave that Kate claimed the old woman had told her tunneled through the cliff and straight into the oasis. It was a long shot, but it was all they had. The light was scant as the penlight flickered off the rocky path. They had more powerful flashlights but this was all they could chance without risking the light might be seen.

"Cover me," he said. "And I'll go in."

"You won't fit," she replied.

"You don't know that." The opening was five feet high by four wide, plenty of room. He bent and entered the tunnel, but within seven feet it became drastically smaller. He shone the light ahead to see that the tunnel curved and realized that he would never get through.

This tunnel was made for a smaller person. Reluctantly he backed out.

"We can go around..." he began.

"And let them know we're here. Ring the doorbell before entering—so to speak," she said and didn't tone down the sarcasm. "I'm sorry, that was uncalled for." She put a hand on his shoulder. "Let me, Emir."

"No..."

"Think of it, if the kidnappers are there, they're protected. If we come in from the oasis, we'd be in the open with no idea as to what their setup is. We'd be sitting ducks. No help to Tara. I can make it through the tunnel. At least, I can try," she whispered frantically. "I need to do this, Emir. We have no choice. You know that."

Reluctantly he nodded. "If she's not near, or if she is and you can't get her attention, come back. Any trouble at all...come back."

"Don't worry." She adjusted her holster, moving it to her back so she could more easily crawl on her belly if necessary.

She took the small penlight then gave him a kiss.

He pulled her against him, his lips ravishing hers, opening her mouth, bending her back as if the passion in the kiss would somehow protect her. When he let her go, they stood looking at each other as if it was the last time they'd get to do that. He pushed that thought from his mind. It wouldn't happen. She was too skilled, too smart, and he cared for her too much.

"Be careful."

"No worries," she said, her lips red from his kisses.

She turned and ducked into the tunnel. He shone his

light on her until she disappeared and all he wanted to do was follow her.

He was left to wait. He couldn't leave his post. He had to remain there, waiting in case she might need him.

He paced.

THE TUNNEL NARROWED almost immediately and then opened up so that Kate was able to walk with her head down. The rock was cool and the passage narrow enough that her shoulders occasionally scraped rock. She could hear faint scratching and movement from somewhere within the tunnel and her flashlight caught sight of a black beetle that froze and then scurried away. She could see why children used this route, but a grown adult wouldn't as at one point she was doubled over and her knees were bent.

The low ceiling and the narrowness had her fighting feelings of claustrophobia and wrestling with the idea of retreating. A minute later she came around a turn and then another going right and then left. Suddenly she could hear male laughter and saw a flicker of light. She turned off the penlight.

The smell of cigarette smoke wafted around her and was intertwined with the smell of burning wood and of what she guessed might be the smoke from a campfire. She squatted, knowing she was near the exit, and waited. If she were able to smell the cigarette smoke over the fire, then the smoker wasn't far from her position. She waited, sniffing the air. Five minutes passed before she could smell nothing but the fire. Whoever the smoker had been, they'd either put it out or moved away. She had to take her chances and hope it was the latter.

She got down on her hands and knees and crawled the remaining distance as the tunnel twisted before she saw another flicker of light. There was a palm tree growing up against the rock, partially hiding the opening. She could see the snap of flames about fifty feet away and as she looked down there was a movement. But she couldn't make out anything in the dark. She squatted back on her heels. As she contemplated what to do next, the night sky cleared and the moon shone bright and revealing. She looked down and met the terrified eyes of Sheikka Tahriha Al-Nassar.

Kate put her fingers to her lips and the woman nodded while avidly watching her. She pointed at Tara and then back at the tunnel where she crouched so that it was clear what she wanted her to do and where she wanted her to go, once she managed to free her. It was a backup plan, nothing else. So that if anything happened to her, as long as she was untied, Tara could still get out and to safety.

Kate looked toward the campfire and saw that there were three men. She could hear their voices and laughter and, as the flames danced, she could also see that they were sitting with their backs to her. The tricky part would be getting Tara free, for they could see in the moonlight as easily as Kate could.

She slid down the path that wound steeply from the tunnel to the hill. She kept low and used her feet to control and steer her way while remaining hidden from the men by the shrubbery growing up against the hill.

With a bump she was on her butt on level ground and the only thing that stood between her and discovery was a grassy bush and another palm tree. She looked over and Tara was watching her. Kate shook her head and the woman looked away.

She could see that Tara's hands were tied behind her back and secured to the trunk of a palm tree. She could also see that they'd only used rope. They obviously hadn't expected much resistance and she hadn't expected that it would be that easy. She fished the knife she always carried out of her pocket. It couldn't be called a pocketknife but it couldn't be called a hunting knife, either. All she knew was that it could slide through any kind of rope with ease.

She held her breath, watching the men. They were caught up in their conversation, and none was paying attention. She'd be in the open for a minute, the time it took to get to Tara. She just needed Tara to back up against the palm tree. She waited until the woman glanced at her and she motioned to the tree. Tara moved until her back was pressed against it.

Smart, Kate thought. So far she was following every cue with ease.

Kate moved in swiftly, keeping low to the ground. Within a minute Tara was free and Kate had given her whispered directions and she was off.

Kate turned on her heels, moving to face the kidnappers; it only took a second but it was enough. As she went to follow Tara she was grabbed roughly from behind.

"What are you doing?" the male voice snarled in Arabic.

"Run!" she yelled at Tara and saw her scramble up the last few feet and disappear into the tunnel.

His grip on her arm was so tight Kate bit her lip against the pain as he twisted her around.

"Where's the sheikka? Where is she?" he roared, his face half hidden by a shaggy beard, his eyes wild, not focusing on her as his hand bit into her arm.

Her other arm was free and with it she quietly moved to reach her gun without drawing his attention to what she was doing.

But as he looked up toward the tunnel, he yanked her arm hard, ramming it up between her shoulders and making her bite back a shriek of pain, causing her other hand to drop from where she had been inching toward her weapon.

"Get her back! Get her now!" he shrieked into her face.

"Run, Tara!" Kate screamed and it was the last thing she did as her captor's fist connected with her jaw.

Chapter Nineteen

"Zafir, I've got her."

Emir gave his brother little time to express his relief or to explain the circumstances. The connection was tentative and could break at any moment. He looked over to where Tara was guzzling the contents of a water bottle. Other than being stressed and dehydrated, his baby sister was fine.

"They've got Kate," he said through clenched teeth. He would have gone in with guns blazing but that wouldn't have done Kate or Tara any good. "I need to go in after her but I need to get Tara out of here, to safety, first."

"Is it Ed?" Zafir asked in a strained voice.

"That's what Tara tells me," Emir said, holding anger back with an iron will as he gave Zafir the coordinates. "How soon can you get here?"

Zafir promised he'd be there soon with Talib, and that they were minutes away. Emir almost sighed. If he lost Kate now, before she knew how he felt about her... The thought trailed. She didn't know that those intimate moments were about more than just lust. It had all been too soon and too fast, and yet it had been like a lifetime. In such a short time, he felt like he'd always known her and, unbelievably, he'd fallen in love with her.

But none of that mattered. What mattered was that they had her, that she was in danger. The thought was killing him as much as the knowledge that there was nothing he could do. He couldn't leave Tara, for they would be looking for her soon, unless somehow they thought Kate was the trade-off. His thoughts were jumbled. He couldn't think clearly and he needed to get it together and get it together now. Kate as a trade-off was a thought he couldn't discard and one that made him every bit as sick as them having his sister.

"She came just in time," Tara whispered as he sat beside her. "He was crazed. Thought I was Mother." She shook her head. "I can't believe it was Ed. He wasn't who I remember. He would have raped me if he'd had much longer."

Or worse, Emir thought as rage rolled through him as he listened and he wanted to kill. He took a few breaths, stilling his emotions. He needed to get through this calmly. After all, Tara wasn't out of danger yet.

Where was Zafir? Emir had to go after Kate and in one crazy moment he considered taking Tara with him.

"Ridiculous," he muttered.

"Em. You're scaring me," Tara said.

Emir looked at his sister and guilt ran through him. She'd been through hell. "It'll be okay, kid. I promise," he said. "Zafir will be here any moment to get you out of here."

"You care for her, don't you," she said in a quiet

voice. "Kate." She said the name as if testing it out. After all, Tara had only learned the name of her rescuer a few moments ago. "She'll make it, Em, she has to."

Has to. Tara's words echoed in their rightness, for he didn't know what he'd do if she didn't.

He took her hands in both of his. "He didn't hurt you? You're certain?" He had two reasons to kill the man now, he thought ferociously. Kate and Tara. It was odd, there were others, but to him it was Ed who had betrayed his family.

"No." She shook her head. "But I never knew… I can't believe… I mean, he loved Mother. He was crazy for her. I mean nutcase crazy. And it made me think about their accident. His face was burned…" She looked at Emir. "You don't think…?"

"Let's talk about that later," Emir said as he thought of the unspeakable act Ed had perpetrated on the House of Al-Nassar. He didn't need to bring down his family, he'd dealt them a crushing blow broadsiding the family, destroying its heart, and no one had known, until now.

Emir shuddered at the thought and again at the thought of what a nightmare this man must have been for his mother. No wonder the mention of letting him go had left her lips when usually she had left employment issues to his father. To think that his parents were dead, partially or wholly, because of this man—rage ran through him.

"I just wanted to go to a party, alone. To look normal, without security trailing me, and I ditched them." She burst into tears, her head in her hands.

"Tara, sweetheart." He put an arm awkwardly around

her, his gun still in that hand, and aware of the importance of time. "It's all right. You're safe and this will never happen again."

"It won't," she mumbled. "I promise."

"Look at me," he said.

She looked up.

"We don't have much time. I need you to take a deep breath and think of where they held you. Tell me what their setup is."

"Emir, you're not..."

"Tell me." He chucked her under the chin with his free hand as he had when she'd been a child. In an odd way it made both of them feel better. "I won't let you down."

"You mean you won't let yourself get killed. Promise me, Emir."

"Promise."

And he listened as Tara explained what she knew of the three heavily armed men who had kidnapped her and the remains of a forgotten oasis where she'd been held. And as he listened, the rage he had tamped down so effectively became like steel, cold and lethally determined.

It was minutes later when he heard the distant whir of a helicopter. He switched on the flashlight and waved it. The powerful light was unlike the minute one that Kate had used on the way into the cave. In fact, it was one used by top scientists working in the desert and threw a powerful beam of light.

Within minutes the helicopter was down and Tara was surrounded. It was only once Talib and Zafir had determined to their satisfaction that she wasn't physically injured that Tara was lifted into a bear hug from which Talib seemed determined not to release her.

"Let's get her out of here." Emir's voice brought everyone back to business. And within minutes Tara was in the helicopter and off with Talib while Zafir stayed behind.

"They've got Kate," Emir said, the anguish clear in his voice as he briefed his brother on all that Tara had told him.

"She's got your heart, man," Zafir said and there was a hint of surprise in his voice. He pulled the safety on his handgun and turned to his brother. "Let's get her."

They didn't have a choice other than to go in from the front, but with the detail Tara had provided, they at least knew how to get close enough unobserved.

When they arrived they found the camp was like nothing Tara had described, instead it was chaos. The fire burned low and cans and empty bottles lay everywhere. In the center of the oasis were the remains of a tent, much of the canvas strewn around the area as if it had been destroyed in a fit of anger.

On the edges, where the desert met the oasis, they could hear the voices of at least two men. Angry but unclear as to what they were saying.

"We've got to locate Kate," Emir said.

Zafir nodded and together they made their way along the perimeter of the oasis.

Twenty feet in, Emir saw her as the moon and the waning fire provided some light. Kate's hands and feet were tied and her shirt was ripped partially off. Her hair was tangled and loose, but it was when he eased closer that he had to use all his willpower to keep silent. Her lip, jaw and cheek were swollen and blood trailed down her chin. He didn't dare go any closer without threatening their cover.

She looked up and, despite her state, smiled. Her eyes shifted to where the men argued. Their voices were getting louder and it was clear they were only focused on each other.

Emir looked back at Kate. She looked toward the men and closed her eyes twice, slowly, deliberately. Then she did it again, this time once, and then she looked up and over the hill.

Emir gave her a single nod. He knew she was telling him that one of the men had already made his escape over the hill, possibly in search of Tara. That thought both enraged and frightened him. They needed to move fast.

He looked at Kate. Any sound could alert the men. He needed to free her, but getting any closer could be tricky. He pulled out his dagger and motioned for Zafir to stay back.

Emir moved in carefully, slipping behind her, using her as a shield to screen his presence. He sliced through the rope that bound her wrists—silently, quietly, desperately wanting to speak to her, to hold her—he could do neither.

There was a shout, garbled words, and he feared they'd been discovered.

"Give me the knife," she whispered urgently.

"Go through the tunnel," he said. "I'll meet you on the other side."

She nodded, taking the knife from him as a beam

of light settled on her and a harsh voice in Arabic demanded to know what she was doing.

Emir moved behind the trunk of a palm tree. He could see the shadow of Zafir across from him. He motioned forward. They needed to get away from Kate—to get her out of the line of fire.

Emir picked up a rock, glanced at Zafir and threw it, hitting one of the men in the arm. He swung around, cursing angrily in Arabic as the other man reached for the rifle slung over his back and the second pulled a handgun. Emir smiled. He didn't want to kill a man by blindsiding him. That wouldn't be fair, no matter what he'd done. He glanced back. Kate was gone.

Despite thoughts of giving them a chance, it was less than a minute before both men were dead.

"One shot," Zafir grumbled. "Too easy."

Emir went over, kicking the one man in the shoulder and pushing the body over. There was no sign of life. He did the same with the other. Neither was the man responsible for it all.

"Where's Ed?" He turned to look at Zafir and alarm raced in unspoken words between them.

"There's no sign of anyone else," Zafir said.

Emir didn't answer, he was on the run, going back—making sure that Kate, too, was gone—safe.

She was nowhere in sight, not at the base of the hills, not in the entrance of the tunnel.

There was no one else in the oasis.

Ten minutes later they were on the other side of the oasis where they'd started out. In the darkness they could see nothing.

"Son of a desert stray, where is she?" Emir growled, his heart pounding at the thought of Ed still on the loose and Kate nowhere to be found.

"We've got company," Zafir said. "Just behind us at ten o'clock."

He'd no sooner said that when a shot came from the hills and echoed through the rocks.

"Ed!" Emir shouted as a means of a diversion as Zafir moved into position to his left. "What are you doing, man? You were my father's friend."

"Damn Al-Nassar!" came the shout from what sounded like near the base of the hill. "You always had everything."

"Give yourself up, man," Emir ordered. He moved forward and to the right as Zafir continued to move in the opposite direction.

"It's not worth it!" Zafir shouted in a perfect imitation of Emir's voice.

Arabic curses followed. "Which one of you bloody look-alikes are you?"

Overhead, the rotors of a helicopter beat the air and overrode their voices.

"Son of a... Talib," Emir swore. Minus a brother, his whole family was here. He hoped Talib had the sense to keep Tara out of this, to have dropped her in a safe place before returning. He couldn't afford to think otherwise.

He moved forward in the darkness, using one boulder and then another for cover.

Where was she?

"Emir?" It was a whisper in the dark. A sound meant only for him, and close, too close.

"Kate," he said. His voice was soft, controlled, so it wouldn't carry. "Get back."

And then he saw her. He moved in beside her. There was no time for discussion. He'd take a hit for her if necessary. The thought, despite the intensity of the situation, startled him. He'd never felt like that about any woman. With the exception of his mother and his sister, there had been no woman he would have taken a bullet for. He felt that and more about Kate.

The light from the helicopter swept the area. It was blinding as bullets cut through the night and he crouched beside Kate behind a rock from where he could see Zafir slowly making his way around, cutting off any chance of escape, using the distraction of the helicopter to his advantage.

"Stay down," he said as he prepared to move in.

Kate nodded. There was nothing she could do. They'd taken her gun.

There was movement ahead and Emir could see the top of Ed's head as he sought better cover. He fired at him and Ed shot back, the bullet whining through the valley. Then there was a shot from the left, as Zafir joined the battle.

A series of shots followed.

"Ed," Emir called when a temporary silence descended. "Mother's been asking about you."

"You're lying," he snarled.

"Stay here," he said to Kate. "I'm going after him."

He moved forward, going from one rock to the next in the direction of the voice. The helicopter had pulled back and they were again in darkness.

"She misses you," Emir said as he moved another few feet forward.

"Why did she run away?"

The voice was just ahead and to his left. Something moved and suddenly he was there, facing the man he barely recognized and who had once been his father's shadow.

Emir didn't wait but instead launched himself at Ed, driving him down with an uppercut to the chin followed by another to the temple. Ed's gun clattered to the rocks as Emir hit him again. This time Ed stumbled and fell.

"Maybe next time you'll think twice about hitting women or destroying families," Emir snarled. But he knew that there wouldn't be a next time. Ed would die before this night was over.

Light bounced over the rock and he could see Kate using a boulder for cover and trying to give him some help as she shone the flashlight at Ed. He was glad of the help as he saw Ed had found his gun. But Emir fired before Ed could raise it into position. Ed tumbled backward, landing heavily in the rocks.

The helicopter had moved in again, preparing to land. The blades were creating a wind that emulated a sandstorm as it threatened to pull their clothes from their bodies.

"I can't believe it, Em," Zafir said minutes later as they stood a few feet from Ed's body. "This piece of camel's offal killed our parents."

"He was in love with our mother and, from what I've pieced together, thought he'd kill our father to have her. In the process he killed them both."

"He was unbalanced to begin with, but he lost all reason as a result," Kate added. "Eventually believing that your mother still lived."

"Son of a desert dog!" Zafir cursed. "I wish he'd lived just so I could have the pleasure of killing him."

"It's over, Zaf," Emir said and threw an arm over his shoulder. "We took him out. Tara's safe."

He let his brother go and moved over to Kate. His finger gently ran along her jaw. "I'm sorry he hurt you. I'd kill him again if it would prevent that."

"I'm okay, Emir, really." She took his face in her hands, pulled him gently toward her and kissed him.

"And the house of Al-Nassar stands to see another day," Talib said as he led the way to the helicopter. "Let's get out of here. Let the authorities clean up this stinking pile of offal."

"I can't believe Ed kidnapped Tara. I mean, I get that he in some crazy way thought she was Mother, who he was in love with," Zafir said as they walked to the helicopter. "But why the blackmail?"

"I can't believe any of this," Talib said. "I wish I'd been the one to kill him. He murdered our parents. And why come after us again six years later?"

Kate looked from one to the other and saw the pain reflected on all of their faces. "From what the police records indicate, your parents' accident was initially just that—an accident. It was what happened after that…" She hesitated, feeling Emir's pain, feeling all their pain. "That became murder."

"It's ugly, guys," Emir said thickly. "Basically when the car accident happened, Ed was there as he usually was to act as bodyguard. My first thought was that he murdered them, that he was responsible, but his last words to me admitted otherwise. And there's no way to prove it. Anyway, he said that he got out of the car and wouldn't let our father out. By the time he got around to trying to help Mother, who was trapped in the back, it was too late. The driver was trapped by the steering wheel. The resulting fire ignited an explosion, and you know the rest. Ed admitted that just before he tried to shoot me."

"Thank goodness you shot first," Kate said.

"Murdering pile of dung deserved a harder death," Talib said with clenched fists.

"You're right," Kate said. "He was a murderer, but he was also sick. I think the guilt of what he did ate at him. I'm not sure when he suffered the next psychotic break but eventually that led him to do what he did. The fact that it took six years." She shrugged. "Hard to predict a broken mind."

She put an arm around Emir's waist and smiled reassuringly at him.

"He thought he could live with Tara, who he saw as Mother, in the lifestyle to which he knew she enjoyed. That's why he needed the money," Emir said. "He was as twisted and broken as his kidnapping plot, and the others were just along for the ride and the money."

"Definitely twisted," Zafir agreed. "And the airport attackers were small-time crooks hired by Ed. They decided it might be easier to get their cash if they took you out, Em. I don't think that was part of Ed's plan."

"Unbelievable," Emir said with a shake of his head. "Ed couldn't keep control of the scum he hired."

"That's why the woman from El Dewar remembered

Ed, not just because of your name, but because he'd recently been there hiring help to take us out. Seems every place has their lowlife," Kate said, remembering the shady man in El Dewar who had looked at her oddly and the bikers that had tried to gun them down, so soon after, in the desert.

Emir shrugged. "That pretty much sums it up."

A HALF HOUR later they were settled in the helicopter and, with Zafir piloting, they began to lift off.

"It was a horrible thing—your parents' accident, Tara's kidnapping. I can't imagine what Tara went through. At least it's finally over." She looked at Emir and her heart beat just a little harder, and despite everything that had happened, she didn't want to leave and return to Wyoming. Not yet. Not without Emir at her side. She pushed back those thoughts. They were ridiculous, her life was there—his was here.

"Is it?" Emir asked. "There's one piece of this whole ugly mess that I'm not so sure I want to be over." His hand ran gently over her rapidly bruising jaw as his eyes met hers, and it was clear that it wasn't Tara's kidnapping he was talking about but the feelings that had grown between them. And despite the time and place— it seemed right, for everything they felt had begun in the heat of this crisis.

"What are you saying?" she asked.

His arm went around her shoulders in an oddly familiar way, as if they'd known each other for a very long time.

"What would you think of spending some time in Marrakech?"

"On assignment?"

"Sightseeing. I think you've earned a vacation," he said as he turned her to face him. His intense eyes met hers and his full lips were… She couldn't look away as he leaned over to claim her lips, his arms bringing her hard and fast against him. "I want you here where I can always see you, where I will never let you go."

"Emir…"

"Later. For now let's just say that I may love you."

"Oh, for the love of Allah, Em. Tell the woman straight up."

"Could we have a moment, Zaf?" Emir said. He turned to Kate and whispered in her ear, "I love you."

And as he bent to kiss her, she met the kiss with all the passion in her heart. "Given some time, I may feel the same," she said, but her heart pounded and seemed to tell her that time wouldn't change anything. She loved him now.

"Then that's all we need," he said as he pulled her tighter against him.

And in the towns and villages of Morocco as he kissed her one more time, the call to prayer was beginning as if the entire country approved of a love that was definitely in the air.

* * * * *

Look for more books in Ryshia Kennie's
DESERT JUSTICE *in 2017.*
You'll find them wherever
Mills & Boon Intrigue books are sold!

MILLS & BOON®

INTRIGUE
Romantic Suspense

A SEDUCTIVE COMBINATION OF DANGER AND DESIRE

A sneak peek at next month's titles...

In stores from 6th April 2017:

Just can't wait?
Buy our books online before they hit the shops!
www.millsandboon.co.uk

Also available as eBooks.